Praise for the Hope Meadows series

'A wonderful heartwarming story . . . I couldn't turn the pages quickly enough' *With Love For Books*

'A gorgeous book to curl up with for a few peaceful hours of reading' *Shaz's Book Blog*

'An adorable read [with] a real sense of village community' *Bookworms and Shutterbugs*

'A stunning, emotional, beautiful tale of friendship, love, and the importance of being who you need to be . . . I laughed, I cried, and I cannot recommend [the novel] highly enough – it really has got it all!' *Books of All Kinds*

'[A] lovely romp through the glorious Yorkshire country-side . . . a really lovely summer read and the start of a promising new series' *Jaffa Reads Too*

'Just the right amount of nostalgia . . . wonderful and very poignant' *The World is a Book Blog*

'An incredibly lovely story' *Rachel's Random Reads*

'The author creates a perfect balance between the human and animal stories in this book . . . this is an absolute must read for animal lovers' *The Book Bag*

About the Author

Lucy Daniels is the collective name for the writing team that created the bestselling children's book series *Animal Ark*. *Hope Meadows* is a brand-new Lucy Daniels series for adult readers, featuring the characters and locations that were so beloved in the original stories.

Sarah McGurk, the author of *Snowflakes over Moon Cottage*, has the twin advantages of being passionate about *Animal Ark*, and a fully qualified vet. Sarah writes fiction related to her work in general practice and in emergency and critical care. Her special interests include anaesthesia and pain relief, and low-stress techniques in small animal handling.

Sarah currently lives in Norway. She has worked for two years in a local veterinary practice and speaks Norwegian fluently.

The Hope Meadows Series

Summer at Hope Meadows
Christmas at Mistletoe Cottage
Springtime at Wildacre
The Lost Lamb on Honeysuckle Lane (eBook only)

Snowflakes Over Moon Cottage

LUCY DANIELS

HODDER

First published in Great Britain in 2018 by Hodder & Stoughton
An Hachette UK company

2

Copyright © Working Partners Limited 2018

A CIP catalogue record for this title is available from the British Library

Paperback ISBN 9781473682412
eBook ISBN 9781473682429

Typeset in Plantin Light 11.75/15 pt by
Palimpsest Book Production Limited, Falkirk, Stirlingshire

Printed and bound in Great Britain by Clays Ltd, Elcograf S.p.A.

Hodder & Stoughton policy is to use papers that are natural, renewable and recyclable products and made from wood grown in sustainable forests. The logging and manufacturing processes are expected to conform to the environmental regulations of the country of origin.

Hodder & Stoughton Ltd
Carmelite House
50 Victoria Embankment
London EC4Y 0DZ

www.hodder.co.uk

Special thanks to
Sarah McGurk BVM&S, MRCVS

To Victoria Holmes, with love

Chapter One

'And that was the last time Mum and Dad ever bought us matching outfits!' Freddie Arnold chuckled. 'So yes, in answer to your question, Phil and I did get up to lots of twin tricks when we were younger.'

Susan Collins laughed as she placed her knife and fork on her plate. She was having a lovely time. Really, for a first date, things couldn't have been going much better. The food at the Fox and Goose was delicious, as always, and the company was excellent. They were sitting at a small wooden table next to a window. Raindrops spattered against the panes, but Susan could see the cheery glow of Christmas lights in the November darkness outside. The heat from the nearby crackling fire made her feel pleasantly cosy, despite the weather. She felt totally relaxed and the butterflies that had set up camp in her stomach for most of the afternoon had all but faded away.

She had met Freddie on LoveSpark, an online dating app, and they had hit it off instantly. He'd made her laugh with a couple of opening quips but had quickly revealed a sweet side that Susan had warmed to. He was even more handsome in person than in his photos. He had dark hair in a neat and tidy cut, and a boyish grin coupled with handsome brown eyes. Susan hoped that she was exceeding his expectations too. For this date, she'd chosen some skinny black jeans, heeled boots and a turquoise blouse. It had become her standard first-date outfit, since it was cute and smart, but not too overdone. To finish off the look, she'd loosely curled her straight brown hair, dabbed on some powder and added a swipe of red lipstick.

'So how about you?' Freddie said. His head was on one side. He seemed genuinely interested. 'Tell me about your family.'

Susan sat very still for a moment. On the surface, it was a simple enough question, but Susan's heart quickened and her chest felt tight. She shuffled in her chair, sitting up a little straighter. 'I'm actually an only child,' she said. 'My dad died five years ago, but my mum lives in Walton. Luckily for me, she also helps out often with my son Jack.'

Let's see what he thinks of that . . .

She watched as he blinked, then glanced sideways. She was growing used to seeing that uncomfortable look. To her son's existence being a bombshell thrown into the middle of an early date, often deciding the outcome of the encounter.

She never mentioned Jack online. Not that she was ashamed of him, but because she felt it was safer that way. However, it complicated things when she did mention it. She always did, as soon as she felt she might want to see someone a second time.

Freddie's jaw clenched for a moment, then unclenched. 'You have a son?'

He sounded quiet, but serious and for a moment, Susan felt optimistic. Maybe it was going to be okay. She found her smile. 'Yes,' she said. 'He's four.'

One side of Freddie's mouth lifted as if he was trying to return her expression but couldn't quite make it. 'And he's called Jack?' he asked.

'Yes.' Susan felt her shoulders relax infinitesimally. Being willing to use his name seemed like a good sign. Although, Susan had to admit to herself that she probably had a very low benchmark for this. Some men didn't believe her when she'd mentioned Jack, some had looked terrified and some had even been angry! The very first man she'd dated since having Jack had stood up, shouted across the table about liars and stomped out. Perhaps Freddie was going to be different.

Freddie lifted his napkin, dabbed his mouth, dropped it on the table, then pushed his chair out. 'If you'll excuse me, I just need to go . . .' he nodded towards the gents. 'Back in a minute.' He stood up and made his way past the bar.

Susan's eyes followed him. She guessed he wanted to process what she'd said in private, but she hoped he wouldn't be long. Then another movement caught her eye. Bev, the landlady of the Fox and Goose, was coming over. Her cheeks were pink in the warm room, but she looked tidy in her smart white blouse and narrow black trousers. She grinned at Susan. 'Was everything okay?' she asked as she gathered the plates.

'It was lovely, thanks,' Susan replied.

Bev leaned a little closer. A conspiratorial grin lit her eyes. 'How's the company?' she asked in a loud stage whisper.

Susan smiled. She had known perfectly well when she came to the Fox and Goose that she and her date would be on display. But the comfort of the old coaching inn, with its open fire and traditional hearty food, was a worthwhile pay-off for Bev's amiable nosiness. Plus, it was close to home. 'It's going well . . . I think,' she said. 'Can you bring us the dessert menus when he comes back, please?'

'Of course.' Bev grinned as she piled the last of the plates and whirled away towards the kitchen.

The room buzzed with the chatter of other patrons. Across the room, Susan could see two old men sitting at the bar, chatting quietly.

She turned her chair slightly so that she could face the room more comfortably. Bev was back behind the bar, polishing a glass. Near the fireplace, a group of teenagers were enjoying a raucous night out. Leaning an elbow on the wide windowsill, Susan propped her head against her hand. She remembered being eighteen, when pubs were still a novelty and every night out had been the best one ever. Another wave of laughter from the teenagers washed over her. They sounded so happy.

For a moment, she envied them their uncomplicated lives. Outside the window, a pair of headlights appeared from the car park behind the pub and accelerated away towards the Walton Road.

After a few minutes, there was still no sign of Freddie. He really was taking a very long time, she thought, a sinking feeling in her chest. *Surely, he wouldn't have . . .* Bev was still at the bar, pulling a pint of ale for one of the old men. Susan pushed her chair out and made her way over.

'Hello.' Bev smiled. 'Do you want to look at the menu?' She glanced across the room and her grin disappeared when she saw the empty table. A crease appeared in the middle of her forehead. 'Is everything all right?' she asked.

Susan leaned against the bar, feeling a flush spread across her face. *You don't know that he's gone,* she told herself. 'Would someone be able to check the gents?' she asked. 'My date went in and he hasn't come back.'

Bev's eyes widened. 'Do you think he's ill?' she asked, looking concerned. 'Don't worry. I'll get Gary to go and look.'

'Thanks,' Susan said. She turned and watched as Bev emerged from behind the bar and walked round the corner towards the snug. Maybe Freddie *was* ill, she thought. Her mind had jumped to scepticism. The timing of Freddie's disappearance had seemed suspicious, coming as it did, just after she had mentioned Jack, but there might be an innocent explanation. But a moment later, Bev returned with her husband, Gary, following close behind.

Gary's hair was standing on end as if he'd pushed his hands through it. His expression was uncomfortable. 'I'm really sorry, Susan. I'm afraid he left a few minutes ago, out the back. I'd no idea you were still here. I thought the two of you were heading home separately or I'd have come and said.'

He looked so guilty that Susan felt even more sorry for him than she did for herself. It was hardly his fault if her seemingly pleasant date had decanted before dessert. She managed a rueful smile. 'Never mind,' she said. 'And thanks for letting me know now.'

'Rotten beggar.' Bev's cheeks were redder than ever and she seemed outraged on Susan's behalf. 'Well, I don't know what happened, but he could at least have had the decency to tell you he was going. If I see him in here again . . .' She trailed off and for a brief moment, Susan felt amused. It would almost be worth seeing Freddie in here again, if it meant that Bev would give him a piece of her mind. Bev was an inveterate gossip, but her heart was in the right place and she was fiercely protective of the young women of Welford.

'Thanks, Bev,' Susan said. 'And thanks, Gary . . . it wasn't your fault,' she added. He still looked doubtful. Their concern somehow made her feel even more humiliated. There was no way she could avoid what had happened; her date had run away from her and now they felt sorry for her. She suddenly couldn't bear being in the pub a moment longer. 'I'd better be off,' she said. 'I'll settle up before I go.'

Bev raised her eyebrows and looked at Gary, who gave the tiniest nod. Bev turned her gaze back to Susan. 'I'll not charge you for his meal,' she said. 'I'll work out how much your bill comes to and we can call it quits, okay?' She reached out a rather awkward hand and patted Susan on the shoulder.

'Thanks, Bev.' Susan willed her voice not to wobble. The kinder they were, the more wretched she felt. Doing her best to smile, she paid her bill and donned her jacket. Pulling the fur-edged hood up, she opened the door and stepped out into the November night. The cool air felt good on her burning red face. *Well, that's that,* she thought, trying to calm herself down as she turned left onto High Street, walking towards the church. The rain had slowed to drizzle, but the wind was getting up. To her right, the village green opened up. A string of chilly white icicle lights hung from the gable end of the old school house. They swayed and danced in the wind. Susan squared her shoulders and tucked her chin into her chest as a flurry of raindrops pattered against her face, and she didn't see the tall figure coming in the opposite direction until it was almost upon her.

'Susan?' The voice was familiar.

'Mandy!' Susan found her smile easily. Mandy Hope was a veterinary surgeon who also ran Hope Meadows rescue centre. She was one of Susan's closest friends.

She and Jack often visited the centre to help out with the rescued animals. At Mandy's heel trotted her much-loved collie Sky, thick fur ruffling in the wind. Despite the wind and rain, Sky began to caper, her tail beating frantically as Susan bent to greet her.

'Are you on your way home already?' Mandy frowned, her face shadowed in the dim light of the streetlamps. 'I thought you had a date? Heel, Sky,' she added as she turned to walk with Susan towards the post office.

Susan groaned. 'Well, I did,' she said, 'until he bailed on me. Just after I told him about Jack.'

'Really?' Mandy sounded scandalised. 'So . . . what? He just stood up and said he was leaving?'

Susan let out a short laugh. 'Worse than that,' she said. 'He said he was going to the gents and never came back. Skipped out the back door, leaving me with the bill.'

'What a shit!' Mandy's exclamation cheered Susan immediately. Mandy always got to the heart of things fast. It was one of the things Susan liked about her. In fact, it had been Mandy's blunt nature that had begun their friendship in the first place when they were only twelve years old. Mandy had believed that something was wrong with Susan's pony, Prince, and had gone to the lengths of hiding him from Susan so that she couldn't compete on him. When it emerged that Mandy had been right and Prince was suffering from the heaves, a sort of equine asthma, Susan had had to thank her for saving Prince's life. Thus, an unlikely friendship had been born.

'It's a shame Bev didn't catch him,' Mandy went on. 'It would have been funny to watch him thrown out on his ear.'

Susan found herself grinning. 'Well, Bev did say she would sort him out if he ever came back but I have a feeling he will be conducting his future dates elsewhere.'

Mandy laughed and then leaned in to give Susan a quick hug. 'Anyway, seems to me like you had a lucky escape. There are better men out there, that's for sure. You're well clear of that one.'

'Thanks.' Susan felt another wave of humiliation washing over her. Having Bev, Gary and Mandy feel cross on her behalf, whilst nice in its own way, did underline how pitiable she felt. When she had set out to join LoveSpark, she hadn't expected it to be easy. But she hadn't expected Jack's very existence to define everything. Only one of her matches had actually made it to the end of their first date and he had said he didn't want to take things further. Two more had walked out. Now Freddie had done the same without even telling her. One of them had referred scathingly to 'her baggage' and had sneered, telling her she would never find a man to 'take on someone else's brat'. It would have been one thing if they'd met Jack and didn't feel it would work out. It was quite another to find herself rejected outright and told she was foolish to even try. Now here she was, walking home to an empty house when the night was only half done.

Mandy seemed to sense Susan's feelings. She reached

out and took Susan's arm, linking it through hers. 'Is Jack at your mum's?' she asked as they continued to walk.

They were nearing the end of High Street. Across the road, Susan caught a glimpse of a Christmas tree in the window of one of the houses. It lifted her a little. She'd always loved Christmas, ever since she was a little girl, living in London. Moving to Welford when she had been twelve had only made it more magical. She had fond memories of pure white fields, village carol concerts and wintery hacks on Prince. 'Yes. He's sleeping over,' she replied.

'Well, in that case, how about you and me have a drink?' Mandy suggested. 'The village shop's still open. We could get a bottle of wine.'

The patter of raindrops on her hood had stopped. Susan pulled it back and turned to smile at Mandy, feeling a rush of gratitude towards her. 'Sounds good,' she said. 'We can go to mine, if you like, seeing as it's closer.'

'Perfect!' Mandy sounded enthusiastic. Susan was so glad she'd bumped into her. Much better than going home on her own.

Five minutes later, clutching a chilled bottle of Sauvignon Blanc, she pushed open the door of Moon Cottage and stepped inside. To the left of the doorway, a small pair of green wellingtons with toad eyes stood neatly on a black shoe-tray. One of Jack's paintings, a picture of a cat, hung in a cheap frame on the wall. For the briefest of moments, Susan was overtaken by a different kind of sadness. Her beloved cat Marmalade had been hit by a car back in September. He had always run to her whatever time of the day or night she had come in. There was still an instant every time she entered the house when she expected him to appear, purring loudly, wrapping himself around her legs.

They kicked off their shoes and the moment passed. Susan collected some wine glasses from the cupboard in the kitchen and handed the corkscrew to Mandy. 'Can you pour the wine, if I light the fire?' she asked.

They walked through to the living room. Susan knelt down beside the mantelpiece. Luckily, she had set the fire before she'd gone out. Within a few moments, the flames were licking up the crumpled newspapers and the kindling was beginning to crackle. When she turned round, Mandy had already sat down in one of the squashy chairs and was leaning forward to open the wine. Jack's well-loved toy, Lamby, sat on the chair beside her, looking with serene indifference out of his one remaining eye.

'Thirsty?' she asked Susan.

'You bet!' Susan felt her spirits lifting. As well as Lamby on the chair, there was a box of toys in the corner of the room. Two rather ugly china dogs stood on the mantelpiece. Left to herself, Susan would have taken them to a charity shop, but Jack loved them. The wine glasses shared the table with several play-doh animals that he'd made earlier. He'd been so proud of them that Susan hadn't had the heart to tell him to scrunch them up and put them away. She had done away with the big fireguard when Jack had turned three, but the house was still unmistakable as the home of a small child. Generally, Susan would have felt awkward to have a guest over when the house was in such a mess, but Mandy was such a frequent visitor that Susan didn't mind. Her friend had seen it, and her, in almost every state imaginable.

As soon as Susan moved away from the fire, Sky edged her way towards it. Mandy was curled in the armchair with a glass of wine in one hand and Lamby on her knee.

Susan lifted her own wine and sat down opposite.

Mandy grinned at her and lifted her glass. 'Here's to us,' she said.

Susan lifted hers. 'Cheers,' she said, sipping her wine, which had a zesty lime flavour. Now she could see her friend clearly and she realised that Mandy was looking rather tired.

'How's your mum getting on?' she asked. Only a few months ago, Mandy's mum Emily had been diagnosed with Multiple Sclerosis. Since then, Mandy had barely had any time to herself. Mandy's parents, Emily and Adam, had run Animal Ark veterinary practice for years. When Mandy had come to join them a year and a half ago, it had seemed things at the Welford practice would settle down. But then Emily's illness had struck and everything had shifted again.

'She's not too bad,' Mandy said. She shifted slightly in her chair and hugged Lamby to her. 'She's not so dizzy any more and the headaches have stopped. She's going to see the ophthalmologist next week for an assessment, but so far so good.'

Susan watched as Mandy stretched out an arm and seemed to be trying to swallow a yawn. 'Tired?' she asked.

Mandy laughed. 'It's worth it to see Mum so much better,' she said, 'but yes. With only me and Dad on the rota, the on-call nights come round so fast. We've a new vet starting soon, though, did you know?' She yawned again and then grinned and shook her head. 'Sorry,' she said.

Susan had heard the rumours, but nobody seemed to have any details. 'So who's your new vet then? Is it a new graduate?' Animal Ark would be a nice practice for someone just starting out. The Hopes were such a nurturing family.

'Actually no,' Mandy said. 'He's been qualified a few years. We thought it'd be better to get someone with experience. That way, he can slot right into the rota. It's still hard to stop Mum jumping in when things get busy, even though it was her decision to stop.'

'Sounds like a good idea.' Susan nodded. 'So will you be having any time off at Christmas?'

Mandy shrugged with one shoulder and shook her head. 'Not a lot,' she said. 'Dad and I are sharing the rota, but Hope Meadows is nearly full.' She paused for a moment to take a sip of her wine. 'People are usually really nice, though, on Christmas Day. If I drank all the glasses of sherry I'm offered, I wouldn't be fit to drive home, never mind calve a cow!'

'What about Jimmy?' Susan asked. 'Are you and he doing anything special?' Jimmy and Mandy had been together for more than a year now. Mandy had spent last Christmas with Jimmy at his old cottage, but now he had moved into Mandy's newly refurbished cottage, Wildacre. This would be their first Christmas there.

Mandy rolled her eyes, though her glance was humorous. 'The twins are coming to stay,' she said.

'Oh! That'll be lovely,' Susan said, then with a smidgeon of doubt, '. . . will it?' She knew that Mandy hadn't had an easy time getting to know Jimmy's children. Abi and Max had resented Mandy coming into their dad's life, but recently things had been much better.

Mandy sent her a look which was halfway between amusement and resignation. 'I'm glad they're coming,' she said. 'It's wonderful now, really it is . . . but hosting Christmas is a big deal. I'm kind of nervous.'

Susan laughed at Mandy's expression. 'Just be yourself and it'll all be fine,' she said and was pleased when Mandy returned her smile.

'So what about you?' Mandy said. 'Apart from tonight, how's the dating going?'

Susan rolled her eyes this time. 'I'm thinking of renaming the cottage "Spinster's Paradise".'

Mandy chortled. 'Is it that bad?'

'Afraid so.' Susan took another gulp of wine. 'I'm starting to think this dating app thing isn't for me. They've all been duds. And that's just the ones I've met in person! There have been dozens more I couldn't even bear to meet.'

'But every bad date is a funny story for your next date, right?' Mandy pressed. 'Come on, tell me the latest ones.'

Susan mused on this for a moment. It was true, she supposed. Some of them had been ridiculous enough to be funny, in hindsight. Even Freddie's back-door escape would probably make her laugh one day. 'Well then, let me tell you about Prince Tarquin from last week.' She smiled at Mandy.

Mandy almost spat out her wine. '*Prince Tarquin?* Tell me that wasn't his real name.'

Susan giggled. 'The name is real but I added the title. Tarquin seemed to think we were still living in regency times. He arrived looking like something out of *Pride and Prejudice*, but with added eyeliner . . .' She paused to show Mandy a picture on her phone. Mandy snorted.

'So, you know I don't judge by appearances. He could turn up dressed as a giant teapot if he was a nice guy, but then we started talking about work. I told him I worked in the nursery and he asked if I would be willing to give up work when I married, because "a married woman's place is in the home".' Susan mimed air quotes.

Mandy whistled. 'How very historical of him.'

Susan laughed. 'That's not all. When I took offence, he assured me he believed working in a nursery was a very *respectable* place to work, like that's what was bothering me. Good practice for when I was a mother, he said. When I told him I was already a mother, thank you very much, I thought he'd explode. He stayed just long enough to splutter that he hadn't thought I was "that kind of woman", and then he rushed out.'

When she looked across at Mandy, her friend had lifted Lamby up and was cuddling him and grinning. 'I guess you didn't see him again?' she said.

'I did not!' Susan snorted. 'Still,' she went on, 'at least he wasn't as bad as Stalkery Steve.'

Mandy, who was taking a slug of wine, choked. For a minute she sat there spluttering, her eyes watering, but when she finally drew breath, she swallowed hard and shook her head with a grin. 'Stalkery Steve?' she said. 'He sounds another real catch.'

Susan rolled her eyes. 'He seemed perfectly normal to begin with,' she said. 'Mostly anyway. He turned up with a hangover. I didn't take much notice. Our date was on a Sunday. I just thought he'd got a bit carried away the night before. He seemed better after he'd had something to eat. I'd told him about Jack and he'd taken it quite well.' She lifted a hand to rub her chin. 'It was only later on, it got weird. He said he needed to go lie down. 'Cos of his hangover. I could "take care" of him, apparently. I suggested if he felt that bad, he should go lie down somewhere else, but he was insistent he wanted to come here.'

Mandy's eyes had opened wide. 'You didn't bring him did you?'

Susan shook her head. 'Course not,' she said. But he didn't want to take no for an answer. I walked out eventually: drove round until I was sure he wasn't following. He called the next day to apologise and ask for another date. He was being all nice again. He called me loads of times. I just put the phone down. He seems to have stopped now, but I know I have to be careful.' She sighed. 'It's not easy,' she said. Her eyes wandered round the room, finishing on the fire. It was getting low. She pushed herself upright, poked the embers and threw on more coal. After a moment, the fire blazed up, sending flames up the chimney. Sky was lying on the rug and didn't stir.

Mandy's gaze was thoughtful. There was sympathy in her eyes. 'That sounds scary,' she said.

'It was a bit,' Susan admitted. She'd kept her voice light as she'd told Mandy, but it had come close to putting her off dating. Especially with Jack being so young. His safety had to come before everything.

'You know I told myself I was going to meet someone this year, and it just wasn't happening naturally. I thought this online dating malarkey might help. But the year's nearly over and I'm no further forward. I know I shouldn't set deadlines, but I'm starting to think if I haven't met anyone yet, it's not going to happen.'

Mandy reached forward and set her wine glass on the coffee table. She settled back in her chair, looking thoughtful. 'It wasn't easy at first with Jimmy. Having children does complicate things. But I'm sure there'll be someone out there who'll accept you for who you are.' She put her head on one side and gave a half smile. 'You'll probably meet him when you least expect it. In the supermarket or something.'

Susan grinned. 'Knowing my luck, he'll appear just as I'm reaching for a supersized pack of toilet roll.'

Mandy laughed. 'If he still likes you after that, you'll know he's a keeper!' She lifted the wine bottle. 'Top up?'

Susan held out her glass and Mandy poured more wine. As she sat back in her chair, the phone in her pocket buzzed. She pulled it out. It was another match from LoveSpark. Douglas MacLeod. She glanced at his profile picture. He had wild red hair and a big bushy beard.

'Everything okay?' Mandy asked.

Susan sighed. 'Everything's fine,' she said. 'It's another LoveSpark match, but he's not my type.'

Mandy smiled, eyebrows raised. 'Really? I thought you didn't judge by appearances,' she said, slyly. 'Can I have a look?'

'If you like.' Susan handed over the phone. 'I just don't think I want to meet him. I've had enough.'

Mandy gazed down at the phone. 'It says he's a children's book illustrator,' she said, looking up. 'That sounds hopeful, doesn't it? He must like children.' She held out the phone.

Susan grabbed the mobile and took another look at the profile. It did indeed say he was a children's illustrator. Further down the page, there were pictures of his work. He seemed to like animals. She read his bio, which was self-deprecating and humorous.

Although I may look like 'Father Christmas before his hair went white', as my nephew kindly puts it, I can assure you that the similarities end there. Except my job also revolves around making children happy, I do have a big laugh and I did get stuck in a chimney once, but that's it, I swear.

Susan laughed. She looked at the photo again. If she looked past the wild hair and beard, she saw he had strong cheekbones, a cheery grin and very piercing blue eyes. He was handsome, if unconventional. He might be fun.

'What do you think?' Mandy asked.

Susan shrugged her shoulders, but she smiled. 'I

suppose I could give it one last go,' she said. 'What do you think I should write?' She leaned forward so that Mandy could see, and together, they began to compose a message.

Chapter Two

Susan clapped her hands and gazed around the nursery classroom. 'Tidy-up time!' she called. 'Bring your brushes and water to the sink, please, then take your paints to Nina.' She glanced over at Nina, her classroom assistant, who was standing at the entrance to the big walk-in cupboard where the art equipment was stored. Nina was a small older woman, whose children were grown up. Her blue eyes were almost always filled with enthusiasm. 'If you can sort the paints out, please, Nina?'

Nina nodded, her smile widening. Chairs scraped all over the room and for a few minutes chaos reigned as the fifteen three- and four-year-olds who made up Susan's class wove their way around the room with their water-filled yogurt pots, paints and brushes. The distinctive smell of poster paint hung in the air.

'Don't forget to wash your elbows,' she reminded Christina. Christina Anderson was four and one of the liveliest children. Her cherubic face belied her tendency to create chaos wherever she went. As ever, she seemed to have paint right up to her armpits. The youngest child in the class walked over. His blond hair was tangled and he had a smudge of blue on his chin. He too held out his brush, a sweet smile lighting up his very round face. 'Thank you, Neil,' Susan said.

Her son sidled up to her, poured his water in the sink and held out his pot to her. 'Thank you, Jack,' she said. She always made an effort to treat him exactly as she treated the others in class.

'Now,' she said, when they had all, finally, come to rest. 'Can you all come and sit down in the story corner, please?'

All the children, bar Christina, trotted obediently towards the story corner and sank to the floor cross-legged, as they had been taught. Susan looked over at Christina. 'Are you coming, please, Christina?' she said.

'Can I go to the toilet?' She was jiggling up and down.

'May I go to the toilet, *please*?' Susan reminded her. 'Yes, you may go, but come straight back.' Christina scurried away. Susan looked down at the children who made up Penguin class. They were, on the whole, well behaved. A few of them had started out in the baby room, but most had joined at three years old. It was a small nursery, based in a converted house near to the church. Susan's classroom was at the front of the house. A big bay window looked out over the nursery garden, which at the moment was filled with fallen leaves. It was much more cheery indoors. The story corner was carpeted and surrounded on three sides with shelves filled with brightly coloured books.

'We're going to do something very exciting now,' she said. 'We're going to learn all about caring for animals.'

A few of the children's eyes widened. Noah, three years old and wearing Harry-Potter style glasses, wriggled to his knees. 'Will we learn about penguins, Miss?' he shouted. There were a few giggles.

'Don't forget to put up your hand, Noah,' Susan reminded him. 'Not penguins, but lots of other animals. We're going to visit Hope Meadows rescue centre.'

There was an outburst of chatter. Christina rushed back into the room and got down, but only to a crouch. Herbie Dhanjal, lively as ever in her brightly coloured kurta, made as if to stand up.

'Sit down, please,' Susan commanded and they quietened immediately. She was pleased they were so excited, but she knew she had to keep their enthusiasm on a tight rein. 'The lady who looks after the rescue centre is a vet. Does anyone know what a vet does?'

Forty-five minutes later, the children walked in a crocodile formation out of the gate and turned onto the track that led through the fields. Susan walked at the front of the class and Nina brought up the rear. Clouds chased across the sky overhead. The air was fresh on Susan's face and she could feel it tugging at her ponytail. The row of trees on the far side of the stone wall were moving, their bare branches swaying with each gust. Luckily the rain, which had fallen all through lunchtime, had stopped.

Mandy was waiting for them at the door. She was wearing a set of dark-blue scrubs, and as often happened, her working clothes were stippled with animal hair. She glanced at the orderly crocodile and grinned at Susan. 'Hello, everyone,' she said.

Susan was pleased to see how much at home she was in front of the children. When Mandy had first come back to Welford, she'd seemed almost frightened of Jack. Now, even with fifteen pairs of young eyes on her, she looked cool and collected. 'Welcome to Hope Meadows! We're going to see lots of animals,' Mandy said. 'It's really important when we go in that you're quiet. Some of the animals haven't been treated very well before they came here. A few of them are really shy. Does everybody understand?' Fifteen attentive heads nodded. Mandy seemed to have them all under a spell.

Susan's eyes wandered over the attractive building, which was built of stone, wood and glass. In winter, from a distance, it seemed almost to merge into the landscape. Mandy and her parents had built it together just over a year ago. As the class walked into the reception area, a few of the children gasped. It was a welcoming room with huge wooden beams and an enormous window that looked out onto the fellside. Susan had been bringing Jack here ever since Mandy had opened her doors to all the unwanted and unloved animals in the area, but now she saw it afresh. It must be lovely for Mandy, looking out every day at that view, she thought.

Mandy was talking again. 'I've someone very special I want to introduce first,' she said. 'But remember what I said about being very quiet. Don't move quickly with any strange animal and don't touch any of them unless I say so, please.' She turned to walk across the room and the children started to twitter. Neil put his thumb in his mouth and reached out with his other hand to grasp Susan's. Susan gave the small fingers a squeeze.

'Okay, all of you.' Susan spoke clearly, raising her voice. 'Settle down now. When Mandy comes back, we all need to listen carefully to what she says. For now, can you all sit down in a circle on the floor.' The circle formed and they all sat down with crossed legs. They were behaving very well, despite their excitement.

A moment later, Mandy reappeared. Sky was trotting at her heel. Mandy sat down on a low chair, and Sky sat down beside her. 'Now,' said Mandy. 'Does anyone know what kind of dog this is?'

Several hands shot into the air. Susan could see that Jack was bursting to give the answer, but Mandy pointed to Neil, who took his thumb out of his mouth. 'It's a Border Collie,' he whispered.

'Well done,' Mandy said. 'Yes, she's a Border Collie and her name is Sky.' She smiled, reaching out a hand to stroke Sky's ear. The collie looked up at her. Susan didn't have time for a dog, but she couldn't help envying Mandy when she saw her and Sky together. 'Sky used to live on a farm,' Mandy went on, 'but her owner became ill. He couldn't look after his animals any more. Eventually we found them all new homes, but Sky was such a special dog that I decided to keep her. Now she comes with me when I go out to look after other animals.'

The class were enthralled. They were all looking at Sky, who was looking up at Mandy.

'Would anyone like to stroke Sky?' Mandy asked. Susan felt very proud as the children waited in turn to go up one at a time and pat the little collie. Mandy must be pleased too, she thought. She had spent so much time socialising Sky. A year and a half ago, it would have been unthinkable even to let the children near Sky, but now she seemed to be coping very well.

Having shown them Sky, Mandy led the children into the dog kennels. As they filtered in, one of the dogs, a small wiry terrier with a very long tail, rushed to the bars and started yammering. Two of the children stuck their fingers in their ears. Though she'd heard it before, even Susan found the racket hard to bear. Moving backwards, Neil slid his hand once more into hers. Mandy took a huge stride across to the door of the kennel. 'Hush, Bounce,' she said, and immediately the little dog stopped yapping and started to wag his tail, bouncing up and down. Mandy reached out a hand and slid the bolt open. 'Now I'm going to get Bounce out,' she said, turning her head to regard the children. 'But I will need you all to be perfectly quiet. Can you do that for me?' A couple of the children edged backwards, but most were nodding. Jack and a few others moved closer.

When he wasn't barking, Susan knew Bounce was a really sweet little dog. She and Mandy had spent a lot of time planning this visit. She was very pleased to see how well most of the children were responding. They were obviously enjoying it and all of them had, so far, been polite and well behaved. Bounce was behaving well too, as Mandy had hoped. Susan knew that in spite of his good nature, Mandy was worried about finding a home for him with all the noise he made.

Once all the children who wanted to had stroked Bounce, Mandy led them all outside. There were two goats in the orchard and an ancient Highland cow out in the paddock. Then she brought them back inside and held up her hands to get their attention. 'And now I have a surprise for you all,' she said. Susan could see Mandy's eyes were twinkling. 'Even Miss Collins doesn't know about this,' she said. The eyes of the class swivelled Susan's way and she raised her eyebrows and made an 'O' shape with her mouth. They giggled at her expression and then turned their attention back to Mandy. 'I'm going to take you in to see some brand new residents,' she said. 'They were brought in yesterday. They're only about four weeks old and they're still with their mum. We'll go in to see them, but please do stay back from the pen so they don't get frightened.'

A wave of whispers ran through the class. Mandy turned and opened the door and led them into the small room off the cat kennel where she kept nursing mothers. The children filed in, their eyes wide. Susan followed them in last, then had to crane her head to see. In the kennel, looking very calm despite the invasion, was a sleek black and white cat. Snuggled into her side there was a pile of kittens. One of the kittens, black and white like its mother, stood up, stretched, then came to the bars of the cage, gazing out with fearless eyes. It put its head on one side, as if to see them better, then gave a piercing mew. As if there had been a signal, three more kittens stood up. There were, Susan saw, two more black and white, one pure black. The smallest kitten was last to wake. It lay close in to its mother, seemingly fast asleep still. With a lazy tongue, the mother cat reached out and started to lick it. It was pure white, Susan saw. Its fur was a little longer than the other kittens' and when it finally opened its eyes, they were a pure bright-blue colour.

Susan had rarely seen the children so enchanted. She glanced over at Jack. He seemed unable to take his eyes off the cage. The little white kitten had now come forward and was sitting daintily at the front of the cage, its blue-eyed gaze both serious and inquisitive.

'We've got a cat at home,' Neil said. 'She was a kitten when she came.'

'I want a kitten,' Christina piped up. 'Please can I take one of them home?'

Mandy laughed. 'They aren't ready to go anywhere yet,' she said. 'They're still far too young.'

Jack was still gazing. His big brown eyes were sad and Susan knew he was thinking about Marmalade. If she had found Marmalade's loss difficult, it had been even harder for Jack. She wanted to reach out and hug him, but instead, with Mandy's help, she led the class back out into reception. Together they began to get the children ready for the walk back.

It was already dark outside the window when the last of the parents arrived to collect their daughter. Susan waved them off, then closed and locked the door and walked back to the classroom. Just a few things to sort out, then she too could go home. Jack was sitting quietly, playing with the big wooden Noah's Ark. It was his favourite toy and Susan stopped for a moment to watch as he marched a pair of giraffes along the edge of a shelf, down a pile of bricks and into the Ark. The classroom door opened with a click. Asa, one of the nursery nurses from the baby room, stuck her head round the door. Her dark-skinned face was serious, as ever, her black hair tied back in a bun.

'I don't know if anyone told you,' she said, 'but you had a visitor this afternoon while you were out.'

Susan frowned. 'Who was it?' she asked. It couldn't have been her mum. Asa would have just said.

'I don't know who he was,' Asa said, 'but he was

very good-looking and he asked for you.' She was smiling, as if this should be good news, but Susan felt a stir of disquiet. Who on earth would come to the nursery looking for her mid-afternoon? Any of her friends would just have phoned, surely?

'What did he look like?' she asked.

Asa thought for a moment. 'As I said, he was quite handsome,' she replied. 'Dark brown hair, brown eyes.' She paused. 'He said he was from York. An old friend, he said.'

Susan felt even more uneasy. Stalkery Steve was from York and the description sort of fitted him, though his hair had a lot of grey mingled with the brown. Would he really come looking for her like that? A shiver ran down her spine but she decided not to mention her worry to Asa. *No need to jump to conclusions.*

'Thanks for telling me,' she said. She kept her voice steady.

Asa smiled. 'Hopefully he'll catch up with you,' she said. Susan nodded, her face bland. She wasn't sure at all if she wanted him to.

Chapter Three

Susan threw her keys down on the little hall table and carried the two heavy shopping bags through into the kitchen.

'Here, Mummy!' Jack came in behind her. He too was weighed down. He had insisted on carrying a third bag home, despite the fact he had to do so with his arms held high.

'Thanks, sweetie.' She took the carrier from him and set it on the side. 'Don't take your coat off,' she reminded him. 'We're going over to Mr Gorski's in a minute, remember.' She pulled a carton of milk from the bag and opened the fridge.

'Can I cuddle Coffee, Mummy?'

Susan smiled as she turned to reply. Mr Gorski was an elderly man who lived across the road from them. Coffee was his equally ancient Border Terrier. 'I'm sure you can,' she said. 'But don't forget to ask Mr Gorski first.'

Jack looked very serious. 'I won't, Mummy,' he said.

Susan turned back to her unpacking to hide her smile. Jack was so very earnest about everything now, especially where animals were concerned. She stowed away the perishable food, closed the fridge, picked up one of the shopping bags and held out a hand to her son. 'Let's go,' she said.

As they crossed the road and made their way down Mr Gorski's front path, it began to rain. Still clinging to Jack's hand, Susan rushed into the shelter of the porch. She rang the doorbell, then for good measure, banged on the door. Mr Gorski didn't always hear so well. Inside, there came a volley of barking.

Jack turned and peered out at the rain and Susan half turned too. It was lashing: droplets bright in the light coming from the porch. Jack looked up at her. 'Will there be snow by Christmas, Mummy?' he asked.

Susan paused for a moment. One of Mr Gorski's gutters was overflowing. The sound of water gushing onto concrete meant she had to raise her voice. 'I don't know,' she replied. 'But even if there isn't, we'll still have a lovely time.'

Jack looked unconvinced. 'But how will Santa's sleigh go?'

'Christmas magic,' Susan said quickly and firmly. Last year, she had indulged Jack's Christmas beliefs and they had hunted for reindeer until the day Jack had decided to go searching alone in a snowstorm and got lost on the moors. The memory gave her chills. She didn't want him to be disappointed, but she couldn't help hoping that if there was snow it would be just a light dusting.

With a loud creak, the door finally opened. Mr Gorski stood in the hallway, beaming. His snow-white hair was carefully combed and he was wearing a warm-looking mustard-yellow cardigan. Coffee trotted rather stiffly onto the porch, her brown tail wagging. She reached up and licked Jack's face as he knelt to greet her.

'Hello, Susan. Hello, Jack.' Mr Gorski stepped back to usher Susan in. They watched as Jack clambered to his feet, then scampered inside after the little terrier. Mr Gorski closed the door.

'I've brought your shopping,' Susan said.

Mr Gorski put a hand behind his ear. 'Sorry?' he said.

'I've brought your shopping.' She turned to face him, repeated her words and held out the bag.

'Oh yes. Thanks very much.' The old man smiled, then turned and shuffled away towards the kitchen. 'Would you like a cup of tea?' he said.

Susan sat down at the little table that stood against the wall. She had got to know Mr Gorski well since she and Jack had moved to Moon Cottage. He'd been a teacher and he had lots of memories that he enjoyed sharing. Conversation had become more difficult as his hearing had worsened, but in every other way, he seemed spry and healthy.

Jack and Coffee trotted into the room. Coffee lay down, her pink tongue hanging out, and Jack knelt beside her.

Mr Gorski looked down at the pair, his eyes bright. 'I've got a favour to ask of you, Jack,' he said. Susan loved the way Mr Gorski spoke to Jack. He never spoke down or treated him as less important. 'There's something I need from the cupboard in the hall and I could do with some help.' He smiled, holding out his hand. Jack stood up and followed. They returned a moment later, carrying a large, dusty-looking box between them. Susan wanted to laugh. Mr Gorski was almost bent double to let Jack 'assist'. They set it down on the kitchen table.

'You see, I usually go to my sister's for Christmas,' Mr Gorski explained. 'So I don't usually bother to decorate my house. But this year, she's coming to me. So I'm going to . . . decorate!' He lifted the lid up with a flourish. Threadbare tinsel topped a pile of faded baubles. A paper angel with a badly drawn face peeped out from the tangle. Mr Gorski's face fell. 'Oh dear.' He looked over the contents of the box with a rueful grin. 'I suppose it's been a while since I used these . . .'

Susan laughed at his expression. 'I'll help you sort them,' she suggested.

Jack's eyes opened wide as Susan pulled out the first piece of tinsel. He loved decorations. 'Can I help?' he asked.

Susan peered into the box. Some of the baubles were broken. 'There's broken glass in here,' she said, 'but you can have a look at this and see if everything's there.' She pulled out a half-buried carton. The picture on

34

the lid showed a miniature wooden Nativity set with brightly coloured, painted figurines.

Jack took it from her, eyes huge, face solemn.

Susan returned to sorting through the debris. Mr Gorski made the tea and then joined her. Most of the decorations were past their best, tinsel that had tied itself into a big knot and old cards that were brown and peeling at the edges. There were a few lovely unbroken baubles, though, and an old wooden toy train piled with brightly coloured presents.

Jack finished checking the crib scene and looked up. 'They're all there apart from there's one sheep missing,' he told Susan. 'Can I play with Coffee now, please?'

Susan smiled as she took the carton. 'Of course you can.' She watched as he sat down beside the little dog and stroked her gently, then returned to her task. She pulled the last decoration from the box. It was a foil star that could be opened to make a circle. Half of it was so squashed that it didn't even unfold. She put it into the almost-full bin.

Mr Gorski looked down at the empty box and the small pile of decorations that lay on the table. He shook his head. 'I'll have to buy some new things,' he said. He lifted up the paper angel that had been near the top of the box. 'One of the last classes I taught gave me this,' he said. 'Christmas was always the best time of year. The children made such lovely things for the classrooms.' For the first time, his expression was a little melancholy.

Susan looked at the lopsided angel. It certainly had character. 'Jack and I could make some new decorations,' she suggested. 'It's years since I've made real old-fashioned paper chains. What do you think, Jack?'

Jack looked up. 'What's a paper chain?' he asked.

Mr Gorski laughed. 'It's a special kind of Christmas decoration,' he said. 'Your mum will show you.'

'Can we make snowflakes for the window too?' Jack's eyes were huge. He loved cutting out paper snowflakes.

'Of course.' Susan nodded. 'We can make all kinds of things.'

Mr Gorski's eyes were twinkling again. 'So will you help?' he asked Jack.

Jack's sweet smile lit up his whole face as he looked over at Mr Gorski. 'Yes please,' he said.

Susan's heart swelled. Making things with Jack was always fun and making Christmas decorations would be better still. She lifted her mug and drank another mouthful of tea, then glanced up at the clock on the wall.

'We should go,' she told Mr Gorski. 'My mother's expecting us for dinner. Come on, Jack, Grandma will be waiting. Say goodbye to Mr Gorski and Coffee.'

'Bye bye!' Jack said, waving madly across the table at the old man, and then giving Coffee another big hug.

It was still raining when Susan pulled up outside her mum's house. Susan's mother, Miranda Jones, lived in a rather grand villa on the edge of Walton. Many years ago, she had lived in London, working as a professional actor in a soap opera. She still popped down to London or Salford sometimes to appear on television, but now she mostly did voice work in Leeds and York. It meant she was free to be with Jack, she said; she didn't want to miss him growing up. Susan pulled open Jack's car door and he rushed across the gravel onto the porch and pushed the doorbell.

'Hello, darlings.' Miranda opened the door and flung her arms wide. Jack rushed into her embrace and she kissed him heartily. Susan smiled. Her mum still enjoyed the trappings and drama of her TV lifestyle. The dress she was wearing, though beautiful, seemed wholly unsuitable for a visit from a four-year-old. It was red and clingy. Her hair looked as if it'd had a team of stylists working on it as well. Yet Susan knew that if Jack spilled something or ruffled the exquisite hairstyle, Miranda would just laugh. She loved Jack so much. Susan still found it hard to believe how lucky she was. Without her mum's help, she would be hard pushed to find any time at all for herself. Miranda let go of Jack, stood up and held out her arms again.

'Mum,' Susan said, stepping forwards into the embrace. She closed her eyes for a moment and was taken back to her childhood. Her mum smelled, as ever, of expensive perfume and Pears' soap. She felt herself relax.

Miranda released her, touched a hand to Susan's face as if she'd never seen anything more lovely, then bent again to Jack with a smile. 'How gorgeous to see you both. Come on in. Let's get that coat off you.' She leaned over to help him with his zip. 'Have you had a good day?' She glanced up at Susan, who had taken off her own damp jacket.

'Pretty good,' Susan replied. 'We took the class to Hope Meadows.'

Miranda opened her eyes wide and looked at Jack. 'That sounds fun,' she said.

'It was!' Jack told her.

'And what was the best animal?' Miranda held the sleeve of first one arm, then the other as Jack pulled out of his jacket.

Jack put his head on one side, then looked up at Miranda. 'They were all lovely,' he said, 'but my favourite was a kitten.'

'Oooooh!' Miranda's voice rose and fell. 'What was the kitten's name?'

Jack frowned. 'I don't know. Do you, Mummy?' he looked up at Susan.

Susan shook her head. 'I'm not sure they even have names yet. Which one did you like?'

'The white one,' he said, then turned his gaze to Miranda. 'It had blue eyes,' he said. 'Really bright blue.'

'That's unusual for a cat, isn't it? I bet it's very pretty!' Miranda reached out a hand to Jack, who took hers and together, they walked through into the warm kitchen.

'Sit down,' Miranda told them, letting go of Jack's

hand and pulling out a chair. 'I've bought your favourite,' she told Jack. Opening the oven, she pulled out a large pie. 'Chicken and mushroom,' she announced, 'and duchess potatoes with peas, followed by jelly and ice cream.' Susan rolled her eyes fondly. Her mum could rarely resist treating Jack to his favourite foods on every possible occasion. At least she'd finally managed to stop Miranda from giving him a whole bag of chocolate buttons on every single visit.

'So what have you been up to, Mum?' she asked. Her mouth watered as her mum set the food on the table. It really did look very tasty, she thought.

Miranda frowned. 'I haven't done all that much today,' she said, 'but I did run into an old friend of yours.' She put some pie on Jack's plate and began to spoon the peas.

Susan stiffened. Another old friend? She forced her shoulders down a millimetre. It was probably nothing.

'Yes, it was Triss Herbert,' Miranda said. Susan breathed out. When Susan had moved to Welford, Triss had taken over the flat she had vacated. Miranda handed Jack his plate.

'And how was Triss?' Susan asked. Not that she and Triss had been especially friendly, but she was relieved her mum wasn't talking about the mysterious man from York.

Miranda pursed her mouth slightly as if puzzled. 'I think she was fine,' she said. 'She certainly looked well, but she asked me if I could tell you that someone came round to the flat looking for you. A man, she said.'

The tension was back in Susan's shoulders. 'Did she say anything about him?' Susan asked.

Miranda paused to hand Susan her plate. 'Yes,' she said, 'he said he was from York and he was looking for you.'

'Did he give his name? Or did she say what he looked like?' Susan tried to keep her voice light as she pushed potatoes onto her fork. Miranda had been encouraging when she started online dating. She wasn't so sure what her mum would think if she heard about Stalkery Steve.

'Dark brown hair and eyes,' Miranda said. 'Very good-looking apparently.' She set her own plate down, lifted her knife and fork and waggled her eyebrows slightly at Susan. 'Anyone I know?' she asked.

Susan swallowed, then shrugged and shook her head. 'If I knew who it was, I could tell you if you know them,' she replied, still trying to sound casual. Of course it might not have been Steve at all. This was the second time dark brown hair had been mentioned. A memory flitted into her head of another man from York, but she batted it away. He had told her long ago that he wanted nothing to do with her. 'This is lovely pie,' she said.

Miranda looked happy. 'Glad you like it,' she said. 'Do you like it too, Jack?'

'Mmmmm! It's yummy, yummy, yummy!' He beamed. 'We're going back to Hope Meadows next week,' he told Miranda. 'Maybe Mummy could take a photo of the kitten. Would you like to see?'

Miranda replied enthusiastically and before long, Jack was telling her all the details of the animals and about a trip they were planning to Rainbow Hill children's farm, where there were llamas and where Holly and Robin, two donkeys that Mandy had rescued last year, lived. After that, he told her about the nursery Nativity. Susan ate slowly and started to relax again. It was a little odd that someone had been looking for her, but for all she knew, it might have been two separate people altogether. There were lots of men in the world with brown hair and eyes.

'Are you finished?' Miranda asked a few minutes later.

Susan smiled as she handed over her plate. 'Yes thanks, it was lovely,' she said.

'We'll go through,' Miranda told her. She led them into the high-ceilinged sitting room. Opening the sideboard, she took out Jack's toy box. Susan sat down on the couch as Miranda set the box down on the floor. Jack knelt beside it and started to pull out his favourites. The phone in Susan's pocket buzzed and she pulled it out, feeling the tiniest wave of nervousness, but it was a message from Douglas, her newest potential match.

'It would be lovely to meet up sometime soon,' she read. 'Please let me know when it would suit you.' It was nice, she thought, that he didn't seem to be pushy.

The rest of the message was amusing, a little flirty, but never overstepping the mark. He'd signed off with a photo of a drawing, a little cartoon pony. It looked a little bit like Prince, the Welsh pony she'd had when she first moved to Yorkshire. She smiled.

'What's that you've got?' Susan had momentarily forgotten about Miranda, but now her mum had sat down on the couch beside her. Susan held out the phone. 'Now there's a handsome face,' Miranda cried. She tilted her head as if to inspect him better. 'And what does he do?'

Her mum always wanted all the details of the men she was meeting. 'He's a children's illustrator,' she replied.

'And is that one of his?' Miranda asked, pointing to the pony drawing. She held the phone closer. 'It's lovely. You know, if only I was twenty years younger, I might have a bash at him myself. He really is very talented, isn't he?'

Susan laughed and took the phone back. Though he was indeed quite good-looking, Douglas had an earthy look about him. Susan couldn't imagine him with her mother, who had always been a stickler for well-brushed hair and a clean-shaven face. 'I'm sure he's not really your type, Mum,' she said. She looked again at the photo: the bright-blue eyes and slightly shaggy haircut. He really did look very friendly. Attractive too in an unconventional way.

'Nonsense, creative and handsome was always my

type!' Miranda waved a hand at Susan, laughing. 'But seriously, darling, I can have Jack tomorrow if you'd like to meet him then.'

'Really?' Susan looked at her mum, who smiled and nodded.

'If you'd like to meet up, I could manage tomorrow,' she typed into the phone.

Within five minutes, Douglas had agreed and they had finalised the details. Susan felt a slight frisson run through her as she put the phone back in her pocket. She wasn't quite sure what it was about Douglas. She was trying not to get her hopes up, but this was the first time she had felt really excited about a date for ages.

Just don't run away at the first sign of Jack, or turn out to be a stalker, she thought. *And we'll go from there . . .*

It was well after Jack's bedtime when they got home. Despite the lateness of the hour, Susan took her time putting him to bed since she was going to miss bedtime tomorrow. She glanced around the room as she helped him into his pyjamas. She had begun to decorate a couple of weeks ago, but like everything else, it took a long time when she had to do it all herself. She had chosen a woodland theme, but as yet, she had only painted the first coat on two of the walls.

Once Jack was ready, he walked round the room, as he did every night, stopping to say good night to all his toys. He stopped at the window to wave to the birds in the garden, to Coffee across the road, to all the animals at Hope Meadows and even to Robin and Holly and the llamas at Rainbow Hill. Lastly, he waved up at the stars. 'Night night, Marmalade,' he said. He remembered poor Marmalade every night and he still looked sad. Susan had only once suggested getting a new pet. Jack had stiffened immediately and shaken his head hard. Susan hadn't tried again.

Once he'd finished at the window, Susan pulled the curtain shut and followed him across the room. He hadn't been a good sleeper when he'd been younger so she always tried to make his bedtime routine as relaxing as possible. She tucked him into the little car-shaped bed that Miranda had bought him before they had realised just how animal-mad he was going to be.

'Night night, sweetheart,' she said, kissing him on the forehead, smoothing his hair back.

'Nighty night, Mummy,' he replied.

She smiled, straightened, walked to the door and switched the light off. 'See you in the morning,' she whispered.

Closing the door, she walked across the tiny landing and into her own bedroom. Leaving the door ajar, she made her way over to her wardrobe. In the mirror on the door, she caught sight of the room behind her. The walls were cream coloured, the furniture rather old-fashioned and heavy. Her bed was covered with a crushed-velvet throw in a rich red colour and there were three paintings on the wall. One of them had been painted by Clive Moon, the former occupant of Moon Cottage. It was an abstract view of the fells as seen from behind Welford Church. It had hung in her parents' house when she was younger. Miranda had given it to Susan when her dad had died.

The only sign of Jack in here was a framed photo that stood on her bedside table. Though she loved being his mum with every fibre of her being, there were moments when she wanted to be just herself. To be Susan Collins, young woman, rather than Susan Collins, Jack's mum.

She pulled open the wardrobe, looked inside and took out a slinky black dress. Slipping it over her head, she looked at herself in the mirror. Could she get away with this tomorrow? She and Douglas were going to a smart restaurant. It would be nice to feel really special. Sidling over to her dressing table, she found a pair of gold-and-pearl earrings and a matching necklace and put them on. She had a smart pair of boots that would be suitable even if it was raining. She walked back over to the mirrored wardrobe door. She couldn't help feeling happy with what she saw. She tucked her brown hair behind her ears to highlight the soft glow of the dangling pearls, then turned round and admired herself from different angles. This was definitely the outfit, she thought. Suddenly, she couldn't wait for the next day.

Chapter Four

'It's your turn at the water table now, Ella.' Susan watched as Ella dropped the saucepan she was banging and rushed over to grab an apron. 'Neil?' Neil, who was emptying a cup of water through the millwheel, appeared not to notice. 'Neil?' Susan said more loudly. Neil looked up. 'That's your time up,' Susan told him.

Neil's chin quivered. 'But I want to play in the water,' he wailed. His bottom lip turned inside out and he began grizzling.

For a moment, Susan wished she could put her fingers in her ears. It had been raining hard all day and they'd been stuck inside. Instead, she put on her brightest smile as she undid Neil's apron string. 'Let's see,' she said and glanced round the room. Her eyes stopped on Noah, who was playing in the toy kitchen. 'Look,' she said to Neil as she mopped him with a paper towel. 'You could go and play in the kitchen, if you like.' The toy cooker with its pots and pans was Neil's favourite and Noah was his best friend. Still sniffling, Neil trudged off.

Susan glanced at her watch. There was a class visit

due at three o'clock. Just a few minutes more and they would have to tidy up. She made her way over to Nina, who was beside the sand table. 'Ten minutes to go till the class visit, Nina,' she murmured.

Nina's eyes continued to scan the classroom, but she glanced sideways at Susan. 'Who's coming?' she asked.

Susan wrinkled her nose. 'I'm not actually sure,' she said. 'It's an author, coming to read a book. Mrs Armitage arranged it.'

Mrs Armitage was the owner of the nursery. She was a lovely woman with a propensity for making last-minute arrangements. There would be paperwork somewhere, but Susan had been caught up at lunchtime when little Kieran had bumped his head and she hadn't had a chance to look.

'Is it a Christmas book?' Nina asked.

Susan gave the tiniest shake of her head. 'I really don't know,' she said with a sideways grin at Nina. 'It'll be a lovely surprise for us as well as the children.'

Nina laughed. 'Ready for anything,' she said. 'That's our motto!'

Susan smiled. 'Ready for anything,' she agreed.

A scream sounded on the other side of the room. Christina and Neil were fighting over a toy car. Noah was yelling. Susan rushed across: better to intervene before anyone was hurt.

Just as she retrieved the car, the classroom door crashed open. A man bounded into the room, clutching a briefcase under one arm. His flame-coloured hair stood on end and a shaggy beard engulfed his lower jaw. Well over six feet of lumbering man-mountain, dressed in a bright red T-shirt, and baggy hiking trousers. Catching sight of Nina, he stretched out a hand and strode towards her. Beside Susan, Christina's howl came to an abrupt halt. All eyes were on the newcomer. He loped across the room, his grin widening.

'Hello!' he boomed. Then as if in slow motion, his foot caught one of the miniature chairs, his body twisted, his arms flailed. Like a falling tree, he crashed to the floor, breaking a chair and upending the art table. His ungainly body lay spread-eagled on the tiles as a cloud of glitter started to descend.

Susan started towards him. Around the room, giggles began to emerge. To Susan's relief, the man sat up. The face under the unruly beard flushed red. As Susan approached, he let out an embarrassed giggle. 'Sorry,' he muttered, with a thick Scottish burr. He eyed the broken chair and grimaced. 'I'll pay for that,' he said.

'Don't worry, it was an accident. Are you okay?' Susan said, offering her hand to help him up. She glanced at him again as he took it. She had seen him before, she thought. For a moment, she couldn't work out why his face was familiar, then in a flash it came to her: it was Douglas MacLeod from LoveSpark. She watched as his open friendly glance turned to wide-eyed recognition. The thought hammered in her head. *Don't say it. Please don't say it.* Her heart pounded in her throat as he stood up, just as Nina arrived beside them.

He gasped. 'You're Susan, right? From LoveSpark!'

As soon as he'd said it, his face turned an even darker shade of red and he glanced around, seeming to realise what he'd just said in front of a whole nursery class. From the corner of her eye, Susan saw Nina's eyes widen. Heat rose in her face. Her cheeks were burning.

'Is that your real name, Miss?' Christina was staring from Susan to Douglas and back again. 'What's LoveSpark?'

Susan glanced at Nina. Nina cringed, but Susan could see the sympathy behind the horror. 'Yes,' she said. 'My first name is Susan.' She cleared her throat.

'LoveSpark's a bookshop,' Douglas said, in a very calm, assured voice. 'I met Miss Collins there.' His eyes were glued to Susan's face, urgently sending his apologies.

Noah frowned. 'That's not what LoveSpark is,' he objected. 'It's on computers. It's where mummies go to find new daddies, that's what my mum says.'

Susan wished she could crawl into the miniature playhouse in the corner of the room and hide until the end of the day. She couldn't bring herself to look at Jack.

'There's a bookshop too.' This time it was Nina who spoke. 'You must be the author.' She held out a hand to Douglas, who shook it heartily, his eyes filled with gratitude.

Susan took a deep breath and pushed her shoulders back. 'Yes, everyone,' she said. 'This gentleman is an

author. His name is Mr MacLeod and he writes books.'
The children were still all eyes. Christina opened her
mouth, but Susan held up her hands. 'I want everyone
to go sit in the book corner,' she said. 'Mr MacLeod,
I'll get you a chair.' To her relief, Christina shut her
mouth with a snap and scurried towards the carpet
with the others.

Finally, Douglas seemed to gather himself into something approaching professionalism. He sat down on the
chair Susan brought him. Even when seated, he towered
above the children like a giant. They stared up at him,
seemingly fascinated with his hugeness and his crazy
hair and beard. 'Hello there!' he boomed. 'My name is
Douglas MacLeod and I'm here to take you on a
magical journey.' He reached down to the briefcase he
had set at his feet and pulled out a book. He held it
up, showing them the cover. '*The Adventures of Frosty
and Snowflake*,' Susan read. Above the title, a pair of
sweet hedgehogs were scampering side by side into a
tangled wintery wood.

Douglas opened the front cover and began to read.
His oversized hands were surprisingly expressive and
he pulled funny faces as he spoke. Each of the characters had a different voice. Susan looked round the
faces of her class. Every single one seemed alight with
interest. Her eyes lingered for a while on Jack. He
seemed just as delighted as the rest.

She looked again at Douglas. Was he really this
scruffy? she wondered. Or had he deliberately messed

up his hair? It looked almost as if he'd gelled it into spikes. That must be for the children's benefit . . . right? Several times he was playing the buffoon so much that he almost fell off his chair. It seemed he was even more wild in person than he'd looked online. She couldn't help cringing a little at the thought of being out with him. Perhaps he couldn't help being clumsy, but he seemed to be revelling in it. He laughed often, a great honking laugh that set the children off, but put her teeth on edge. Would he turn up on their date in the same unkempt state?

She pictured herself sitting opposite him in a nice restaurant and winced. She had built him up into something special in her mind, but now she was filled with doubt. Could she tell him she'd changed her mind? She wracked her brains for something that she could say that wouldn't embarrass him.

His story drew to a close. He looked round and grinned at Susan and in an instant she knew she couldn't say a word. For all his ungainliness, she couldn't escape the feeling that he was kind. She wouldn't hurt his feelings, she thought. She would see him tonight and then back out. Lots of pairings never made it past the first date.

She smiled back, then looked at the class. 'Well, children, wasn't that lovely?' she said. 'I'd like you all to give Mr MacLeod a round of applause, please.' She and Nina started to clap and the children joined in, climbing to their knees, faces glowing.

Douglas smiled and held up his hands for silence. 'Thank *you*!' he said to the class. He turned to Susan. 'And thank you, Miss Collins, for agreeing to have me. It really has been a pleasure.' His honest blue eyes crinkled, lighting up his whole face. Susan accompanied him to the door. 'Thank you very much for coming,' she said, then very quietly, 'I'll see you later.'

He smiled again. 'I can't wait,' he whispered. Susan was relieved when he left and she could close the door behind him. Nina walked over as she returned to the room. Susan could see that she was bursting to say something, but she sent a warning look.

She was glad when it was time to go home. She had, one way or another, avoided being alone with Nina. She didn't want to talk about LoveSpark and Douglas. It was all too embarrassing.

The last thing in the world that she wanted to do tonight was go on that date. *But there's no excuse I could give,* she thought to herself, desperately. *He's seen me today!* She realised that aside from Douglas's buffoonery, she was feeling uncomfortable about her dating life being so close to Jack. Then and there, she decided that she would do the date and tell Douglas that she wasn't going to be dating any more. She would take down her LoveSpark profile. Online dating wasn't for her.

She walked home with Jack along the edge of the

green under the streetlights. It was still drizzling. Each lamp was surrounded by an orange halo of mist. Jack was holding her hand. He seemed weary. It was a pity she was going out, she thought. A lovely evening, reading stories in front of the fire with Jack, then a couple of hours of TV, seemed so appealing. Much better than donning her glad rags and meeting a near-stranger in a bar. She knew how it would be, searching for things to say: wondering what would happen this time when she mentioned her family. It felt odd this time. Douglas had met Jack, but not known he was her son.

It doesn't matter either way because I'm only seeing him this once, she told herself as she pulled the front-door key from her bag. She fitted the key in the lock but then a voice called from behind her. 'Susan?' She turned. It was Mr Gorski, standing without a jacket, looking lost. Susan felt immediately that something was very wrong.

'Susan, I'm sorry but I need help. Coffee's not well.'

Worry filled Susan's mind. Coffee wasn't a young dog. 'Oh, I'm sorry! What's wrong with her?' she asked. 'What do you need?'

'She's laid in her basket and whimpering and there's blood on her blanket. I called Animal Ark and they've said to bring her in but it's a long way to carry her. Please . . .' The old man's voice cracked. He was close to tears.

She reached out and gave his hand a squeeze. He

was so cold. 'Of course I'll take you,' she said. She glanced down at Jack, who was gazing at Mr Gorski. He loved Coffee. How would he take it if she was seriously ill? But Mr Gorski needed help. There was nothing for it but to get the little dog to Animal Ark. 'Come on, Jack,' she said. 'Mr Gorski needs us.'

Chapter Five

Susan pulled into Mr Gorski's driveway and parked as near to the door as possible. She opened the rear door. Mr Gorski would have to sit with Coffee in the back seat. Jack could sit in the front for now. She took Jack's hand again and followed Mr Gorski up the drive and into the house. He led them to the kitchen. Coffee was curled up in her basket, but she didn't look comfortable. She was panting and her face was anxious. Usually when Jack came in, Coffee would leap up and rush to him. Now, though she managed to wag her tail, she didn't try to move.

'Can you wait there with Mr Gorski?' Susan asked Jack.

Jack nodded, his eyes solemn. 'Is Coffee going to be all right, Mummy?'

Susan squeezed his small fingers. 'I'm not sure yet,' she said. 'We have to take her to Animal Ark.'

Mr Gorski held out a hand and Jack took it. Susan walked over and knelt down beside the little terrier.

'Will Mandy be able to make her better?' Jack asked. He sounded worried.

She glanced over at him. 'I hope so,' she said, 'but we'll have to wait and see, okay?' She turned her attention back to Coffee. If the little dog was in pain, she needed to be very careful when she moved her. As Mr Gorski had said, there was blood on the cushion where she was lying. Susan reached out and stroked Coffee's head. Her stumpy tail moved again. There was nothing for it. She was going to have to look.

As gently as she could, she rolled the terrier onto her side, then lifted her hind leg. Coffee's eyes were white-rimmed, but she made no attempt to resist. For Jack's sake, Susan stopped herself from crying out. There was blood everywhere. Near the back, in line with the teats that ran the length of her body there was a ragged looking wound. Coffee gave the tiniest whimper as she rolled back.

'Will you be able to lift her?' Mr Gorski looked down at her. He looked so worried that Susan wanted to hug him, but she had to stay practical.

'Yes,' she said. She put both arms under Coffee's bed. She would lift the whole thing, she thought. Coffee would be more comfortable.

Mr Gorski steadied the little dog's head as Susan manoeuvred the basket into the back seat of the car. He climbed in beside her and pulled on his seat belt. It was still raining hard. Susan could feel the rain on her back as she moved Jack's booster and helped him into the front seat. Then, with the windscreen wipers lashing back and forth, she drove the short distance to Animal Ark.

The lights were still on. Susan opened the car door and lifted Coffee's bed again. By the time she had Coffee in her arms, Mr Gorski had gone round and helped Jack out.

Helen Steer, Animal Ark's veterinary nurse, was sitting behind the reception desk. Her long brown hair was neatly tied back. She glanced up as they dashed in. Her welcoming smile froze when she saw Susan's face. 'What is it?' she asked.

'She's bleeding,' Susan gasped. 'Underneath.'

Helen was at her side in a second. It took only a moment for her to lift Coffee's leg and see the awful wound. 'Mandy's free,' she said. Her voice was so calm that Susan felt her heart slow a little. 'Come on through,' Helen said. She opened the consulting-room door and ushered them inside.

Mandy was sitting at the computer, but she stood up as soon as they walked in. 'What's up?' she asked. She sounded just as composed as Helen had.

Susan put Coffee's basket down on the black-topped table. 'It's Coffee,' she said. 'She's bleeding.'

'Okay then, let's have a look.' Mandy's voice was soothing. She reached out and stroked Coffee's head, then checked the little dog's mouth. 'Her gums are still nice and pink,' she assured them. 'I know it looks as if there's a lot of blood, but she hasn't lost a dangerous amount.' The sure hands continued to explore. She shifted Coffee's head onto her blanket, then rolled the quivering little body over. Susan felt a shock run through her. Under the bright lights, the ragged cut looked worse than ever. She sent a worried glance towards Jack. Helen, who had followed them through caught her gaze and held out a hand to Jack. 'Would you like to come with me?' she asked. 'I've got a sweet cat through here that loves being stroked.'

To Susan's relief, Jack grasped Helen's hand and trotted away. Mr Gorski moved closer to the table. Mandy looked at them both. 'I'm afraid Coffee has a tumour,' she said. 'It's on her mammary gland. It's burst open, which is why it's been bleeding.'

Susan heard Mr Gorski's gasp. He grasped the edge of the consulting table. For a moment, she wondered if he would fall, but he steadied himself. 'Can you operate?' he said. 'She's an old lady, but I'd like to try if possible. Please.' Susan could hear the pain in his voice.

Mandy was stroking Coffee's head, but she looked up at Mr Gorski and smiled. There was so much sympathy in her eyes. 'She's ten, isn't she?' she said. Did Mandy know all her patients so well? Susan wondered. The intensity of Mandy's professionalism and love of animals still amazed her.

Mr Gorski nodded. Mandy was checking over the rest of Coffee's body. 'I'm just going to check her lymph glands,' she said. 'It might be possible to operate, but I need to check if there's any sign that the tumour's spread.' Reaching for a stethoscope, she spent a couple of minutes listening to Coffee's lungs. She was very thorough, Susan thought, and wonderfully gentle. Coffee was a darling. Though the examination must have been uncomfortable at times, the little dog had only whimpered once. She even licked Mandy's hand as if she understood Mandy was trying to help.

Mandy took a step back, her eyes serious. 'There's no reason we can't operate,' she said. 'The tumour itself isn't too big. I'd like to take some chest X-rays first, though. The lungs are one of the places we check to see if there's any spread through the body. If her chest is clear, we can remove the lump itself. Better to do it now as it's been bleeding.' She looked up at them with her head on one side, giving Mr Gorski time to understand and consider.

'Thank you,' Mr Gorski said finally. Susan could see that tears were threatening to overflow from his eyes, but he stood firm. 'Do everything you need to.'

Mandy reached for a form. The next few minutes were taken up with explanations about what she would do and how much it was all going to cost. Susan listened as Mandy and Mr Gorski discussed what to expect. Coffee was in the best possible place to get help.

A few minutes later, she and Mr Gorski were sitting in the waiting room. Jack was huddled beside her. Helen and Mandy had taken Coffee through to prepare her for her anaesthetic. She would need to be asleep for the X-rays. Susan glanced up at the clock on the wall. There was no way she could desert Mr Gorski. Not while Coffee's life was hanging in the balance. She pulled her mobile phone out. 'I just need to call someone,' she said. 'Can you keep an eye on Jack for me?' she asked.

'Of course I can.' He managed a small smile.

Susan disentangled herself from Jack. 'Wait here. I'm just going to phone Nana,' she promised.

The rain was still lashing down. Susan pulled her hood up and made a dash for her car. She would phone Mum first, she thought. Hopefully Miranda would come and collect Jack. She didn't like to ask her to come out in this awful weather. The rain was battering against the windscreen, gusts of wind driving flurries across the glass. On the other end of the line, the phone was ringing. *Pick up, pick up, pick up.*

'Hello, love.' Miranda's voice was warm. 'Have you been held up?'

Through the bleary windscreen, Susan could see the dark bulk of the fells that rose behind the clinic. A solitary lane was marked by a string of lights slanting up the hillside. 'I'm not going to make it,' she told her mum. 'You remember Mr Gorski who lives across the road?'

There was a momentary pause, then Miranda's bright voice. 'The one with Coffee the Border Terrier? That Jack's always talking about?' She sounded as if she was smiling.

Thank goodness for Jack and his animal chatter, Susan thought, with relief. She wasn't going to have to explain the whole thing. 'Yes, that's the one,' she confirmed. 'Coffee's been taken ill. We've brought Mr Gorski to the vet's but she's probably going to have an operation.'

'Oh . . . poor little thing.' Miranda paused. Susan could imagine her mum looking at the clock or at the front door as she spoke. 'Would you like me to come and pick up Jack so you can stay with Mr Gorski?'

Susan gave a sigh of relief. She had hoped, but had been worried about asking. 'Would you?' she said. Warmth rose inside her. *How does Mum always know exactly what I need?*

'I'll be there in twenty minutes,' Miranda assured her. 'But does that mean you'll be missing your hot date? That's a shame, isn't it?'

'Yes, isn't it.' Susan crossed her fingers as she replied.

'Never mind, though, I'm sure it can be rearranged. See you soon.' She rang off.

Susan let the hand holding her phone drop into her lap. Calling her mum had been the easy part. Now she had to let Douglas know she wasn't going to make it. What to say? She rubbed her chin. In the distance, a pair of round headlights topped the brow of the hill and began to descend along the line of lights. The rain was easing. She had to get on with it.

She called up Messenger and began to type. She still wasn't sure what she wanted to tell him. Should she offer a different date? She paused to think. It would be polite, but the memory of his spiky hair and loud guffaw filled her head. She had wondered how to let him down gently. They really weren't suited. Was fate stepping in?

Quickly, she finished the message and read it back. It was short and to-the-point:

Hey Douglas, I'm afraid I can't come tonight. Elderly neighbour's dog needs an emergency operation, he hasn't got anyone else to stay with him. So sorry for the late notice.

There was a good chance he wouldn't reply. Taking a deep breath, she clicked 'send' and it was done.

Goodbye, Douglas. Goodbye, LoveSpark, she thought. Despite the awful situation with Coffee, she felt a little lighter as she made a dash back into the clinic.

It was lucky Miranda had come quickly, she thought an hour and a half later. Mandy had come through just after Jack had left. She'd explained that the X-rays were clear and she was going to operate. Susan had sent a quick text to her mum and got one back. They were safely home, Miranda had assured Susan. Jack was ready for bed. She would give him the news in the morning.

And now they were waiting. Susan's eyes wandered yet again round the room, taking in the carefully grouped chairs and the plants that kept the cats and dogs apart.

Mr Gorski sat beside her. His head had fallen back to rest on the window. His eyes were closed. How exhausted he looked. For a long time there had been silence, broken only by the distant barks of Bounce in the Hope Meadows kennels, but now Susan heard movement: the sound of a door opening and closing and the muffled sound of voices. The door to the waiting room opened and Mandy walked in. She looked drained, Susan thought. No wonder. It must be exhausting to tackle an emergency at the end of a full day's work. Mr Gorski stirred, opened his eyes and sat up.

'The operation went well,' Mandy said, pulling one of the chairs towards her and sitting down. 'I'm pretty sure I got the whole thing. I'll get it sent off to the lab. I'm going to keep her in overnight.' She gazed at them, eyebrows raised, waiting for questions.

'Can I see her?' Mr Gorski asked. Susan wanted to reach out and hug him. His eyes were pleading.

Mandy smiled. 'Of course,' she said. 'I'll take you through. She's still very sleepy.'

Coffee was in the recovery ward. She lay on her side, eyes half closed under a fluffy blue blanket. A drip led to her foreleg, which was neatly swathed in a red bandage. Helen was standing at the open door of the kennel, stroking the rough little head.

With a cry, Mr Gorski rushed over. Helen shifted to the side to let him in. Coffee's short tail banged on the metal kennel and she blinked her eyes, but she didn't lift her head.

'There are painkillers in her drip,' Helen explained. 'We'll keep her on them overnight, then we can see in the morning about moving to tablets.'

Mr Gorski was stroking Coffee's head over and over. He turned to look at Mandy and then Helen. There were tears in his eyes. 'Thanks so much,' he said. He let out a long, shuddering breath.

Mandy's eyes were on Coffee. 'We'll keep her comfortable,' she assured him, 'and we'll wait and see what the lab says and after that, we'll have to wait and see what happens. I'll not be in tomorrow,' she sent the tiniest smile towards Susan, 'but Helen'll be here. She'll give you an update.'

'Thank you,' Mr Gorski said again. With a sigh, he gave Coffee one last caress, then turned and trailed across the room. Susan followed him outside and helped him into the car. He seemed very much older, all of a sudden.

She drove her car right up the driveway to his front door and stopped.

'Do you want me to come in?' she asked. She was relieved when he shook his head.

'Thanks for everything, Susan,' he said, sounding exhausted as he climbed out.

She felt bone weary too. She drove back onto the road, parked the car and climbed out. She turned and paused for a moment outside the front door of Moon

Cottage to look at the sky. The rain had finally cleared. The air was wonderfully fresh after hours in the heated waiting room. She turned back, put her key in the door and shoved it open.

There was an envelope on the mat. Bending, she picked it up and turned it over. The handwriting was familiar, but for a moment she couldn't place it. Then a cold feeling filled her chest. The mysterious man was no longer a puzzle. For a long moment, she couldn't take her eyes off the letter. The stamp was bright and Christmassy: sickeningly inappropriate.

Scrunching up the envelope, she shoved it into her coat pocket. It had been a long night, she thought. It had been four long years since she'd heard from him. She didn't have to deal with his letter now.

Or ever. She slammed the front door shut.

Chapter Six

Susan slept surprisingly well. She woke in the morning to the rising sun and jumped out of bed. She was halfway through making a cup of tea when she remembered the letter in her coat pocket, and for a moment she hesitated, feeling almost as if it was watching her through the fabric. But then she shook the feeling off. She wasn't going to let it ruin her day – she was going to York with Mandy, and they were going to have fun. She washed and dressed in record time, then headed outside.

Cold air nipped at her fingers as she rushed to the car. Climbing in, she drove the short distance to Animal Ark. She'd been looking forward to this for days. York was beautiful all year round, but now it would be filled with decorations. There would be a huge tree in St Helen's Square and festive stalls in the Shambles Market.

Every year since Jack was born, Susan had bought a special decoration for the tree to celebrate. Each one reflected the things he loved that year. There were presents to buy too, and an outfit for Christmas Day.

She would be spending it with Miranda and Jack. Her mum always made a special effort, and of course she was always stunning. It would be lovely to have something equally special to wear.

She pulled up outside the veterinary clinic. Mandy had told her to come to the old cottage next to the surgery where Mandy had grown up and where her parents still lived. Emily Hope opened the door. Emily smiled when she saw Susan. 'Mandy's not quite ready,' she said. 'She's out in the clinic if you want to go through.'

'Thanks, Emily.' Susan returned her grin. She was looking well, Susan thought. Mandy had been desperately worried when her mum had been diagnosed with MS. But for now, everything seemed to be going better than anybody had hoped.

Susan stepped across the gravel, opened the door and stopped. Standing close to Helen behind the reception desk was a young man with blond hair and blue eyes. He was smooth-shaven with a very attractive smile. His hair was carefully coiffed into meticulous spikiness. He was leaning over Helen to point to something on the computer screen and Helen was laughing. Two pairs of eyes swivelled towards Susan as she walked in. Helen smiled a greeting and the young man pulled himself upright and moved away from Helen a little.

'Hi, Susan,' Helen called. 'Mandy'll be through in a second. She's just washing her hands.'

Sure enough, a moment later, Mandy rushed in.

'Sorry, Susan,' she said. 'One of the goats in Hope Meadows had a sore eye. It took ages to catch her.'

Susan grinned. 'You're here now,' she said. 'How's Coffee doing?'

Mandy waved to Helen and the young man. 'Bye,' she called. 'Have a good day.' Pulling open the door, she ushered Susan back outside into the sunlight. 'Coffee's doing okay,' she assured Susan as she closed the door behind her. 'She's had her breakfast and the wound's fine. She can go home later, all being well.'

Susan unlocked the car and dropped into the driver's seat. Mandy climbed in beside her.

'So what do you think of Toby Gordon, our new vet?' she asked as Susan turned out of the lane and swung onto the Walton road. 'He was by far the best candidate that we interviewed, with loads of experience in anaesthetics and exotic animal practice. We're lucky to have him! And Mum feels much better about stepping back now there's someone to share the work with me and Dad.'

Susan risked a sideways glance at Mandy. Mandy looked amused, as if this was some kind of test.

'Toby eh?' she said. 'Well I think . . .' She paused, pretending to frown and then grinned. 'I think . . . that he's going to be the subject of a very great deal of village gossip!'

Mandy laughed. 'Never a truer word . . .' she admitted. From the corner of her eye, Susan could see that Mandy was looking at her. She thought she knew what was coming next.

'Spit it out,' she said. 'Whatever it is you're thinking.'

Mandy grinned with delight. 'You're far too perceptive,' she said. 'Well, I was thinking what about you? Will you be part of that gossip?'

Susan rolled her eyes and gave a firm shake of her head. 'Not my type,' she said. *Too pretty,* her mind added. She really hadn't felt any kind of spark when she'd seen him. 'So he's single?' she asked. He would cause havoc in the village if so.

'He is,' Mandy said, 'though I must confess Mrs Ponsonby seemed very keen to see him yesterday when she brought Fancy in to have her nails clipped. Maybe he won't be on the market for long.'

It was Susan's turn to laugh. Mrs Ponsonby was Welford's most redoubtable widow, and a regular at Animal Ark with Fancy, her much loved Pekinese. The idea of that slick young man and the very upright older woman together was hilarious. 'Imagine her with Fancy under one arm and Toby under the other,' she said.

'Or she could keep him in her handbag,' Mandy shot back, then groaned. 'Poor Toby,' she said, then clapped her hands down on her knees. 'Speaking of new couples,' she said, 'how about you and that Douglas? You were meant to meet last night, weren't you? Was he okay about it? Have you rearranged a time yet?'

Susan sighed as she came back to earth. 'No,' she said, 'and I'm not going to. I didn't get a chance to say, but he turned up at the nursery yesterday for a visit. You know he's a children's illustrator. He brought one of his books to read. I had no idea he was coming. My boss set it up . . .'

Mandy frowned. 'And . . .' she prompted.

'And it was awful.' Susan put her foot on the brake as she approached the turning onto the main road. She glanced to left and right, then pulled out. 'He was like some kind of buffoon,' she said when they were moving again. 'He was so wild-looking,' she wrinkled her nose, 'and stupidly loud. He laughed like a seal. I wanted to tell him I didn't want to meet, but it seemed so rude.'

'So you weren't too disappointed you had to cancel?' Mandy asked. The teasing tone had disappeared from her voice.

'Not at all.' Susan was definite. She would be happy if she never ran into him again.

Below them, the Plain of York stretched into the distance. It was beginning to cloud over, a thin high layer of cloud that looked very far away. Presently a few flakes of snow appeared. 'Was this forecast?' Susan asked Mandy.

Mandy shook her head. 'Mum said they were talking about a cold snap on the TV last night, though.'

The snow was coming faster now, the flakes swirling in eddies over the windscreen.

'Jack will be pleased!' Susan said, happily. She squinted at the clouds. 'Looks like it might be heavy, though. Do you want to turn back?'

Mandy looked out for a moment, assessing the sky. 'Not unless you want to,' she said.

'We'll see if it gets any worse,' Susan said. The snow was beginning to lie. By the time they reached York, the ground had turned properly white. Susan turned in at the entrance to a multi-storey car park near the castle. At least the car would be under cover. It was a good thing she'd worn her fur-lined boots.

The city had a magical look. The snow had stopped for now and the sky was clearing a little. They tramped through the narrow streets, surrounded on all sides by fairy lights and glitter. Christmas music floated through the air. Stalls had been set up all round the town centre. Mandy stopped at a stall selling brightly coloured candles. Susan stopped beside her. There were all different shapes and sizes from tiny tea-lights to massive pillars with multiple wicks. Susan lifted a red candle in a glass to her nose. It was scented with cinnamon and apple.

She breathed in deeply, then held it out to Mandy, who sniffed it appreciatively. 'Smells like Christmas,' she said.

They walked on to see the Minster. Every ledge and spire was edged in white. As they looked, a ray of sun broke through the clouds, lighting up the rose window. Susan felt a shiver run down her spine; it was so beautiful. The sun went in again and the moment passed. As one, they turned.

'Where next?' Mandy asked. 'I need to buy some

presents for the twins,' she added, 'though I've no idea what. I should have asked Jimmy.'

'Why didn't you?' Susan asked.

Mandy waved an airy hand and grinned. 'Didn't want to admit I'd no idea what I was doing.' Susan found herself smiling back. Mandy's cheeriness and honesty were infectious.

'What are they into just now?' Susan asked.

Mandy looked up at the sky, then back to Susan. 'Well they love the kittens,' she said.

Susan smiled. Abi and Max had adopted the two young cats from Hope Meadows at the end of the summer. Susan knew they'd been a great hit. She thought for a moment.

'What about,' she said, 'buying them a stocking each and filling it with little bits and bobs? Mini calendars and pens and stuff. You could get things with kittens on.'

Mandy opened her eyes wide. 'That's a brilliant idea,' she said. 'Maybe a little soft toy each. And some chocolate coins . . .' she trailed off. 'You're a genius,' she added a moment later.

'Well in that case,' Susan said, 'we can start in here.' She steered Mandy towards the entrance of a large department store. 'I need to find a white toy kitten for Jack too. He's so taken with that kitten at Hope Meadows, that I think it will be the perfect present. And I want a special ornament for him to put on the tree.' They walked in and took the escalator up to the second floor. There were lots of small gift items. The whole shop was beautifully decorated. There was music playing in the background. It really was very Christmassy, even though November still wasn't quite over.

There was a whole section dedicated to soft toys. 'Did you say you wanted a white kitten?' Mandy called. She was next to a stand where there were all different shapes and sizes of cats. Susan walked over. Some of the toys were truly enormous, bigger than Jack. But the one Mandy was holding out was quite small. 'Look,' she said, wiggling her hand so the kitten danced. 'This one's a bit like the kitten I've got in at the moment.'

Susan reached out and took it. It really was the sweetest thing. It had wide blue eyes and tufty fur. Best of all were its realistic pink nose and incredibly long whiskers. 'It's perfect,' she said. She stroked it. It was silky soft. 'Thanks, Mandy.' Jack would love it.

'What about Abi and Max?' she asked Mandy. Do you think they'd like soft toys, or are they a bit old?' What were they now? Ten, she thought.

'They still like them,' Mandy replied. 'Maybe dogs, though, rather than cats. Huskies if they had any.' As well as the kittens, Mandy's partner Jimmy Marsh owned two huskies. 'Especially if they have some small enough to fit in a stocking.'

They wandered a little further. With Susan's help, Mandy chose several small presents for the twins. Susan also found a lovely umbrella for Jack with sheep all round the outside and a wind-up penguin that waddled and flapped its wings.

They made their way back downstairs and Susan

caught sight of a lovely deep red dress. It was a skater style, overlaid with red lace. She walked over, took it off the rack and held it up. 'What do you think of this?' she asked Mandy.

Miranda had slipped some money into Susan's hand when she'd collected Jack from Hope Meadows last night. 'Treat yourself to something nice,' she'd whispered.

Mandy smiled. 'Lovely,' she said.

Susan wanted to laugh at Mandy's expression, which held nothing more than polite interest. Her friend wasn't a great lover of clothes and didn't go in for dresses at all, but she seemed happy enough to follow Susan to the changing room.

It was the most fantastic dress. Susan gazed at herself in the full-length mirror. Despite the unforgiving light she could see, as she turned this way and that, that it hugged her figure in all the right places. It wasn't the most practical of dresses; lace sleeves weren't great at keeping out the cold. *But Mum said something nice . . .* Susan reasoned to herself. It would be lovely, for once, to buy something just because it was beautiful and not because she had calculated how much wear she could get out of it. She pushed open the curtain and twirled out to show Mandy.

'It looks great,' Mandy said. She looked genuinely impressed.

Susan put her hands on her hips and gazed down at the dress. It really made her feel good. 'It actually does, doesn't it?' she grinned. 'Yeah. I'm going for it.'

Perhaps she didn't have anywhere exciting to wear it, but it would be fantastic to feel glamorous on Christmas morning.

Ten minutes later, they were back outside. Though there was still snow on the ground, it was becoming slushy. Clutching their bags, they explored the stalls, looking for Christmas decorations. Susan had just handed over the money for a little robin ornament for Jack to hang on the tree when there came a crash of thunder. She glanced up at the sky. Huge black clouds were closing in. Within a minute, large raindrops began to fall.

'We should have bought ourselves umbrellas too,' Susan joked. She had to raise her voice for Mandy to hear. They were sheltering under an awning for now. The stall was selling mulled wine. It smelled wonderful, but Susan was driving. 'Should we make a dash for it?' she suggested. 'Find lunch somewhere. Hopefully this won't last too long.'

Mandy glanced out at the rain. It seemed to slow a little. 'We could go to James's,' she suggested.

James was a childhood friend of Mandy and Susan's. He ran a little café-cum-bookshop in York. Susan had heard a lot about it but had never been. 'Where is it?' she yelled. The deluge intensified again, thrumming on the canvas over their heads.

'It's just round the corner on the other side of the road,' Mandy bawled. 'I was going to suggest it anyway, if you didn't have anywhere else in mind. James is working, but he might have time to have lunch with us.'

'That would be lovely,' Susan shouted. It was ages since she'd seen James, and Mandy often talked about the little café.

They waited a moment longer until the rain eased again, then after a nod, Mandy made a dash for the end of the street. Susan scurried after, bending her head against the driving rain. Round the corner, under a bridge. Ahead, Susan saw an old-fashioned shop front with bow windows: small panes of glass criss-crossed with white-painted bars. A moment later, she and Mandy stood in the doorway panting and laughing. Mandy straightened first. She slicked a hand through her blonde hair, pushing it back out of her eyes and blinking. Susan stood up, rubbing away the drips from her own forehead.

The glass in the door was misted. Mandy grinned as she pushed it open. 'Hope James doesn't object to drowned rats coming for lunch,' she said.

Susan followed Mandy inside. The little café was just as cosy as Mandy had promised. Its walls were lined with bookshelves. Tables were tucked into booths and there were nooks and crannies filled with artwork and paintings. But she stopped dead as she heard a booming voice from the back of the café. 'Snowflake rushed to the edge of the frozen lake. Frosty was stuck in the ice!'

From the alcove at the back of the shop there came a roar of children's laughter. A huge man with flame-red hair pranced into view, gurning madly and waving his arms. It was Douglas MacLeod.

Chapter Seven

There was no time to back out. Douglas had seen her. The grin widened to watermelon proportions and he waved both arms in the air. 'Hi there,' he mouthed, and disappeared again.

Beside her, Mandy was frowning. 'Do you know him?' she asked.

Susan managed a weak smile as she looked at Mandy. 'That's Douglas,' she admitted.

The gangly figure hove back into view. He was singing a bouncing song and jumping up and down. Susan's face was hot. She felt embarrassed on his behalf, although he certainly didn't seem to be. She was glad when Mandy guided her to a seat. Douglas was now letting out his honking goose laughter. The song continued, culminating in the most enormous leap and a farting noise. Some of the children joined in and the café rang with the sound of competitive raspberry blowing.

She could turn away, but she couldn't close her ears. How had she ever thought of him as attractive? The idea of them sharing a quiet romantic evening appeared absurd. He seemed wholly undateable. *See what I mean?* The words got as far as her teeth, but she stopped them as she turned back to Mandy. Mandy was watching him too, but she looked fascinated. She laughed out loud. Susan closed her eyes. *Don't encourage him.*

A shadow fell over them. Susan looked up. James was smiling down at them. His brown hair was flopping over his forehead as it always did, and his glasses were halfway down his nose. He pushed them up. 'Mandy, Susan! What brings you here?' he asked.

Mandy stood up to hug him. 'We're on a girly shopping trip and we thought you might like to have lunch with us! If you have time, that is?'

James grinned, leaning his hands on the table. 'I'd love to,' he said. 'Give me five minutes. I'll be free once story time's over.' He followed Susan's gaze towards Douglas's antics and grinned. 'Enjoying the show?'

Susan resisted the temptation to grimace. This was James's café. Under all other circumstances it would be delightful. 'Oh, yes,' she managed.

'Can I get you some drinks?' James asked.

Susan asked for a latte and Mandy a hot chocolate. Mandy's attention was still on Douglas whenever he capered into view. Now and then, she turned to address a remark to Susan. Susan found it difficult to concentrate. In a few minutes Douglas was going to bound over. He would ask when he could see her. How could she tell him she didn't want a date? She could hardly say she was busy the whole time between now and Christmas.

She lifted her coffee to her mouth and took a sip. It tasted wonderful, but she felt it would choke her. She set it down again. Today had started so well. Now everything just seemed awkward and difficult.

Douglas finished his story with a final roar. There was a burst of enthusiastic clapping from the children, then they began to appear from the alcove as Douglas bent to put his props back into his briefcase. As Susan had predicted, once he had tidied up, he made a rush for their table. Pulling out a chair without asking, he sat down.

'Do you mind if I sit down?' he asked. He sounded breathless. No wonder, Susan thought. Did he ever sit still?

James came over too. He clapped Douglas on the back and pulled up another chair. 'That was great,' he said. He glanced round the table and frowned. 'Do you guys know each other?' he asked.

Susan felt the familiar heat rising in her face. Would Douglas blurt out about LoveSpark again? But Douglas glanced at her with the hint of a smile. 'Sort of,' he said to James. 'I did story time the other day at the nursery where Susan works.'

'Great!' James turned to Mandy. 'Douglas is our most popular storyteller,' he said. 'Every time he comes, we get a bigger audience. The parents get a break and a coffee and the kids have a whale of a time. Bet he was a hit at your nursery,' he said to Susan.

'He was,' Susan replied. She wished they could talk

about something else. She searched her mind for a change of subject.

'How's the dog doing, Susan?' Douglas's voice startled her and for a moment she had no idea what he was talking about. 'The dog from last night?' he added after a moment.

'She's doing well,' Mandy said.

Douglas looked at Mandy with his head on one side as if wondering how she had guessed which dog he was talking about.

'I'm the vet that operated on Coffee,' Mandy explained and his expression turned from mystification to understanding.

'I was really sorry to hear about her,' he said. The twinkle had gone from his eyes and he looked genuinely concerned. Susan watched him as he questioned Mandy about Coffee. The buffoon seemed momentarily to have disappeared. He looked sympathetic as he listened.

'Well done, you.' He reached out a little awkwardly and patted Mandy on the shoulder as she finished. 'Sounds like Coffee's in good hands.'

There was a moment's silence, then James turned to Mandy. 'So how are things at Hope Meadows?' he asked.

'Well I've got lots of animals in just now . . .' A minute later, they were deep in conversation.

Susan sent a tentative smile towards Douglas. Her mind had gone blank again.

He leaned forwards, resting an elbow on the table.

'I'd love to rearrange our date,' he said, keeping his voice low. 'I was sorry when you said you couldn't make it.'

For a moment, Susan was tongue-tied. What could she say that wouldn't be cruel? 'I'm sorry I had to cancel,' she said. It was sort of the truth.

'So what about it?' he said. His eyes looked so hopeful, but she really didn't want to go. She had to let him down gently.

She took a deep breath. 'I don't actually have my diary here,' she said. 'I wasn't expecting to run into you.' She waited for him to look disappointed. He would get the hint, wouldn't he?

But Douglas's grin was back. 'No worries,' he said. 'In that case I'll drop you a message later and you can let me know.' He scraped out his chair, leaned back and looked around as if he was quite satisfied. 'I'll have to go,' he said, putting his palms down on the table. 'Enjoy your lunch.' He pushed himself upright, patted James on the back and thanked him, lifted his briefcase and walked out. Though nothing was resolved, a wave of relief washed over Susan as he left. At least that was over.

As the door closed behind Douglas, James turned to her. 'So how are you, Susan?' he asked.

'I'm fine,' she replied, finding her smile. James was always kind. It would be lovely to see him more often, she thought.

'It's good you've met Douglas,' James said. 'He's

great, isn't he? He comes in, sometimes, just for a chat.' He paused, then frowned slightly. 'Has he been to your nursery a few times?' he asked. 'He seemed very keen to talk to you.'

Mandy looked at Susan, a question in her eyes.

Susan sent her a rueful glance, then she put her cup down, smiling slightly. 'I'm supposed to be going on a date with him,' she confessed. 'I've been using LoveSpark and it matched us.' She felt herself go red yet again as she spoke, but there was nothing but polite interest on James's face.

'That's nice,' he said. 'Like I said, Douglas is lovely. You've done well to get such a good match.'

Susan let out a sigh. 'I'm sure he's lovely,' she said. 'I just don't think he's for me. He isn't my type.'

'He was a little . . . boisterous,' Mandy said, with a glance at Susan. Susan sent her a weak smile.

James laughed. 'All part of his act,' he said. 'He's quite different once you get to know him.'

'I liked him too,' Mandy admitted. 'I know what you mean,' she said with a wry glance in Susan's direction. 'He was being silly, but the children were loving it. I guess that's what his job is all about.'

They seemed so enthusiastic, that Susan found herself wavering a little. Children were often quite good judges of character. She lifted her cup and drank the last of her coffee. She didn't have to decide anything now, she thought. She should just concentrate on enjoying the rest of her day off.

'So are you both ready?' James asked. 'I know a lovely little restaurant just round the corner if you'd like to try it. It'll be nice to get out and eat something somebody else cooked for a change.'

They walked out, around the corner and into a small Thai restaurant. It was dimly lit inside with black walls, and leather furniture scattered with brightly coloured cushions. There was a great choice of food. All of it sounded lovely. Susan finally settled on some stuffed rice balls and a red curry. She was really hungry, she realised as she gave her order.

'So how has it been with LoveSpark?' James asked her as they waited for their food to arrive. 'Is Douglas your first match?'

Susan shook her head. 'I wish he was,' she said with a twisted grin. 'He's the fifth one I've actually tried to go out with, but the rest have been a write-off. As soon as they hear about Jack, they disappear in a puff of smoke. I never hear from them again.'

James wrinkled his nose and pushed his hair back off his forehead. 'Sorry,' he said, leaning his elbows on the table. 'Still, you know what they say about kissing a lot of frogs, right? Has Mandy told you about the awful date I had here?'

'She hasn't,' Susan replied. 'What happened?'

James grinned. 'Well, I'm pretty sure he'd been drinking,' he said. 'He suddenly yelled that he needed to pee, stood up and knocked the waiter's plate flying. Next thing I knew, I was wearing noodles on my head.

He was very apologetic. Said he'd take me home for a shower, but then took offence when I said "no thanks". I thought he was going to thump the waiter on the way out.' He glanced heavenwards. Susan wanted to laugh at the enormousness of his eye-roll. She knew just how he felt. She glanced at Mandy. She was grinning. James made it sound hilarious, though it must have been mortifying. 'Luckily Josh who runs the restaurant just laughed when I tried to apologise next time I was in,' James finished. 'But the moral of this story is, never take your date to your local.'

Susan laughed. A pity he hadn't given her that advice a couple of weeks ago. 'I can't beat that for sheer slapstick,' she said. 'Though I agree about not dating on your own doorstep. My last ended with me sitting alone in the Fox and Goose. I think he climbed out of the window. At least Bev didn't charge me for his food. It could have been worse.'

Mandy stirred. 'Do you remember that weird guy I dated for a while at university?' she asked James.

'The Hairdresser?' James's eyebrows disappeared under his fringe.

'That's the one,' Mandy admitted. She leaned back as their starters arrived. The waiter set out the plates, then left. 'Yum!' Mandy said and lifted her fork. She took a mouthful, chewed for a moment, then turned back to Susan. 'He wasn't a real hairdresser but he was *very* taken with my hair. I think it was the first thing he commented on. He said he had a bit of a thing about hair,' she said. She shook her head and frowned at the memory. 'I had no idea what he meant. He asked if he could brush it.' She shrugged. 'I thought it was a bit . . .' Mandy paused, '. . . well, unusual,' she went on, 'but harmless enough. He was so perfect in every other way: easy to talk to and funny and he had these amazing eyes. My friends were dead jealous.' She stopped for a moment, her face contemplative. 'The hair thing wouldn't have been a problem in itself,' she said finally, 'only he was obsessed. He just wouldn't stop stroking my head! I felt like a cat! I had to end it.' She waved her fork. 'It's odd,' she said, 'but right from the beginning, even though he looked perfect, there were alarm bells ringing. Kind of the opposite of when I first met Jimmy. On the surface, I was telling myself he was awful. An ignorant forest-wrecker with a side order of arrogance.'

She laughed at her own description and Susan found herself joining in. 'Poor Jimmy,' she said.

Mandy looked down at her vegetable satay, then lifted her eyes to look straight at Susan. 'I guess what I'm trying to say,' she said, 'is that from the outside, the Hairdresser seemed perfect and Jimmy the opposite. But somewhere inside I knew I had things the wrong way round. I never once felt unsafe with Jimmy. Even though he rubbed me up the wrong way, there was a feeling of trust. Whatever James and I think about Douglas, it's not about us. You have to work out what your own instincts are telling you.'

Susan looked down at her plate. Mandy was right, she thought. Douglas seemed loud, even irritating. But every time they'd spoken directly, his kindness had shone through. She would never know what he was like on a date unless she gave it a try. If she ended up with chow mein in her ears, so to speak, they didn't have to meet again.

'I guess I could give it a go,' she said slowly. 'After all, a public noodle shower is embarrassing, but not the end of the world.'

James laughed. 'I suggest a burger place.' His face became serious again. 'Mandy's right, though. You need to listen to your instincts. If something seems too good to be true, it probably is. I like Douglas, but it's about how you feel. I almost didn't go out with Raj. It didn't seem like the right time.' Susan hadn't met Raj yet, but she knew James had met him when he'd injured an owl with his van, and they'd brought it to Hope Meadows for treatment. James and Raj had fallen for each other. Susan studied James's face. A year and a half ago, James had lost his husband Paul to bone cancer. Susan had seen him a few times since and his eyes had been haunted. Now the black rings had faded, and there was an easy contentment in his face. 'Raj is coming to Mum and Dad's for Christmas,' he told them.

Mandy grinned and reached over to squeeze his shoulder. 'That's fantastic,' she said.

Susan shut her eyes for a moment, then opened them. 'I give in,' she said. 'You've persuaded me. When

I get home, I'll send him a text and tell him I've found my diary after all.'

'Well in that case,' James said, 'I hope you have a lovely time.'

'Me too,' Mandy said.

'You should,' joked Susan. 'I'm holding you responsible otherwise!'

Chapter Eight

Susan glanced over her shoulder at the mirror. It had been one week to the day since her conversation with James and Mandy. Today she was going out with Douglas.

She'd abandoned her traditional first-date outfit. It was starting to feel like bad luck. Left to herself, she would have worn her nice black dress, or one of the dresses she'd bought in York, but Douglas had told her to wear trousers. They were going to be outside, he'd said. She turned and tilted her head, still gazing at her reflection. She'd chosen a pair of dark green slim-fit cords and a fitted golden-brown jumper. The cords looked great with the black knee-high boots she'd pulled on.

With a last glance, she made a face at her reflection, then walked out of her bedroom and down the stairs. She'd been close to cancelling – once she'd gone so far as to type in a message. All her other dates had met her in bars or restaurants. Everything about Douglas seemed different, and not necessarily in a good way. She sighed. It would be fine, she told herself. It wasn't impossible that she'd enjoy it. And if she didn't, in a couple of hours she'd be back here. If she and Douglas didn't click, that would be it.

The hallway was a bit of a mess. She and Jack had been out that morning. Jack had collected several stones from the edge of the stream and brought them home. They lay on the hall table in a higgledy-piggledy pile. She plucked them up along with a stray plastic giraffe and two felt-tip pens that had somehow found their way under the radiator. She put them in the kitchen, then inspected the hall again. Jack's wellies were lying on their side where he'd left them in the rush of being collected by Miranda. She stood them up. Not that she had any intention of inviting Douglas in, but when he picked her up, she didn't want the place to look as if a bomb had hit it.

She heard the sound of footsteps outside and a second later, there was a loud knock. She stood very still for a moment. She didn't want him to think she was waiting just inside the door for him to arrive.

When she opened the door, she was pleasantly surprised. Though he wasn't dressed smartly, his clothes were unobjectionable. He had somehow tamed his hair and he had an unexpectedly pensive look on his face. She'd expected the same brash confidence he had when he was telling stories, but his smile was nervous.

There was an odd smell. She almost wrinkled her nose. What on earth could it be? she wondered. Presumably it wasn't Douglas. Maybe they were spreading something on the fields? He reached into the pocket of his waxed jacket and pulled out a small wooden box. 'I got you a present,' he said, waving it at her.

Susan reached out a hand and took the box. 'Luxury French Camembert,' she read. The less-than-pleasant aroma was almost overwhelming. She resisted the temptation to hold it away from her face.

'It's lovely,' Douglas said. 'I discovered it last year.'

Susan lifted her eyes from the brown lettering on the box. She'd never been given cheese on a date before. 'That's very thoughtful,' she said, stifling a laugh. *Other girls get flowers, I get . . . cheese?*

They stood in silence for what felt like several minutes. Douglas looked down at his feet for a moment, then glanced again at the cheese. His eyes widened as they returned to Susan's face. He drew in his breath as if he'd thought of something. 'You look lovely,' he said. He glanced down at her boots. 'You might want to change your footwear, though. You need something more practical.'

What on earth *are we doing?*

Susan looked at Douglas's feet. He was wearing trail shoes. 'Would trainers do?' she asked.

'Trainers would be perfect,' he replied. For the first time since she'd opened the door, he smiled that boyish grin, slightly lopsided and filled with enthusiasm.

Susan nodded, feeling confused. Two minutes in and this was already the oddest date she'd had yet! 'I'll just put this in the fridge,' she said, wiggling the aromatic cheese. She unzipped the glamorous boots, kicked them off and walked through to the kitchen. She opened the fridge and shoved the cheese inside, then grabbed her ratty old trainers from beside the back door. She regarded them, feeling ridiculous. What on earth was she doing, going out with this man-child who brought her cheese and took her to places where she couldn't wear nice things?

When she got back to the door, Douglas had walked up the road and was waiting beside his car. It was an old shooting brake Morris Minor with wooden trim. It was painted bright green, like a radioactive lime. Susan swallowed as she closed the door behind her. If she was feeling shy about being seen out with Douglas, this wasn't the car to travel in.

Though the interior wasn't exactly untidy, the back seat was filled with boxes of Douglas's books. He was holding the door open for her. Somehow, he even made that look awkward.

Soon they were rumbling along the edge of the village green. The bare trees were stark against the grey sky and the surface of the pond was ruffled. 'Where are we going?' she asked, turning to face him.

He grinned. 'It's a surprise,' he said. 'It should be fun. Just as well the rain's holding off.'

He slowed to turn right at the crossroads beside the

church and a moment later, they were scudding up Welford High Road towards the Beacon. Susan looked at the leaden sky. It might not be raining right now, but going by the past few days, there was every chance it could pour down any minute.

Where on earth was he taking her? she wondered. This road led up to Welford Hall, then up onto the moors. Would he take her walking up the fells? Susan had walked to the Beacon, the ancient Celtic cross, many times as a child. But it was hardly the place for a first date. Though she was wearing her trainers and a warm jacket, she wasn't kitted out for hiking. Even though last week's early snow had passed quickly, Susan knew it was important not to go out onto the moors without the right equipment. *And with all the rain we've been having, the ground will be like a bog!*

She glanced out of the window. The road zig-zagged upwards. Already they were climbing out of the village. A trail of smoke rose from the chimney of the Fox and Goose. It wouldn't be her first choice for a date either, after her previous disaster, but for a moment, she wished they were heading there. At least it would be warm. There would be a log fire and Bev and Gary behind the bar and quiet chatter.

'Here we are.' Douglas's voice brought her back from her reverie. To Susan's surprise, they had turned in to the entrance to Upper Welford Hall. Her heart rose a little. There was a café here now, she remembered. Mandy had told her about it. You could get coffee and a scone and watch the Upper Welford pedigree cows being milked in their rotary parlour. That would be a bit weird, but not bad at all. Perhaps a walk in the grounds, and then coffee . . .

But to Susan's dismay, when they got out of the car, Douglas didn't lead her through the stone archway. He led her the other way, down through a gate and into a paddock.

He turned to her and grinned. 'I hope you like climbing,' he said. 'I've arranged for us to have a go on the rope course. I don't know about you, but I've been on some *really* boring LoveSpark dates. Anything to avoid another mediocre plate of spaghetti carbonara, right?'

Susan's breath caught in her throat and she stopped. Mandy had told her all about the rope course. It lay on the edge of the wood right beside the paddock. She had never felt the slightest desire to try it. She hated heights. For a moment, she thought about turning and running back down the hill.

Douglas had stopped too. 'You haven't done it before, have you?' he asked. A worried line formed between his eyebrows.

Susan shook her head, forcing herself to smile. 'I haven't,' she said.

'Thank goodness.' He heaved a sigh as if enormously relieved.

Susan's stomach churned. She couldn't do this. She just couldn't. She ought to tell Douglas about her fear of heights, but he seemed so delighted that she hadn't done it before. His expression was that of a pleased puppy.

'Hello!' A new voice sounded behind them and Susan turned. It was Jimmy Marsh. He looked happy to see them, grinning at Douglas, then turning to Susan and giving her a little wink. Susan felt herself blush. Was he laughing at her and Douglas coming here for a hot date? Probably not, she reminded herself – it was Jimmy's own place, after all, and Jimmy had brought Mandy here for their first outing. He probably thought it perfectly suitable. She felt sick nonetheless. It was bad enough that she was going to do the rope course at all. Doing it in front of Jimmy as well as Douglas was mortifying. What if she couldn't even make it up to the first platform?

Douglas's smile had returned to full wattage as he held out a hand to Jimmy. 'Afternoon,' he bellowed, looking delighted. 'Good to see you again.'

'Hi, Susan,' said Jimmy.

Douglas glanced from Jimmy to Susan and then back again. 'Do you two know each other?' he asked.

Susan managed a tight smile. 'We do,' she admitted. 'Hi, Jimmy.'

Douglas had finished pumping Jimmy's hand. 'Really?' he said. For a second he looked bewildered. So much so that Susan suddenly wanted to laugh despite her nerves.

Jimmy cleared his throat. 'Through her friend Mandy,' he offered. 'She's my girlfriend.'

'Oh! Mandy, the lady I met in York! The vet!' Douglas's face had brightened again.

'That's right.' Jimmy led them into the little wooden hut. 'You'll need some gloves,' he said. He held out a pair of lightweight leather gloves to Susan, then rooted in a drawer for some larger ones for Douglas. 'Okay?' he asked.

Susan nodded her thanks.

'Great.' Douglas beamed.

Susan put on the gloves and then donned the helmet that Jimmy gave her. If she'd been worried about her trainers, it was nothing to how she would look with this on, she thought. She'd spent ages doing her hair. There was nothing for it, though.

They walked outside and made their way across the paddock to the edge of the wood. Susan couldn't help but feel a little bit reassured. The rope constructions looked sturdy and safe. But she almost gasped when she saw how high the first platform was. There wasn't much of a breeze down here, but the topmost branches were moving. A narrow set of wooden steps led up to it. Jimmy clipped a safety rope onto each of them.

Douglas gave her a bright smile. 'Would you like to go first?' he asked, pointing.

'No! Thanks. You go on,' Susan said, through gritted teeth. Douglas practically bounded up the ladder-like staircase onto the little wooden stage. He turned round with his arms outstretched, whooped loudly, then waved. 'Fantastic,' he yelled. 'Come on up, Susan. There's a brilliant view.'

Susan could barely bring herself to look up. Douglas wasn't even holding on.

'Okay, Susan,' Jimmy said. 'You next.'

It's fine, she told herself. *You can do this, it'll be great.*

Her heart was in her mouth. She put her foot on the first step. She was half expecting it to collapse, but in fact it was firm under her foot. She lifted her other foot, stepped up. By the time she was halfway up, her knees were so shaky that she had to stop. Jimmy was close behind her. She had to resist the temptation to turn and cling to him. Why were there no handrails? Above her head, there was a low branch. It was swaying. To go any further, she was going to have to duck underneath it.

Nope, I can't do it, she thought. *I just can't.*

Behind her, Jimmy was waiting. 'Are you okay, Susan?' he asked. There was nothing but patience in his voice.

'No.' The truth was out before she could even think.

'Is there anything I can do?'

Susan was frozen. Her head was spinning. Above her helmet, the branch was moving to and fro, just at the edge of her vision.

'We can go back down,' Jimmy said.

Susan frowned, trying to calm down and focus on the ladder in front of her. If she said yes, he wouldn't judge her. But a wave of sudden determination passed over her. If Douglas was going to make her come on this terrible idea for a date, she definitely wasn't going to let him see her frightened or embarrassed.

She closed her eyes for a moment, then opened them again. The momentary dizziness had passed. 'You can go up on all fours if you prefer,' Jimmy suggested. 'There's no right or wrong way to do it. I'm right behind you. You're quite safe.'

'Thanks, Jimmy.' Taking a deep breath, she leaned forward, placed her hands on the steps in front of her, and clinging tightly, she made her way past the swinging branch and on upwards.

She had half expected to find Douglas standing on his hands, or doing something equally crazy, but when she finally made it and put her palms on the platform, there was worry in his eyes.

'Are you okay?' he asked. 'I'm so sorry, I never thought to check if you didn't like heights! We don't have to carry on. If you'd rather go somewhere else or go home, it's quite all right.' He crouched down and took her hand.

With his help, Susan eased herself upright and onto the platform. If she didn't look down, it wasn't as bad as she'd thought. They were right next to the solidity of the tree trunk.

'I'm really sorry,' he repeated. He hadn't let go of her hand. He was holding on tightly as if he knew just how scared she was. 'Would you rather go back down?'

Though her legs were trembling, with her hand in

Douglas's and her back against the tree trunk, Susan risked a look round. Her heart was in her mouth but it was certainly an experience to be right up here in the branches. He'd been right about the view – to one side she could see right into the canopy of the wood, and to the other they could look over and see the roofs of Upper Welford Hall poking up between the branches.

Ahead of them was a cargo net. It was nice and wide. Susan took a long, deep breath. Maybe it would actually be easier to go on than to navigate her way back down those stairs. Douglas squeezed her fingers and she felt a little strength returning. 'Yeah. I want to carry on,' she said. If she sounded sure enough, perhaps even she would begin to believe it herself.

'You're doing really well,' Douglas said.

'You really are,' said Jimmy, who had arrived on the platform beside them. Douglas held on to Susan's hand until she gripped the rope and began to climb the net. He followed after her, and a few moments later they had eased themselves over the top and were sitting on the platform at the far side.

There was a rope bridge next. 'How would you like to do this?' Douglas asked. 'If I go first, I can wait for you on the other side?'

Susan nodded. Her knees felt a bit weak again as she glanced down.

'Don't look,' Douglas urged her. He smiled, sending her reassurance. 'Hold on with both hands and look straight ahead.'

He went first, swinging across the bridge, making it look effortless. Then it was Susan's turn. She did as he'd said, holding on to the guide ropes with both hands. The bridge was wobbly, and it was an incredibly long way down . . .

Don't look. One foot forward, then the next. Douglas was waiting for her at the far side. She looked up at him, and saw that he was pulling a funny face at her. She laughed, despite herself, as he did a little jig on the platform. He looked like an idiot, but he was doing it to keep her attention off the long drop to the ground, and weirdly, it actually helped.

He took her hand again as she stepped off the bridge. 'You're so brave,' he said.

'Oh shut up,' she replied. 'You're just saying that because I nearly had a heart attack coming up the ladder.'

'Well, yeah.' His fingers were warm and steady. Susan felt as if some of his courage was flowing into her. 'It's not brave if you're not scared.'

He smiled. There was real warmth in his gaze. For a moment, she felt butterflies in her stomach.

Douglas let go of her hand as Jimmy caught up with them and the moment passed. Susan felt a swoop of disappointment, but then she wanted to laugh. What had she expected? That he would kiss her right there and then, halfway up a tree with Jimmy watching? And . . . why did she suddenly feel like that might be okay?

By the time they got to the final section, Susan's muscles were aching. She had made it up and down several more nets, crossed what had felt like hundreds of swinging logs and slithered upside down along a kind of rope tunnel. Douglas had stopped to help her several times. Each time there had been that gentle smile, or a funny face. Now they had reached the final element. Susan's heart was in her mouth. It was a rope swing into a cargo net. Despite her success so far, Susan couldn't help but feel a twinge of terror at the huge gap.

'Hold on here,' Jimmy showed them, 'just above this knot. When you let go, the net will catch you.'

Susan was suddenly shaking again. What would happen, she thought, if she couldn't hold on and let go too soon? Would she crash down to the forest floor?

'May I go first?' Douglas asked.

'Be my guest,' Susan said. She wasn't at all sure that she would be able to do it. Her hands were shaking and her grip felt weak.

'Thanks.' He seemed genuinely grateful, as if she'd done him a favour.

He grasped the rope and pushed off, swinging crazily across the divide, then as he reached the end of his swing, he let go with a yell of delight. A moment later, he landed squarely in the centre of the net, bounced once, then stood up. 'Brilliant,' he shouted. Before Susan knew what was happening, he made his way to the edge of the net and dropped to the ground. He rushed across the gap. Hand over hand, he climbed back up the ladder to the platform where Susan was waiting with Jimmy.

'How are you feeling?' he asked Susan.

She shook her head slightly. 'Really quite sick,' she said and he laughed as she pulled a face.

'Would you mind if I had another go?' he asked. The puppy-like enthusiasm was back in full force. He couldn't help himself, she thought. He was throwing himself into this, heart and soul.

She shook her head. 'Of course I don't mind,' she said. 'You go on.'

'But you will give it a go?' he urged. 'It really is fun.'

Susan nodded. 'I will,' she said.

She watched as Douglas swung again, flinging himself into mid-air as if he hadn't a care in the world. What would it be like to be him? Susan wondered. Not that she was a coward. She had always prided herself on her strength – and it had got her up those damn steps right at the beginning, after all. But Douglas seemed fearless. He landed in the net again, then swung down over the edge and landed on the ground in a heap. He clambered to his feet, laughing. 'Oops,' he called.

'How about it?' Jimmy had waited with Susan. He had pulled the rope back over and was looking at her. Susan took hold of the rope. Her weight was back against the net, leaning away from the drop. She was trying not to look down, but Douglas appeared below her and she couldn't help herself. He was gazing up and smiling. To her amazement, he raised an arm, opened his mouth and began to sing. His voice was strong, a fine baritone, surprisingly sweet.

'Swing, Susan, swing. Have no fear.
Across the divide. I will be here.
Swing, Susan, swing, though your heart is aflutter.
And to go with your cheese I will buy you some butter.'

Susan laughed. It was ridiculous but she couldn't deny that it was funny. She grasped the rope more tightly. Taking a deep breath, her fingers gripped. She pushed herself off with all her might. Then she was swooping through the air. The wind was freezing, but she felt amazing – as if she was flying! It wasn't hard to keep her grip on the rope at all. She finally let go and her heart skipped a beat as she tumbled into the net, landing on her back, then bounced once, twice, then came to a stop.

She felt breathlessly happy. In the distance, she could hear both Douglas and Jimmy cheering. Her cheeks felt hot as she slithered to the bottom of the net and swung down to the ground. Douglas was waiting for her. He hugged her, and for a brief moment he held her close. 'Fantastic,' he said.

'It actually was.' He loosened her and she stood firm:

trembling but exhilarated. *She had done it*. By the time Jimmy arrived, she was breathing easily again. They walked back through the trees, across the paddock and back into the little hut.

'That was wonderful,' Douglas said, grinning at Jimmy. 'Thank you.'

'You both did really well,' Jimmy said. He looked happy as he took their helmets and gloves. ''Specially you Susan. It's not easy if you don't like heights.' He turned to Douglas. 'You should come back another day,' he said. 'I think you'd enjoy the high-wire even more.'

'That sounds great,' Douglas said.

'That . . . sounds like something I'd probably enjoy, *with advance warning*,' Susan said, giving Douglas a sly, gentle elbow in the ribs.

They walked back up to the car park. Though Susan was feeling great, her footsteps were slow. She hadn't looked forward to this date, but now it was almost at an end, she realised it had been wonderful to have a few hours doing something utterly different.

'Can I interest you in a coffee?' Douglas said. 'I hear there's a nice café here.'

'Yes please,' she said.

Douglas smiled as if her reply was the most satisfying thing he'd ever heard. He ushered her through the stone archway. On the far side, there was a small cobbled courtyard. There were little shops to one side selling cheese and woollen goods and other local items. In the centre there was a Christmas tree. There was a stall selling toffee apples and the sweet scent reached her on the chilly air.

She'd hoped for this, she thought. Right back at the beginning of their date. And now they were here.

Directly opposite, there was an even higher archway that looked as if it had once been the entrance to a barn. It was glassed in.

Douglas led her across and into a friendly looking café with a row of tables and chairs against another huge window. Through the glass, she could see down into the most enormous milking parlour. It was like a huge wheel, turning slowly. As she watched, a cow walked into one of the gaps on the revolving platform and on the other side, another was released. A red-haired dairyman in blue overalls was attaching the milking machine to the first cow's udder. It was a strangely fascinating sight to watch over coffee, even for Susan who had lived in rural Welford for years and years.

'Cappuccino?' Douglas suggested.

Ten minutes later, they were sitting at one of the tables, sipping coffee. Beyond the glass, the cows strolled in and out and the man in the boilersuit worked away.

'Mesmerising, isn't it?' Douglas said eventually.

'It's kind of great,' Susan said. She turned her full

attention to him. This really was turning out to be the most unusual date she'd ever been on. 'Almost as good as that rope swing.'

Douglas laughed, ran a finger round the handle of the coffee cup, then looked up and into her eyes. 'I hope you enjoyed it,' he said. 'I'm so sorry I never thought to ask if you liked heights.'

Susan smiled. 'It was okay in the end,' she assured him.

'That's good,' he said. His voice was earnest. 'So how long have you been in Welford?' he asked.

Susan found herself telling him about herself easily. About how she had come here when she was twelve with her parents. About Welford and Mandy and Hope Meadows and her mum. He gazed at her as she spoke as if everything she said was fascinating. She needn't have worried that he would be loud or embarrassing. Finally, she took a deep breath and mentioned Jack.

Douglas's eyes widened. 'The Jack I met in your nursery class? He's a lovely little chap! You must be very proud of him.'

And just like that, the moment was over. Like it was no big deal whatsoever. A feeling of warmth flooded through her. *He really is a great guy*, she thought to herself as they chatted on.

'Would you be able to show me Hope Meadows sometime?' he asked. 'I'm always looking for inspiration for writing. And Mandy seemed lovely, from what I saw of her in York.'

'She is lovely,' Susan agreed. 'I'll get in touch with her. I'm sure she'd be happy to show us around.'

Douglas glanced at his phone. A startled expression leaped into his eyes. 'Goodness,' he said, 'I didn't realise it was so late. I'm awfully sorry, but I'm going to have to go. I've an evening session in Walton library.' He looked flustered. 'I can drop you off,' he said. His blue eyes were mortified. 'I'm really sorry to have to rush you.'

Susan smiled at his consternation. 'It's no problem. It's nice that you're in such high demand.'

Susan pushed her chair out and lifted her jacket. Douglas helped her put it on and she thanked him. She hadn't expected him to be a gentleman, but somehow it seemed the most natural thing in the world.

He dropped her off beside the church near her cottage, and as she turned the corner, she felt the first drops of rain against her face, but the change in the weather didn't dent her mood.

It would be nice to see him again, she thought. She had utterly misjudged him. Even if he was sometimes a bit awkward, his heart was in the right place, and there was a grown man behind all the puppy-like capering. She smiled to herself as she rounded the final bend. The rain was falling faster, but she pulled her collar up around her neck.

Then she stopped dead. Despite the dimness of the light, she could see a form just ahead, and it was painfully familiar. She felt her heart miss a beat.

Jack's father was standing on her doorstep.

Chapter Nine

He was standing very still and for a moment, Susan couldn't move either. Michael Chalk, Susan's ex and Jack's biological father, who had deserted them both before Jack was born, was outside her house. Fury rose like a hot wave through her body. She barely felt her feet as she marched towards him.

'What the hell are you doing here?' Despite her anger, she spoke in a furious whisper. The last thing she wanted was for her neighbours to witness this meeting. She had built a wonderful life without him. She would not let him waltz back and destroy it. 'How dare you?' She shut her mouth with a snap and stood there, glaring into his ludicrously handsome face.

'Susan, I'm sorry. I tried to write, but . . .'

He seemed dismayed by her ferocity. She almost expected him to turn tail and run. He took a step back, but then stopped.

The rain intensified. Huge droplets hissed onto the paving slabs and gurgled in the guttering. Michael's carefully styled brown hair flattened. Rivulets of water began to run down his tanned face.

'What do you want?'

'Just to talk. I've . . . been having a hard time of it lately.' Susan clenched her teeth. Her eyes raked over his smart waxed jacket and pressed trousers. A shiny Mercedes stood on the road in front of her battered Twingo.

What would he know of hard times? Had he spent the past four years caring for a baby, and then a toddler? Jack was a wonderful child, but that didn't mean there'd been no sleepless nights. The panicked trips to the doctor, the tantrums, the ache and worry when they were apart too long. Michael had made it clear he wasn't interested in any of that.

Well, she wasn't interested in hearing his life story. How could he turn up here snivelling after all these years?

'My father died. A month ago.' He stopped then dropped his gaze to the floor. For a fleeting moment, Susan saw pain in his expression, but she pushed her sympathy aside.

In her mind's eye, she could see Michael's father. Like Michael himself, Angus Chalk had sported well-chiselled cheekbones and a decisive chin. He'd never shown her an ounce of kindness. Whenever Susan had veered into his eyeline, his expression had been stony. She had never been sure what crime she had committed, but she was certain that in Angus's eyes, she'd been beneath the notice of his son and heir.

'Sorry to hear that,' she lied. She kept her voice low.

She would not give him the pleasure of knowing how much he'd hurt her.

He lifted his eyes again and tried a smile. His gaze took on a beseeching look that didn't sit well with his aquiline features. 'I've been wanting to reach out to you for a while,' he said.

Susan stiffened. Did he think he was doing her a favour? 'You needn't have bothered,' she muttered. Her voice felt thick. 'We're fine without you.' She continued to stare.

He dropped his eyes first, but he raised them again with a sideways glance at the house. Susan felt herself getting hot. She was acutely aware of the shabby paint on her front door and the bulging window frame with its blistered white wood.

'I . . .' His eyes finally met hers. 'I was hoping . . .' He paused again. Susan waited. Whatever he wanted to say, she wasn't going to help. 'I'd like to get to know my son . . .' he said '. . . Jack. I know I don't have any right . . .'

'Correct!' Susan snapped out the word before he could go any further. 'You've no right to anything.' She stopped. Her mouth was trembling, but she squared her shoulders. 'I'd like you to go away now and leave us alone.'

He took another step back. His eyes raked her face as if searching for even the slightest sign of pity. Susan stood firm. The rain had slowed now and he was beginning to have a defeated look, standing there, soaked to the skin. 'Did you get my letter?' he asked.

Susan pursed her lips. She slid her hands into her pockets. The letter was still there, screwed up and unopened. 'Yes.' She swallowed. 'I threw it away,' she lied.

He sighed. Susan felt her annoyance surge again. He had always sighed, whenever she was 'being unreasonable' as he put it. That put-on air of saintly patience sickened her. 'I thought you might,' he said. 'I brought you a copy.' He held it out. When she failed to take it, he moved closer as if to try to thrust it into her hand.

Susan stepped back. 'I don't need it,' she said.

He held up his hands, and then put the copy of the letter down on the doormat. 'Please will you read it?' he asked. 'Please?' he said again.

'Fine.' Susan shivered. Water was running down her neck. 'Now will you go? We don't need anything from you.' The rage had left her. She was beginning to feel weak.

For a moment, she thought he was going to say something more, but with a final glance, he turned on his heel, pulled a key from his pocket and strode along the pavement to his car. Susan stood very still as he climbed in, then drove away. The car turned the corner and slid out of sight. Susan pulled out her own key. Her hand was shaking as she opened the front door.

She picked up the copy of the letter and crumpled it up, shoving it into the pocket beside the unopened first copy. It was freezing inside the house so the first thing she did was nudge the thermostat up. She should go and change out of her wet things, but instead, she slumped against the wall.

How could he come here? She'd not expected to see him again. He hadn't changed, she thought. He was still the handsome, privileged, oblivious man he always was. There had been a time she had loved that about him. Everything seemed easy when she was with him.

Despite her disquiet, a memory of better times rose out of the fog of regret. They had made love on a summer's evening in the sand dunes on a remote beach. She closed her eyes: felt his hands on her skin. Her trembling reaction. Her head fell back against the wall.

Reality returned. She remembered other times too. His rejection and the coldness of his eyes. Her fear for the child growing inside her. Bile rose in her throat. She glanced down again at the letter with its neat handwriting. She would read it, she thought. Then she would know what he had to say. There was nothing that would make her want him in her life again.

She shifted over until she was against the radiator. She was shivering, though her face was hot. Her fingers fumbled with the damp paper and she nearly dropped it, but then she ripped at it with a ferocity that almost tore the letter inside. Dragging the pages out, her eyes devoured the fusty sentences. How *Michael* it was. Dry and practical: devoid of emotion.

I would like to take up my legal rights as Jack's

father. I am aware that as his legal guardian, and the only person on his birth certificate, you, Susan Collins, are the only person who can grant me this right. I very much hope that you will allow me this contact, and that I can start to take the role I should have played since he was born.

It felt like one of his legal documents. The only personal touch was his signature: tidy blue writing on the bottom of the page. Could he not have made more effort?

She screwed the paper up and threw it on the hall table.

Thank goodness Jack was still with Miranda and hadn't been here to witness this. She might not have been able to stop Michael from seeing him. And if Jack had seen a man claiming to be his father, what then?

She wandered through into the kitchen and put the kettle on, standing there while the hissing sound filled the silence.

Jack was the most important thing in her life. She wouldn't let anything hurt him. And knowing that his father was a spoiled, selfish, cold man who'd abandoned him before he was even born could only hurt him.

But now, there was a sinking feeling settling in her stomach. The kettle finished boiling and clicked off, and Susan didn't move.

What would Jack have thought if he'd been here?

And what would he think years from now, if he found that his father had wanted a relationship and she, Susan, had denied him that?

She thought about her own dad, and how close they had been, especially when they first moved to Welford and Miranda was still travelling a lot for work. She thought about Michael's dad – as horrid as he'd been to Susan, the two of them had been close. Michael must be feeling guilty. Maybe he'd only just understood what he'd taken from Jack by leaving them the way he did. 'We don't need him,' Susan told the empty kitchen.

Chapter Ten

She was still there an hour and a half later when the doorbell rang. A shiver ran down her spine as she stood up from where she had slumped down against the kitchen cupboards. Surely he hadn't come back? She put her hands on the table and dragged herself upright. It seemed a long way to the front door. Her heart was thudding as she pulled the door open, but there, under the lamp, hair damp from the rain, stood Mandy Hope. Her collie Sky was beside her. Behind Mandy, Miranda was opening the car door and helping Jack out.

'Hi! How did the date go?' Mandy's voice was bright. Her grin fled as she looked into Susan's eyes. 'Is everything all right?' she asked.

And now Miranda was approaching, holding Jack's hand. 'Oh dear,' she said, looking directly at Susan. 'Does Mummy have a headache?' she said, her voice bright. Susan nodded and swallowed hard. Her mum could always tell when there was something up. Miranda bent to speak to Jack. 'Well Jack, it looks like Nana is going to put you to bed tonight. Mandy will help Mummy with her headache, won't you dear?'

She turned her well-meaning gaze on Mandy, who looked a little surprised, but nodded.

'Now go give Mummy a good night hug.' Miranda spoke to Jack again.

Susan crouched down as Jack let go of Miranda's hand. He rushed forward, then stopped and moved carefully to her, snuggling in, his arms tight. Susan buried her face in his small shoulder. He was so precious. She didn't want to let go. She breathed in deeply, dropped a kiss onto his neck, then loosened her arms and looked directly at him. How big his brown eyes were. She managed a smile. 'Good night, sweetie,' she told him. 'Nana will take you up now, okay?'

'Love you, Mummy. Get well soon.' His face was solemn. She wanted to hug him again, but she let Miranda take his hand and lead him across the hall. Together they trailed upstairs. Jack turned halfway up to wave and blow a kiss. 'Nighty night, Mummy,' he called.

'Nighty night.' She watched until he was out of sight.

Once he had disappeared, the empty feeling returned. Susan felt Mandy's hand on her back, urging her gently towards the kitchen. 'Can I make you a cup of tea?' Mandy asked. She sat Susan down again, then reached out a warm hand to check her fingers. 'You're freezing cold,' she said, frowning. She turned and disappeared into the living room, returning with a plaid blanket, which she draped round Susan's shoulders.

The hollow feeling persisted as Mandy set to, boiling

the kettle, opening and closing cupboards as she searched for mugs and teabags. Sky seemed to know something was wrong. She sat very close to Susan, leaning her warm body against Susan's leg. How comforting it was. As if understanding, Sky reached round and laid her head on Susan's lap. Her coat was so soft. Susan ran her fingers down the collie's neck. Sky was so trusting. She had been so frightened when Mandy first got her. For a moment, Susan was reminded of Marmalade. He would have been there for her, just as Sky was now. She buried her fingers in Sky's coat and bent over to kiss her head.

The kettle came to the boil. With a click, Mandy switched it off, poured the tea and added milk. A moment later, she placed two steaming mugs on the table and sat down. 'You look like you've seen a ghost,' she said. 'Do you want to talk about it?'

Susan reached out her hands and wrapped them round the mug. 'I kind of have,' she said. 'Seen a ghost, I mean.' She let out a long sigh.

Mandy looked puzzled. 'Was it something with Douglas?' she asked. 'Jimmy said you seemed to be having a good time . . . not that he was gossiping . . .' she added with the tiniest shake of her head.

Susan looked down at her mug. The tea was steaming. She shook her head very slightly. 'It wasn't Douglas,' she said. She paused for a moment, closing her eyes, then opening them again. What could she say? She'd never told Mandy the whole story of what happened with Michael. She'd never told anyone the whole story, really, except Miranda, who had been by her side throughout, of course.

Mandy sat on the far side of the table, leaning back as if she felt at home. Speaking quietly, she began to tell Susan about her Hope Meadows charges. Now and then, she sent Susan a reassuring smile. She seemed quite willing to wait until Susan was ready to talk.

Footsteps sounded on the stairs. A moment later, Miranda slipped into the room. 'That's him in bed,' she said, softly.

Mandy lifted her mug and drank the remainder of her tea. 'Would you like me to go?' she offered. 'If you'd rather be alone with your mum . . .'

Susan swallowed. It wasn't easy to talk, but suddenly, urgently, she wanted Mandy to stay and hear. 'Don't go,' she said. 'I want your help.' She looked up at her mother. 'Michael came by,' she said.

Miranda's eyebrows shot up. 'Here?' she said. She sounded outraged, as Susan had known she would.

'Yes,' she replied. She was glad Mandy was still there. Much as she despised Michael, her mum's reaction was troubling.

Mandy frowned. '. . . Jack's dad, Michael?'

Under the table, Sky licked Susan's fingers. Susan drew her shoulders back, looked straight at Mandy and nodded. She wanted to tell her everything. 'Michael and I were together for a year,' she explained. 'I was working as a nursery nurse in York. He was a law student.' She stopped for a moment. She could picture the flat they'd shared. It had been small, but cosy. Susan had supported Michael in his studies: had never once questioned his love. She pressed her lips together. She was not going to cry. She drew in breath and steadied herself.

'I got pregnant with Jack,' she said. 'It wasn't planned, but the timing wasn't awful. Michael's course was almost done.' The words were coming easier now. 'He'd be finished before Jack was due. He had a job lined up with his dad's firm.' She managed for the first time to find a smile, though there was a bitter edge to it. 'I was so happy,' she said. 'I thought he would be too.' She paused, stroked Sky's ear, looked back up.

'He was so angry when I told him,' she said. The pain was still raw. She couldn't keep the bewilderment out of her voice. 'He was just starting out, he said. He didn't have time for a child. It wasn't in the plan. He wanted me to have an abortion.' Her voice quivered. She would never judge any other woman, but she couldn't have aborted Jack. Not in a million years. From the moment she'd known he was growing inside her, she had loved him. 'I said it was me and the baby or nothing.' She stopped and swallowed hard. 'So he picked nothing. I moved back to Walton. I thought he'd change his mind,' she blinked hard, 'but then his *father . . .*' her voice wobbled as she spat the word, '. . . sent an official letter from the firm. It said Michael didn't want to be on the birth certificate. He renounced any claim on Jack, and he didn't want me to contact him ever again.'

How could a memory be so painful? The image of Michael on the doorstep came back to her with a jolt. Angus was dead. But his legacy lingered. How could Michael have been so pathetic, to hide behind his father's law firm when dumping the woman he'd supposedly loved, and their unborn child? She sat back, overwhelmed again with that sense of unreality. 'I never saw him again. Not till today.' She stopped.

'So what did on earth did he want?' Miranda's voice pulled her back to the moment. Her mum still looked scandalised. She held up a finger. 'Before you answer that, I think we all need a glass of wine.' She pulled open the fridge.

'There's no wine there, Mum,' Susan said, finding a smile. Much as she loved her mother, there were times when she wished she was less theatrical.

Miranda emerged holding a bottle of white wine. 'Nonsense, darling, I slipped one in there earlier in case you wanted to celebrate your date.' She closed the fridge triumphantly and poured them each a glass.

'So what did he want?' Mandy asked Susan, eyebrows raised.

Susan sighed. 'He wanted me to read this.' She picked up the letter and handed it to Mandy who took it and read it, concentrating hard. Miranda leaned over to read too.

'He wants access to Jack?' Mandy looked across the table at Susan a few minutes later.

Miranda seemed speechless.

'So he says,' Susan admitted. 'What do you think of the letter itself?' she asked. It wasn't as cold as the one she'd received from Michael's father four years ago, but for someone wanting to get to know his child, it was worded very stiffly.

Mandy looked thoughtful. 'Well it's very . . . polite,' she said, glancing down, then back up at Susan. 'He sounds just like a lawyer.' She sent Susan a smile, and Susan couldn't help smiling back.

Miranda, who had been rereading the letter, dropped it on the table with a disgusted scoff. 'Awful man.'

Susan drew in a long breath, then let it out slowly. 'I don't know what to do,' she said. 'He's been so horrible. I don't want him back in my life. But the only reason he's not seen Jack is because he didn't want to. If he'd asked when Jack was born, I'd have said yes, even if we were broken up.' She shook her head, reached out a hand, picked up the letter, glanced through it again then put it back down. 'Should I stand in his way now? If he really wants to get to know Jack?' She picked up her wine and took a sip. She didn't really want it. She needed to see clearly.

'Well, what's changed?' There was still antagonism in Miranda's voice. 'Why's he come to find you now?'

'He said his dad had died.' Susan looked across the table at her mum's angry face, then at Mandy's calm expression. 'I've always thought his dad put pressure on him. He never liked me, even before Jack was in the picture.'

Miranda gave a short laugh. 'It's not much of an argument for Michael's strength of character,' she pointed out, 'if he can't say no to his father when his own child is at stake.'

Susan sighed. 'I agree,' she said. 'But it's not about Michael, or me, not really. It's about Jack and what's best for him.'

'That's true,' Mandy said, her voice thoughtful, 'but it has to be your decision. You're the only one who knows Jack and Michael. It's quite possible to grow up normal without access to your biological parents.' She wiggled her eyebrows. 'Just look at me. But . . . for Jimmy, it's important to have contact with the children. For Abi and Max too. Even when things go wrong, they know he cares. It comes down to whether you think Michael will be good for Jack.'

'At least he isn't on the birth certificate.' Miranda was looking through the letter again. 'He says himself he'd have no legal case to force you.'

'It can't have been an easy letter to write,' Mandy pointed out. She reached out to Susan. Her fingers were warm and strong as she squeezed Susan's hand. 'As long as you feel safe, I think it might be worth trying to find out what he wants. Talking to him won't hurt Jack. If it all goes wrong, Jack doesn't have to know.'

Susan squeezed Mandy's hand in return. Susan was glad she was there. Mum was amazing, but Susan needed someone neutral to help her with this. She had never felt unsafe with Michael. But then he'd put himself before Jack once before – what was to stop him from doing it again?

Reluctantly, she realised she needed to speak to him. If there was a chance that he really wanted to become a part of Jack's life, then she had to consider it. And she couldn't do that without knowing more.

Chapter Eleven

Susan tucked a holly stalk into the base of the wreath she was holding and tilted her head, looking at her creation. She couldn't tell if it was good or not; her mind wasn't really on the job. She was finding it hard to shake the sense of impending doom that had settled on her since she had seen Michael. It was like she was standing on the edge of a ravine and if she took one wrong step, she could go tumbling down into places unknown. It wasn't a feeling that lent itself easily to Christmas spirit.

She reached for another sprig of holly and pricked her finger on a leaf. 'Ow!' she exclaimed, sucking the hurt fingertip.

'Careful, Mummy!' Jack giggled as he looked up from the paper chain he was making. 'Remember: "Leaves that prick, berries make you sick!"' He repeated the rhyme Susan had made up that morning when they had gone to collect the holly from the woods.

'That's right!' Susan smiled back at him. 'Silly Mummy!' She carried on looking at him as he went back to his paper chain. *His hair needs cutting*, she thought, fondly. He looked ridiculously sweet with his hair falling into his eyes. His head was bent forward, and he was concentrating hard as he smeared glue onto the paper. She wished that she could just enjoy this moment but it felt impossible. In two hours' time, she was going to be meeting Michael. For all she knew, that could be a moment when everything changed. It had felt important to her to spend a morning doing fun activities with Jack, even if her mind was elsewhere. Besides, they had promised Mr Gorski some Christmas decorations.

Jack looked up again and grinned, his brown eyes shining. 'Look how long it is now, Mummy,' he said. He held up the chain for her to inspect.

Susan put her head on one side to assess his handiwork. The chain didn't quite reach the ground yet, but he was working hard. 'It's lovely,' she said. 'Mr Gorski will be pleased.'

'Mummy?'

He sounded more hesitant and thoughtful this time. 'Yes?' she asked.

'Is Coffee all better now? Can we go visit soon?'

Susan paused before replying. She had to think what to say. Coffee was home again after her operation. Her wound had healed well, but Mr Gorski still seemed worried about her. She wasn't her usual self, he said. 'She is better after her operation,' she said carefully. 'But in doggy years, she's a very old lady. When we go visit, you should check with Mr Gorski if you can play with her.' She didn't need to add that he should be gentle. She knew he would.

'Can we go to see her today, Mummy?'

Susan shook her head. 'You're going round to see Herbie and Kiran,' she reminded him. Herbie Dhanjal was in Susan's class at nursery. Susan was friends with Roo Dhanjal, Herbie and Kiran's mum.

Jack's face lit up. 'Oh yeah! We can play with Somia and Shahu!'

Susan knew Jack loved the Dhanjals' cats, whom they had adopted from Hope Meadows over a year ago. She had a sudden urge to fold him in her arms and hold him tight: protect him from everything. He was so innocent, she thought. He knew he was going to Herbie's, but it had not crossed his mind to wonder what she would be doing.

Was she doing the right thing? she wondered. She had never once mentioned Michael to Jack. It didn't seem to have occurred to him yet that he must have a father, but one day it would. The last thing Susan wanted to tell him was that she had denied Michael access when he'd asked. And she wouldn't lie; she tried always to be honest with him. So there was nothing else for it; she had to meet Michael to try to find out what he was offering. There was a slightly sick feeling in her stomach. Up until now, all decisions about Jack had been hers to make. If Michael became involved, that would change.

'Mummy?' Jack's voice startled her out of her reverie. He was gazing at her, looking very serious.

She found herself wondering whether he could divine her thoughts. Or her feelings, at least. *Can he sense I'm nervous?* 'Yes, sweetheart?' She managed a smile, though her heart was beating faster than usual.

'Can I have a glass of milk, please?'

Susan stifled the relieved laugh that bubbled up. 'Of course you can, lovey,' she said.

I just need to stay calm. If it all goes wrong, Jack will never know.

It was almost as if time had stood still in Zio Toto's. The scents of freshly baked garlic bread and sweet tomatoes met her as she opened the door. When she stepped inside, the ancient wooden tables with their rustic cloths greeted her like old friends. And there he was, sitting at their old table beside the window, as if the four years that had passed had been compressed into a bare week. He stood up as the waiter ushered Susan towards him. He was wearing smart beige trousers with a green jumper. His dark brown hair was neatly combed, and his strong face was smooth-shaven. He'd always been a very stylish man and Susan felt glad that she'd chosen one of her smarter work dresses. The last thing she wanted was to feel frumpy and flustered.

'Susan.' He smiled at her.

'Hello, Michael,' she replied, attempting a smile back. He reached out a hand to grasp hers and leaned towards her for an air kiss near her cheek. Even his aftershave smelled the same. It was like being in a strange dream; a mix of memories and the present, although her dry mouth and thumping heart made her certain that she was very much awake.

As he stepped round and pulled a chair out for her, Susan tried to calm herself. The anger from her first meeting had dissolved into nerves. She had no idea how a meeting like this was meant to go.

She sat down in the chair, then watched as he whisked round to his own place. *I have the power here,* she reminded herself.

The waiter handed over the menus and for a few moments, they sat across the table from one another, in silence. What was she going to say to him? She pretended to concentrate on the menu, even though she didn't feel hungry at all. The words on the page in front of her blurred as she stared at them.

When she looked up again, he had put down his menu and was waiting. He seemed to be watching her intently, but he'd made no effort to speak yet either. Was he nervous too? He had always been difficult to read.

'See anything you fancy?' he asked. He was smiling, a little tentatively. Susan was acutely aware that the last time they had been face to face, she had yelled at him. She hadn't regretted it, but she supposed an apology was in order if they were going to make any progress today. Besides, now that the shock was over, she found that she didn't feel angry at him any more. She'd felt that for so long when they had first broken up, and then it had faded over the years, until she'd never bothered to think of him. She had finished mourning for the future she'd never had.

'Are you ready to order?' The waiter had arrived and was looking her way.

Michael too was gazing at her. She scanned the menu quickly. 'I'll have the chicken and mushroom risotto,' she said.

Michael smiled up at the waiter. 'I will too,' he said. 'And a bottle of the Pinot Grigio, please.'

Ordering without asking me, just like he always used to, Susan thought. She remembered how she'd found it charming at the time, like he was taking care of her, but now, it irked her.

She cleared her throat. 'I don't want anything alcoholic,' she said. She had arranged to stay with James, but she needed a clear mind. 'Just some sparkling water, please.'

She waited for Michael to object. He'd always insisted on wine with every meal. He looked up at the waiter. 'In that case, I'll just have the water too,' he said. 'Thank you.'

Susan couldn't help raising her eyebrows in surprise as the waiter took their menus.

Well that's a change . . .

'How have you—'

'I wanted to—'

They both started speaking at the same time. Susan closed her mouth, feeling her face redden and then he nodded with an unusually gentle smile. 'You first,' he said.

She closed her eyes for a second, gathering herself, then looked up. 'I wanted to say I was sorry,' she said. She paused for a moment, searching for the right words. 'The last time we met, I was . . .' She stopped.

He held up a hand and shook his head. 'Please don't apologise,' he said. 'You didn't say or do anything that wasn't totally justified. Not after . . .' It was his turn to trail off, but he took a deep breath and began again. 'You must have been surprised to see me again, after all this time,' he said. 'And I'd have to be a fool to expect you to welcome me with open arms.' He smiled, his eyes crinkling with self-deprecation. Another small wave of curiosity ran through Susan. Even amongst his law student friends, Michael had always had a confidence that made him stand out. Would that Michael, the one she remembered, have admitted he had been in the wrong? She didn't think so.

That unusual smile was still in place. He seemed even more handsome than she'd remembered. To her younger self, he had seemed impossibly glamorous. She'd been so happy when he had chosen her. He could have had anyone he pleased.

He was gazing at her still. There was admiration in his eyes. 'You haven't changed,' he said. 'How have you been?'

For a moment, Susan was about to say that she'd been fine. But then she thought of all the sleepless nights, the stress, the money worries that had become part of her life since becoming a single parent. That hadn't been fine; that had been difficult. Then, she thought of all the delicious cuddles, the magical moments of discovery and all the laughs she had shared with Jack, ever since the day he'd been born. How could she convey all that to someone who hadn't been part of it? Who had never felt those things?

Take it slowly, she thought to herself. 'I've been okay,' she replied.

'And where are you working now?' he asked.

'I'm working in the nursery in Welford,' she replied.

'Oh yes?' He sounded as if he was genuinely interested. 'How did you end up there?'

Under the table, Susan rubbed the edge of the tablecloth between her fingers. It was linen and smooth under her fingertips. 'Well . . . before Jack was born,' her voice had the tiniest of tremors as she mentioned Jack's name, but Michael's face was open and encouraging, 'I had a flat in Walton,' she went on. 'But it was tiny and Jack and I were going to outgrow it in no time. I needed to stay near Mum, so that she could babysit. So, when Moon Cottage came up for rent in Welford, I moved in there. Then the job came up at the nursery and I applied. Luckily I got it.'

The way she said it was casual, but it had been a stressful time before she had found work. It had been the perfect position for her. Mrs Armitage, the nursery owner, had immediately offered Jack a place. Without her and Miranda, Susan would never have managed.

'That was lucky,' Michael replied. 'It's good to live so close to your work.'

Susan felt a spike of annoyance at his offhand comment. It wasn't just *good* for her to live near her work. It was *essential*. She couldn't have afforded the time or money for a long commute.

He doesn't get it. But then, how could he? At least he seemed interested now and maybe, in time, he would grow to understand.

The waiter arrived with their water and Susan took a sip. 'So how about you?' she asked, following his lead. 'Are you working at Chalk and Manders?'

It had always been Michael's plan to join his father's firm when he qualified. 'I am,' he said. 'I've been there since I qualified. I'm going to become a partner shortly.'

He stopped. Susan could see the muscles in his jaw working. She'd hit a nerve, she realised. Perhaps the partnership had only come up due to the death of Michael's father.

'I was sorry to hear about your father,' she said, and she knew as soon as she said it, that she'd hit the nail on the head. He frowned a little, staring down at his side of the tablecloth, his jaw still clenching. 'I know you were . . .' she paused, 'you were close,' she finished. It hadn't been easy to say. She had long suspected their break-up had been closely related to his father's expectations for Michael's career and for her part, she had found Mr Chalk to be a cold, judgemental man. She stopped fiddling with the tablecloth and rested her hand on the table instead.

Michael looked back up at her. 'Thank you for saying so.' He sounded sincere. His hand twitched, as if for a moment, he'd thought about reaching out and taking hers, but then it stilled again. 'It's not been easy,' he admitted. 'I wasn't thinking straight when I just turned up on your doorstep. I should be the one apologising. There's nothing I want less than to force anything on you. I just want to talk.' His brown eyes were steady. 'I know it's probably too late,' he said, 'but I've realised opting out of Jack's life . . . and yours . . . well it was a mistake.'

There was a tremor in his voice, but he took a deep breath and started again. 'It sounds stupid,' he said, 'but until my father was gone, I hadn't realised how important it was to have him there. It made me think about Jack.' He stopped again, lifted a hand to his mouth and pinched his top lip between his finger and thumb. Then he sighed. 'I have thought about him in the past . . . of course I have. I thought he was better off without me. But when Dad died . . .' again the slight spasm, '. . . I think it was wrong of me to deny Jack the bond that I had. He deserves more.' This time, he really did lean forward and put a hand over Susan's, gazing into her eyes with calm solemnity. 'But I only want it, if you feel it's the right thing. You're his mum and you know him best.'

Susan couldn't help but feel astonished. This was the most sincere and vulnerable she could ever remember Michael being. *Perhaps he really has changed?* Maybe losing his father had caused him to grow up.

His hand was warm. They'd sat there like that so many times in the past. It was too intimate and unease washed through her. She shifted her hand: tugged it away and let it fall into her lap, away from his grasp.

'Can I ask you,' she said, '. . . honestly . . .' She paused, thinking hard. 'Did you leave me because of your father? Did he tell you to . . .' She had been going to say 'abandon us', but she pulled up short and frowned. 'I know you're remembering your relationship with him,' she amended, 'but isn't it partly because of him that you and Jack don't have a bond?' Despite her best efforts, she could hear the tone of bitterness that had crept into her voice. The old Michael would have been furious that she had even implied such a thing. Would he douse her with cold anger, as he had four years ago?

But he only looked sad. 'You're right,' he replied. 'And I do see the irony. I know he was far from perfect. I was too. But it's made me realise that I want to be a father as well. I want to do better . . . if I can, that is.' The sides of his mouth twitched upwards, though the sadness was still there.

Of all the things Susan had expected from this meeting, this wasn't it. This man was apologetic, gentle, humble and open about his feelings – the complete opposite of the ambitious, suave, alpha that she had known four years ago, who could never accept criticism of himself or his family.

He must have misread her silence, because he rushed on. 'You don't have to decide right now. We can just . . . catch up today. I want to know about Jack and about you and what you've both been doing.' He smiled now. 'What are Jack's favourite things?' he asked. 'What does he like to do?'

She had forgotten this about him, Susan thought. He had always been easy to talk to. Always filled with questions, even faced with someone shy. He'd been a great asset when they were out together. Susan sometimes found herself tongue-tied in strange company. Michael could talk to anyone.

There were so many things to tell him. All about Jack's love of animals and about the birds in their garden that he fed every day. Jack knew so much about them. They had learned together, looking at pictures in books Susan had bought. If she'd thought that Michael would quickly become bored, she needn't have worried. He listened intently, asking questions that showed he was paying attention. The food arrived but they ate slowly as they chattered.

'Football eh?' Michael said, looking pleased. 'Which team does he support?'

'Manchester United,' Susan told him. 'His shirt is his favourite thing to wear. If he had his way, it would never be washed!'

Michael's eyes were shining. 'Manchester United was my favourite team when I was small! That's who I wanted to play for when I grew up. I spent hours and hours out on the playing fields, taking pretend penalties.'

He laughed and Susan could tell he was relishing the small point of contact.

Dessert had come and gone. Susan had barely noticed it, though she had eaten it all and they'd even stayed for a coffee. Susan glanced out of the window beside her and realised that it was already late afternoon. Soon it would be dusk, and the Christmas lights that were strung between the houses were swaying in the wind. Just as well she was staying over.

And still they talked.

She told him about the time Jack had chickenpox so badly that he still had the scars and about how he had gone on a reindeer hunt last year and got lost out on the moors in the snow.

Then, she shared happier moments. Jack's first steps, his first word: 'kitty', the first time he'd won a race at the nursery sports day. Michael's reactions were giving her the smallest inkling of what it might be like to have a co-parent by her side. It felt like it would be nice.

It had been so much better than she had expected, Susan thought. She had come here filled with worry about herself and about Jack. But Michael seemed truly to have changed.

He leaned forward and looked her straight in the eye. 'So what do you think then?'

The time was finally here, she thought. He wanted to know what the future would hold. For a moment, Susan thought about throwing caution to the wind. The afternoon had gone so well. Why would she say no to him seeing Jack? But she had decided earlier that however it went, she wouldn't make up her mind tonight. She should sleep on it and talk it over with someone. Then it would be time to make up her mind.

She sighed with relief. The tension that had filled her earlier was long gone. 'I've really enjoyed this,' she said. 'I'll think it over about Jack and let you know.'

He sat back in his chair. She had half expected him to press her, but he seemed satisfied. *Another positive change.*

'That would be great,' he said. 'I was so worried you'd just say no.'

They'd been there so long that the waiter had lit the candle on the table, ready for the evening service. She could see its light reflected in Michael's large brown eyes. Those eyes that were so much like Jack's. She had never allowed herself to see it before.

'I've missed you,' he said. She hadn't expected him to say it, but her breath caught in her throat. Had he really? They'd had some good times. A wave of longing rushed over her. If only she could go back to those uncomplicated days, when the sun had shone on everything and the future had seemed so clear. How much of the blame for what had happened lay with

Michael's father? It was hard to stand up to parents sometimes, even as an adult.

'I missed you too, sometimes,' she admitted.

The words hung in the air and for a moment, she wanted to call them back. But, she reasoned, it was the truth. They owed each other that.

'I'm glad,' he said. 'Thank you for this afternoon.'

They pushed out their chairs and made their way to the door. The waiter brought their coats and Michael helped Susan put hers on.

'Thank you very much,' Susan called out to the waiter, who nodded and smiled.

They paused in the lane under the old-fashioned street lamps, which had now lit up in the dusk, and the trembling Christmas lights. 'Can I offer you a lift?' he asked.

Susan shook her head. 'No need. I'm staying just around the corner,' she said.

'Well in that case, I'll walk you there,' he said.

They walked side by side along the pavement. The wind was swirling, chilly on Susan's face. Overhead the sky was dark grey. The sounds of their feet echoed in the narrow street.

'This is me,' Susan announced a few minutes later. She pressed the buzzer beside the door, then turned to face him. He looked so good under the peach-coloured light. For a moment, she wondered if he would kiss her, but he just stood and gazed into her eyes. When the answer came, and the buzzer sounded, he nodded, then turned and strode off. Susan had a sudden feeling of emptiness as she pushed the door open, which alarmed her. She closed the door and stood with her back against it for a moment.

I cannot *fall for Michael again!*

Chapter Twelve

'We've brought your decorations!' Susan stood on Mr Gorski's doorstep, clinging tightly to the cardboard box into which she had loaded the paper chains, the wreath, some cut-out snowflakes and several ornaments for Mr Gorski's mantelpiece.

Mr Gorski pulled the door open wide. 'Come on in,' he said, then to Jack with a grin, 'you'll help me put them up, won't you?'

'Course I will.' Jack bounded into the hall. 'I can show you which ones I made!' He sounded excited. Susan was too. They'd made a real effort. Susan was especially proud of the mini fir trees they'd made from string and sequins. She stepped into the hall and Jack rushed over to take Mr Gorski's hand. 'How's Coffee?' he asked, gazing up into the old man's face.

Mr Gorski smiled, though Susan could see it was an effort. 'I think she's a bit better,' he said. 'Would you like to come and see her?' He led them through to the living room, where Coffee was lying in her bed. 'I moved her here,' Mr Gorski said, 'so she'd be nice and warm.' The little terrier was lying huddled in her bed, which was close to the fireplace. She wagged her tail as they went in, but she didn't stand up.

'She still barks to let me know when the door rings,' Mr Gorski told them. 'But she doesn't rush through like she used to.'

Coffee gave Jack a cursory lick. Susan was sad to see the little terrier so dejected. She had always raced around the house and arrived noisily at the door long before Mr Gorski himself made it there.

'Well now.' Mr Gorski was looking in the box that Susan had set on one of the chairs. 'Isn't this a lovely thing?' He pulled out Jack's paper chain and held it out in his hands. 'Where do you think we should put it, Jack?'

'Ummmmm.' Jack gazed about the room. 'Over the mirror!' He pointed to the large mirror above the mantelpiece.

'Marvellous!' Mr Gorski pulled a step stool next to the mantelpiece. 'Would you do the honours, please, Susan?'

Susan took the paper chain and draped it over the heavy gilt frame that hung over the fireplace.

Mr Gorski grinned at Jack. 'Oh, what a clever idea, Jack. The reflection makes it look like there are two lovely paper chains!'

Jack nodded. His big eyes were glittering with happiness.

'What next?' Mr Gorski asked.

Jack trotted over to the box and pulled out the snow-flakes. There were a lot of them and for a moment, Susan wondered what the old man would do with all of them. But he set to with Jack and a few minutes later, there was a white paper snowflake stuck in every one of the small panes in the large bay window. Susan popped out to hang her wreath on the front door.

They put the string trees on the mantelpiece. Susan had also brought some fir-branches and holly. They trimmed them with the baubles and tinsel that Mr Gorski and Susan had rescued from the dusty old box they'd looked at before. By the time they'd finished, Mr Gorski's room looked very cheery. He stood nodding as he gazed round with satisfaction. 'It's beautiful,' he said. 'My sister will love it.'

'Would you like me to send her a photo?' Susan asked. 'So she can see what she's coming to?'

Mr Gorski beamed. 'What a lovely idea,' he said.

Susan pulled out her phone. She would take a picture of the fireplace with its trees and the paper chain. Coffee's basket was close by as well. Susan lined up the camera and took the picture. It looked very festive. She showed it to Mr Gorski. 'Shall I send it?' she asked.

'Yes please,' he said.

Susan typed in Mr Gorski's sister's number. 'That's it sent,' she said. She glanced round the room. Now that the decorations were done, Jack had settled himself on the floor beside Coffee and was stroking the little terrier's head. Both of them seemed contented.

While she had her phone out, she thought, she should ask Mr Gorski for a shopping list. 'Is there anything you need me to buy?' she asked.

'That would be very kind.' He really was a lovely man, Susan thought. He never took anything for granted.

He started to list the things he would need. Susan was typing in the list when a message came through. It was from Douglas.

Hi Susan, it read. *I had a great time the other day and I hope you did too. I'd love to meet up again sometime. Maybe visit Hope Meadows as we discussed. I hope you're doing something fun right now. Douglas. x*

She stared at the screen for a moment, reading the message again. He was very polite. He wasn't pushing her and despite her reservations, their trip to Upper Welford Hall and the rope course had been fun. But what about Michael? His reappearance complicated everything. She sighed internally. Why did life have to be complicated? Maybe this wasn't a good time to be dating.

'And a packet of mince pies please.' Susan looked up. Mr Gorski was looking worried. 'Did you get all that?' he asked. 'Sorry if I went too fast.'

She shook her head slightly. 'I missed a couple of things,' she admitted. 'Sorry.'

He smiled. 'Please don't be,' he said. 'Coffee and I really are very grateful for everything you do.'

★

Susan knelt down next to the chicken coop, lit by the dim overhead light of the barn. Mandy crouched next to her and they peered into the coop. Inside there were five chickens. All of them were peacefully asleep. They looked very cosy, huddled together. There were three with red feathers and two with white. One of the white chickens had lifted its head, opened an eye and gazed at them without fear.

'So these are your new arrivals,' Susan whispered with a smile, referring to a cryptic message Mandy had left on her voicemail when she'd invited her up for dinner at Wildacre.

'That's right.' Mandy grinned at her. 'I rescued them. They won't start laying until spring, but after that we should have lots of lovely eggs. Jack can meet them next time you come. I thought there wasn't much point showing him when they were asleep. They're much more fun awake!' She closed up the coop and stopped in the barn doorway before turning off the light. 'Jimmy and I have finished renovating in here too,' she said. 'I think he's hoping to use it for cars, but I'm determined it should stay free. What if a horse needed a lovely new home?' Her eyes were so wide and innocent that Susan laughed.

'They're very sweet,' she replied. 'You rescued them, you said?'

'Seb brought them in to Hope Meadows,' Mandy said. Seb Conway was Welford's animal welfare officer. Susan knew that Mandy and he often crossed paths.

'They weren't well when they came. One of them had lost most of its feathers, but they've come back, thank goodness. I thought at one point I was going to have to learn to knit so I could make a woolly jumper.'

Susan found herself laughing again. Mandy really was crazy about animals.

It was completely dark outside. Once Mandy switched the light off, it seemed like the lights in her cottage, Wildacre, were the only ones on for miles around. They walked back into the cottage and Mandy led Susan to the living room, where they had been sitting before the chicken excursion. Susan could hardly imagine a more homely place. The walls were painted creamy white and a fire burned brightly in the grate. A pile of dogs lay in front of it: Mandy's collie Sky, Simba the German Shepherd, Zoe the husky and her six-month-old puppy, Emma. It was very peaceful. Jack was asleep upstairs, in the bedroom Jimmy's twins stayed in when they were over. Luckily, he was familiar enough with Mandy and Jimmy that he could happily go to sleep in Wildacre. It meant Susan could have dinner with her friends, without having to find a babysitter and she was grateful to Mandy for suggesting the arrangement.

A few minutes later, they were sitting around the little scrubbed oak table in the kitchen. There hadn't been a peep from Jack. Susan had checked him just before they'd sat down. He was fast asleep, snuggled up to Lamby, just as cosy as the chickens had been earlier.

Jimmy's veggie Bolognese was very good, Susan thought. Cooking had never been one of Mandy's strong points. She was lucky Jimmy seemed to enjoy it. Mandy was looking a bit less tired. Maybe it was the help of that rather dashing blond vet. 'How are things at Animal Ark and Hope Meadows?' she asked.

Mandy chewed a mouthful of her Bolognese, then took a sip of wine before she answered. 'It's going well at the practice,' she said. 'Toby's slotted in perfectly. It almost feels like he's always been here. Hope Meadows?' She lifted her glass again and put her head on one side, inspecting her drink. 'It's much better now we've got the grant,' she said. Susan knew Mandy had won a grant from the Walmey Foundation back in the summer. 'We can cover the running costs now, but . . .' She set her glass down and paused to scoop up some spaghetti, stopping with her fork halfway to her mouth. 'I still need some new kennels,' she said. 'And I'd love to have better spaces for wildlife and rearing kittens and so on.'

'So you need some fundraising ideas?' Susan asked.

'You're just like Mandy,' Jimmy told her, laughing. 'Getting straight to the heart of things.'

Mandy grinned. 'I'll take any ideas you've got,' she said.

'Maybe I could organise something through the nursery?' Susan suggested. 'A sponsored walk or something. The kids get so much out of their visits, I know they would love to do something to help the animals.'

'That's so kind of you, Susan. Maybe you could do something after Christmas, when your Nativity play is over?'

Susan nodded. Mandy knew just how hectic Christmas could be for her. 'New Year fundraising it is!' she said, raising her wine glass.

'In the meantime, Toby had a few ideas,' Mandy said. 'Open evenings, sponsorship, that kind of thing. He knows lots of people in our industry and some of them are quite important. I'm waiting to see whether he'll organise them. I don't want to push him too hard. Not when he's just arrived.'

Susan swallowed her last mouthful of the Bolognese and sat back in her chair. 'I'll see what I can do,' she said. 'Jack and I love coming to visit.'

Mandy had finished her meal as well. She and Jimmy stood up and started to clear away the plates. Susan tried to help but they flapped her away, laughing.

'Our guest doesn't lift a finger!' Jimmy insisted as he disappeared into the kitchen.

'By the way,' Mandy said, as she sat back down. 'I know it won't make any money, but how about having a little competition with your class? They can all suggest names for the kittens, then you and I can choose the best ones.'

'That's a lovely idea,' Susan said. 'Good that you

and I get to choose, though. Otherwise, we'd end up with one called Kitteny McKittenface!'

Mandy laughed. 'Yes,' she agreed. 'Our decision is final. Definitely not a vote.'

Jimmy had just returned with dessert bowls and ice cream when Susan felt the phone in her pocket vibrate. She knew that Miranda had driven to London that night to see old friends, so she thought she'd better check it wasn't some sort of motorway SOS. ''Scuse me a moment. Just have to check this,' Susan said.

It was another message from Douglas. Susan felt a jolt of surprise and guilt as she realised that she'd forgotten to text him back. She'd put it off before, not knowing what to do in the wake of her Michael meeting, and then it had slipped her mind. Somehow, with Michael back on the scene, it almost felt like she couldn't just carry on with her dating life . . . could she?

'Anything important?' Jimmy was smiling at her over his bowl of ice cream.

'It's from Douglas,' she replied.

'Oh, great!' said Jimmy. 'He's a good guy, I like him.'

'What's he say?' Mandy's eyes were shining. She, too, obviously thought a message from Douglas was a good thing.

Susan gave the tiniest of shrugs, twisting her mouth to one side as she reread the message:

Hi Susan, sorry to bother you again, but I was wondering if you might be willing to show me around Hope Meadows? I think the animals would be great inspiration for my writing. I'm having a bit of a block at the moment. Obviously, I'd like to see you again, too, but this wouldn't have to be a date unless that's what you want. Douglas

'He'd like to come to Hope Meadows,' she replied. Was he a little pushy in texting so soon when she hadn't replied? She mostly responded to texts really quickly, though.

Mandy grinned. 'Well that's no problem,' she said. 'Honestly, you know you're welcome any time.' Susan felt uneasy for a moment. Mandy had obviously mistaken her hesitancy for concern about asking for a favour.

'It's not that,' Susan admitted. 'It's Michael. You know I saw him the other day?' Mandy nodded. 'Well I just feel a bit odd about seeing him and Douglas at the same time.'

Mandy frowned. 'But you're not *seeing* Michael,' she objected. 'Just talking to him as Jack's father, no?'

Susan felt her face redden. There was no way she should be thinking of Michael in anything other than those terms. But ever since she'd seen him, she'd been confused. She had loved him so much all those years ago. If he'd really changed, it would be so easy to fall for him all over again.

'Is Douglas pushing you too fast?' Jimmy put in.

Susan shook her head. 'No,' she said, truthfully. 'He even says it doesn't have to be a date.'

'Well then.' Mandy leaned forward and put her elbows on the table. 'Bring him but tell him it can't be a date because you want to bring Jack. Then see how it goes. Nothing wrong with getting to know him better.'

That was true, Susan thought. She typed a reply to Douglas and he swiftly agreed that they could meet tomorrow. His message was filled with enthusiasm. Susan shoved the phone back into her pocket.

'Coffee?' Jimmy asked. 'I'll make it. Why don't you guys go to the fire and get comfy?'

Susan pushed her chair back. She was still feeling a little uneasy, but it didn't have to affect the rest of this evening. 'Thanks,' she said. 'That would be lovely.'

Jack was delighted when he opened the door the next day and found Douglas on the doorstep. 'Mummy, Mummy,' he shouted. 'Come and see. It's the nice story man.'

Susan walked out into the hallway.

'Hello!' Douglas beamed as he held his arms out and bellowed his greeting. He grinned and winked at Jack, then raised his eyes to Susan. 'Ready to go?' he asked.

Jack looked up at her, his eyes wide. 'Is he coming to see Mandy with us?'

'Yes, he is,' she replied and was rewarded with grins from both Jack and Douglas.

They set off towards Hope Meadows. The walk through the village was lovely. A huge Christmas tree had been erected on the village green. The Fox and Goose had now been decorated with greenery and lots of the front doors sported festive wreaths. Fairy lights flashed in the windows.

'Can we put our decorations up today?' Jack asked, tugging at Susan's sleeve.

'Probably not today,' Susan said. 'But soon, I promise.'

'So what do you like best about Hope Meadows?' Douglas asked, looking down at Jack. Jack had taken Douglas's hand, to Susan's surprise. It usually took Jack a while to get to know strangers and Douglas was a very loud stranger. Perhaps it was because of story time, she thought.

'I love the kittens.' Jack's little face was thoughtful as he looked up. 'And last Christmas there were baby donkeys called Holly and Robin and I loved them too. But I don't really have a favourite.'

'Quite right!' Douglas's voice boomed forth again. He really was larger than life in every way. Would he frighten the animals? Susan wondered.

'You must remember to be very quiet, Jack, and gentle with the animals,' she said.

Jack looked at her, his eyes wide. 'I know that, Mummy,' he objected, looking a little hurt.

Susan knew that he did. She'd been aiming her

comment at Douglas and hoping to be subtle about it.

'Almost there,' she said with relief as they turned in under the old wooden Animal Ark sign. They walked past the clinic and round to the back where Hope Meadows stood. Mandy opened the door as they arrived.

'Hello and welcome,' she said. She held the door open and they walked through. 'I've been waiting for you,' she told Jack. 'There's something I need help with.' She held out her hand and Jack skipped across and took it. 'I hope you don't mind, Douglas.' Mandy turned her head towards him. 'I know you came here to do research for your books, but I'm a bit worried about one of the kittens. I have a feeling he might be deaf. There's some tests I can do, but it's easier with help.'

Douglas gave a broad shrug and smiled. 'Fine by me,' he said. 'It's all inspiration.' Thankfully, his voice was more muted than it had been on the walk. *Looks like my warning worked,* Susan thought to herself, with a small smile.

They followed Mandy and Jack into the room where the kittens were. The mother cat was lying in her bed, but all the kittens leaped up and rushed to the front of the cage. Five pairs of wide eyes gazed out at them, filled with innocence and curiosity. Which one of them was Mandy worried about? Susan wondered.

Mandy let go of Jack's hand, opened the cage and lifted out the white kitten with the blue eyes.

'What makes you think he can't hear?' Douglas asked

the question that was in Susan's mind. All the kittens had raced forward. Surely if the little white one couldn't hear, it wouldn't have responded when the door opened.

They took the kitten out into the examination room. Mandy was cradling him in her arms. He was a lively little thing, crawling up her chest in a purposeful fashion, determined to explore. In a moment, he was standing on Mandy's shoulder, snuffling into her ear. Mandy reached up and grasped the tiny body. With a smile, she uncoupled his claws from her scrubs, then offered him to Jack to hold. As Jack began to stroke the soft white fur, Mandy looked up and answered Douglas's question. 'I've been watching him since he was born,' she explained. 'There's a genetic link to deafness in white cats with blue eyes. Not all are deaf, but some are. He's starting to show the signs. He sleeps more deeply than the other kittens. He's almost always the last to wake. And if he doesn't see me coming, he jumps like crazy. I hope I'm wrong, but we need to check it out. He'll need a very special home if he does turn out to be deaf.'

Jack was snuggling the tiny creature. 'You'll be all right, little kitten,' he whispered. 'I'll look after you.' The kitten began to purr as Jack's small, deft fingers stroked his head.

Mandy fetched a toy fishing rod with a stuffed gold-fish on a string. She handed it to Jack. 'Can you pop him down on the floor,' she said, 'then keep him distracted with this? I'm going to make some noises to see if he reacts.'

Jack knelt down on the floor. He was taking his role very seriously. The little white kitten gazed around with his head on one side. He seemed wholly unafraid. Jack held up the toy fishing rod, dangling the fluffy orange fish just out of the kitten's reach. The kitten's blue eyes widened. He reached out a paw, batted the fish, then watched in seeming fascination as the toy swung from side to side. He was so cute with his pricked ears, his head swaying from side to side as he watched the fish swing.

'I'm going to make some different noises.' Mandy had gone out of the room and had come back in with a number of different items. 'You keep him distracted, Jack, and then we'll see what he can hear.'

Jack nodded without taking his eyes off the kitten. He jerked the fish up and down and the little head followed, the blue eyes unblinking.

Mandy lifted a bunch of keys from the table. Making sure she was out of the kitten's line of sight, she shook them not far from his head. They made a loud jingling noise. Susan's eyes were on the kitten. There was no sign the little animal had heard.

Mandy picked up a piece of paper. With a sudden movement, she ripped it from end to end, keeping her eyes on the kitten, which was still entranced with Jack's fish. 'Different pitch,' she murmured, but the kitten remained oblivious. Mandy clapped her hands, hissed loudly then took out a cardboard box, beating on it with an empty syringe case. Nothing.

She put the box down with a sigh. 'One last test,' she said. Careful not to go to close, she stamped her foot hard on the floor behind the tiny cat. The response was immediate. The little animal turned its head, gazed at Mandy's foot, then slowly upwards. Then with deliberation, he turned back and pounced on the fish, which had dropped to the floor.

Jack looked up at Mandy, an appeal in his eyes. Susan could see how much he wanted the kitten to hear, even if only a little. 'He heard that, didn't he?' he asked. 'When you stamped your foot.'

Mandy pressed her lips together, then sighed and shook her head. 'I'm afraid not,' she said. 'He felt the vibrations through the floor. If he had heard it, he would have jumped out of his skin, and he didn't react to any of the other sounds at all.'

Jack looked from Mandy to the kitten. He blinked twice, his chin quivered and tears gushed forth, running down his face unchecked. Susan wanted to reach out and hold him, but Mandy was already kneeling down beside him. She put an arm round his shoulders, though she still had her eyes on the kitten. Douglas reached out a tentative hand, and when Mandy nodded, he scooped up the little white fluffball so that Mandy could concentrate fully on Jack.

'There's no need to cry,' she said. 'He might be deaf, but he can still have a good life. I'm going to read up more about cats that can't hear and then I'll be able to find him the perfect home.' She dried Jack's tears and Douglas handed the kitten back to Jack with a sympathetic smile. Susan watched as the little animal nuzzled up under Jack's chin. It was almost as if the tiny creature sensed his distress. A moment later, the kitten began to purr loudly again.

'See,' Mandy said. 'He's quite happy. He doesn't know any different.'

Jack looked up at Mandy, then across at Susan with a watery smile. The kitten butted his head against Jack's chin and tickled him with his whiskers and Jack let out a shaky laugh.

An hour later, they stood at the front door of Hope Meadows. Douglas held out his hand to Mandy. 'Thank you so much for showing me round,' he said. 'You've given me more inspiration than I know what to do with.'

Mandy held out her hand and shook his. 'It's been a pleasure.' She grinned.

'Is there any way I can thank you?' Douglas asked. Susan glanced down at Jack. He was holding on to Douglas's free hand as if he really didn't want to let go.

Mandy had her head on one side as if she was thinking. 'Publicity's always good,' she said. 'If you do write any stories about us, maybe you could give us a little shout out in the books?' She left the question hanging in the air. It was obvious she didn't want to put pressure on Douglas, but Douglas beamed.

'What a lovely idea,' he said. 'Better still, how about if I go one better and donate five per cent of the profits?'

Mandy shook his hand more heartily than ever. Susan had rarely seen her look so pleased. 'That would be fantastic,' she said. 'Thank you so much.'

Chapter Thirteen

The walk home was far more comfortable than the way there. Douglas and Jack seemed very much at home with one another and chatted like old friends. Snippets of the afternoon ran through Susan's mind. There was the way Douglas had quietly lifted up the kitten when Jack was upset and handed him back at just the right moment. He had been so calm and quiet that Susan felt ashamed that she'd worried that he would scare the animals. He'd helped Mandy with cleaning out the kennels without being asked. Once again, she felt like she'd misjudged him.

At one point when Mandy and Jack were busy, Douglas had sat down and pulled out a sketch pad. Susan had watched him. It seemed as if he was transformed as he began to draw. His normally ungainly movements had tightened. His fingers on the pencil were skilled as he added detail and shading. His concentration was so fierce that it was almost as if he had entered another world. Susan hadn't wanted to disturb him, but when she accidentally stepped on a metal bowl and made him jump, he had merely smiled up at her, then returned to his work.

They were back at the village green almost before she knew it. Though it was still early, the lights on the tall Christmas tree were lit. Their reflection danced on the surface of the pond beside the war memorial. Overhead, the sky was growing dim and grey. It looked like rain might come later. Susan had put a bag of birdseed in one of her pockets. She and Jack often stopped to feed the ducks. Jack and Douglas were standing at the edge of the water. Susan dug into her pocket and pulled out the little bag of seeds. 'Here,' she said to Jack. After a moment, she held a second bag out to Douglas. 'Would you like to feed the ducks as well?' she asked.

She had worried that he might think it silly, but she was not too surprised when he took it and thanked her gravely.

'I used to go and feed the ducks with my mum when I was little,' he told Jack. 'But we always used bread.'

Susan grinned as Jack frowned. Douglas was about to get a lecture. 'You shouldn't feed ducks bread,' Jack said. 'It's bad for their tummies.' She wondered how Douglas would respond. Jack had been perfectly polite. Had he been rude, she would have corrected him, but she knew that some adults would be offended.

But Douglas just raised his eyebrows and looked interested. 'Is it really?' he said. 'Well, in that case, I'm very sorry.'

'That's all right.' Now Jack was looking concerned. 'I only know because Mummy taught me about feeding them special seeds instead. Maybe your mummy didn't know. It's not your fault.' He was so serious, Susan found herself smiling again. She lifted a hand to cover her mouth. She didn't want Jack to think she was laughing at him.

She could see that Douglas was also trying to keep a straight face with difficulty. 'Thank you, Jack,' he said. 'And don't worry. In future, I'll always make sure I use special seeds when I feed the ducks.'

Jack beamed up at Douglas. It was lovely to see them getting on so well together. Susan found herself struck by the thought that perhaps Jack was missing out on a father figure, after all. But Michael didn't have the years of practice at talking to kids that Douglas had. Would Jack have the same, easy rapport with him? She tried to ignore those thoughts for now.

'So do these seeds taste nice?' Douglas asked.

Jack tilted his head, a puzzled look on his face. 'I don't know,' he admitted.

'Maybe I should try them . . .'

Jack's eyes were enormous as he turned to look at Susan. She'd told him when he was much younger not to put seeds in his mouth. But Douglas grinned at her and winked. He folded up his arms like wings and stuck his bottom out. Jack's gaze was no longer on Susan. Douglas was waddling in circles, flapping his 'wings'. A moment later, he bent his head and sucked up some of the seeds into his mouth. Pursing his lips, he gave an astonishing rendition of a confused duck, holding up his head, smacking his lips. And then he was strutting again. He wiggled as if readying himself to sit down as he let out a series of contented-sounding quacks.

Jack was lost in giggles. Tears were running down his face. Susan found herself joining in. Douglas grinned as his impression came to an end. He reached out a hand towards her, palm outstretched. 'Please may I have some more seeds?' he asked, then added with a sheepish look, 'Promise I'll feed them to the real ducks this time.'

Susan laughed. 'I'll let you get away with it this time,' she said, handing him the bag.

Just as Douglas took the bag, there was a flash of lightning. Susan glanced upwards as it started to pour with rain: droplets cascading, hissing on the ground, stippling the smooth water of the pond. The thunder arrived, growling in the distance.

Susan grabbed Jack's hand, ready to run. 'Will you come back to ours?' Susan called to Douglas over the roar of the storm. She lifted her free arm over her head, trying to protect herself from the lashing rain.

Douglas threw his arms up in the air, whooping. 'Why don't we stay out and enjoy the rain?' he boomed. He had water running down his face, and his hair and beard were already soaked, but he was smiling. 'I don't think we can actually get much wetter. And look at them.' He pointed at the ducks. 'They're loving it!'

Susan looked. The ducks did indeed seem to be

enjoying the downpour. They were swimming in circles and shaking their tails. A female mallard climbed onto the bank and started preening. She bent, dipping her beak into a puddle, lifted it and shook her head before twisting round again. Douglas crouched down beside Jack and pointed. 'They have a preen gland beside their tail,' he said. 'They reach round to it, then use the oil to coat their feathers. That's why the water flows off.'

Jack leaned in to look. Susan was about to protest but then she thought to herself: why not? Douglas was right. They were already soaked through. Droplets gathered on the brown feathers on the mallard's back, merged into miniature puddles, then flowed off.

Douglas and Jack started waddling around, pretending to be preening ducks.

'I love being a duck!' Jack cried.

'Me too,' said Douglas. 'Maybe that nice lady has some more seeds for us?'

Jack giggled as they waddled towards Susan. As she held out the bag, a trickle of water went down Susan's neck and she shivered slightly. It wasn't frosty cold, but it was chilly.

'We should go now,' Douglas said, straightening up, as if he had seen her movement. He grinned at Jack. 'Shall we do a rain dance on the way home?' he suggested. He set off, hopping on one foot, stamping his feet into puddles and laughing.

Jack followed his lead. 'Look, Mummy!' he shouted, jumping right into the middle of a huge puddle. It was much deeper than it looked! The water splashed up, soaking his already wet trousers and for a second he looked as if he might scream at how cold it was, but Douglas lifted him out effortlessly and set him down.

'Choose your puddles wisely, young duckmaster,' he said in a booming tone and Jack's face uncrumpled. After a moment, he scampered on with Douglas in hot pursuit.

By the time they arrived home, they looked like they'd been swimming with their clothes on. 'You will come in, won't you?' Susan said to Douglas. 'You can't drive home like that.' She unlocked the door and pushed it open.

After only a moment, Douglas stepped inside. 'If you're sure?' he said. His eyes were on her face, double-checking that she meant what she said.

'I'm sure,' she said. 'I'll find something you can put on and put your clothes in the drier.' She turned to Jack. 'Upstairs . . .' she said, '. . . now.' She followed Jack up, found him a towel and some dry clothes, then dug around for something that would be big enough for Douglas. *There really wasn't much. What was I thinking? I don't have any clothes that would fit a man that size!* She had reached the bottom drawer. It was almost empty except for some old T-shirts and jeans that she kept for painting. Underneath the jeans, there was something red. She pulled it out. It was a pair of pyjama trousers. She pulled out the top. It too was red, trimmed with white. On the front was a picture of a reindeer. She'd bought them at the last minute for a Christmas party a couple of years ago. They were far too big for her and she'd ended up not wearing them after all. She stood up and inspected them. She stifled a laugh as she tried to picture Douglas wearing them. *They'll have to do!* She grabbed a towel, then rushed back downstairs, holding them out.

'I'm really sorry—' she began and then burst out laughing at his surprised face.

He took them, held out the top with its cute reindeer, complete with velvet antlers and a tartan nose, and laughed. 'I know my dress sense is a little eclectic but this is something else!'

'They're from a fancy dress party and they're the only thing I've got!' Susan admitted. 'Unless you want to try some of Jack's clothes . . .'

'No, no, I'll keep these, thanks,' grinned Douglas. 'I think I'm going to look absolutely stunning!'

'In one sense of the word,' Susan agreed. She took him into the living room and drew the curtains. 'Change in here,' she said. 'I've just got to go and give Jack a hand.'

She went back upstairs. Jack was in the bathroom. He'd managed to strip to the waist and was wiping at his face with the towel. Susan quickly helped him dry his hair. He too could get into pyjamas. Once he was dry, she went back into her room and dug out some dry clothes for herself. She pulled a comb through her damp hair and checked the mirror before heading back downstairs with Jack.

Douglas had found his way to the kitchen. Susan put his wet clothes in the dryer while he switched the kettle on. Susan couldn't help but snort when she saw the pyjamas. They stopped halfway down his calves, revealing a pair of very white legs. The sleeves made it past his elbows, but only just. Jack took one look and roared with laughter. Douglas stood with his hands on his hips, giving him a mock-glare. 'I'll have you know this is the height of fashion,' he said.

'Go on then,' Susan teased. 'Give us a twirl.'

Douglas put an arm in the air, as if he was doing a highland fling, and hopped round in a circle. Jack was laughing so hard he could barely stand. Susan put a hand up to her mouth, but she too began laughing as he stood on one leg like a ballerina and stretched upwards.

'Very graceful,' she said, once she had caught her breath.

The kettle had boiled. 'Tea?' she suggested.

'That would be lovely,' Douglas replied.

She threw teabags into mugs and poured on the hot water. 'Would you like some milk, Jack?' she asked as she added a drop to each cup.

'Yes please.' She poured him a small glass and watched as he drank it, then wiped off his milk moustache with the back of his hand. Then looking up at

Douglas, he asked, 'Do you want to see my bedroom? Mummy's painting it.'

Susan cringed inside. She had started to paint the bedroom weeks ago, but somehow, there just hadn't been time to finish it. Douglas was looking at her, asking with his eyes whether she was happy for him to follow Jack upstairs. 'It's nowhere near finished,' she said, feeling her face redden.

He smiled, his eyes reassuring. 'I started decorating my kitchen two months ago and so far, I've only painted half the cupboards,' he said. 'I don't know where the time goes.'

Jack led Douglas up the narrow staircase and Susan followed. They trooped into Jack's room. Susan had painted two of the walls with golden-yellow paint, but the other two were still plain white with grubby marks.

'Mummy's going to make it like being in a wood,' Jack announced. 'It's going to have trees and animals and everything.'

Douglas smiled at her. 'I bought these,' Susan told him. She held out the pack of decals she had bought. There were two tree trunks and lots of leaves to attach. There was a mummy owl and a baby owl to sit in the branches of one of the trees and a family of squirrels for the other. There were little birds, and butterflies with patterned wings.

'They're great,' Douglas said, looking at them one by one. He handed them back, then pointed at the white wall. 'You're going to paint over that, right?'

Susan laughed. 'I certainly am,' she said. 'Though Jack'll be helping.'

'I love painting,' Jack told Douglas.

'I see you have some paints there.' He pointed to the small pots of paint Susan had bought. She was intending to paint some background for the decals and there were lots of different colours, as yet unopened. 'Would you mind?' he asked.

'Be my guest,' Susan said. She watched as he picked up a paintbrush. This was turning out to be one of the most unusual non-dates she'd ever had.

Douglas knelt down and started to paint. A few moments later, there were two little hedgehogs, standing on their hind legs and holding paws as they looked up at a bumble-bee.

'Snowflake and Frosty!' Jack was thrilled. Susan wanted to laugh at the awe on his face.

'That's right,' Douglas said. 'Your very own.'

'You know I won't be allowed to paint over that now.' Susan smiled.

'Can you do Barty the Badger?' Jack asked. 'And Archie Rabbit?'

Douglas laughed. 'Only if Mummy says so,' he said.

He looked at Susan, who nodded. 'Of course you can,' she said. 'Though if you start taking requests, you'll never hear the end of it.'

There was silence for a few minutes as he set to and painted several of the other characters from the book. Then he sat back on his heels to inspect them. 'You know,' he said, 'I could help with the painting if you like. I've done one mural in my office and another in the hallway outside. I could paint a whole woodland scene on this wall.' For the first time since they'd arrived back, he was speaking hesitantly, as if he wasn't sure if he was overstepping the mark.

Susan felt almost as uneasy as he sounded. 'I'm sorry,' she said. 'I'm not sure I'd have the money to pay . . .' She trailed off.

Douglas's eyes widened and he shook his head. 'I didn't mean that,' he said. 'I meant as a friend . . . of Jack's.' His voice was unexpectedly flustered.

'Please, Mummy?' Jack looked as if Christmas had already come.

Susan looked from Douglas to Jack. Two pairs of eyes, one blue, one brown.

'I guess that's a yes then, so long as you're sure,' she said.

Relief spread over Douglas's face. 'It shouldn't take too long,' he promised. 'We can set up a time. Whenever you like.'

'That would be lovely,' Susan admitted. It would be much easier to finish the room with his help. And Jack would have the most wonderful bedroom at the end. 'I've just thought,' she said. 'Would you be able to do some painting at the nursery? They're looking for someone to paint some new scenery for the Nativity play. Mrs Armitage will pay. I can recommend you, if you'd like?'

'That would be great,' Douglas said.

The beep-beep-beep of the dryer sounded down-stairs. 'That's your clothes,' she said. The three of them trooped down the stairs together. Susan opened the dryer and pulled out Douglas's clothes. 'Here you go,' she said, handing them to him.

'Thanks,' he said. He left the room, then reappeared a few moments later, back in his normal clothes with the red Christmas pyjamas bundled neatly under one arm. 'I'd better head off,' he said, handing them back to Susan, who couldn't help letting out another chuckle. He headed back out into the hallway and Susan opened the door. He turned on the doorstep. 'Thanks for a lovely afternoon,' he said. He hesitated, glancing over his shoulder into the gathering gloom. The rain had stopped. He turned back to Susan. 'I'd like to take you out again,' he said. 'If you wouldn't mind. I've had a great time.' He smiled, looking suddenly shy. 'Doesn't matter if you'd rather not,' he said. 'I'll still paint the mural. I told Jack I'd do it . . .' He trailed off and looked at her, his face open. He really was . . . Susan sought for the right word. Decent. The old-fashioned concept swum into her mind. For all his bumptiousness when he was working, he really was incredibly kind. Whatever was happening with Michael, she shouldn't let it interfere.

'Yes please,' she said. 'I would like to go on another date.'

She was rewarded with that enormous smile. 'That's great,' he said. 'In that case, I'll get planning.'

Susan closed the door behind him, then leaned back on it, looking down the hallway. Jack appeared on the landing. 'Will Douglas be coming back?' he asked. 'He won't forget, will he?'

Susan shook her head. 'He won't,' she said. She found herself grinning at nothing. He was coming back and she was looking forward to it just as much as Jack.

Chapter Fourteen

The children sat cross-legged in the book corner, looking up at Mandy and Susan. Excitement was simmering. It was time for the parts in the Nativity play to be announced, and after that Mandy would tell the class the results of the kitten-naming competition. They'd had a lot of fun looking at the suggestions. Some had been very traditional, such as Kitty. Others had been more unusual. Susan wondered what would happen if a new owner was presented with a kitten called Floofylegs or Santa Claws. Mandy had eventually shared the names with James as Susan had felt that with Jack involved, she wouldn't be able to judge in an impartial way. There were five kittens, so several of the children would have their names used, but there would be one overall winner.

Susan had also spent a long time discussing the Nativity with Nina. It was always difficult to keep things completely fair, but they did their best. Jack had been asking for days whether she thought he would make a good Joseph. It had been a difficult question to answer. Though she was sure he would have been fine in the part, it had gone to Armando. Jack was to be one of the shepherds. She had fudged a reply, saying she was sure he would play any part well. She had reminded him too that all parts were important. Now she just hoped he wouldn't be too upset.

'Okay, everybody. Shush.' She put a finger on her lips and one-by-one the children followed. They were still shuffling, but at least they were no longer in uproar. 'I'm going to read out the parts now, so I want you all to listen carefully. Firstly, Herbinder, you will be Mary.' Her eyes fell on the sweet oval face with its dark-brown eyes. Herbie had breathed in and was sitting up very straight as she looked round proudly. Christina, who was sitting beside Herbie managed a smile, though Susan could see she was disappointed.

Her eyes dropped back to the list in her hand, though she had no real need to read what it said. 'Next, Joseph.' It was the boys' turn to sit up straight. Several of them crossed their arms as if to tidy themselves in the hope they would be chosen. 'Armando, you will be playing Joseph.' From the corner of her eye, she saw Jack's shoulders slump. This was the downside of being Mum to one of the class. Much as she loved being able to spend so much time with Jack, it was hard too. She knew that she was often so careful not to show favouritism that she sometimes leaned towards favouring any other child over Jack. It was such a hard thing to balance.

She began to speed up. She raced through the

angels and the kings, then came to the shepherds. 'Three shepherds,' she read, 'Neil, Jack and Kendall.' Jack sent her the tiniest of smiles and she sent him one back. Kendall also had a small smile on her face, but when Susan looked at Neil, she saw trouble brewing. He looked as if he was about to bawl, and indeed as Susan watched, his mouth opened wide and he started to howl.

To Susan's relief, Nina scooped him up. 'What's up, Neil?' she asked.

Neil was sobbing still, but now he was making an attempt to speak. '. . . not fair,' he gasped. '. . . wanted to be Baby Jesus.'

Christina burst into a loud fit of giggles and Susan wanted to laugh as well, but she quickly shushed the class again. 'I'm very sorry, Neil,' she explained. 'But Jesus is a tiny baby and we'll actually be using a dolly. Mary has to hold Baby Jesus, you see.'

Neil's chin was still shaking. He was clinging on to Nina. With a final glance, Susan moved on. He would get over it in a minute or two. It was better not to pay too much attention.

Once all the parts had been allocated, it was time for Mandy to speak.

'We had a lovely time looking at all your names,' she said. 'Some of them were very unusual indeed and all of them were good, so thank you. We've chosen our five favourites.' She held up a photo of the largest black-and-white-kitten. 'We're going to name this little guy Joey,' she said, and looked up. 'Who was it that came up with that name?'

A little girl called Naomi raised a shy hand. 'Well done,' Mandy said. She put down the photo and picked up one of the little black male kitten. 'And this little boy is going to be called Fiddlesticks! Whose idea was that?'

Susan was pleased to see Noah raising his hand. He was one of the shyer boys in the class and she knew this would give him a boost of confidence.

Next, Mandy held up a picture of the two black-and-white female kittens. 'These two are going to be called Ana and Elsa. Who came up with those lovely names?'

Herbie and Christina put up their hands, exchanging beaming smiles.

Susan noticed that Jack was leaning forward, his face a picture of hope. *He must be hoping to name the little white kitten,* she realised. She found herself desperately wishing that he had won. She knew it would mean so much to him, since he already had a bond with the little thing. *And it would soften the blow of not getting the Nativity part he wanted. . .*

'And finally,' Mandy looked around the class and held up a photo of the little white kitten. 'We come to the last name. One of our kittens is rather special. The smallest of the litter is the white one and he's actually deaf.' There were one or two murmurings around the class. 'But that doesn't mean he won't be able to have a lovely life,' Mandy assured them. 'We wanted him to have a very special name and there was one that really stood out.' She smiled again. 'The name for the little white kitten is . . . Frostflake.'

There was a gasp from Jack. 'That's my name,' he said in a loud voice. 'I chose it.'

Mandy smiled. 'Well done, Jack,' she said. 'It's a great name. It really suits him.'

If Jack had been disappointed over Joseph, he was thrilled now. Susan had rarely seen him look so happy. His eyes caught hers and he sent her a beaming smile, which made her heart swell. Frostflake. He'd put together Frosty and Snowflake, the names of the hedge-hogs in Douglas's book. What a wonderful name for a white cat. She would have to tell Douglas, she thought. He would be pleased.

'Well, thank you very much, Miss Hope,' she said. 'It's been lovely having you here and we're all looking forward to our next visit to Hope Meadows, aren't we?'

'Yes!' the class chorused, even Neil, whose disappointment in not being Jesus seemed to have worn off in the face of Mandy's kittens.

She began to clap and the class joined in. Jack clapped hardest of all, and Susan felt her heart swell.

The taxi was late. Susan had waited at her mother's house, patiently at first, then less so. She was going out for the evening with Michael. It was purely a business meeting, she reminded herself as she glanced at herself in the mirror for the fourteenth time. She had put on a plain black dress, then had added gold earrings and a necklace. It was important to feel good, she told herself. This was to be a negotiation. If she felt comfortable, she would find the evening much easier.

She sat in the back of the cab, trying not to think too much about Michael himself. They were going to discuss his future relationship with Jack. It would be filled with practical conversations about where and when they would meet and for how long. And about how he intended to parent Jack. It was important that she set the right boundaries.

But in spite of her good intentions, her memory kept drifting back to the last time they'd met. There had been a spark between them, hadn't there? Or had she imagined it?

The different versions of Michael in her head clashed awkwardly whenever she thought about him. There was the old Michael, the fun-loving and hard-working man she'd fallen in love with, and there was also the cold and selfish man who'd broken her heart and abandoned Jack, whom she'd hated for so many years . . . and now there was this new, improved, serious Michael who just wanted to make things right. It was hard to believe they were all the same man.

She looked out of the window. She was almost there. They were meeting at Sheep from the Goats, a bar in Walton that had opened last year. It was Michael that had suggested it. Susan had never been before. The taxi pulled up outside an upmarket building with its name spelled out in brightly lit letters. The interior was equally stylish. Very Michael, she decided as she cast her eyes over the white leather seats and black lacquered tables. Although she was a little late, he didn't seem to have arrived. She pulled her mobile from her handbag and checked her messages. She was in the right place. He'd be along in a minute.

It was busy at the bar. Susan had to wait until two men had been served before she even managed to get an arm on the counter. Even then, it seemed like the barman would never notice her. Three times he whisked past, carefully avoiding her eye. She eyed the rows of bottles as he flitted past again. What should she drink? she wondered. She didn't fancy wine. It would be nice to have a cocktail, but she shouldn't get carried away. Just one, then she'd stick to orange juice.

'How about an Old Fashioned?' The voice came from behind, as cool and smooth as the marble surface of the bar. She felt a hand on her shoulder.

'Michael.' She swung round and found herself smiling. He'd looked good last time they'd met, but this time he took her breath away. He was wearing chinos again and a fitted cashmere sweater that accentuated his broad shoulders. His brown hair was brushed back from his forehead.

'Hi.' His voice was slightly husky. He raised an eyebrow and smiled. 'Well?'

'Yes please,' she said. It was years since she'd had an Old Fashioned. Back when they'd been together it had been her go-to drink.

Michael turned to the barman. 'Two Old Fashioned, please,' he said.

The barman responded immediately. It was as if there was nobody else in the bar that mattered. He grabbed two glasses and began to mix their drinks. Michael stood there smiling, as if the barman's reaction was nothing more than he expected. Susan felt torn between irritation that she'd been ignored on her own and amusement that Michael could drift in so easily and get served first.

'Why don't you go and sit down?' Michael said, turning to Susan and nodding towards a booth that had just been vacated. It was more of a command than a suggestion. Susan felt suddenly flustered. She had meant to stay in charge of this conversation.

'I'll pay for this one,' she said, reaching for her purse.

'I'd like to pay.' His words were polite but firm. Susan didn't know how to refuse. She didn't want to start this meeting with them squabbling over money, so she nodded and went to the table.

Two minutes later, he set down the two glasses on the table and slipped into the booth beside her. It was tucked away in the corner, and unlike the other booths, which had longer seats opposite one another, this had only one curved bench. Susan shuffled along a few inches. He was a little too close for comfort.

Jack, Susan thought. They were here to discuss Jack. She lifted her drink. The ice clinked as she lifted it to her lips. It was delicious: sweet and bitter with a kick that warmed all the way to her stomach. She could feel herself relaxing.

'So how have you been?' he asked.

'I've been fine,' she replied. It seemed suddenly impossible to rush into all the issues about Jack. She could have a drink first. She lifted the glass again. The flavours mingled in her mouth, taking her back in time. 'How about you?' she asked and he smiled.

'Much better for having seen you,' he said. He lifted his glass and inspected the amber liquid, then put it to his lips and took a sip. He set it back down with a sigh, as if it was completely satisfactory. 'Do you know,' he said. 'I ran into Matthew the other day. He and Julie are married now.'

Susan frowned, casting her mind back. Matthew and Julie had often been a part of their circle when they had been out and about in York. They were both lawyers as well, although they worked in different firms from Michael. Together, they'd been quite a crew of pleasure seekers. Long weekend brunches, mid-week drinks, mini-breaks galore. Those memories barely felt like her own any more, they were so different from her life now.

'We had some good times together, didn't we?' Michael said. 'Do you remember the weekend away in Pickering?'

Susan did. The four of them had stayed in the Silver

Hart, an old coaching inn in the centre of the little market town. She and Michael had splashed out on a tiny suite with a four-poster bed and thick white carpets. That had been just before Christmas too. They'd drunk mulled wine in the Swan. Afterwards, she and Michael had walked up the hill towards the castle and had kissed in the lee of its ancient stone walls.

'Do you remember it had snowed when we got back?' she said. The heating in their flat had broken and there had been ice on the inside of the windows. 'You had to light a fire.' They had huddled together on the couch sharing a blanket. They'd drunk whisky cocktails that night too. Julie had offered to let them stay over at hers, but Michael had whispered to Susan that he wanted time alone with her.

They had shared the most wonderful little flat. It had been on the top floor of an old Georgian house. Their windows had peeped out from under the roof and ancient ivy had tapped on the glass when it was windy.

'That was one of the best weekends of my life,' he said softly. He lifted his glass. 'Cheers to good times.'

Susan raised her glass to meet his. He began to chat again about the memories they shared. Summer days on the beach at Scarborough. An autumn trip to Scotland. They had another drink, and then another. It was years since she had laughed like this. So long since she had felt this free.

She was aware that she should be turning the subject

back to Jack, but she couldn't bring herself to end their fun reminiscing. It felt so natural, and besides, all their chat was helping her get to know Michael again. To learn who he was now. As she had thought last time, he really did seem to have changed. He was still confident and self-assured, but he seemed to have lost the arrogance and temper that had marred their relationship before. As she was thinking this, their eyes met and she felt suddenly, uncomplicatedly happy. A shiver ran down her spine. He was the only man she had ever loved and here they were, back together. Hadn't this been her dream? That he would come back to her and accept Jack? It was all she'd ever wanted.

When Michael shifted in his seat and slipped an arm around her, Susan didn't pull away. *Friends can sit like this too,* she reasoned, but really, she knew that she was enjoying feeling like a couple again. Sitting in this pose that they had sat in hundreds of times before, comfortable with one another. It just felt *the same*. Even his aftershave was familiar and that, mingled with the smell of the whisky meant that if Susan closed her eyes, she could believe it was still five years ago.

When it was time to go home, he helped her up as if it was the most natural thing in the world. She felt a little unsteady as she walked to the door, but he held her elbow.

'Here's your taxi,' he said as a sleek silver car drew up beside them. Had she forgotten his efficiency? Everything ran like clockwork when Michael was at her side. He pulled open the door. His hand was still there, warm and steady. He leaned in to kiss her and by instinct, she turned at the last moment so that it landed on her cheek, but he laughed at the near miss and she reached out and hugged him.

'I'm so glad you're back,' she whispered in his ear, then sighed as she pulled away. 'I'm sure Jack would love to get to know you too.'

He helped her into the car and leaned in, touching a lock of her hair that had escaped from the band that was holding it back. He smiled. 'I'll be in touch,' he promised. 'I can't wait to see you again, and to meet Jack.'

He closed the car door and stepped back.

'Where to?' The driver was looking at her in the mirror.

'Torsdale House,' she replied and the driver nodded and put the car in gear. Susan turned as they drove off, but Michael had already disappeared.

Chapter Fifteen

Susan stood in the reception area of Hope Meadows, clutching the stem of a wine glass. She had taken a sip of the wine when she'd first been handed it, but then she'd stopped. Not that it wasn't good: it was expensive enough. She just couldn't face any more alcohol after yesterday.

At the front of the room, a man with a rather plummy voice was telling them all about the different wines available, but Susan was distracted. Her mind kept wandering back to the previous evening with Michael. She shouldn't have drunk so much. She had almost kissed him. The meeting should have been all about Jack and they had barely mentioned him. Though she was willing for Jack and Michael to have a relationship, she had wanted to keep boundaries in place. Now he seemed to be creeping back into her life as well.

'If anyone is interested in buying the Tempranillo . . .' The voice at the front droned on. It had been Toby Gordon's idea to have a wine-tasting fundraiser. He had invited a few colleagues and friends from college in the hope of making some money for Hope Meadows.

Susan had come to give Mandy moral support. She knew Mandy had agonised over whether to charge for entry. Toby had assured her that the money from the wine sales would be topped up with donations, but as far as Susan could see, there had been very few of either.

Her mind wandered again. The situation with Michael would have been bad enough in itself. But then there was Douglas. The last time she'd seen him, when he'd offered to paint Jack's bedroom, she had felt very much at ease. She had begun to feel that their friendship might have a future. They were supposed to be meeting up on Thursday. Now her feelings for Michael made everything complicated. They were such different men. Michael, with his expensive tastes and city living, was from her past. Douglas's goofy demeanour and laid-back attitude slotted perfectly into her Welford life.

Around her, people were shuffling their feet and starting to chat. The lecture had ended. Several people were huddled round the table where the wine was being shared. Nearby there was a table with several plates of rather expensive nibbles supplied by the wine company. There were definitely more people standing around with miniature egg-wraps and canapés than buying anything, Susan thought. Poor Mandy. She really should go over and chat.

The phone in her pocket buzzed and she pulled it out. It was a message from Michael.

Thank you for yesterday evening. I had a great time and it was lovely hearing all about Jack. I look forward to meeting him. I am free on Thursday if that would suit. Please let me know as soon as possible.

Susan felt worry rising in her stomach, which did nothing to help her hangover. She *had* told him at the end of the night that he could see Jack. *Why did I say that?* She mentally scolded herself. Now she'd created a pressure she didn't need to have. She could have left things vague, at least until they'd had a proper conversation about Jack, instead of tipsy reminiscences. Besides, Thursday was her date with Douglas and she couldn't cancel on him again.

Would it be possible to do a different day? Tuesday or Wednesday would work better for me. She typed in the words and hit 'send'. She wasn't going to gush about yesterday evening. Not until she'd had time to think about what she wanted.

A text pinged back almost instantly. *I'm afraid not. Big case starting in the crown court next week and Thursday will be the only possibility in the near future. Possibly next week on Saturday, if that isn't too long?*

How long was the 'near future' she wondered with a frown? A week, a month, a year? Couldn't he be more specific? It wasn't really fair on Douglas, but she guessed it wasn't fair on Michael to make him wait too long after she'd said he could meet Jack. The Saturday wasn't possible either. Jack was going to a Christmas party at the Dhanjals'. Susan sighed and looked up.

Mandy was now chatting to Toby. They appeared to be deep in conversation. She didn't really know anybody else.

Okay, let's do Thursday, she typed back. *Jack has a party on the Saturday afternoon.* A few more messages and they had agreed on the details. Susan tried to ignore the queasy feeling in her stomach at the thought of the meeting. *I knew this was coming and I'll worry about it later.* She just hoped Jack would be okay.

In the meantime, she had to rearrange her meeting with Douglas. She took a gulp of wine. What should she tell him? Jack meeting Michael would be a perfectly valid reason to give. She could explain to Douglas that Jack's dad had contacted her and wanted to spend some time with Jack. A stray memory from last night slunk into her mind. Michael's arm had been round her. She hadn't pushed him away. Why hadn't she?

Sorry, Douglas, she typed quickly, *I forgot I was taking Jack to the dentist's on Thursday. Would it be possible to meet up another night?* Again she clicked 'send' before she had time to think. She stared at the screen a moment later. Why hadn't she just told him the truth? Should she tell him now? She couldn't. She lifted the glass again. The wine was almost gone.

No problem. The message popped up with a cheery emoticon. *How about the Thursday after? Maybe we could go for a ride? I know you love horses.*

That would be lovely, thanks. She felt a little breathless as she sent it. By the time she saw him again, the first meeting with Michael and Jack would be over. She would tell Douglas all about it then, she thought. She knew she didn't exactly owe him anything, but she hated lying.

When she looked up, the room had started to empty, though several people were still standing around chatting. The wine-salesman was packing away his wares and the plates of nibbles had been stripped bare. Mandy was coming towards her, flanked by Toby. Susan shoved her phone back into her pocket.

'How did it go?' Susan asked. She couldn't read Mandy's face.

Mandy shrugged and glanced at Toby. 'So-so,' she said.

Toby grimaced. 'I'm sorry,' he said to Mandy. It sounded as if it wasn't the first time he'd said it.

'I think people had a good time, but we didn't make anything.' Mandy managed a smile.

'Actually, it made a loss,' Toby admitted. He looked sad as he looked straight into Susan's eyes. His hair wasn't quite as fiercely styled today, she noticed.

'It doesn't matter,' Mandy assured him. 'I'll come up with another idea. It's good to try different things.'

'I can have a think too,' Susan said. 'I'd really like to help. You've been so good to me and Jack.' She shuffled her feet. She had worn high heels and they were starting to nip.

'You're looking very nice,' Mandy said, looking her up and down. 'That dress really suits you.'

'Thanks.' Susan smiled. She was wearing a shimmery green number that she'd owned for a few years now and she'd been hoping it wasn't obvious that it was old. She glanced down and brushed a speck of dust from the skirt. Would Douglas ever see it? she wondered. It wasn't the sort of thing she could wear to go swinging around on ropes or horse-riding. Michael would like it, though. They were two very different men, she thought, smiling to herself.

The moon was high in the night sky by the time she arrived home. Miranda came out into the hall as she opened the front door.

'How did it go?' she asked. 'Did you buy anything?'

Susan shook her head. 'Sorry,' she said. 'I should have brought you something. For looking after Jack.'

Miranda smiled. 'No you shouldn't,' she said, putting her hands on her hips. 'You know I enjoy it.'

'Mummy!' There was a cry from the top of the stairs and a moment later, Jack rushed down and flung himself into her arms. Susan snuggled him for a moment, enjoying the tightness of his little arms, wrapped around her neck.

'Love you,' she murmured, dropping a kiss on his soap-scented cheek.

She set him down and he tugged her into the living room. The coffee table was strewn with felt-tipped pens and half-finished drawings. Jack pulled out a paper from under the pile. 'This is for you, Mummy,' he said.

Susan took the picture. Though it wasn't easy to see exactly what he had drawn, there seemed to be a ginger cat and something that looked a bit like a scrubbing brush on legs. 'Tell me about your picture,' she said, crouching down beside him and holding out the drawing.

'That's Marmalade,' he said, pointing to the cat.

Susan smiled. 'He's lovely,' she said.

'And that's Frosty.' Susan looked at the brush figure. It was wearing a red bow, she realised. It was Frosty the little white hedgehog from Douglas's books.

'It's really very good,' Susan told her son.

She handed the paper back to Jack. 'Can you give me a minute?' she asked. 'I need to talk to Nana.'

Jack nodded, his face solemn. 'Can I draw another picture?' he asked. 'One for Nana?'

Susan wanted to kiss his earnest little face. 'Good idea,' she said.

Miranda raised her eyebrows as Jack trotted off and knelt down at the table. 'What is it?' she asked.

'Come into the kitchen?' Susan suggested. She glanced down at Jack, who was already concentrating hard.

Miranda looked surprised. 'Yes, of course,' she said.

Susan led her through, leaving the doors open. She no longer needed to have her eyes on Jack every minute of the day, but she liked him to know she was there if he needed anything.

She put the kettle on, then stood leaning on the worktop. Miranda wasn't going to like what she had to say. She knew that from their previous discussion when Mandy had been here. Though her mum had made it clear she would respect Susan's choices, Susan had been able to tell she would much rather Michael went away and never came back.

'I've spoken to Michael,' she said. Miranda pursed her lips a little, but Susan ploughed on. 'I've told him he can meet Jack. He's coming here on Thursday.' Her mum's frown deepened. Susan wasn't too enamoured herself with the idea of letting Michael into her home, but she had thought about Jack. He would be more relaxed in his own place. 'I haven't talked to Jack about it yet. I was wondering if you would mind staying a few minutes longer while I tell him?'

For a moment, Susan wondered if Miranda was going to object. She had said many times that even if Michael deigned to return, Susan shouldn't give him the time of day. The frown on Miranda's face was replaced after a moment with a small smile. 'Of course I will.'

Susan felt the tension in her shoulders ease a little. It would be better to have her mum there, she thought. An extra layer of comfort if Jack seemed worried. He loved his Nana so much. 'Thanks, Mum,' she said and reached out to give Miranda's hand a squeeze.

Jack was still drawing, but he stopped and looked up when they walked in. 'Come see, Mummy,' he said.

Susan walked round to where he was sitting on the

floor, but her eyes barely registered Jack's picture. 'Come and sit with me over here,' she said. She took the two steps over to the couch, sat down, and patted the seat beside her. Miranda sat down in the chair nearest the fire. 'I want to talk to you about families,' she said, looking down into Jack's big, dark eyes. 'Lots of families have a mummy and a daddy don't they?' She smiled at him and he smiled back at her.

'You mean like Herbie's mummy and daddy?' he said.

Susan nodded. 'Yes,' she said. 'Like Herbie's mummy and daddy.' She paused for a second. She had to get this right. 'Well, you know some families only have a mummy or a daddy? And some families have a mummy and daddy who live in different houses?' Jack's eyes were still gazing at her, filled with innocence. He had never once asked about his father and he didn't have an inkling where this conversation was going, but there was no going back. 'Well you have a daddy. Do you know that?' She stopped and held her breath. Jack was staring at her. 'He's a very nice man.' She rushed on. 'He's a lot like you,' she said.

From the other side of the room, she heard Miranda shift in her chair. She glanced over, but her mum's face was unreadable.

Susan reached out her arm and put it round Jack, pulling him in closer, smiling to reassure him. 'So what do you think?' she asked. 'Would you like to meet him?'

Jack had screwed up his mouth into a tight 'O' shape

and he was frowning. Susan waited. 'My daddy isn't like Harrison's daddy, is he?' he said.

Susan shook her head. Harrison's mum and dad were going through an acrimonious divorce. Poor Harrison had confided in Susan that his daddy was often very cross. She hadn't known Jack knew about it. 'Not like that,' she assured him. 'Your daddy is good,' she said, 'and he and I are friends.' For a moment she wondered if he would ask why his daddy hadn't come round before, if they were friends, but he was staring at her, his face serious.

Susan felt suddenly nervous. She didn't want him worrying. 'You're so yummy, I just wanted to keep you all to myself,' she told him, grinning, trying to lighten the apprehension in his gaze. She reached out a hand and gave his tummy a tickle and he smiled, so she leaned down and started to smother him in kisses, ending up with blowing a raspberry on his stomach. Jack was laughing now, the tension dispersed. She put her arm round him again and hugged him. 'Whatever you want,' she said, 'it'll be fine. Nothing else will change, okay?'

He reached out to Lamby, who was sitting in his usual place at the other end of the couch, then holding Lamby tightly, he snuggled into Susan's side.

'So you'd like to meet your daddy?' Susan had to be sure it was what he wanted.

Jack looked up at her and nodded. 'Yes please,' he said.

'That's good,' Susan replied.

Jack was still leaning on her. He could think about it as long as he wanted. She wasn't going to move until he was quite ready. He sat quietly for a minute, then looked up. 'Can I draw again?' he asked.

Susan glanced at the clock. It was well past his bedtime, but a bit more drawing wouldn't hurt this once. 'Of course you can,' she murmured, and watched as he slid off the couch and padded across to the table.

Susan remembered that the kettle had boiled. 'Cup of tea?' she asked, glancing across at Miranda.

Miranda smiled. 'I thought you'd never ask,' she said.

Chapter Sixteen

Thursday afternoon had come round all too quickly. Michael had taken the afternoon off work and was due to arrive at two. Susan's morning had passed in a haze of Nativity preparations. They had been running through it every day for several days now. Herbie Dhanjal was the only one who actually knew all her lines and Susan was beginning to despair, as she did every year, of them being ready in time.

She hadn't slept much last night. Her brain had been on a weird loop of Michael and Jack scenarios. None of them had been good. In one, Jack was terrified of Michael. In another, Jack behaved so badly that Michael said he never wanted to see them again. The worst one, though, was that Jack and Michael would get on so well together that Jack would decide he wanted to go and live with Michael. Michael had all the legal representation he would ever need if he decided to make things difficult. Letting him meet Jack was an acknowledgement of his fatherhood.

Don't be dramatic, Susan, she told herself. Why would he do that? He didn't seem to be here to cause trouble.

And he had never indicated he wanted Jack to live with him. Yet she couldn't help but feel nervous as she cleaned away the lunch things.

Jack seemed quite happy. Susan had expected him to be nervous, but he had chattered away about all kinds of things as he ate his sandwiches. It's going to be fine, she thought. There was a part of her that felt excited too. If it worked out well, it would be good for all of them.

The doorbell rang. Susan put the last of the cups on the side and reached for the towel. She glanced round the kitchen for what seemed to be the hundredth time. Everything was tidyish. She had half expected Jack to rush to the front door to open it, since he had seemed so excited, but instead, he appeared in the doorway of the living room as she walked out into the hall. His face was pale. He followed her along the hallway and she took a second, running a calming hand over his hair before she opened the door.

Michael's clothes were more casual than they had been on the other occasions they'd met. Susan ran her eyes over the chic sweater and fitted jeans. They both looked brand new and probably were designer, knowing Michael. He still looked almost comically out of place at their cottage, despite his attempt at 'off-duty'.

'Hello, Michael,' Susan said. 'Jack, this is your daddy.'

Jack was standing very close to her, almost hiding behind her legs. It was a long time since he'd done that, she thought. She wondered whether Michael would bend to try to hug him, or even just talk on his own level, but Michael didn't seem to have any idea what to do.

'Hello, Jack,' he said. 'It's nice to meet you at last.'

He sounded as nervous as she was feeling, Susan thought with a lurch of compassion. She'd always assumed he would be confident in every situation. She crouched down beside Jack, holding both of his hands and looking directly at him. 'Do you want to say hello to Daddy?' she asked.

She sent him a reassuring smile and he looked up at Michael with those huge eyes that were so much like Michael's own. 'Hello,' he said.

Susan stood back up. Michael was looking more worried than ever. 'It's okay,' she mouthed, placing a hand on Jack's head.

Michael was carrying a bag in his hand. He reached in and drew out a spherical parcel, wrapped in bright orange paper. 'I've brought you a present,' he said, holding it out to Jack, though even that looked awkward.

Jack took the parcel. 'Thank you,' he whispered, then backed behind Susan again.

'Come in, Michael,' Susan said. They couldn't stand on the doorstep all day. 'Why don't you take Daddy through to the living room, Jack,' she added. 'You can open your gift there.'

She closed the door and led Jack through. He still seemed more inclined to stare at Michael in silence than open his parcel. Michael didn't seem to know what to do either. He stood beside one of the chairs, looking utterly out of place among the evidence of Susan's daily life as a mother. 'Won't you sit down?' she suggested. She sank down onto the couch and was relieved when Michael subsided into the rather worn chair that she normally sat in when she was on her own.

'Would you like a drink, Michael?' she offered, trying her best to act like he was a normal guest.

'Oh, no thank you.' Michael shook his head, but his eyes were fixed on Jack, who was still just clutching the parcel.

'Are you going to open your gift?' Susan asked Jack in a gentle voice. He had stayed very close to her throughout and now he came and leaned on the couch to tear off the wrapping paper. It was a football.

For a first gift, it wasn't a bad choice. But Michael's forehead creased when Jack remained silent. 'I thought you liked football,' he said. Jack was looking at the football as if he didn't know what to do with it

Susan sent Michael a reassuring smile as she reached out and put her arm round Jack. 'He does, don't you, Jack?' she said.

Jack nodded, though he still seemed overwhelmed.

Susan looked across at Michael. 'How about we all go out into the garden?' she asked, then cringed. The voice she had used was a bit too much like the encouraging tone she used at the nursery. 'We can play with the ball. You'd like that wouldn't you, Jack?' she added, directing her question directly at him to try to cover her embarrassment.

'Great idea.' Michael's voice seemed a little too hearty

as well. He stood up nonetheless and followed Susan and Jack out into the back garden. Susan grabbed coats for herself and Jack, noting that Michael didn't seem to have brought one.

The garden was small and mostly lawn. Stone walls marked the boundaries. Though Susan kept the grass trimmed, climbing plants ran rampant. In summer, the garden was a tiny oasis of Golden Showers roses and purple wisteria. Today it looked tired, though the grass had not yet turned winter yellow. Offset from the window, there was a bird table filled with seeds and festooned with hanging feeders.

For the first time, Jack looked animated as he set the ball down on the ground and kicked it so it rebounded off one of the stone walls.

'Over here!' Michael called, raising an arm.

Jack paused for a moment, then kicked it to him.

'Great left foot!' Michael said, controlling the ball and then sending it gently back.

Jack received it and kicked it back once more. When he looked up, Susan could see he was smiling.

They kicked the ball back and forth, occasionally sending it in Susan's direction. Michael was becoming more enthusiastic. Susan sent the ball back. He caught it on his foot, bounced it twice, then booted it. It arced upwards. For a moment, Susan felt her head prickling as it veered towards the window. It missed by only an inch, hit the angle of the wall, ricocheted off at a crazy angle and smashed into the bird table.

The carefully arranged seeds went flying as the table fell. Jack let out a strangled yelp. Susan made a rush for the table and picked it up. It was undamaged, but most of the seeds were lost in the grass.

'I'm so sorry.' Michael's face was red as he lifted up one of the seed-feeders and set it back on its hook.

'That's all right.' Her voice had that over-compensatory cheery tone again. Though her comment was directed at Michael, she was trying to reassure Jack. He had looked for a moment as if he was going to cry, but now he seemed to have retreated into his shell. 'We can give the birds more. We've plenty.' She pulled open the door that led into the kitchen, stepped inside and pulled the bags of bird food from the cupboard. 'Jack and I feed the birds every morning,' she explained to Michael as she returned outside.

'So you like birds then, Jack?' Michael asked as they placed the new seeds on the table. He was trying, Susan thought. But Jack was busy arranging the food and didn't respond.

'He loves all animals,' Susan interjected.

'That's good,' Michael said. 'I like animals too. What's your favourite animal, Jack?'

Jack looked up at Susan. She smiled at him, trying to send him reassurance. 'Cats are his favourite.' Jack was standing behind her again, as if he had returned to toddlerhood.

'So do you have a cat?' Michael asked Jack.

Again there was a moment when Susan thought Jack

was going to burst into tears. Though he still said goodnight to Marmalade up in heaven every night, Jack almost never mentioned him otherwise. He didn't like Susan talking about Marmalade, though she did so now and then.

'No cat,' she said, shaking her head. The stark words hung in the air. 'There are lots, though, at Hope Meadows,' she added, '. . . the rescue centre we visit. They've some lovely kittens too, just at the moment.'

There was a long silence. Despite the December chill, Susan's face was hot. She thought longingly of Mr Gorski and Douglas. Both of them knew how to chat to Jack and put him at his ease. That Michael had no idea how to talk to children was painfully obvious and her own nerves weren't helping. The nightmares that had plagued her last night were coming true. The painful future stretched out in front of her. Would Michael disappear again, leaving Jack more confused than ever? She had to think of something that would make things easier for both of them, but what?

A vision of the deaf white kitten came into her head. Sometimes you had to find different ways to communicate. Jack was always at his most relaxed around animals. Mandy had found it hard to talk to Jack to begin with too, but animals had brought them together.

'In fact, why don't we go to Hope Meadows now?' she suggested. It would give them something to talk about. Even if nobody else could find anything to say, Mandy could talk to anyone about the animals in her care. It came with the territory of being a vet and running a shelter.

Jack came out from behind her. For the first time since Michael had arrived, he looked excited.

But Michael was frowning. 'Can we just pop in like that?' he asked. 'Won't they be busy?'

Susan crossed her fingers. 'I'll give Mandy a call,' she said, 'but even if she isn't there, there are animals outside in the paddock.' It would be better to get out of the house, even if they were just walking.

'Really?' Michael looked interested. 'It isn't just dogs and cats?'

Jack shook his head vigorously.

'There's a cow and goats in the paddock,' Susan explained.

Jack folded his arms. 'Mandy has rabbits and guinea pigs too,' he said. 'And last summer she had an owl called Frank.' For the first time since Michael had arrived, Susan felt a laugh bubbling inside. That was the longest sentence Jack had strung together in front of Michael so far. He seemed outraged at the suggestion that Mandy would only have cats and dogs.

She glanced at Michael, wondering if he would take offence, but he still looked interested. 'Really?' he said, looking directly at Jack. 'An owl called Frank? What are the other animals called?'

Jack's eyes widened and he drew in a deep breath.

'The cow's a Highland cow and she's called Dawn. The goats are Minnie and Mike. . .'

Susan pulled her phone out of her pocket. Listing the animals would take some minutes. She dialled Mandy's number, but there was no reply. Should she phone Animal Ark? Mandy was probably busy. If they walked over, she might be there and if not, they could stroke the outdoor animals. Even Dawn, who had been very shy to begin with, came over to investigate now when Susan and Jack arrived.

'I can't get Mandy,' she said, shoving her phone back into her pocket a couple of minutes later, 'but we can wander over there. There's always something to see.' It would be something to do anyway. Better than going back into the house and trying to chat.

They set off up the road and turned left onto the green. A gust of wind blew a stray lock of hair over Susan's face and she tucked it behind her ear. The air was beginning to have an icy edge. The surface of the pond was ruffled. There were only two ducks this morning, a male and female teal. They were well camou-flaged in their winter plumage, but Jack saw them immediately. He stopped and watched them with his head on one side. Michael halted too. He bent forward and Susan thought he was going to talk to Jack about the ducks, but he brushed away some mud from his expensive jeans and straightened again. The image of Douglas lifting his head to gobble down birdseed in the rain swam into her head. Things would be so much easier if Michael was like Douglas. She thrust the thought away. She had to deal with the situation as it was. Wishful thinking helped nobody.

They walked on. Though Jack was still not talking to Michael directly, he seemed more himself. He climbed up on a gate to scan the field beyond for rabbits and seemed delighted when a flock of sheep rushed towards him, bleating loudly. Michael watched quietly, though he stayed well back from the wooden gate.

Mandy's RAV4 was parked beside Animal Ark when they arrived. 'Looks like Mandy's here after all,' Susan told Michael. She felt relieved as they made their way round to the entrance to Hope Meadows itself. The visit would take much longer if they could go inside and look round. The centre itself was so lovely. Michael couldn't help but be impressed with what Mandy was doing. Jack had run ahead and was holding the door open. That was a relief. Michael was finally seeing the good manners Susan had taught him.

She walked into the reception area. Mandy was sitting at the desk and for a moment, Susan thought she must be talking on the phone. 'Come any time,' she said. For the first time, Susan became aware there was a second person, standing leaning against the wall with their back towards the newcomers. He turned to see who had come in and the familiar grin froze on his face. It was Douglas.

Chapter Seventeen

Susan felt her entire body cringing. The *one* person she didn't want to run into today was standing right in front of her. She felt like cursing her luck. *But it wouldn't be a problem if I hadn't lied,* she reminded herself, uncomfortably. There was confusion on Douglas's face as he glanced from her to Michael and back again.

'Hi, Douglas!' Jack went in to give him a hug. This time, it was Michael's turn to look confused as he watched his son hugging the other man.

Susan wished the floor would swallow her up.

Mandy stood up, smiling.

'Hi.' Mandy looked at Jack and raised her eyebrows. 'Who's this you've got with you today?'

'It's my dad.' Jack was watching Mandy, as if to see how she would react.

Mandy's eyes widened ever so slightly and she glanced again at Michael, then smiled at Jack. 'Well then, he's very welcome,' she said. She held out a hand to Michael. 'Hello,' she said. 'Mandy Hope. Welcome to Hope Meadows.'

Michael took her hand and shook it, courteously bowing his head. 'Lovely to meet you. I'm Michael.'

Susan risked another glance at Douglas. There were clouds in his usually clear blue eyes. She felt sick. She and Douglas had only been out twice. The second meeting hadn't been a real date because of Jack, but he'd still made it fun. She could have told him about Michael, explained that there wasn't another day he could meet Jack. Instead she had taken the easy way out.

And now Douglas was moving. He pushed himself away from the wall and held out a hand to Michael. 'Hello,' he said. 'Douglas MacLeod.'

Michael took Douglas's hand. For a moment, surprise crossed his face as if Douglas had gripped his hand more tightly than he had expected. 'Michael Chalk,' he said after a moment.

'Douglas is a local author and children's illustrator,' Mandy explained. 'He's been sketching.'

The pad Douglas had been using was dangling from the fingers of his other hand, Susan saw. He'd been drawing the kittens. The drawing showed them asleep in a pile. He was so skilled. Michael was looking at Douglas. Douglas's eyes were still on Susan. 'I did a reading at Susan's nursery recently,' he said, as if in explanation. Susan felt a fresh wave of guilt. If she had been honest with Douglas, he wouldn't be meeting Michael unprepared. 'I understand you are a dentist?' Douglas said to Michael, his eyes darting back to Susan again.

Susan felt like a worm as she heard him refer to her lie of taking Jack to the dentist. *He's cross. And he has every right to be* . . .

Michael was frowning. 'No I'm not a dentist. I'm a lawyer actually, in York.'

'Ah, my mistake,' Douglas replied. Susan had never seen him so reserved before.

'When are you coming to paint?' Jack was looking at Douglas. His eyes were filled with hope.

Michael was looking at Susan now. For a moment, she was tempted to tell him Douglas was coming to the nursery to paint scenery, but then she'd be lying to Michael as well. Not that she owed Michael anything, she thought. It hit her suddenly that she didn't want Douglas to see her lie to Michael. The feeling was unexpectedly fierce. What did it matter? She'd already been caught lying to Douglas himself.

'Soon.' Douglas managed to smile at Jack.

Jack seemed reassured by Douglas's presence. He returned Douglas's smile, then looked up at Michael. 'Mummy and Douglas are friends from LoveSpark,' he said.

Susan's face was burning. Jack must have overheard that at nursery and stored the information away. He announced it in such a matter-of-fact tone that Susan couldn't have denied it, even if she'd wanted to. Now Michael was staring. She had no idea what to say.

'So what would you like to do today?' Mandy interrupted the painful silence. She looked at Jack. 'I've been working on some techniques to train Frostflake. Would you like to come and help?' She held out a hand to Jack, who trotted over to take it. 'Your daddy can come too,' Mandy added in a firm voice. She walked over to the door of the cat room, opened the door and held it open for Michael in a way that he would have been hard-pressed to refuse. Susan realised that Mandy had understood the situation and was giving her a chance to speak to Douglas.

Douglas. He looked almost as uncomfortable as Susan herself was feeling. He was gazing at his feet. Susan took a deep breath. 'I'm sorry,' she said. She stopped. Her voice sounded unsteady. She straightened her spine and looked at Douglas. There was nothing to do but be honest now and hope he would understand. 'As Jack said, Michael is his father. He got in contact recently, after a long time and wanted to get to know Jack. This is their first meeting. He couldn't manage a different day. I should have told you, but . . .' she paused, then took another unsteady breath. 'It's complicated,' she said finally, knowing her words were inadequate.

If she had hoped for his understanding, she didn't get it. He was looking at her as if he couldn't quite believe what he was hearing.

'It doesn't really matter,' he said. Susan winced at the disappointment in his voice. 'I like you very much,' he said, 'but if you can lie to me so easily, I can tell you don't feel the same.' His eyes were on hers and for the first time, there was no trace of a smile. 'I don't like people who can't be honest. It's fine. No more dates.'

He reached over and grabbed his briefcase from the desk. Flipping the top open, he wedged in the drawing of the kittens, then closed the bag. 'I'll see you round,' he said. He paused and for a moment, Susan thought he was going to say something else, but he turned on his heel and strode out.

Susan stood there, reeling. She felt as if she had been slapped in the face. She wanted to feel anger at Douglas, but this was entirely her doing. And now she had to pull herself together: go back to Jack and Michael. Jack needed her. She had just started to walk towards the kennel-room door when it burst open and Jack rushed through, holding Frostflake.

'Mummy, Mummy,' he shouted. His eyes were huge. 'Frostflake knows sign language.'

'Really?' Pulling herself together, Susan looked at Mandy, who nodded.

'Yes,' she said. 'I've been showing Jack.'

Jack was grinning so much that he hardly seemed able to get the words out. 'We had to wake him up by tapping on the floor next to him,' he said. 'You have to make sure he's looking at you before you touch him. Otherwise he might get scared.'

'Oh yes?' Susan was fascinated in spite of what had just happened. Mandy always found a way to help the animals she cared for.

'Yes. And Mandy showed me the signal to call him.' Frostflake was nuzzling under Jack's chin, thrusting his small pink nose upwards. Jack laughed and Frostflake began to purr that enormous purr that seemed so big, coming from his tiny body.

'How do you call him?' Susan asked.

'It's a hand movement . . . like this.' Jack reached out his hand and made a beckoning motion. 'He has to be looking at you first, though,' he explained. 'And now we're going to put a harness on him.'

Susan had the sudden image of Frostflake pulling a tiny cart.

'He can't go outside,' Mandy explained. 'Not unless he's on a lead, so we have to get him used to it nice and early.'

Oh, that kind of harness!

Michael was smiling. For the first time since he'd arrived that afternoon, he looked at ease. However awful the meeting with Douglas had been for Susan, it had been the right thing for Jack to come here. Mandy had handed Michael the miniature harness and together, he and Jack managed to get it onto the squirming kitten.

'Now this,' Mandy said, and they clipped a lead onto the little harness. She set Frostflake down on the floor. 'You can hold the lead,' she told Jack, 'and just keep up with him wherever he wants to go. For now, I just want him to get used to how it feels.'

Jack seemed pleased with the task, as he always was when Mandy asked him to do something. Susan felt proud as he patiently followed Frostflake round the room, never once tugging on the lead. When the kitten stopped and scratched at the harness, or tried to twist round, he made sure the soft leather didn't get tangled. At the end of the session, Mandy stood across the room from Frostflake and flapped her arms. When he looked across at her, she made the beckoning motion that Jack had shown Susan earlier, and the little white shape set off across the room in a series of bounds with Jack chasing after, laughing with happiness.

Mandy bent over and held out a tiny piece of food. Frostflake sniffed at it, then licked the morsel off her finger. 'Tuna,' she told Jack. 'It's his favourite. But I think that's enough for now. We have to stop while he's enjoying it.'

Jack lifted up Frostflake. The kitten seemed a little tired after all his exertions. He snuggled into Jack's arms.

'May I stroke him?' Susan asked, once Mandy had removed the little red harness.

'Just make sure he sees you first,' Mandy reminded her. Susan held out a hand and tapped on Jack's shoulder beside the kitten's front paw. Frostflake looked round. His blue eyes were huge. Susan reached out her fingers and stroked the soft fur on the side of his neck and his tiny little face. And there was that super-loud purr again.

'He seems a happy little thing,' Susan said.

'He is.' Mandy nodded.

'No wonder you like coming here so much,' Michael said to Jack, as Mandy lifted Frostflake out of Jack's arms and carried him through to put him back in with his brothers and sisters.

Jack looked pleased. 'Can we go in and show Daddy the dogs next?' he asked Susan.

Susan smiled. 'We'll have to ask Mandy,' she reminded him.

Mandy reappeared. 'Did I hear someone mention dogs?' she asked. Jack reached out a hand to Michael. For the space of a beat, Susan wondered if Michael would ignore the invitation, but a moment later, the pair were making their way hand-in-hand towards the dog kennel room. Susan swallowed. For a moment, she felt oddly excluded, seeing the two of them like that.

Don't be silly, this is what you wanted, she told herself. It was great that they were getting on. She could wish all she liked that Michael had never turned up, but she was committed now.

The afternoon wound on. Jack seemed much more like himself as he showed Michael round. The stilted questioning from earlier had stopped. Michael seemed more comfortable too, though once or twice, Susan caught him looking bemused and several times he pulled a super-clean handkerchief from his pocket to wipe his fingers. They went outside and looked at the animals in the paddock. Michael stood well back from the fence as Jack explained all about the goats eating hay and about how Highland cows had so much hair to keep them warm up in Scotland. Michael was obviously out of his comfort zone, but he was trying hard.

Finally, it was time to go home. 'I'm afraid I have to go,' Mandy told them. 'Evening surgery starts in half an hour. Though you're welcome back any time you're out this way,' she added to Michael.

'Well, thank you very much, it's been lovely,' Michael said, shaking her hand again. He seemed, all at once, very formal again. Susan wondered whether he had really enjoyed himself or was secretly relieved that the afternoon was over.

The walk home was more relaxed than the way there had been. They stopped again to look at the pond. There were more ducks now, and a goose had joined them. Michael looked a little alarmed as the goose waddled out of the water and came towards them. It stopped short and stood very still with its head a little to one side. Susan could see the fine white edges to the grey-brown feathers and the smoothness of its webbed feet. It observed them for a long moment as if wondering whether they had any food. Susan wished again that she had remembered to fill her pockets with seed. Next time, she thought.

They walked on and a few minutes later, they were home.

'I won't come in,' Michael announced, and Susan felt relieved. She had been wondering for the last ten minutes whether she should invite him back in. Jack had stopped just inside the gateway. For the moment, he seemed oblivious to Susan and Michael as he watched a snail making its way over the soft ground of the small flowerbed to the right of the path.

'Thanks for coming,' Susan said.

Michael smiled. 'Not sure how much of a success it was,' he said. He was back to his normal self, now he was addressing her and not Jack, but Susan was surprised at his honesty. He had rarely admitted to feeling discomfort, even in the most trying situations.

'It was fine,' she assured him. 'I don't think it could have gone much better.'

Michael didn't look convinced. He stood there for a moment, looking at her, then turned to Jack. 'Goodbye, Jack,' he called.

Jack straightened up and came over. Susan wondered if he would ask Michael to stay longer, but he seemed inexplicably shy again as he stopped a little short, standing very close to Susan.

Michael leaned over and held out his arms, and with only a moment's hesitation, Jack walked over. It was one of the most awkward hugs Susan had ever seen. It didn't seem to cross Michael's mind to crouch down properly. He let go of Jack, then almost as an afterthought, he reached out and ruffled Jack's hair.

'I'll see you again soon,' he said with a half-smile.

'That would be lovely,' Susan replied. Jack nodded. He seemed to have lost his tongue again now they were home. He made his way back to Susan's side and held out a hand for her to hold. They stood together and watched as Michael got into his Mercedes, started the engine and drove off.

'Let's go in,' Susan said. 'I'm starving. You starving?'

Jack grinned up at her and nodded again, his eyes wide.

'Pizza?' Susan asked. It was a special occasion, she thought. Jack loved making pictures with the toppings before it went in the oven.

'Yay, pizza!' Jack clapped his hands.

There was a squeal of tyres from the corner of the road and for a moment, Susan thought that Michael had forgotten something, but it was Mandy's RAV4 that rounded the corner. She pulled up in front of Mr Gorski's driveway and jumped out to open the gate. Susan grabbed Jack's hand, looked quickly to check there were no cars coming, then they hurried across.

'What's up?' Susan gasped. 'Is it Coffee?'

Mandy nodded. 'Would you mind coming with me?' she asked. 'It sounds as if we might need another pair of hands.' She rushed back and climbed into her car, slammed the door and drove onto the gravel. Susan followed, leaving the gate open. If Coffee was very ill, Mandy might need to rush her back to Animal Ark.

Susan made her way to the door with Jack. Mandy was standing on the doorstep. The house seemed very silent. Susan found herself wondering if Mr Gorski would hear the bell, but the door swung open as Mandy reached for it. He must have been waiting. Should she take Jack in? Susan wondered, glancing down at him How would he take it if Coffee was very poorly? But he seemed calm as he looked back up at her. 'Coffee doesn't bark any more,' he said. 'She always barked. She must be very ill.'

Susan swallowed, taken aback by how matter-of-fact he was. 'She must be,' she agreed.

His hand gripped hers a little more tightly. 'Is Coffee going to die, Mummy?'

They had reached the door and Susan stopped and crouched down. 'She's very old,' she said, looking straight into Jack's eyes. 'She might die, yes. Would you rather not come in?'

She half expected him to ask to wait in the garden, but he squared his little shoulders. 'If Coffee dies, Mr Gorski will be sad, won't he?' he asked. 'Like we were sad when Marmalade died.'

He held out his hand again and Susan stood up and they walked together into the familiar front room.

The brightly coloured paper chain still hung on the mirror over the white-painted fireplace, but Susan only had eyes for the kneeling figure of Mandy, who was bending over the little bed beside the fire holding her stethoscope against Coffee's chest. Susan saw Mandy's shoulders droop. She knew what was coming.

'I'm really very sorry.' Mandy lifted her head and looked up at Mr Gorski, who was hovering beside the hearth, clasping his hands together. 'I'm afraid she's gone.' Susan felt a tremor go through her. The little body in the basket was very still. Though Coffee could no longer feel, Mandy was stroking her, as if offering comfort, even in death.

Susan felt Jack's fingers holding on to hers very tightly. She glanced down. There were tears on his face.

Mandy shuffled back, then pushed herself upright as if it was a struggle. She had looked the same when she'd announced Marmalade had died, Susan thought. Mandy must see death more often than most, but she had tears in her eyes as she regarded Mr Gorski. 'You gave her a great life,' she said. She reached out and touched Mr Gorski gently on the arm. 'I'm sorry,' she said again.

A spasm crossed Mr Gorski's face, but he pressed his lips together and nodded. 'Thanks, Mandy,' he said. 'I know you did your best.'

There was so much dignity in his eyes. The folds around his mouth seemed deeper than ever as he looked down at the small brown bundle. 'Will you be able to take her?' he asked Mandy.

Mandy nodded. 'For cremation?' she asked. 'Will you want her ashes?' Susan knew how difficult Mandy found it to discuss practicalities when her patients died, but it had to be done. There was nothing but compassion in her voice.

Mr Gorski shook his head. 'No thanks, lass,' he muttered. Very slowly, he lowered himself to his knees. He bent down and laid his wrinkled cheek against

Coffee's flank. 'Goodbye, old lady,' he whispered. Then he sat back on his heels and watched as Mandy reached down and gently scooped up the still little figure.

'Could you come out and open the door of the car?' Mandy's words to Susan were uttered sotto voce as she passed. Susan nodded her head. The little dog looked serene as Mandy cradled her carefully. All the pain had gone from her face.

'Will you be okay here with Mr Gorski?' Susan whispered to Jack, who nodded. His tears had stopped for now, though Susan could see his huge eyes were still swimming. She pressed a hand on his shoulder, then followed Mandy out.

'Back door please,' Mandy said. Susan pulled the car door open, then watched as Mandy manoeuvred Coffee into the back seat of the car. Mandy stopped to pull a blanket over the little dog, leaving her head clear. Coffee looked as if she were sleeping. Much more comfortable than she had the last time Susan had seen her. Back then, she had lain panting. Perhaps Mandy had the same thought, because she gave a tight little smile. 'They always look so peaceful,' she said.

She patted Susan on the shoulder as if to reassure her. 'Thanks,' she said. 'I'm glad you're here for him. I hate leaving people alone when . . .' She trailed off, then turned and closed the door of the car. 'I'm sorry I have to rush off,' she said. 'Dad's had to go back out and it's Toby's half day.'

Susan watched as Mandy climbed into her car and

drove off. It was hard to imagine dealing with the death of a patient, and then having to rush back to evening surgery. It was chilly out in the garden. The sky overhead was grey. She'd better go back in. Mr Gorski would need her.

But when she walked back into the living room, Mr Gorski was in his usual chair. Jack was standing beside him, leaning over the armrest. His arms were wrapped tightly around the old man's neck as if he would never let go. Mr Gorski's arm was round Jack's back. His eyes were closed, but when he heard Susan come in, he opened them. He reached out a hand to her and smiled. 'Thank you for coming,' he said, 'and for bringing this wonderful young man with you. He's been a great comfort.'

Chapter Eighteen

'I'm sorry, there is no room in my inn, but I do have a stable,' little George proclaimed loudly, throwing his arms out wide.

'Great, George!' Susan called from the corner. 'Now we need all our stable animals, come on!' A donkey and a couple of sheep scuttled into the stable. Susan frowned. 'We're missing our ox! Samira? Samira!' She spotted Samira playing in the Wendy house, her ox horns catching on the curtains. 'Come on, Samira!' Susan shooed her up onto the stage. Really, it was like herding cats. 'Mary, where have you gone?'

Herbie stuck her head out through the hole in the cardboard scenery and grinned. She had been standing inside the inn all the time.

Susan was feeling tired. She had got up extra early this morning to make sure she had time to see Mr Gorski before coming to nursery. It had taken him a long time to come to the door and for a few minutes Susan had been worried. But he answered eventually, and he had seemed okay. 'We'll come over soon,' she told him. 'Today or tomorrow.'

At least at work, there was little time for thinking. Susan had been keeping an eye on Jack, who was a little subdued, but the rest of the class seemed excited.

A movement in the stable area caught Susan's eye. She turned to see Samira gripping the horns that were attached to her headband. Lowering her head, Samira charged at Neil. Neil fled across the classroom, dislodging the tea towel he was wearing as a shepherd and shrieking.

'Come back, Neil. Stop that, Samira.' She put her hands on her hips. 'Bring me the horns, please.' Susan was holding on to her patience by sheer effort of will. She had hoped they could run through the Nativity with costumes this morning, but she was starting to think it had been a mistake.

She held out her hand, looking at Samira, waiting without comment. Samira's dark eyes lingered on Susan's face for a moment. Then with a conspicuous sigh, she took off the headband and handed it to Susan.

'Can you put this back in the cupboard, Nina, please?' Susan handed the horns to Nina. She kept her voice matter-of-fact. She displayed no anger, but actions had consequences.

Armando, who had been holding Baby Jesus by his heels and had been on the point of swinging him in the air, quietly pulled the doll back into position, cradling it in his arms as Susan had told him.

'Right then, shepherds.' She looked round. Jack, Kendall and Neil, all dressed in tunics and tea towels gazed back at her. 'It's your time to come in. Jack can you—'

Across the room, the door opened. A tall, red-haired man walked in: instantly recognisable. Susan's stomach dropped.

He was here. In spite of everything, he'd come, just as he'd said he would. For a moment, her heart lifted. Perhaps she might be able to make up for her lie after all. He was standing in the doorway still, as if unsure of his welcome.

The three shepherds were still waiting for Susan's instructions, but Christina, her king's crown askew, set off across the room at a gallop. Several of the others followed.

'Mr MacLeod!'

'Have you come to read another story?'

'Will you tell us about Frosty and Snowflake again?'

'Please read to us.'

The voices rose, filled with excitement. Douglas smiled and bent to greet them. There was something different about him, and for a moment, Susan found it hard to place. He had combed his hair and trimmed his beard, she realised. And his clothes? The baggy trousers and rainbow T-shirt had gone, replaced with black trousers and a white shirt. Instead of bouncing around, he seemed subdued.

Was he sad? she wondered. Was this what her lie had

done? Though she had worried about his flamboyance, this new Douglas seemed much smaller somehow.

'Okay, Christina, Neil, Armando and all of you, please come back over here,' Susan called, then turned to Nina. 'Can you take over for a few minutes, please? I need to show Mr MacLeod where the scenery boards are.'

'Of course!' Nina sent her the slightest of winks as she replied. Susan pretended not to see as she headed across the room.

'This way, Mr MacLeod.' Susan kept her voice professional. She led Douglas into the smaller room where sundry pieces of heavy cardboard were lined up against the wall. He left the door onto the main nursery open. Susan had hoped he would close it so they could chat, but it seemed overly officious to go back to do it herself.

'What would you like me to paint?' His polite quietness still jarred. 'And was there any particular style you'd prefer?'

The hope she'd had when she first saw him was dissipating. He wasn't here to talk to her or offer another date. He really was just upholding his commitment. Susan felt silly for hoping otherwise. She glanced back at the open door. None of the children were close enough to hear.

'I know you're here to paint,' she said, 'but I just wanted to say again that I was sorry, for . . .' She paused and swallowed. The words, 'for seeing Michael' were on her lips. Wasn't that the real problem? Her feelings for Michael. She felt her face reddening. Douglas was gazing at her, eyebrows raised. His eyes were courteous, but there was no warmth. '. . . for what happened the other day,' she said finally. She tried for a smile. It didn't really work.

'Thank you for your apology.' His voice was grave still. 'Now about this painting . . .'

From the doorway, Susan heard a whisper. She turned to see the Three Kings standing in the doorway, staring up at her and Douglas. 'What are you talking about?' Christina asked, playing with her crown.

'Mr Douglas is here to help with the scenery,' Susan explained. 'We're talking about painting.'

'What about painting?' Christina's cherubic face was smiling. The other two kings, Ben and Harrison, looked on with interest. She should send them back through, Susan thought. Even if they weren't in the current scene, they should be watching.

Her mind flipped back to Douglas. Though he had thanked her for her apology, he had moved the conversation on, as if he hadn't really wanted to hear. Maybe there was a chance to make him understand. 'We were just talking about making mistakes,' she said. Though her eyes were on Christina, she could feel Douglas's gaze burning into her. 'How they don't always have to spoil things. If you do something wrong when you're painting, you can let it dry for a few days and then paint over it.'

It wasn't a very good analogy, she thought. If you painted something wrong, you didn't hurt anyone's feelings. But it was the best she could do . . .

Christina was staring at her. The crease between her eyebrows was deeper than ever. 'Even if it's dark green?' she said. 'Or black.'

The image of a child's picture came into Susan's head. Poster paints, smeared together. Why had she started this? 'Even if it's green or black,' she confirmed, 'with special scenery paint. Mistakes don't have to spoil things forever.'

Ben had his head on one side. Dark curls spilled from under his crown. 'What if you paint it wrong again?' he asked. 'What if you have to do it again a million times?'

For the first time since he'd come in, Douglas laughed. It wasn't his usual booming guffaw, but a tight, unfriendly sound. Susan glanced at him. He had raised a fist to his mouth. Was he finding this funny or not? She couldn't tell.

She turned her gaze back onto Ben. 'Some people aren't very good painters,' she said, 'but even they probably wouldn't make a million mistakes.'

'If they have made a million mistakes, they might be better off if they stop trying. Maybe there is something else they can do better.' Douglas had his eyes on Ben, but his words hit Susan like a slap. Was he saying there was nothing she could do that would make things okay? Sadness welled up inside her. Despite her feelings for

Michael, she'd liked Douglas too. Why had she worried about his clowning? Now his sense of fun had disappeared. It was cold, as if the sun had gone below the horizon.

'Run along now, you three. Nina's calling.' Could he hear the brittleness in her voice? she wondered. Her eyes followed the three cloaked children as they retreated. She turned her eyes back to Douglas. He was smiling now: a gentle smile as if he was trying to be kind.

'Look,' he said, 'I appreciate your apology, but I can't pretend what you did didn't hurt. In my last relationship, my ex lied to me a lot. It started with small things and they seemed harmless, but then there were more and more. I'm not up for something like that again.'

Susan felt shame welling up inside her. He had been kind and she'd hurt him. But could he really not find it in himself to forgive her? It had only been one little lie. She had regretted it as soon as she'd said it. She would have told Douglas next time she saw him.

'I'm sorry,' she said. 'I was going to tell you . . .'

He held up a hand, cutting her off. 'If it was just that Michael was Jack's dad,' he said, 'you would have told me. I saw how you looked at him when you saw me. I don't know what's going on between the two of you, but I won't compete. Not with the father of your child.'

Susan felt hot and embarrassed. *How could he see that so clearly?* There was no denying that she felt torn between them. Until this moment, she hadn't realised just how much she had been growing to care for Douglas. Now that he was removing himself from the equation, the feelings she had been ignoring threatened to overwhelm her. She liked him very much – and in trying to control the situation, she had driven him away and lost her chance to choose.

Why had she lied? He was right about that. If she'd felt nothing for Michael, she could have just been honest. But Michael was her past, not her future . . . or was he? What she needed was time. 'Please . . .' she began, but Herbie Dhanjal rushed in.

'Please come, Miss Collins. Naomi cut her leg and Mrs Wilson took her to the sick room. Samira's got Baby Jesus and she won't give him back.' With a last glance at Douglas, Susan turned and trailed back through into the nursery.

Chapter Nineteen

Susan glanced around the living room. It looked more lived-in than tidy, and for a moment, she had the urge to rush round and clear all the surfaces. There were paintings left out to dry and a half-built Lego house on top of the toy box in the corner. But they were Jack's things and he loved them. If Michael wanted to be part of Jack's life, it was important he didn't see a sterilised version.

Jack seemed to have fully accepted that he had a father now. He and Susan had counted down the days until 'Daddy's coming again'. When she'd told him today was the day, he'd rushed round the bedroom, collecting toys. 'Daddy will love this!'

Susan was better prepared too. She had pulled the table football from the cupboard. Miranda had given it to Jack when he was far too young, but now was the perfect time to bring it out. She had also grabbed his Guess Who? game. It was another favourite that she liked to keep for special occasions. They could play indoor games for a while and if the weather held, they might feed the ducks.

'He's here, Mummy!' Jack jumped down from the chair beside the window where he had been waiting. He rushed at Susan, his eyes wide, then turned round and ran to the front door. By the time Susan reached the hall, he was already dragging the door open.

She had half expected Jack to rush into Michael's arms for a hug, but once the door was open, the reality seemed to overwhelm him, and he just stood very still with an uncertain smile on his face. Michael was looking very smart again. He was smiling too. He looked far more at ease than Susan felt. She could feel her face reddening. How could he still have this effect on her?

'Hello,' he said. He was holding out a gift again. Generous as it was, it would be better if Jack didn't think Michael would always arrive with presents. She would have a quiet word with him later.

Jack took the parcel, gazing down at it. 'Can I open it now, please, Mummy?' he asked.

'I think we should let Daddy come inside first,' Susan said. She put a hand on his head and stroked his hair as he stared up at her.

Together they moved back. Susan took Michael's coat, then Jack took hold of his hand and led him into the living room. Susan followed.

'There's something for you too,' Michael murmured as Jack sat down and began to rip the wrapping paper. He reached into his pocket and drew out a blue velvet box. Susan frowned. Not that she didn't like gifts, but it seemed a little over the top. He's just being generous, she told herself.

She took the box and opened it. Inside, nestling on white silk, lay a fine rose-gold bracelet with a small dog charm, complete with an engraved S. 'Thank you very much!' she said.

Jack walked towards her, holding out his gift. It was an iPad and he looked up at Susan, wide-eyed. There was a computer station at the nursery, which all the children enjoyed. But Susan hadn't bought him a computer or tablet at home. She would when he was older, of course, but for now she wanted him to play with other things. A couple of the children in her class had to be torn from their gadgets when they arrived every morning.

Seeing her hesitation, Michael stepped in. 'It's an iPad. You turn it on using this button here,' he said, taking the iPad. He switched it on, then handed it to Jack. Jack was looking confused, Susan thought. He knew what it was but had no idea how to use it.

'Wow, aren't you a lucky boy?' Susan tried to sound enthusiastic. 'What do you say to Daddy?'

'Thank you, Daddy,' said Jack, smiling at Michael, though Susan could tell he still wasn't sure what to do with it. He sat down on the couch and started pressing buttons on the screen.

'How do you like your bracelet?' Michael asked Susan. The easy smile was back in place. He seemed to think everything was going fine.

Susan didn't know what to say. She liked gold. He had that right, but the little dog wasn't her style. She liked animals, but not on jewellery.

'It's lovely.' She looked up at him.

He had a kind of proprietary look on his face and he nodded as if he was quite satisfied. 'I know how much you like dogs,' he said.

I do? Susan was perplexed. She looked at the bracelet again. She liked dogs well enough, but they'd never been her favourite. She preferred horses and cats. 'It's very nice,' she lied. A memory came to her from the time when they had first dated. There had been gifts galore then too. She had been flattered by how much money he'd spent, but even back then, he had often missed the mark. There had been expensive chocolates in a flavour she'd told him she didn't like and a huge bunch of lilies he'd forgotten she was allergic to.

She needed to bring the conversation back on to Jack and what they were going to do. 'I got some games out, if you'd like to play,' she said to Michael. 'Jack?' He looked up from the screen. 'Would you like to play table football?' she asked. 'It would be nice to play with Daddy while he's here.'

She held out a hand for the iPad and Jack handed it over, though he looked as if he would rather not. He had already found a cartoon. Susan switched it off.

'We can play games if you like,' Michael said. 'But I thought you might both like a trip to York. Did you see my car, Jack? It's a Mercedes GLE Coupé.' In her mind's eye, Susan could picture the rather flashy silver car Michael had driven away in last time. Jack hadn't said anything about it, but she knew he liked cars. She had a sudden feeling of helplessness. She'd thought she was organised for today. Why hadn't she discussed plans with Michael? It hadn't crossed her mind that he would suggest a trip.

Jack was jumping up and down. 'Can we, can we?' He tugged at Susan's hand. She felt strangely reluctant to go. Not that she felt in any way unsafe. Michael was a good driver and she knew he wouldn't do anything to harm them. She just felt . . . off balance . . . that was it. Surprise trips had been another of Michael's specialities. But they were only going to York. It wasn't that far and Jack would enjoy the Christmas market and all the stalls.

The car trip was surprisingly enjoyable. Wedged into the heated bucket seat beside Michael, Susan felt herself succumbing once again to his charm. He seemed to fit the car: expensive and well built, just the right side of flashy. To her surprise, he'd also programmed in a playlist of children's Christmas songs. It must have taken him some time to find them all. She found herself joining in as Jack and Michael sang along to 'Jingle Bells' and 'Rudolph the Red-Nosed Reindeer'. The drive passed by in a flash. As they drove through the edge of the city, Susan turned to Michael. 'Shall we go to the Christmas market?' she suggested. 'Jack would love to see the decorations.'

Michael reached out a hand and turned down the music. 'That would be great,' he said, 'but there's something I want to show you first.' He indicated right and turned into a side street, then pulled up in front of a red-brick townhouse. Susan peered up at the façade. It was rather grand: three storeys high with a porticoed blue front door.

'Where are we?' she asked.

Pulling on the handbrake and turning off the engine, Michael twisted round in his seat to grin at Jack. 'This is Daddy's house,' he announced. 'Would you like to see inside?'

Jack was almost hopping up and down in his excitement. 'Yes please, Daddy,' he said. There were a million thoughts rushing around Susan's mind. Michael hadn't said anything about this. And yet she hadn't thought to ask, so in a way, wasn't she also at fault? What would he have done if she had? He would have told her . . . wouldn't he?

She looked up at the house again. There was nothing she could do about it now. Not without looking like the bad guy. *What is he trying to do here?* Michael climbed out of the car and walked round to open the back door to let Jack out. Susan could see how excited Jack was. She felt sick as he put his hand in Michael's. The nightmares she'd had before – the ones where Michael and Jack bonded and she ended up left out

– surged back into her head. She shook herself, trying to be calm. Michael had seen where they lived, after all. Perhaps it was natural for him to want to show Jack where he lived.

They walked up the steps and Michael took out his key. Behind the classy front door, there was a rather grand hallway. Ivory tiles with smaller black diamonds stretched back to an archway. To the left there was a stairway with a cream-coloured carpet. Two dark wooden chairs stood with their backs to the duck-egg blue walls and there was a huge mirror on the wall on the landing high above them.

Jack was still holding Michael's hand. Now he reached for Susan's as well. Was he feeling a little overwhelmed too?

Michael seemed pleased by their reaction. 'Nice, isn't it?' he said. 'I'll show you round.'

He led them through the first of the doorways that led off the hall. It was another lofty, high-ceilinged room. There was an original Georgian fireplace, intricate cornices and a picture rail with paintings. The carpet was a tasteful blue colour and the walls were white. It was four times the size of the tiny living room at Moon Cottage. Large leather sofas and a mahogany coffee table completed the feeling of opulence. Yet it didn't feel as if anyone lived there. The carpets were unmarked, as if recently vacuum cleaned. Jack's eyes were huge.

'Do you like it, Jack?' Michael asked.

Jack nodded. He was still holding Susan's hand.

'And this is the kitchen,' Michael said, a couple of minutes later. It was wonderful as well, Susan thought. Far bigger than Michael could possibly need. It stretched across the width of the house. Two massive windows abutted graceful French doors. Through the glass, she could see a small garden. The floor was wooden, as were the doors of the cupboards. Michael walked across and leaned on the island in the centre of the room, looking out of the window. 'Come and look,' he said, turning to look at Susan. After only a moment, she went and stood beside him. They were in the city, but the windows looked out onto a small walled garden. It was unexpectedly wild, with ancient trees and creepers on the walls. It would be lovely in summer, Susan thought.

There was a clatter behind them. Susan whirled round. Jack was looking down, his face filled with alarm. On the floor, lying on its side, was a large bottle. Champagne, Susan realised, reading the label. Dom Perignon, 2004. It had fallen from a built-in wine rack that seemed to be filled with other expensive bottles. Jack's face was red and his pupils were huge and black. 'I just wanted to look,' he said. His voice was defensive.

Thank goodness it hadn't broken. For a moment, Susan wondered whether Michael would shout. He looked angry, although she could tell he was trying to control himself. She rushed over to Jack and bent to pick the bottle up. 'No harm done,' she said, sliding it back into place. 'Just don't touch anything else, okay?'

Jack nodded. He seemed relieved now he knew he wasn't in trouble. He walked over to the French doors and peered out. 'Can we go out in the garden?' he asked.

'In a minute,' Michael promised. 'There's something else I want to show you.' He grinned, then led them back through into the hallway and up the stairs. Four doorways led off the landing, then there was another flight of stairs. They glanced into two big double bedrooms, each neatly made up with matching furniture and king-sized beds. There was a lovely bathroom too with an enormous bathtub, two sinks and a separate shower. 'Heated floor,' Michael announced. His smile was filled with pride. He seemed to be enjoying himself.

Susan thought again of Moon Cottage. Though it was tiny, it was cosy and it was home. Michael's house seemed more like a show home. 'Beautiful,' she said.

Michael smiled that smile again.

'And now,' he announced, 'the *pièce de résistance*.' He led them through another doorway. Susan found herself in a small bedroom with a single bed. Like all the other rooms in the house, it was pristine. Michael walked over to the window, which looked out over the garden, then turned round and waved an arm. 'This can be Jack's room,' he said.

Susan felt for a moment as if the floor had disappeared from under her feet. Jack was looking around the room with interest. *Jack's room?* Her throat was closing. 'Can I have a word?' It was difficult to speak, but she had to know what Michael thought he was doing. She was a long way from being ready for Michael to have the kind of contact that would involve Jack staying overnight. She glanced round the room. Single bed with a white duvet cover. White chest of drawers and wardrobe. White desk. Nothing friendly or warm, but nothing breakable, nothing that Jack would hurt himself on. 'Can you stay here a minute, Jack,' she said.

For the first time, Jack looked worried, but he nodded.

'You can look out of the window,' Susan suggested. He moved over obediently.

Susan strode out onto the landing. Not far enough away, she thought. She stepped into the doorway of the huge front bedroom. It would have to do. She had to be able to see if Jack came out. Michael was looking at her. He was wearing his hurt expression. Memories flooded back into Susan's mind. Whenever she questioned anything, he always looked hurt as a first line.

'What did you mean?' she asked. 'Jack's room?'

The hurt look intensified. 'Well, you know . . .' he said. 'Down the line. Jack can stay over here sometimes. I'd like that.' He smiled, though Susan could see there was something else behind his eyes. 'And maybe one day,' he said, 'both of you could move in. There's plenty of space.'

Not in a million years, she thought, furiously. Any

remaining trust she had retained in Michael had disappeared. Hadn't they agreed to take this slowly? He'd said he would be guided by her, but he was pushing them towards the goal he'd chosen. Worse still, he was using Jack to do it. He should have discussed this with Susan long before saying anything to Jack. Now she was going to have to deal with the fallout.

But wasn't this Michael all over? she thought with a shiver. She'd hoped he had changed, but he was just the same. Everything had to be arranged as he wanted it. He had sent Susan away because Jack wasn't part of the perfect life he'd planned. Now he'd changed his mind. He wanted to play at being a father. But that had to be done his way too.

Worse than that, he had decided he would move her here as well as Jack. Michael had made up his mind and she had only to agree. She wasn't to play a part in the decision. She'd fallen right into his trap, she thought. She had spent the evening with him, drunk too much and ended up snuggling with him. Mixed messages. Hadn't there been a part of her that wanted this? She felt sicker than ever.

She was shaking, but she had to be clear. 'I can tell you that's not going to happen,' she said. 'Jack and I are happy in Welford. We're not moving anywhere.' She paused. 'You and I will not be getting back together,' she said. 'We had a great time the other night and I hoped you'd changed. But instead of talking to me about this, you brought Jack over here and started suggesting things I hadn't agreed to. Now I guess I'm going to have to be the bad guy who has to tell him it's not happening.' She stopped and swallowed as she saw the angry look flash into Michael's eyes. More memories tumbled back. She'd never been allowed to contradict him. Their relationship had only ever been wonderful when she complied.

'Nobody has to be the bad guy.' His voice was filled with contempt. 'I'd forgotten how everything always had to be done *your way*.' He was sneering now; his voice was rising. 'You certainly didn't make it clear you didn't want a relationship when we were out together. The exact opposite, in fact. What made you change your mind? Was it that red-headed giant? Is he your type now?'

Susan felt heat rising. Her heart was hammering.

'I'm not with Douglas. I don't need to be with anyone,' she hissed back. 'Jack and I are fine on our own. We're going to go now. Don't you dare make a fuss.'

He seemed shocked that she was daring to fight. Susan glared at him for a moment, then turned on her heel, walked back across the landing and opened the door to the little bedroom, still shaking.

'We're going, Jack.' She held out her hand and he took it. He looked frightened. *Bloody Michael. Why had she ever thought this would work?*

Michael didn't appear as she led Jack down the stairs. He couldn't even bring himself to come out and say goodbye to Jack, she thought. She pressed her teeth together. She couldn't make him care about Jack. There was no way she was going to let him hurt her son, as he'd hurt her.

Once outside the house, she looked left and right, then turned towards the main road. York was not that big. She could find her way to the centre and they could go round the market as she'd suggested.

Jack had followed her without question, but when they were on the main road, his pace slowed. 'Is my daddy mean like Harrison's daddy after all?' he asked. He had stopped altogether now and stood looking up at her with those innocent brown eyes. When he looked at her like that, she wanted to hug him and make all the bad stuff go away.

What should she say? This morning had been awful, but she wasn't going to start badmouthing Michael. 'No,' she said eventually, swallowing her anger. 'Daddy isn't mean. He and Mummy just had an argument about something, okay?'

Jack nodded. It wasn't really okay, Susan thought. It should never have happened. She should have been clear with Michael from the start. Then she should have stayed calm. 'I'll try and talk to Daddy again,' she said, though she wasn't sure there was any point.

Ahead of them, she could see Christmas lights and a couple of stalls. 'How would you like to go to the Christmas market?' she said. 'I was there with Mandy last week. They had freshly cooked doughnuts.'

Jack's eyes brightened immediately. 'Will Santa be there?' he asked.

'I don't know,' Susan said, 'but we can have a look and see if we can find him.'

Jack set off again. All she wanted was for Jack to be okay, Susan thought. *Why is it so hard?*

Chapter Twenty

Even without snow, the Christmas market was pretty, but Susan was in no mood for fairy lights. Nor could she find any joy in the Salvation Army band, carolling merrily. The flat grey sky overhead matched her feelings exactly. Jack had been almost overly chatty as they walked. Susan wondered whether he would ask about what had happened between Michael and her, but he seemed to have adopted a brittle kind of cheeriness. She glanced at him a few times, wondering if he was masking the kind of worry that he never normally had to face. This trip, which had started out so well, had turned into a waking nightmare. She didn't know how they were going to get home. She could ask James, but she didn't want to bother him. Nor did she really want to start explaining herself and how they'd got here.

They stopped at the first doughnut seller they saw. Susan usually tried to restrict Jack's sweet tooth, but the freshly made doughnuts came in packs of five or ten. Susan asked for five. Moments later, Jack was clutching a white paper bag with a slowly spreading, translucent grease mark and sucking sugar-coated fingers.

He gasped suddenly and Susan looked round in alarm, thinking perhaps Michael had followed them. But Jack was pointing at a street performer. He was in the middle of an acrobatic routine that seemed to involve a great many handstands and flips. The movements looked effortless, which was all the more amazing, given that the man was dressed in a full Father Christmas outfit, right down to a large black pair of wellington boots. Jack tugged at her hand and she looked down into his wide eyes. He obviously wanted to say something, so she leaned over.

'Is that the real Father Christmas?' he whispered. He sounded so awestruck that Susan wanted to laugh, despite the horrible situation they were in.

She thought quickly. 'That's one of his special helpers. Father Christmas can't be in every town at this time of year, so his friends help him spread Christmas spirit.'

'So he *knows* Father Christmas,' Jack whispered, sounding almost as awestruck as if the man were the real deal.

Susan pulled her mobile phone from her pocket. While Jack was distracted, she really needed to sort out how they were going to get home. With a sigh, she flipped through her contact list and stopped on 'Mum'. Miranda would be furious with Michael of course. She'd also be angry with Susan for letting herself be fooled by Michael again. But at least Susan wouldn't have to start and explain the whole situation from the beginning.

'Hello, Mum?'

'Hello, darling!' Miranda's voice held surprise. 'I thought you . . .' She trailed off. 'Is everything okay?'

Susan glanced down at Jack. He still seemed mesmerised with Father Christmas's unexpected athleticism, but she didn't want to get into a major conversation with Miranda right now. 'We're fine,' she said, 'but we're kind of stranded in York. Is there any chance you could come and pick us up, please? Jack's here and he's fine too. I'll explain later if that's okay.'

'Oh!' There was still a trace of worry in her mother's voice, but her tone became brisk. 'Yes, of course. I'll meet you in the car park near the castle in about an hour. You know the one I mean?'

'Yeah. Thanks, Mum,' Susan said.

The next hour was expensive. She and Jack went from stall to stall. By the time they met Miranda, Jack had drunk a large hot chocolate topped with cream and they were clinging to a number of bags containing cat Christmas cards, several wooden decorations for the tree, a packet of snowman jellies and a scarf with polar bear pom-poms on each end. Jack had remained happy at least. The bustle of the street market seemed to have done the trick. The last thing she wanted was for him to have awful memories of the last time he saw his dad. He seemed sleepy as she strapped him into the back of Miranda's car.

Susan dropped a kiss on his forehead and he smiled. 'Love you, Mummy,' he said.

By the time they reached the outskirts of York, his eyes were closed.

'Thanks so much for coming to pick us up,' Susan said in a low voice, turning to Miranda.

Miranda took a brief glance in the rear-view mirror. 'Is he sleeping?' she asked.

'Fast,' Susan replied.

'So what happened?' Miranda took her eyes off the road again to take a sideways glance at Susan.

Susan took a deep breath. There was no point in hiding what had happened from her Mum. 'I told you Michael was coming round?'

Miranda nodded.

'Well, I had a few things planned, but he offered to bring us to York for the afternoon. He hadn't told me, but he made it sound fun and he said it in front of Jack . . .' She paused for a moment. She really had been played, she thought. 'I thought it'd be fun so I agreed. But then he pulled up in front of a house . . . his house. He showed us round.' She swallowed. 'He had a room he said was for Jack.'

Miranda muttered something below her breath. Susan saw her fingers tighten on the steering wheel. 'You hadn't even talked about overnights, had you? You were nowhere near that stage.'

Susan shook her head and sighed. 'Definitely not,' she agreed. 'It was only the second time Jack had met Michael.' She closed her mouth, pressing her teeth together. Why had she let herself be pushed into the trip to York? She should have said no right away, but it had always been hard to say no to Michael. And it had sounded so harmless. Should she tell Miranda the rest? she wondered. Her mother's expression was already grim, but she wanted to be completely honest. 'He talked about me moving in as well,' she admitted. 'About us being a family.' She stopped.

Miranda made a kind of growling noise in her throat. 'He really is a shit,' she said, then glanced in the rearview mirror again.

Susan twisted her head to look at Jack.

'He's still asleep,' Miranda confirmed. Her lips were pursed into a disapproving pout, but to Susan's relief she fell silent as they drove on. She felt bad enough about what she'd put Jack through. It was gracious of her mother not to rub it in. Miranda had been wholly against Jack meeting Michael. Susan leaned her head back on the headrest. She wished she too could fall asleep, but so many things were whirling in her mind that she couldn't relax. She was glad when they turned into the side road off High Street and pulled up beside Moon Cottage.

Susan hadn't slept well. Memories had flickered through her mind all night. Michael arriving with the not-quite-right gifts. His grin as he'd suggested the trip to York in his sporty car. Why hadn't she just said no? Her face had been grey when she'd risen in the morning.

Now she was standing in the reception area at Hope Meadows. It was another nursery trip. This time she had brought only half the class. Mandy had suggested they could do more if the group was smaller, so Susan and Nina had split the class between them.

To Susan's delight, Emily Hope had also appeared, looking quite well. 'I'm having a good day today,' she said. Now she had a small group clustered round her, helping to socialise a litter of baby guinea pigs that had been born a few days earlier. Susan was amazed at how advanced the tiny creatures were. They looked just like miniature versions of their mum with their sweet shining eyes. They were already incredibly docile.

Mandy had brought the litter of kittens through, and she and the remaining children were sitting in a small pen as the kittens ran around.

'Would you like to hold Frostflake?' Mandy lifted up the little white kitten and held him out to Jack. Susan and Jack had visited several times to help out with the deaf kitten. Jack reached out his hands to take Frostflake. His whole face was filled with joy. Frostflake seemed happy too. He climbed his way up to press his fluffy white head up under Jack's chin. His extra-loud purr sounded, as it always seemed to when he and Jack were together.

Jack looked up at Mandy. 'Where is Frostflake's daddy?' he asked. His voice was quiet. Susan moved a little closer. If Jack was talking about fathers, she wanted to hear.

Mandy smiled at Jack. 'I don't know where Frostflake's daddy is,' she replied. 'Most kittens stay with their mummy until they are old enough to go away to homes of their own. The daddy cats don't normally live with them.'

Jack frowned. 'Why not?' he asked.

Mandy glanced briefly at Susan, but she turned her gaze back to Jack before answering. 'That's just how cats like it,' she said. Her tone was matter-of-fact. Susan couldn't help but feel grateful towards her friend. Mandy had no idea what had happened, but she was always straightforward with Jack. She treated him as if he was a miniature adult, never speaking down to him, presenting the truth in an honest way.

'Just like Mummy and me.' Jack's voice was quieter than ever. He too sounded pragmatic. He seemed satisfied with Mandy's reply.

Mandy turned away and lifted up one of the other kittens. 'Now, Armando', she said. Would you like to hold Fiddlesticks?'

Armando's eyes opened wide. He looked as thrilled as Jack had a few moments before. Susan's eyes wandered back to Jack. Frostflake was standing on Jack's shoulder, delicately nuzzling Jack's ear. He reached up a hand and gently lifted the furry little body round onto his chest. Leaning over, he began to whisper into Frostflake's ear. Susan smiled. Jack seemed to love chatting away to the kitten, even though he knew Frostflake couldn't hear him. She moved closer still.

'You're the best cat ever.' Jack's hands were busy, stroking and petting. Frostflake rubbed his face against Jack's hand, then looked up and gave a silent mew, as if in reply. Jack leaned his head closer to the silky white ear. 'You and me are the same, Frostflake,' he said. 'Your daddy doesn't live with you and mine doesn't live with me.' He paused, blinking a little. He didn't seem distressed: only intent as he snuggled Frostflake in his arms, but Susan knew it must be bothering him a bit for him to be talking like this. 'We can look after each other, though. Don't worry, Frostflake. I'll take care of you.'

Susan felt a rush of emotion. Tears formed in her eyes and she gripped her hands into fists. Damn Michael. If it hadn't been for him, Jack and she would still have been perfectly happy in their own little world. She blinked away the tears and breathed in and out slowly. If Jack noticed something was wrong, it would only upset him more.

'Are you okay?' Mandy took a quick glance round the peaceful kitten pen, then moved over to stand beside Susan.

'Yesterday was a bit rough,' Susan admitted in a low voice. Her eyes were on Jack, but he was still chatting away to Frostflake.

'With Michael?' Mandy guessed.

Susan nodded. She opened her mouth, then closed it again.

'If you need to talk,' Mandy said, 'you can come

over later. I'm having tea with Mum and Dad today, I'm sure they'd love you to come for a chat. It's Jack's day with your mum, isn't it?'

Susan nodded again. It wasn't easy to speak. 'I'd like that, thank you,' she managed finally.

Mandy reached out a hand and patted her on the shoulder. 'It'll all be fine,' she said. 'Now, I'd better go back in and help these young kitten wranglers.' She sent Susan a sympathetic grin, then turned and climbed back into the pen.

It was dark by the time Susan walked up to the back door of the cottage attached to Animal Ark where Mandy had grown up. Susan had been to the house often enough that it felt familiar and friendly. She knocked on the door and it opened.

'Come in,' Mandy said. 'The kettle's on.'

Susan stepped into the warm kitchen. After the chilly night air, it felt very cosy with its scrubbed pine table and black stove.

Emily was sitting at the table knitting something that looked almost like a baby jacket. She smiled when Susan said hello and held it up. 'Hi, Susan, I'm knitting jumpers for penguins that have been caught up in oil-spills,' she said. 'What do you think?' She waved the warm-looking mini-sweater, which was a cheery bright-red colour. 'I have to rest far too much these days. I had to find something useful to do with the time.'

Susan couldn't help but smile. How typical of Emily. Though she could no longer work as a vet, she was still using her skills to help animals.

'It's lovely,' she said. 'I'm sure any penguin would be happy to wear it.'

She suddenly felt very much at home as she moved over to the table and sat down. The Hopes had always been so kind to her.

She greeted Adam, who was standing beside the kettle, waiting for it to boil. 'How do you like your tea?' he asked Susan. Still white no sugar?'

'Yes please,' Susan said. Adam turned away to organise the mugs. Once the tea was ready, he brought Susan and Mandy's mugs over and set them down. 'It's great actually all being able to sit down together and know we're not going to be called out,' he said. Still standing at the end of the table, he raised his mug in the direction of the wooden door, beyond which the surgery lay. 'Cheers, Toby!' he said.

Mandy was looking at her. 'Is it okay if we all sit together?' she asked. 'If you need to talk privately, we can go in the other room.'

Adam looked from Susan to Mandy, eyebrows raised. Mandy obviously hadn't said anything to her parents about the reason for Susan's visit. 'You don't need to move anywhere,' he said. 'If you need to chat on your own, Emily and I can go through and leave you to it.'

Emily looked up from her knitting and smiled. She put a hand on the table, as if to push herself upright.

'Don't go.' Susan lifted a hand and held it up. 'Actually I'd be happy to have your perspective as well.'

Emily sank back into her seat and Adam pulled out a chair, but then paused, opened a cupboard and pulled out a cake tin. 'I think this calls for cake,' he said.

'Gran's Christmas cake. She always makes a trial one and this year she gave it to us,' Mandy explained. Susan's mouth started to water. Mandy's grandmother's baking was famous in Welford.

Adam carved off four large slices of fruitcake and set them out on the table. He added a few lumps of Wensleydale cheese to the plate, then sat down. 'Help yourself,' he urged Susan and pushed the plate towards her.

'So what happened?' Mandy, having taken a sip of her tea, leaned forward and put her elbows on the table. 'I thought it was going well with Michael?'

Susan sighed. 'I thought so too,' she said. She glanced at Emily and Adam. 'Has Mandy told you who Michael is?' she asked, raising her eyebrows as she looked at them.

'Only that he's Jack's dad,' Emily told her. She sent Susan an encouraging smile. 'It must be difficult, when someone appears like that, out of the blue.'

'It certainly is,' Susan agreed. She looked down at the cake on the plate in front of her. She hadn't eaten anything since lunchtime. She took a mouthful of cake and a sliver of cheese and chewed. Dorothy Hope's cakes really were just as good as everyone said they were. It was rich and delicious.

'I did think it was going fine,' she said. 'The first time Michael and I met, we got on like a house on fire. It was almost like old times. Then he met Jack. It wasn't great at first. Michael's not used to children,' she added. *Why was she making excuses for him?* 'But then we came round here and Jack was less nervous and . . .' She glanced at Mandy, who nodded.

'Yesterday he came round again. I had a few things planned this time. Board games and so on. But he suggested we could go to York. He said it in front of Jack. It was difficult to say no.' She looked up, but all three faces held sympathy. They weren't judging her. 'So we went,' she said. 'I suggested we could go to the market. I thought Jack would like it. But Michael stopped at a house, then said it was his and we could go in.' She found herself crumbling bits of the cake onto the plate and stopped. 'I should have said no, but I didn't,' she said. 'It was the path of least resistance, I guess. And then he showed us a bedroom and said it could be Jack's. He had all kinds of plans. He wanted us to move in with him.'

Emily looked shocked. Adam was wrinkling his nose. Mandy reached out a hand and placed it on Susan's arm. 'That's not great,' she said. 'Like he was trying to push you into it, telling you in front of Jack.'

Susan nodded.

'He should have checked with you first,' Emily agreed.

'So what's going to happen now?' Mandy asked.

'I'm not sure what I should do,' Susan said. She glanced up at the ceiling, then back down. 'I wanted to do the right thing. I thought it was better for Jack to have two parents, but now I'm not sure. Not if he's going to end up hurt.' She leaned an elbow on the table. It was good to be able to talk this through properly.

Adam had his head on one side, as if considering. 'We brought Mandy up without any input from her biological parents,' he said.

It was true, Susan thought. Mandy's parents had died in a car crash when Mandy was a baby, so there had been no choice.

'I mean, she turned out to be a disaster,' Adam added, sending a cheeky sideways grin at Mandy. 'So maybe view her as the worst-case scenario.'

Mandy mock-glared at him. Narrowing her eyes, she lobbed a piece of cheese across the table at him. Adam just opened his mouth and caught it neatly. His expression was so smug that Susan wanted to laugh.

'There were two of us, though,' Emily put in. 'It must be tough for you on your own,' she said to Susan.

Susan pulled a wry expression. 'It was fine until Michael turned up,' she said. 'I'm lucky to have Mum nearby.'

Mandy ate the last piece of her cake, then sat back in her chair with a thoughtful look on her face. 'As far as I see it,' she said, 'there aren't any hard and fast rules. Look at Jimmy and his twins. They have two loving homes and it works. Jack has a loving home with you. It's all about creating the right atmosphere, isn't it? So the child knows they're loved. It doesn't really matter if there's one parent or four. It doesn't matter if they're related or not, so long as there's love and security. You can provide those on your own. You've proved that. After that, you have to decide whether to let anyone else in. And only you can decide who's suitable for you and for Jack.'

Emily was nodding. 'I think Mandy's right,' she said. 'If you feel it's better for Jack that he doesn't meet Michael again, then that's the right decision. Jack's young enough to accept it for now. And when he's older you can explain. You just have to be happy in your heart that you're doing the right thing for the right reason.' She smiled again. Her kind eyes were filled with warmth. Mandy was so lucky, Susan thought. Miranda was wonderful, of course she was. But Emily had always seemed so wise. And now Mandy was the same.

'Thank you so much,' Susan said. 'For the tea and the advice and everything.' She sat back in her chair and took a sip of tea. Then she put a piece of the crumbled cake into her mouth. It really was delicious. Maybe if she asked nicely, Adam would give her another piece.

Half an hour later, Mandy pushed out her chair. 'I'm going to have to go,' she said. 'I'm on surgery this evening.'

Susan stood up and Mandy ushered her over to the back door. Susan expected Mandy to close the door behind her, but Mandy stepped outside and stood on the doorstep. The sky had cleared and stars shone overhead. 'I didn't want to ask in front of Mum and Dad,' Mandy said, 'but what happened with Douglas?'

The happy feeling in Susan's chest subsided a little. Even if she had it worked out what was happening with Michael, her relationship with Douglas, such as it had been, was over. 'I ruined it,' she said. 'I had to cancel my next date with him because it was on the only day Michael was free to meet Jack. But I lied and told him Jack had the dentist instead of the truth . . . And, well, you saw what happened at Hope Meadows. We were supposed to be going riding at Molly's next Thursday, but now he doesn't want to talk to me . . . which is understandable,' she added.

Mandy looked at her sadly. 'You liked him, didn't you?' she said.

Susan sighed. 'I did,' she said. 'I wasn't sure at first. But I definitely did.' They stood there for a moment in the darkness.

'I really must get on,' Mandy said. 'Try not to worry. I'm sure it'll all turn out in the end.' She patted Susan on the arm, then turned and stepped back inside.

Chapter Twenty-One

Susan pushed aside the half-finished pile of Christmas cards, sat back in her chair and looked around the living room. Before sitting down with the cards, she had put up some Christmas decorations. She'd wanted to surprise Jack when he came home, but she had got fed up halfway through when she couldn't get a garland to hang right. The room looked depressingly messy with its unfinished tree and the half-completed wreath lying on the table. It had been pouring with rain for the past three days and it was hard to get into the Christmas spirit.

Behind her, she could hear the rain hurling itself against the window. Now and then a gust of wind backed up in the chimney and a small cloud of smoke billowed from the fireplace. The acrid smell filled the room.

She pulled out her mobile to check the time. It was almost midday. She'd had breakfast early. She might as well take a break for lunch. Her eyes strayed to the messenger icon despite her better intentions. No new messages. She tried to stifle the swell of disappointment that coursed through her. Today was Thursday. If circumstances had been different, she and Douglas would have met this afternoon for riding.

With a sigh, she pushed herself up out of the chair, walked through to the kitchen and opened the fridge. She held her breath as she did so. Every time she'd opened the fridge in the past couple of weeks, a smell like old socks had greeted her; it was coming from Douglas's Camembert cheese. She had considered throwing it away but hadn't been able to bring herself to do so. Instead, she had been haunted by the cheese aroma all week.

The scent of another failed dating attempt, she thought to herself, wryly. She took it out and examined the use-by date. It was tomorrow. Her stomach rumbled. Perhaps it would be fine, despite the smell. Douglas had said to bake it. She lifted out the packet and read the instructions, then took out some baguette-style rolls from the freezer. She could put them in the oven together.

While she was waiting for them to heat up, she went through to the living room to carry on writing her Christmas cards. She looked at the picture on the top card as she laid them on the table. Jack had chosen them in the market in York. As ever, his preoccupation with animals had won through and the cards were filled with sledging penguins and snowy reindeer.

She picked up one of the penguin cards and addressed it to Mr Gorski. She would take it round later, she decided. His sister had arrived so he had company, but he was still missing Coffee. He would enjoy a chat with Jack.

Mandy would like one of the reindeer cards, Susan thought. She opened it up and wrote Mandy's name inside. Should she address it to Jimmy too? she wondered. She frowned. What about the children? It was hard to know whether to send things to one person or the whole blended family. She plumped for adding them all, as well as all the animals.

She glanced out of the window. To her surprise, the rain had stopped. The scudding clouds that had darkened the sky for days were dispersing. She felt suddenly more cheerful. If it did clear up, she decided, she wouldn't sit here moping all afternoon. She would go out and get some fresh air. *I could post the cards if I finish them all.*

She selected a penguin card for James, wrote it and then paused, realising she didn't know his home address. Pulling her phone out of her pocket, she dialled Mandy's number. There was a good chance Mandy wouldn't be able to answer right now; she might, quite literally, be up to her armpit inside a cow, but she could leave a message if so.

'Hi, Susan.' Mandy sounded as if she was smiling. There had been a few times in the past months when she had been under a lot of pressure, but she always seemed to bounce back. Susan was determined to take a leaf out of her book.

'Hi, Mandy,' she said. 'I was just writing my Christmas cards and I realised I don't have James's address. Could you send it over when you get a minute?'

'Oh.' Mandy sounded surprised. 'You're writing Christmas cards? At home?' she said after a pause.

'Yes,' said Susan. 'It's my day off so I'm getting some Christmas admin done while Jack's at nursery.'

'Oh I see,' Mandy said. There was a moment's silence, then Mandy spoke again. 'I'm really sorry about Douglas.'

'So am I,' Susan said, trying to smile. 'But it didn't work out and that's that! Christmas waits for no woman. Me and Jack have always been fine by ourselves. We don't need a man to be happy.' She hoped she was managing to sound positive. *Fake it 'til you make it . . .*

'That's good.' Mandy sounded as if she meant it. 'You were meant to be going riding with him today, weren't you?' She sounded thoughtful. 'Can I give you a ring back in a few minutes? I might be able to sort something out. Would you still like to go if I can manage it?'

'That would be great!' Susan felt her spirits lifting as she put the mobile down on the table. Outside the window, the sun had broken through. For the first time in three days, sunshine flooded into her kitchen. If the sun stayed out, it would be lovely to go for a ride. The ground would be waterlogged, but there was a good track along the bottom of the valley where it wouldn't be too windy. Mandy loved horses as much as she did. It would be fun to spend the afternoon together.

The buzzer on the cooker beeped. Susan went and opened the door. To her surprise, the scent of the French bread and the savoury aroma of the cheese smelled marvellous. She lifted them out and decanted them onto a plate. Her mouth watered as she dipped the mini-baguettes into the soft cheese. It was truly a wonderful combination. The crunchy bread and the pungent oozing cheese somehow came together and were utterly delicious. For a moment, she felt sad. Instead of thanking Douglas properly for his gift, she'd half dismissed it as weird. *I wonder how much I've missed out on over the years by avoiding weird stuff?* she thought. Maybe this would be what she would take from her brief time with Douglas: a more open mind and being more in touch with her sense of fun?

She was so lost in thought that she jumped when the phone buzzed on the table beside her. It was Mandy again. 'Hi, Susan,' she said. Her voice was breathless as if she had been rushing around. 'It's all sorted. Can you get to the stables for two?'

Susan grinned. Her spirits rose to the ceiling. 'Yes I can,' she declared. She put the phone down on the table and put her plate into the dishwasher. There was just time to take Mr Gorski's card round and see if he needed anything. She paused as she passed the living room. It was still a complete mess and she felt an urge to tidy it before she left. But then she remembered what she had just been thinking about. *Life's too short to worry about mess,* she told herself. *I can finish it later, and that way, Jack can join in too!*

She arrived at Six Oaks stables just before two. The sun was still shining brightly, even though some grey rainclouds hung stubbornly around it. The wind was gusting now and then, but Susan was wearing a warm jacket and thick jodhpurs. The yard was alive with the sounds of horses. Several heads appeared over the stable doors as she walked in. A dappled grey Shire with a broad white blaze whinnied his greeting and Susan went over to stroke his velvety nose. 'Hello, Bill,' she said as he snuffled into her ear. His whiskers tickled her cheek and she reached up a hand to stroke his neck. Bill was one of Mandy's rescues. Molly Future, the owner of Six Oaks, had adopted him. Mandy thought he might be thirty years old or more, but he seemed to be enjoying his retirement.

Leaving Bill, Susan set off across the yard to see whether Coco was ready to go out. Coco was the chunky bay gelding Susan normally rode. He reminded Susan a little of her childhood pony, Prince. As she walked, her eye was caught by two figures coming out of one of the stables to her left. One of them was Molly Future. The other was Douglas.

Susan felt the breath go out of her body. What on

earth was he doing here? she wondered. He looked very much at home as he led Munro, a tall Clydesdale cross gelding, out of the stable.

'Hi, Susan,' Molly greeted her with her usual easy smile. 'I'll just go finish up with Coco.' She flapped a hand towards Coco's stable, then set off across the yard at a jog.

Douglas stared at her, seeming to have lost the ability to move. Susan couldn't take her eyes off him. His hair was flattened again, as it had been the last time she'd seen him at the nursery. He looked surprisingly good in his riding gear: a padded jacket and olive breeches above long riding boots. Susan glanced towards Coco's stable. Molly had disappeared inside. However weird the situation was, she had to talk to Douglas before Molly reappeared. Her knees felt wobbly as she made her way over. She couldn't help but feel a little guilty. It was Douglas who'd suggested riding. He'd obviously decided to come on his own. Now she and Mandy had gatecrashed his party.

Her face was hot as she walked towards him. 'I'm sorry,' she said, feeling the redness in her cheeks intensify. 'I arranged to come riding with Mandy. I'd no idea you'd be here. I thought when our date was off . . .' She trailed off. She didn't want to talk about the reason their date had been cancelled.

Douglas stared at her, a line creasing his usually good-tempered forehead. 'You arranged to come with Mandy?' he said. 'But . . .' He paused, then shook his head. 'Mandy called me earlier. She told me we'd go out. There were some wild hedgehogs she wanted to show me . . .' He stopped again.

It was Susan's turn to frown. She pulled her phone from her pocket and consulted the messages. Sure enough, there was one from Mandy.

If you're mad, then I'm sorry, it read. *If not, you're welcome.*

She felt breathless as she looked up from the phone. Douglas was watching her still. 'I'm afraid we've been set up,' Susan said. Her eyes were on his face. Would he turn round and put Munro straight back into his stable? He looked, if anything, even more disconcerted than she felt.

The sound of hooves came across the yard and Molly appeared, leading Coco. Susan's heart lifted a little, as it always did when she thought of their many happy days out, hacking around the dale. She turned quickly to Douglas. 'I'm sorry,' she said. 'I honestly had no idea. I'd love to ride with you if . . .' She paused, then continued in a hurry, '. . . if you could forgive me for lying.' She held her breath, but Douglas had no time to reply before Molly was upon them. 'It's a lovely day for it,' she said, her voice cheery. 'Nice of Mandy to set it up.' She winked at Susan, who was feeling ever more embarrassed. She hoped Douglas hadn't seen. The last thing she wanted was for him to think she'd lied again and that Mandy had set up the date with Susan's blessing. But Douglas had turned away and was tightening Munro's girth.

Molly looked Susan up and down, then inspected Douglas, who had finished buckling. 'I was going to get you a hat, wasn't I?' she said, seeing Douglas's uncovered head. 'Wait there a minute.' She rushed off again, this time in the direction of the tack room.

'So is it okay?' Susan asked.

The nod he sent her seemed tentative. 'We might as well ride, now we're here,' he said, with the tiniest hint of a smile. Susan felt relief course through her. Awkward as it would be to go out, it would have been worse if he'd turned and walked away. Molly appeared with a couple of hats and held on to Munro while Douglas tried them on. He ran his hands through his hair before setting the first one on his head. He clipped the chin-strap into place, shook his head a little and nodded. 'This one's fine,' he said. Molly went round to hold the stirrup on Munro's saddle, and with surprising agility, Douglas pushed off, landing lightly in the saddle. He gathered in the reins in a business-like fashion, then sat very still as Molly came over to give Susan a hand.

'You should stay away from the low path along the valley bottom,' Molly said, looking up at Susan. 'There's a risk of flooding after all the rain we've had. Walton Bridleway should be fine but stay on the high ground when you come to the field with the big oak. You know the one I mean?'

'I do, thanks. Don't worry, we'll be careful.' Susan smiled down at Molly, who clapped a hand on Coco's neck.

'Have a good ride,' she said.

A few minutes later, they turned right out of the driveway, then crossed over the road. So far, they had not exchanged a word since they mounted their horses. It felt strange to be riding out with Douglas. Susan didn't get to ride as often as she would like, but when she did she went out with Molly or Helen Steer, the Animal Ark nurse. Coco was quite tall enough for Susan, but she felt dwarfed beside the hefty Munro. She glanced up at Douglas, who was riding easily, his body moving in motion with the steps of the large Clydesdale cross.

'Have you done much riding?' she asked. Douglas certainly looked happier, now they were out and moving.

He looked down at her and for the first time, sent her an echo of the huge grin that she had been missing recently. 'I grew up on a smallholding in the Highlands,' he said. 'I didn't have a pony, but the neighbours on either side did. I used to ride with them after school. I don't really remember a time before I could ride.'

It sounded idyllic, Susan thought. She had lived in London until she was twelve. When she'd first come to Welford, she had hated it. Now she wouldn't want to live anywhere else. She waited for a moment, hoping he would ask her about her childhood, but instead, he looked around, taking in the scenery. 'It always looks so different from horseback,' he said.

They had turned off the road and were riding along

the bridleway that skirted the edge of the valley. The river did indeed look swollen, Susan thought as she gazed down into the gully. In summer, it was shallow, chattering over rocks. In springtime, it rose as the snow melted from the high moors. Now it was close to bursting its banks. 'It does,' she said, searching for something more to say, but coming up blank.

Douglas put both reins into one hand and reached up with the other to move his hair out of his eyes. His new style, with his fringe brushed forwards, made him look a little smarter, Susan thought, but it didn't suit him nearly as well as the wild look he used to sport. 'You've changed your hair,' she said.

Douglas gave a kind of shrug. He looked, if anything, unexpectedly shy. 'Do you like it?' he asked.

Susan's mind was still treacherously empty. How could she answer truthfully? She didn't want to upset him. She was lucky to be here talking to him at all. But she had promised herself she wouldn't lie. 'It's nice,' she told him, 'but I kind of liked it the way it was before.' She tried to smile as she spoke to take the sting out of the words, but he looked away again at the view and didn't smile back.

'There's something I want to tell you,' she said. He turned and looked straight into her eyes. She was jolted by the pain in his. Had he been trying to please her with his new look? She'd obviously hurt him again. She had the sudden feeling that this was it: her chance to make things right or fail forever. She took a deep breath then began. 'I want to apologise properly,' she said. 'And I wanted to explain something.' She stopped. It was difficult, but he was listening. 'You were right,' she said, 'to be suspicious when you saw me with Michael. I was head over heels in love with him when we were together.' She paused. Though it was past history, it was still hard to talk about. 'Back then I thought we'd spend our lives together and have a family and share everything.' Her voice was shaking. 'Then Jack came along,' she said. 'It was the wrong time for Michael.' She stopped again, pressing her mouth together in a thin line. *The wrong time?* What an understated way to describe the devastation he'd made of her life. She swallowed, giving herself time.

'I built a new life,' she went on, when she had her voice under control again. 'Just me and Jack. We were happy, but obviously I was looking for someone – I was on LoveSpark, I tried dating. Then Michael turned up again, just as I met you and I somehow got caught up in this . . . dream.' And now the words were rushing out. 'I'd always wondered how it would be if Michael and I had stayed together. Brought Jack up as a family. It felt like a second chance, you know?' She stopped in desperation. Would he, could he, understand?

They were riding along steadily. The path narrowed as it descended further into the valley and there were trees either side of the track. Susan felt a shiver run down her spine. Douglas was so close beside her that their knees were almost touching. She wanted to reach out her hand for comfort, but she didn't know how he would react. They rode on for another minute, side by side and a million miles apart. She had to continue, she thought. She had to make him see.

'But just like the first time, it turned out to be more of a nightmare than a dream.' Her voice sounded grim as she spoke. 'I thought he'd changed, but he hadn't . . . We've built a new life together, Jack and me. I know now that Michael isn't for me. I don't want his life. I want the one I have now. I can't go back.'

The path opened out again. Susan could see the river rushing over the rocks fifty feet below. The pouring water sounded loud. There was only a low wall between them and the torrent beneath. She pressed Coco gently with her foot, moving away from the edge.

There was a softer look in Douglas's eyes when she looked at him again. He gazed at her with a tentative smile and reached out a gloved hand. Susan stretched hers out and for a moment, their fingers touched. She felt strength run into her. 'Thanks for telling me,' he said. 'It can't have been easy. I do understand.'

Susan screwed up her face and shook her head. 'I'm so sorry I lied to you,' she said. 'It was stupid and on the spur of the moment when Michael said he couldn't do another day. I was ashamed as soon as I'd said it. I knew it was all wrong. I was going to tell you the very next time I saw you, but then when we met at Hope Meadows . . .'

Their fingers were still touching. For a moment, he

gripped hers. 'I'm glad you told me,' he said. 'It's tough when too many things come up at the same time. And I can see it's complicated with Jack. I know you must always be trying to do what's best for him.'

They had reached the bottom of the hill and now the roar of the torrent filled her ears. Ahead of them, a narrow stone bridge led across the river. Beyond it, there were fields. They could canter, Susan thought, once they'd crossed the water. Then they could go back along the other side of the valley, or if the fields were flooded, they'd come back the way they came. They had broken the ice. It would be easier from now on. Her spirits lifted as she encouraged Coco towards the bridge.

They managed to get the horses across, though the wall of sound was deafening. *Just as well Coco and Munro are quiet.* On the far side, the noise retreated as they walked onto the field. The smooth stretch of grass was inviting. Susan could feel Coco becoming restive. He wanted to run.

'Race you!' Douglas turned to her, waited for her to nod and gather her reins, then leaned forward in his saddle and urged Munro on. A second later, Susan and Coco were chasing them across the field, the wind in their hair and a laugh in Susan's throat.

Chapter Twenty-Two

Susan crouched over his withers, balancing like a jockey. The wind rushed in her ears and she couldn't help grinning. Beneath her, Coco surged and stretched, hoofbeats thudding on the wet turf. There was no way she could catch Douglas on the much taller and faster Munro, but she was having a fantastic time trying.

He slowed as they approached a line of fir trees beside the wall that marked the field boundary. They ended at a comfortable canter. Douglas leaned back in his saddle. 'Woohooo!' he yelled. He made a motion in the air as if he was circling a lasso. 'Could've been a cowboy, me,' he cried. Susan laughed as she caught her breath. Both horses were breathing hard and snorting. Douglas grinned, exhilaration filling his eyes. 'What now, Calamity Sue?' he asked in the most exaggerated cowboy accent imaginable.

Susan blew out her cheeks. 'I don't mind,' she said. 'Have we got time to go a bit further?'

Douglas glanced at his watch. 'Should do,' he said. His eyes were sparkling and Susan felt a surge of joy. The old cheery Douglas was back. If they hadn't been on horseback, she would have reached out to hug him.

They began to make their way along the trees towards the gate into the next field. In the distance, Susan heard the bellow of a cow. Douglas reached the gate first. He gathered the reins into one hand and opened it, backing Munro round to let Susan through first.

Susan's breath caught in her throat as she looked out across the field. The gate was the highest point in it, and most of the rest was completely waterlogged. A herd of Highland cattle were huddled in the far corner, penned in on two sides by walls. On the third side, brown water was lapping towards them. They were trapped!

Douglas came through the gate and stopped beside her. 'Oh no, we've got some trouble here,' he said, a note of worry in his voice. Even as they watched, the area of land upon which the cattle were sheltering shrank. The water was rising fast. Susan looked down the field to see that the river had broken its banks downstream from where they had crossed. *That's where the water is coming from.* The cows were milling in circles. They reached down to sniff at the water, then jumped back, eyes wide, as if alarmed.

'What should we do?' Susan's heart was racing. There was no longer space for all the cattle. The water was lapping at their hooves. One of them raised its head and bellowed again, stretching out its neck.

'We have to get them out of there,' Douglas said. He frowned. 'Ring Mandy,' he said. 'She'll know whose they are.'

Susan pulled her phone from her pocket. She was relieved when Mandy replied on the first ring. 'Hi, Mandy?' She pressed the phone to her ear. Douglas was circling on Munro. The horse was unsettled, shaking his head up and down and snorting. 'We're on Walton Bridleway,' she said loudly. 'Second field after the bridge. We've found some Highland cattle. The field's flooding. The water's rising fast.' Even as she spoke, she could see the flood water spreading. The moat that separated them from the cows was widening.

'They must be Jeremy Loxhill's' Mandy's voice was clipped. 'I'll give him a call. We'll be there shortly.'

'They're on their way,' Susan called out. Munro seemed to have calmed again.

Douglas nodded. 'That's good,' he said, 'but we can't wait. We're going to have to get them out of there before the water gets any higher.' There was determination in his voice. Susan felt courage surging into her. She looked across the field, trying to work out the safest route. She had ridden here a thousand times before. 'We should follow the line of the track there,' she pointed to the track, which lay on a ridge. Though it too was submerged, the water there would be shallower. 'Then we can drive them along the wall. Once they're out of the water, we can bring them up here.'

Douglas nodded once. Side by side, they rode down the slope. The water was still rising, creeping towards them. When Susan looked over at the cows, there was no land left to see. Their feet were submerged beneath the rising brown tide. They rode into the water. She could hear Coco's hooves splashing. The water was at Coco's knees, then Susan's feet.

The brown water was swirling. For a moment, Coco faltered, but Susan urged him on. Douglas rode by her side. Munro seemed to be taking the unusual ride in his stride.

'What'll we do when we get there?' Susan asked.

Douglas had a grim look on his face. He was riding forward nonetheless. 'They may not want to move,' he said. 'We'll have to drive them. Shout at them. Wave your arms if you think Coco'll take it.' Susan had never seen him look so serious.

Beneath her, Coco stumbled and lurched, and for a moment, Susan felt panic rising, but then the gelding found his feet again. Munro, easily two hands taller, was still striding forward. The cattle were eyeing them and snorting, milling round on their now submerged island.

'Okay?' Douglas looked down at Susan. How steady his blue eyes seemed. 'Ready?' he asked and then they surged forwards. They were close to the cattle now.

'Wooo! Go on!' Douglas roared at the herd and waved his left arm in the air.

The nearest cow looked at him. Her eyes were frantic.

'Get on!' Susan too found her voice.

The herd were milling faster and for a moment, Susan wondered if they would break through the wall, but Douglas drove Munro forward again, close to the wall and the cattle began to turn, reluctant at first, but then they too were fully in the water up to their elbows, swimming for a moment, then swishing and splashing as they reached the slope that led up to the gate.

'We'll drive them round the wall,' Douglas shouted. 'You stay behind them and I'll go alongside to keep them moving in the right direction. You're doing great!'

They should have left the gate open, Susan thought as they drove the cattle up the slope. Not that the other field was safe from flooding if the water continued to rise, but the way out lay in that direction. There was no way the cattle could stay here safely. She and Coco trotted behind the herd and Douglas controlled their direction as he'd said he would. *He really* is *like a cowboy!*

A movement up ahead caught her eye. The gate was opening. For a moment, Susan thought she caught a glimpse of Mandy waving, then her attention was back on the cattle in front of her. They were moving steadily now. Douglas moved out a little. They reached the gate and he circled round to turn them through it. He was still chattering soothingly the whole way. 'Come along now, ladies, off to dry land. You all right there, Susan? See, they're going to be fine.'

For a moment, Susan thought the cows would turn easily. They slowed. Then the lead cow snorted at something unseen, tossed her head in the air and set off again up the hill.

Douglas did not hesitate for a moment. Kicking

Munro into a gallop, he roared ahead of the cows. 'HeiYA!' he whooped. 'GET ON!'

The cows checked. They stared for a moment, snorting, then turned and trotted through the gate as if the outcome had never been in doubt.

'You did it!' Susan cheered.

Douglas flashed her a grin and Susan felt a flutter in her chest that wasn't entirely to do with the adrenaline of herding the cows. 'We did it,' he corrected her.

Mandy was standing on the far side of the gate, hiding behind the wall. As Susan slowed to a walk, she saw Mr Loxhill rushing down the hill on a quadbike. His face was worried. He drew to a halt beside Mandy.

'Brilliant herding!' Mandy grinned up at Douglas. 'Where'd you learn to do that?'

Douglas beamed. 'I used to help out with the North Country Cheviots that belonged to my neighbour. They're sheep, but they're just as thrawn as Highlanders. I've never herded anything on horseback before, though. Think I'd have made a cowboy? Howdy, pardner!' He seemed amused, now the cows were out of danger.

Susan laughed. 'I think you might need to practise your accent,' she said.

Mandy chuckled, but Mr Loxhill didn't join in. He still looked concerned. 'Thanks very much for bringing them out,' he said, 'but I've no idea what I'm going to do with them. If that field's flooded, the whole valley's at risk. It's already lapping at the door of my barn.' He put his hands on his hips and glanced around, as if hoping an answer would present itself.

'There's probably space up at Wildacre,' Mandy suggested. 'I've an empty paddock and plenty of space in the barn if they don't mind sharing with a few chickens.'

Mr Loxhill looked at her. 'Are you sure?' he said. 'It really would be a help.'

'Of course,' Mandy smiled.

'What's the best way to get them there?' Mr Loxhill asked. He glanced around as if trying to decide. 'We could go along the road, I suppose, but it's busy at this time with the Walton traffic and it's getting dark.'

It was, Susan realised as she glanced upwards. The sky had clouded over again. Dusk was falling. 'We came along the bridleway,' she said. 'If we can get the cows over the bridge, we could take them along that way.'

'Good idea,' Mandy said. 'It's only a couple of hundred yards from there to the Wildacre turnoff. I'll take the car round and stop any traffic.'

The cattle were nervous crossing the bridge, but with Douglas, Susan and Mr Loxhill all urging them along, they soon had the cattle heading along the bridle path. Douglas managed to pass them before they got to the road. Mandy was waiting there as promised, headlights beaming. It was starting to rain again.

Mandy followed them along the road in the RAV4 and together, they drove the exhausted cattle all the way up to Wildacre. Jimmy appeared as they reached the top of the track. 'Barn door's open,' he shouted.

A few minutes later, all the cows were safely inside Mandy's barn. Now that the emergency was over, Susan suddenly remembered Molly. She'd be wondering where on earth they'd got to. 'Mandy,' she called out. 'We'll need to head back before it's completely dark. Could you let Molly know where we are, please?'

Mandy, who had closed the door of the barn and was discussing the logistics of feeding the cattle with Mr Loxhill, looked up at her. 'Of course,' she said. 'I'll tell her you'll be back in a few minutes. Are you sure you're okay?'

'I'm fine,' Susan assured her. Despite being wet and a little tired, she was feeling astonishingly cheerful. A few minutes later, she and Douglas had made their way down the road and back into the stable yard. Susan couldn't stop herself from stealing covert glances at Douglas. As he rode confidently through the rain he looked like a romantic hero. *Who would have thought it?* She smiled to herself, remembering her first impression of him in the classroom.

Molly came rushing out to meet them. 'Are you okay?' she asked. 'I hear you've been rescuing Mr Loxhill's cattle.' She came over and held Coco's head as Susan pulled her feet out of the stirrups and dismounted. She landed rather stiffly. It had been a long time since she'd spent quite so long in the saddle. Douglas dismounted as well and Molly returned to put Munro in his stable.

'You too should go home and get dry,' she ordered with a nod. 'Nicole's here. We'll get them sorted out.'

Susan smiled and Douglas saluted. 'Yes, boss,' he said to Molly, who grinned.

'It's not every day I get to welcome back two heroes on horseback,' she said. 'Give me your hat, Douglas, and I'll put it away for you.'

She took Munro and Douglas's helmet and disappeared at a run. Susan found herself alone with Douglas. She felt suddenly shy. He had been so brilliant back there with the cattle. He moved closer to her. His eyes were shining in the dim yellow lights that dotted the yard. 'You were amazing,' he said softly. He smiled down at her and reached out to take her hand. Despite the rain that was still falling, Susan had no wish to move away.

'No,' she said. 'You were amazing . . .' She felt suddenly breathless. His body was so close. Desire coursed through her.

The phone in her pocket buzzed and she cursed softly under her breath. 'I'm sorry,' she said. 'I'd better get this.' She pulled the mobile from her pocket.

It was Miranda. 'Where on earth are you?' Miranda trilled. 'Jack and I are waiting outside the door. I forgot to bring the key. Will you be long?'

'Sorry, Mum. Long story but I'm on my way.' Susan sighed as she pushed the phone back into her pocket.

Douglas was still smiling, but the moment had passed. 'Mum duties calling. Thanks for this afternoon,' she said.

Douglas shook his head. 'It's Mandy you should thank,' he said. 'I'm glad she set this up.'

'Me too,' Susan admitted. She paused for a moment, gathering her nerve. 'So, do you think you might want to try again? This dating thing, I mean . . . I'd like to if you would.' She felt herself flushing bright red.

Douglas smiled. 'I'll give you a call,' he said. 'Very soon.'

He opened the door of her car and waited while she climbed in.'

'So long, partner,' Susan joked.

Douglas beamed and closed the car door with a hearty, 'Yee ha!'

Susan laughed as she started the engine.

Who says a romantic hero can't be a bit silly too?

Chapter Twenty-Three

'Hello, Susan? Douglas here!'

Even though she had to hold the phone away from her ear because the booming Scottish voice was so loud, Susan was smiling widely to herself and struggling to contain her excitement. *He's called!* 'Hi, Douglas,' she managed, as casually as she could. 'How are you?'

'Oh I'm fine,' Douglas said. 'Just about dried out after yesterday! But I'm actually ringing up about a rather serious matter.'

Susan wondered what on earth it could be. He sounded almost as serious as he had when he'd been herding the cows.

'Of course, I would love to take you on another date, if you'd like,' Douglas went on. 'But before I can, there is another very important commitment I must honour. Can I come over and paint Jack's mural someday soon?'

Susan felt pure happiness rising in her chest. Had she finally found a man whom she liked, who liked her and accepted Jack? Not just accepted, but seemed to actively want to get to know him and be kind to him?

'That would be amazing!' she replied. 'We're free tomorrow evening. Would that work?'

'Sounds perfect,' said Douglas. 'I'll come at six. I can't wait to see you again,' he added, softly.

The next day, Susan sat beside the window, watching for Douglas's car. He was due in a few minutes. Jack knew he was coming but he was upstairs. Susan hoped she would be able to grab a minute or two alone with Douglas. She rushed to the door as his car drew up. Stepping out onto the doorstep, she pulled the front door to behind her and grinned as he climbed out of his car and strolled towards her.

'Hi,' she said. A wave of happiness was flooding her body.

He smiled down at her as he reached her side. She couldn't help but smile back as she gazed up at him. His hair was back in its old style, a happy medium between its tousled primary-school-author-visit state and too-stern slickness. He looked wonderful. He came to a stop so close that she felt breathless. He lifted a hand and placed it gently on her waist. He was going to kiss her, she thought. There were butterflies in her stomach. She lifted her face to his as he leaned forward.

'Hi, Douglas!' The yell came from the doorway. Jack pulled the door open wide with a welcoming grin. 'Come in.'

Douglas straightened then laughed. He removed his

hand from Susan's waist and sent a rueful shrug in her direction.

They trooped upstairs together. Susan had readied the room. Sheets covered the floor and furniture. Jack had some paper and paints ready so that he could paint as well. Susan watched as Douglas set out his painting things. He seemed very efficient as he took out several different-sized brushes and a number of small pots of paints.

'So what should I paint, Jack?' he asked. A moment later, they were deep in discussion about seasons and plants, animals and insects.

Susan had brought up the last of her Christmas cards to write. She sat down at the covered desk with good intentions, but it was distracting having Douglas in the room. Her eyes were drawn to him continually. She had watched him sketching before. He painted with the same intensity. His usually wild movements were contained and controlled. After only a few minutes, she set the cards aside and put down her pen to watch.

Despite his fierce concentration, Douglas seemed able to manage a running commentary as Jack asked him question after question.

'Do you like football, Douglas?'

Douglas frowned very slightly as he inspected the flowing line he had just added. Then he glanced in Jack's direction with raised eyebrows and a smile. 'I do like football.' He nodded once, then bent again to add another brush stroke.

'What's your team?'

Again the pause as he inspected the line he had added. It was amazing how his pictures took shape. He glanced again at Jack. 'Manchester City,' he said.

'Boo!' Jack's voice rose to a shout and Douglas sat up and looked round properly. He was grinning. 'Don't tell me you're a United fan,' he said. He feigned a look of horror, his mouth turning down as he held his hands in the air and he waved the paintbrush as if in disdain.

Jack glared at him. 'Well, look at these,' he said and pulled up the hems of his trousers to reveal a pair of red and white socks. 'United are way better than City,' he declared.

Douglas wrinkled his nose and shook his head with a mock grimace. 'They are not,' he growled.

Jack narrowed his eyes. He was holding a paintbrush in his hand. It was full of red paint. 'Are!' he shouted and stamped his foot. With a cheeky glance at Susan, he turned back and flicked the brush at Douglas.

Susan gasped. Douglas sat there looking surprised. His face and beard were spattered with scarlet paint.

'Jack!' Susan yelped. 'You mustn't flick paint. Say you're sorry to Douglas, please.'

Jack hung his head. 'Sorry, Douglas,' he muttered.

Douglas, still decorated with random red spots, grinned. 'It really doesn't matter,' he said to Susan. 'I'm often covered in paint and your dustsheets have protected everything that matters. We're all in old clothes, aren't we?'

'True.' Susan glanced down at the jeans she was wearing. They were almost worn through at the knees. Her T-shirt was also ancient. 'Well then, in that case . . .' She reached out for one of Douglas's paintbrushes that was propped on the top of a jar of white paint. A huge grin spread across her face as she carefully took aim and flicked the brush at Douglas. 'Red and White,' she said. 'Now you're going to have to support Man U.'

Douglas opened his eyes wide in mock outrage. 'Right!' he said. He bared his teeth and growled, then dipped his brush in the light blue paint that he had been using to paint the sky.

A few moments later, the room was filled with flying paint. Susan was laughing so hard, she could barely breathe. Douglas looked crazier than ever, spattered with every colour of paint under the rainbow. Jack had watched for a second, his eyes wide with shock at the way his mum was acting, and then he had joined in, flicking paint at both Susan and Douglas with glee.

'Look at me, Mummy!' Susan was almost too distracted to look, but at the last minute, her eyes swivelled to Jack. He stood poised with a whole tin of paint. In another second, he would launch it at Douglas.

'Stop, Jack!' she yelled as she rushed towards him, but Douglas was quicker. He reached out and grabbed the pot.

Jack looked surprised, then he crossed his arms and stuck out his bottom lip.

'Sorry, Jack.' Douglas put the paint out of arm's

reach, then knelt down in front of Jack, whose face was still mutinous. 'We've had a lot of fun,' he said, placing a hand gently on Jack's shoulder, 'but if you throw the whole pot, it'll make so much mess it'll soak through the sheets and spoil the carpet. Do you understand?' He smiled at Jack, making it clear he wasn't angry.

Jack's face slowly cleared. He looked at Douglas and nodded.

'Shake?' Douglas held out his enormous, paint-stained hand. Jack reached out his own small one and they shook. 'Now,' said Douglas. 'I think we need to help Mummy clean up, don't you?' He glanced up at the walls. Susan looked too. The mural they had painted was fine, but one of the cream-painted walls was spotted with flecks of colour. Douglas looked at Susan, his face rueful. 'Sorry,' he said.

Susan laughed. 'I don't know what you're sorry for,' she said. 'It was me that started it.'

Douglas smiled, his eyebrows lifting. 'That's true,' he admitted, 'but I'll help you paint again. It was at least partly my fault.'

Jack was looking up at the spattered wall with something approaching awe. 'I like it,' he said. 'Can't it stay?'

Douglas grinned at Susan. 'Maybe we should listen to Jack,' he said. 'It is a bit like modern art.'

That enormous smile. It was irresistible. Susan laughed. 'It does look a bit Jackson Pollock,' she said, making a square with her fingers and thumbs and peering though it to inspect the dotty wall from different angles.

'More a Banksy by the time I'm done,' Douglas replied. He dipped the paintbrush into one of the pots and a moment later, several of the dots had been joined together to make a cow.

Susan wondered whether Jack would protest. A cow didn't really fit with their woodland theme, but Jack was wide-eyed, seemingly as awestruck as Susan when Douglas painted anything.

'Is it one of the cows you and Mummy rounded up?' Jack asked. 'Mummy told Mandy you looked great on a horse,' he added in a matter-of-fact tone. Susan could feel a tide of pink rushing across her face. *I'm going to have to be more careful about him listening to my phone calls!*

'Did she now?' Douglas raised his eyebrows. Susan could see the effort it was taking him to keep a straight face. 'I must go riding more often in that case. Thank you, Jack.'

'You're welcome,' Jack said. Susan could feel a giggle rising. She put a hand to her mouth and pressed her lips together and wanted to laugh all the more. There was a definite taste of paint. Douglas was even more covered. Maybe he would have to don the ridiculous Christmas pyjamas again, unless he wanted to drive home with paint all over him.

Douglas held up a finger and put his head to one side as if trying to hear. 'I think there's a phone ringing,' he said.

Susan listened. Sure enough it was her mobile. She

grabbed a towel, wiped her hands, then followed the sound through to her bedroom. The phone lay on the bedside table.

'*Michael*'. The name flashed on the screen and she stopped. For a moment, she wondered if she should ignore it. Hadn't she decided he should never see Jack again? But she had stormed out of his house in anger. She hadn't told him her decision. He needed to know. She pressed the button to answer the call.

'Susan, I hope you got home safely after you dashed out the other day.'

Though his tone was arrogant, Susan's reply came almost automatically. 'We did,' she said. Her mind worked furiously as soon as she'd answered. He was blaming her for dashing out, not himself for putting her in an impossible position.

'Well, I hope next time we meet, you'll be a little more rational,' he said. His voice was sardonic. Susan felt about six inches tall. Why did he do this to her?

'I'm not sure I want you to see him again,' she said. Even as she said it, she couldn't keep the tremor out of her voice.

'Don't be ridiculous. I want to see my son.' The voice on the other end of the line was unequivocal. 'I'll come Saturday afternoon.'

'He's at a birthday party,' she said. She spoke without thinking, then kicked herself. She had to take a firmer approach. It didn't matter whether Jack was in or out. She didn't want Michael coming round any time. 'And even if he wasn't,' she said, 'it's not going to work. What happened the other day upset Jack.'

'You're not being fair. It's important—' Michael began, but a loud shriek from Jack's bedroom sent Susan scurrying onto the landing.

She had thought from the scream that Jack had hurt himself, but when she arrived, he was grinning and standing on a chair on one leg. 'Look at me, Douglas,' he yelled at the top of his voice.

Susan was about to go in and intervene, when Douglas lifted him down. 'Be careful, Jack,' he said.

Michael had stopped halfway through his sentence. There was silence for a moment, then a single word. 'Douglas?' There was outrage in his voice. 'You told me you wouldn't be seeing him again. Not only are you bringing strange men into the house, but you lied to me. How dare you?'

Susan quailed. Had she said that? She could barely think straight. She ducked back into her bedroom. 'It's really nothing to do with you,' she retorted, as quietly as she could, 'but Douglas is less of a stranger to Jack than you are. You've only met him twice. Your own son. I'll decide who's suitable to be around him.'

'He's my son too, whether you like it or not.' Michael's voice dropped to a dangerous-sounding hiss. 'And I will see him, even if I have to take you to court. In the meantime, I'm going to ask you politely to send that man away.'

Susan felt rage boiling up. Polite? How dared he call

his demands polite? Michael rarely yelled when angry. His fury was icy cold.

'I have no intention of asking Douglas to leave,' she spat. 'And no judge is going to take my son off me. All I want is to be left alone.'

She ended the call filled with rage, but within a few moments she felt nausea rising. Could he take her to court over this? Surely no judge would side with a man who had only seen his son twice and wasn't on the birth certificate. But Michael had some powerful friends.

Her hands were trembling as the mobile clattered down on the bedside table. She glanced down at her paint-spattered clothes. She should get herself cleaned up, she thought miserably. Why had she ever let Michael back in? A few minutes ago, she had felt uncomplicatedly happy. Now everything was upside down.

She turned to go to the bathroom, then stopped. Douglas's worried face was peering round the open bedroom door. How much had he overheard?

'Was that . . . Michael?' he asked. His eyes were sympathetic and worried at the same time.

Susan nodded her head.

'I'm so sorry, I didn't mean to eavesdrop,' Douglas said. 'I heard my name and I thought you were calling for me and well – it was hard not to overhear.'

'It's fine,' Susan said, with a bitter laugh. 'Better that you know about the drama sooner rather than later. Full disclosure in case you want to run for the hills.'

'Did he threaten you?' Douglas looked concerned.

Susan shrugged. 'He was trying to pressure me into letting him see Jack, but then he heard you in the background and lost it. Started talking about taking me to court. I guess he felt jealous or something, of another man with his son.'

As soon as she'd said it, Susan wished she could call the words back. There was shock on Douglas's face. 'I'd better go then,' he said. 'You can't take that risk.'

Susan could feel tears welling up as she gazed at him, standing there looking helpless. She didn't want Douglas to go, but what if Michael meant what he said?

Douglas crossed the room in an instant and took both her hands as the painful tears began to roll down her face. 'Look,' he said. 'It's a lot for you to take in, but it's better that I go for now. You go clean yourself up. Jack and I will tidy the bedroom. Try not to worry. You just have to stand firm.' He squeezed her fingers, rubbing her hand with his thumb. 'Focus on sorting things out for Jack before – well, before anything else . . .' he said. He gave her knuckles a final squeeze, then let go of her hand and walked out of the room. A moment later, she heard him talking to Jack as they began the clean-up operation.

By the time she came out of the shower, Douglas had gone. The house seemed silent and empty. Jack was downstairs, watching TV.

'I like Douglas, Mummy,' he said. 'When will he be coming back?'

Susan took a deep breath. She was not going to cry again. Not in front of Jack. 'I'm really not sure,' she said. 'But hopefully soon.' She could still hope, couldn't she? Somewhere on the far side of this, there must be sanity? It was just hard to see it right now.

Jack seemed quite satisfied with her response. 'Good,' he said. He turned back to the TV. Susan stood for a long minute, just watching him. She loved him so much. The very idea of him being taken away from her was unbearable. Douglas was right. It wouldn't do to wind Michael up. She wandered through to the kitchen and looked out of the window to the spot where Douglas's car had been. She wanted to wail at how unfair life was. She'd finally found a wonderful, kind, funny, handsome man, after all this time, and *now* Michael decided to rear his ugly head.

I just can't win.

Chapter Twenty-Four

'Night night, robin redbreast. Night night, Marmalade.' Jack edged backwards and climbed down from the window seat where he had been kneeling to gaze into the cold, wet darkness beyond.

Susan held out her hand to him. 'Come on now. Into bed,' she said, grasping his hand and giving his small fingers a squeeze.

He obediently clambered into bed and lay down. 'Night night, Mummy,' he said, smiling up at her.

Susan pulled the covers up to his chin. 'Nighty night,' she said. She bent forward to drop a kiss on his forehead. He looked so sweet.

'When will Daddy come round again?' he asked. 'Will he be here for Christmas?' His eyes were filled with innocent curiosity.

Susan felt as if something was shifting in her belly. She hated having to be less than truthful with him, but how could she tell him Daddy wouldn't be coming back ever? She wanted to explain, but what could she say that he would understand? It would have to wait until he was older. 'I'm not sure when he's coming again,' she told him, and then before he had time to react, 'I love you very much. Sleep well, sweetie.'

She felt torn as she walked downstairs. She didn't want Michael to see Jack again in case he hurt him. Yet she and Michael had never discussed the situation properly. Both their recent conversations had descended into anger. Should she contact him, if Jack was missing him? But wouldn't that be madness, considering what he'd threatened last time they had spoken?

Downstairs in the kitchen, she put the oven on. Mandy was coming round for mince pies. Even if she couldn't help, it would be a distraction from the thoughts that kept circling Susan's head. Michael ruining her budding relationship with Douglas had made her feel angry. For her part, she'd be happy if she never saw him again. But then, it had been Douglas's decision to step away. Several times over the last twenty-four hours, she'd been tempted to ring him and say to hell with Michael and ask him if they could carry on regardless. But she'd always paused, fearful that the answer would be 'no', that Douglas's backing off was more to do with his not wanting the drama, than out of consideration for her situation. She kept replaying his final words in her head. What had he meant by them? That he didn't want to see her at all for now? Or he just wouldn't see Jack? She was glad when the doorbell rang.

'Hello!' Mandy grinned at Susan as she stood on the doorstep. Her blonde hair glistened with droplets from the fog that was hanging in the air. She held out a bottle. 'I've brought some mulling wine,' she said. 'I thought it'd go well with mince pies.'

Susan reached out and took the bottle. 'Thanks,' she said. She led Mandy through to the kitchen. The aroma of warm mince pies filled the air. On the table, Susan had lit one of the scented Christmas candles she'd bought in York.

Mandy breathed in deeply, lifting her head and closing her eyes as if in ecstasy. 'It smells like a Christmas bakery in a fir forest,' she said.

'That's spot on! It's called "North Pole Kitchen".' Susan laughed, pulling out a pan from the cupboard. She emptied the contents of the bottle Mandy had given her, then dug in her store cupboard for a cinnamon stick and some cloves. She dropped them into the saucepan, then took an orange from the fruit bowl and added a few slices.

Mandy had pulled out a chair at the kitchen table. Susan sat down opposite while she waited for the wine to heat through.

'So how are things?' Mandy placed her elbows on the table and leaned forward. 'How did everything go after your cattle-herding date?'

Susan's eyes dropped. She hadn't seen Mandy since the horse-riding session. When she looked up again, there was concern in Mandy's face.

'It was okay, wasn't it?' she asked. 'I thought your date went well. You're not angry with me for setting you up?'

Susan managed a smile. 'I'm not at all angry with you,' she said. 'The ride went really well. In fact, if my mother hadn't phoned at just the wrong moment, I think we might have kissed.'

Mandy tilted her head. Her eyes were steady on Susan's face. 'I sense a "but",' she said. 'What went wrong?'

Susan sighed. 'He came round yesterday,' she admitted. 'Michael phoned while he was here and Douglas overheard the call.'

Mandy shook her head. The crease on her forehead had deepened. 'And?' she said. 'What does that have to do with Michael?'

Susan gazed across the table feeling gloomy. 'Well, you know when Michael was trying to pressure me into some ridiculous family situation with him? He was refusing to accept when I said no, and he implied that it was because of Douglas.' She replayed the incident in her mind. She hadn't been able to recall what she'd said yesterday, but now it was as clear as day. 'Douglas was barely speaking to me at the time, because I'd lied to him about what we were doing the day Michael met Jack.' She felt a welling of misery inside her as she recounted the whole mess. 'So I didn't think I was ever going to see him again, so I told Michael I wasn't seeing anyone and I didn't need or want a man. That worked to shut him up, but now of course he thinks I lied as well. He said Douglas had to go. I said it was none of his business and the next thing, he was telling me he wanted Jack back and would take me to court.'

Mandy was staring at her now. 'He said he'd take you to court?' she repeated.

Susan nodded, her shoulders slumped.

'And now you're worried that if you see Douglas again, Michael will try to take Jack away?' Mandy asked.

Susan felt sick. How had everything become so complicated? 'Yes,' she admitted. 'And Douglas overheard and said he should go. It wasn't worth the risk, he said.' She swallowed. It had taken her far too long to realise what a good person Douglas was. Now she might have lost him forever.

Mandy shook her head again. 'But that's all wrong,' she objected. 'Michael might be Jack's dad, but it's nothing to do with him if you see someone else.'

Susan lifted her eyes to the ceiling. There was no answer to that. The situation was *all wrong*, but she couldn't see a way out of it.

'You have to try to talk to Michael again,' Mandy urged. She reached a hand across the table, grabbing Susan's hand. 'It's not as if you can avoid Douglas forever. I haven't sent out the invitations yet, but I'm having a Hope Meadows Christmas party and you're both invited. And what if he comes to school to paint again? You can't live your life like that – not for *Michael's* sake!'

Susan didn't know what to say. Mandy was right, but how could she even begin to discuss this with

Michael? Every time they talked, it felt like she was further and further into the mire.

There was a sizzling sound from the cooker. Susan turned her head. The mulled wine was boiling over. Mandy jumped up and removed the pan from the heat, then reached for a cloth. 'Don't panic,' she said with a grin. She wiped up the spilt wine, threw the cloth back on the side of the sink, then stretched out to grab the ladle that Susan had left on the side. 'And in the meantime,' she turned to Susan, waving it in the air, 'you should tell Douglas you don't want him to stay away. You can't give in to that kind of blackmail. Michael's not even on the birth certificate, is he?'

Susan took a deep breath to voice her fear. 'I actually wonder if Douglas staying away is more something that he wants to do, rather than to help me. Who wants to be involved with this much drama?'

Mandy waved a hand. 'Nonsense. I've seen the way Douglas looks at you. He likes you too much to just walk away. Besides, he's a hero cowboy! Do you think some mean-spirited lawyer is going to scare him off? You need to talk to him to know for sure, but I'd be willing to bet he's just waiting for his chance to be by your side again.'

For the first time since Douglas had left, Susan felt her heart lift a little. Mandy's no nonsense way of looking at the world always made things sound so simple. 'You're right,' she said. 'I don't have to do what Michael tells me. I'll ring Douglas later.'

'Great!' Mandy clapped her hands.

Susan pushed her chair out and stood up. 'But right now, we've got even more important things to think about! Would you like some ice cream with your mince pie?'

A few minutes later, they were ensconced on either side of the living-room fire. In the corner beside the door, the Christmas tree lights sent their warm light into the room. Susan dug her spoon into her mince pie. 'I do love mince pies,' she said. She put a sliver of the pastry in her mouth. The warm mincemeat was wonderful with the cool ice cream 'So tell me about your Hope Meadows party,' she said.

Mandy looked pleased. 'Well, after the great wine-tasting debacle,' she said, 'I thought maybe I needed to go back to basics. Welford's always supported Animal Ark and now Hope Meadows too. I wanted to thank everyone who's helped out or donated or adopted.' She grinned. 'I'm hoping that people will come feeling Christmassy and generous.'

Susan found herself smiling back. Mandy's enthu-siasm for life was cheering. 'Well, I'll definitely be there,' she said. 'And if you like, I can donate some mince pies.'

Mandy looked down at her empty bowl. 'If they taste as good as these,' she said, 'I'm sure everyone'll throw money at us.'

'So how are things at Animal Ark?' Susan asked. 'How's Toby settling in?'

Mandy laughed. 'Very well indeed,' she said. 'He's very popular. Especially with certain clients.' She waggled her eyebrows up and down.

Her expression was so funny that Susan felt like laughing too. 'Who exactly?' she asked, though she thought she could perhaps guess. 'Has someone taken a "Fancy" to him?'

Mandy raised her glass in a salute. 'Exactly so,' she said. 'Mrs Ponsonby does indeed keep bringing Fancy in to see Toby. It's amazing how many times that poor Pekinese needs to have her ears checked because she shook her head or has an awful cough because she choked on her evening biscuit.'

'Poor Fancy.' Susan could picture the fluffy little dog in Mrs Ponsonby's arms.

'Luckily she's very patient,' Mandy said. She leaned forward and put her empty bowl on the coffee table. 'I miss her actually. Mrs P used to bring her in to me before Toby won her heart.'

'Pity,' Susan commented, but then she grinned, holding up her glass. '. . . but it must be good for business,' she added. She took a sip of the mulled wine. Despite having been overheated, it still tasted delicious. She was feeling much more cheerful. It was great that Mandy had come round.

'Must be,' Mandy agreed. She was grinning so hard it looked almost painful. 'Mrs P's not the only one either. All her friends also keep turning up with their little handbag dogs. Toby can't understand how all these dogs have so many strange symptoms, but nothing that ever shows up when he's looking at them.'

'Ah, the many mysteries of unrequited love,' Susan said. She glanced at Mandy, who caught her eye and they both burst into laughter.

An hour later, as Susan mounted the stairs to her bedroom, she remembered she hadn't contacted Douglas. Should she call him? she wondered. Mandy was right in one way. She shouldn't be giving in to Michael. It really wasn't any of his business who she saw. She paused on the landing, then pushed open the door to Jack's bedroom and wandered over to stand beside the bed. Jack was fast asleep and dreaming. He stirred a little, reached out a hand for Lamby and snuggled deeper under the covers. Outside the window she could hear the rain. Mandy must be home by now, thank goodness. What was it Douglas had said about Jack? She pictured him standing in the doorway. 'You can't take that risk.' A wave of weariness washed over Susan.

Her eyes dropped again to Jack's sweet little face. Douglas was right, she thought. There was no way she could risk this. Before she could see anyone, she was going to have to speak to Michael. The only problem was that she had no idea how. She reached out a hand and smoothed a lock of hair from Jack's forehead. There was nothing she could do tonight anyway. She made her way through into her own bedroom. It had felt like a sanctuary before. She had always been firm with Jack about sleeping in his own bed. Yet now her own double bed seemed very cold and empty. She lay awake a long time.

Chapter Twenty-Five

'Did he go in okay?' Miranda called from the living room as Susan opened the front door of Moon Cottage and stepped inside.

'He was fine.' Susan had just dropped Jack off at the Dhanjals' house for Kiran's birthday. It was the first time Susan had left him alone at a party. Miranda had agreed to come over and keep her company. 'I think I was more worried about it than he was.'

'I brought your panettone,' Miranda said, appearing in the doorway. She had been to York that morning and had picked up a few things from James's café. She'd called Susan while she was there. James had recommended the sweet Italian bread that his boyfriend Raj had imported from Italy. 'He sent a Christmas bombe recipe too. In case you have leftovers. And he said thank you for the Christmas card.'

Susan took the paper from Miranda and read through the instructions. It seemed very complicated. She was nearly sure she wouldn't need it. Both she and Jack loved panettone. 'Thanks, Mum.'

'Oh it's no problem,' Miranda replied. She smiled.

'I must say, James was looking well,' she said. 'And he seems very upbeat. He's coming over to Welford for the Hope Meadows party. Raj and he are bringing food.'

Susan hung her coat up. 'I must buy some more mince,' she said. She walked through into the kitchen and made a note on the pad she left by the fridge. 'I promised Mandy I'd take some mince pies to her Christmas party,' she explained. She put down the pen and picked up the kettle. 'Tea?' she asked.

'That would be lovely,' Miranda replied. She pulled out a chair and sat down facing Susan, leaning an elbow on the table beside her. 'So what did Mandy have to say the other night about that young vet . . . what's his name again . . . ?' She gazed at Susan, eyebrows raised to quizzical, head on one side like a bird.

Susan resisted the urge to roll her eyes or laugh. Miranda must be pretending she'd forgotten Toby's name. Her mum loved all kinds of gossip, but especially if it was about attractive young men of Susan's age. Sometimes she seemed more like a friend than a mother. 'You mean Toby?' she said.

'Oooh yes.' Miranda pulled her chin in with a self-satisfied look. 'Toby, that's right. How's he getting on?'

Susan paused to set out a mug for herself and a bone china cup and saucer for Miranda, then turned and put her hands on her hips. 'Mandy says he can hardly move for middle-aged ladies chasing him round the consulting-room table.' She grinned, then turned again to grab teabags from the cupboard and milk from the fridge.

If Miranda had been hoping for romantic gossip, she must have been disappointed, but she hid it well as she raised a single eyebrow. 'I'm not surprised,' she said with a little laugh. 'Middle-aged womanhood can be lonely, you know.'

Susan stifled a chuckle as she looked at her mother. There was no way Miranda was lonely. She had often said as much herself, surrounded as she was with friends and admirers as well as Susan and Jack. 'Maybe you should pop in and see him yourself,' she suggested, her voice dry.

'Maybe I will,' Miranda said and laughed again. 'Although I'd need to acquire a pet. Maybe a cute little bunny?'

'I think a cougar would be more your style,' Susan teased, with a grin. Her mother was incorrigible. Susan had to admire her optimism.

'So rude about your own mother!' Miranda mimed being shot in the heart. 'Oh darling, I've been meaning to ask, how is Mr Gorski doing?'

Susan held on to her smile, though a wave of sadness pushed through her. 'He's doing okay,' she said. 'His sister's there now till after Christmas, so he has company at least.'

She and Jack had been round to see Mr Gorski a couple of times. Even the presence of his very chatty

sister couldn't hide the gap that Coffee's cheery presence had left. And Mr Gorski was starting to have
trouble hearing the doorbell. Fine while his sister was
there, Susan thought, but what would happen later?
She and Jack would have to keep a good eye on him
when Christmas was past. The New Year could be a
difficult time when you were alone.

'Poor fellow.' Miranda sighed. 'It's terrible to lose
your companion. Life is just no fun alone. Speaking
of which . . .' Miranda sat up straight and looked Susan
right in the eye. 'How's your love life going?' she asked.

Susan had to smile at her mother's ability to hop
from comedy to tragedy and then back to gossip again
in the space of a minute. Miranda had always been this
way: no subject too delicate and nothing off limits. All
the same, she had hoped this wouldn't come up. The
last time they'd been together, she had told Miranda
all about the cattle round-up with Douglas. Miranda
had clapped her hands together and talked for hours
about attractive cowboys. But Susan hadn't had a
chance to tell her about the awful phone conversation
with Michael, or the fact that Douglas had overheard
and then left.

She sighed. 'It's not going anywhere much,' she said.
She paused for a moment as the whole thing rushed
through her head again. She didn't want to talk about
it, but it was better that Miranda knew everything.
'Michael called to talk about Jack when Douglas was
here. Jack was playing with Douglas. Michael overheard

them talking.' The words were flooding out too fast. She stopped to take a breath, then began again. 'Michael got stupidly angry that I had someone else here.'

Miranda's eyes opened very wide, then she frowned. 'Michael thinks he can still order you about?' she said, shaking her head. 'I hope you didn't listen.'

Susan felt her shoulders sag. Back when she and Michael had been together, it had always been hard to tell him when something was wrong. Nowadays, she aimed always to speak her mind, but with Michael's return she was back there again, unable to tell him what she wanted. Miranda was gazing at her. Was that pity or disapproval in her eyes? Susan couldn't tell, nor did she want to ask. She turned away, opened a drawer and took out a teaspoon. Much as she loved her mum, she'd always had the feeling that Miranda felt she hadn't stood up to Michael properly in the first place.

The kettle was boiling. She picked it up and poured the hot water onto the teabags. She had to start standing up for herself, she thought. Susan knew her mum loved her, but if even Miranda thought she was a failure, then perhaps she really was. 'He mentioned taking me to court over Jack,' she said, looking over her shoulder. It was the only defence she could think of that might exonerate her from being to blame.

To her relief, this time Susan could tell Miranda's wrath was entirely aimed at Michael. 'He threatened that, did he?' Her tone was grim. 'Well I wish he was here right now. I'd love to give him a piece of my mind.'

Miranda's fingers were tapping the table as if she was itching for a fight. Susan had the oddest feeling that she might laugh. The idea of Miranda facing up to Michael was much better than the idea of Susan herself having to do it. She knew she would have to eventually, but things were so bad already that she barely knew where to start.

Miranda was looking at her thoughtfully as she brought the tea over and set it on the table. 'What about Douglas?' she asked. 'Where does he come in all this? You didn't tell him, did you?'

Susan shook her head, feeling miserable. 'I didn't tell him,' she said, 'but he overheard me on the phone. He stayed to tidy up, but said it would be better if he didn't come back.'

'He thought it would be better if he stayed away? Maybe he's not the brave cowboy I took him for.' Miranda's voice was dismissive.

Susan could feel her face reddening. This time it was anger rising. She glared at Miranda. 'He *is* brave,' she replied. Her voice was tight with tension. 'He wasn't backing out because he was scared. He said it wasn't worth the risk that I'd lose Jack.' *At least, I hope so . . .*

Miranda seemed surprised at Susan's vehemence. They stared at one another in silence for a moment. Susan searched in her mind for a new topic of conversation. She really didn't want to carry on with this one. She lifted her mug to take a sip, then almost spilt her tea when the doorbell rang.

'Are you expecting someone?' Miranda asked.

Susan put her mug down and shook her head. 'Don't think so,' she said, pushing her chair out.

She walked along the hallway. It would probably be someone selling something, she thought.

To Susan's horror, Michael was standing on the doorstep. Susan felt sick as she looked at him. He looked as dapper as ever. Every hair was in place. His suit was impeccable. How could he look so perfect when everything was awful? For a moment, Susan considered slamming the door in his face. What was he doing here? Her hands were shaking as she held them tightly balled into fists at her sides. She took a deep breath, trying to quell the fear and rage that had risen. Mandy had said she should try to talk to him and she was probably right. Susan had been trying to dredge up the courage for the confrontation. She had picked up the phone, even got as far as calling up his number, but she hadn't known where to start. And now here he was.

She wasn't ready. Her mind was blank.

'What do you want?' she said. 'I was . . . you said—' She bit off the words and shut her mouth like a trap. She might not know what to say, but she wasn't going to say the wrong thing.

Michael frowned. He was looking directly into Susan's face as if trying to read her thoughts. He seemed different, she thought. Last time she'd seen him, he'd been so angry. On the phone too. Now his expression was guarded. It was as if the uncertainty he'd had when he first came back had returned. 'I wanted to talk about Jack,' he said.

Susan pressed her teeth together. She wasn't sure if she could speak, even if she wanted to. Michael had paused as if waiting for her to say something, but when she said nothing, he pushed on. 'I didn't want to talk again over the phone.' Again the hesitation, the searching look.

Susan's mind was frozen. This was her chance to tell him what she wanted. Would her mum think better of her if she just laid into him? But she could no more do it than if someone put a knife in her hand and told her she should hurt Jack.

'I think I owe you an apology.' Michael said the words so quietly that Susan barely heard them.

'You think?' she said slowly. She stared at him. What on earth did that even mean? She shook her head, trying to lift the fog. Did he actually want to apologise? He sounded so half-hearted. There was a noise behind her in the hallway. The door, which she had been holding half open, was pulled out of her hand and opened wide.

Miranda stepped up and stood beside Susan. Standing on the step, she looked straight at Michael. Her eyes were blazing. Susan would hardly have been surprised if she had pulled out a cross, exorcism style. She looked ready to cast out any demon. When she spoke, Susan was surprised by the calmness of her tone. 'I'm not sure what you think you are going to achieve by coming here,' she said. 'Four years ago you walked out on my daughter and threw away your chance to become a father.'

How was her mother so emphatic, yet still composed? Susan was trembling. Out of sight, a cool hand reached for hers and squeezed her fingers, sending strength into her. She pulled her shoulders back and tried to stand tall.

Miranda was speaking again. 'I watched my daughter as she rebuilt her life and rediscovered the strength you'd taken away,' she said. 'I've never been so proud of her as I was when she became a mother. She is bringing up my grandson on her own. She's doing a wonderful job.'

Miranda squeezed Susan's hand again and the shakes Susan had been feeling subsided even more. It was amazing how much comfort was coming from that small contact.

'And now you waltz back into her life without a care: wanting everything your own way.'

Michael was gazing at Miranda as if mesmerised. Susan herself was astonished at her mum's dignity and power. 'You are dishonest and pushy.' And now the voice had grown a little louder. 'You have used every trick in the book to get her to do what you want. Nothing is too low for you.'

Michael's eyes widened for a moment. 'But I . . .' he stammered, then gave up.

Miranda was in full flow again. 'You took her out and plied her with alcohol so she didn't know whether she was coming or going.' Her eyes flashed. 'Then you tell her you want a trip to York as if it's some innocent request. Once there, you dare to announce your intentions to Jack: show him your fancy house with your fancy bedroom and tell him all this can be his. You never once thought to check with Susan whether it was okay. What kind of man would do that? Use the excitement of a child to force his mother into doing something she doesn't want?'

Michael was looking more and more taken aback. Miranda took a slight step forwards and he inched away.

'Don't you think you should have asked for her permission before you told Jack anything? You have no respect for her, but you should. She is the woman who raised your son. She's done it on her own with no help from you. Don't you think you should have checked every single detail before you acted?'

There was a brief pause and again, Michael opened his mouth, but Miranda spoke over him. 'You have shown her no respect whatsoever. Even today, you've turned up here. You had no idea whether Jack was here. Were you trying to use him again to get your way? That truly is despicable.'

Susan couldn't imagine what else there was to say, but Miranda showed no sign of stopping, as if she had been storing everything up, just for this moment.

Michael looked so cowed now that Susan almost felt sorry for him.

'Having bribed her and tried to coerce her into agreeing. Having used your own son as a weapon, you have the *temerity* to tell my daughter how to live her life and who she might invite into her house. Where were you all this time? Where were you when she needed you? And yet even then, you dared to use the threat of legal action to try to get your own way. Do you really think the courts would help? You, who have been absent all through Jack's life?' The scorn in Miranda's voice burned like acid. She took another step forward, still holding on to Susan to Susan's hand. She raised her arm so that their linked fingers were in view. 'This is my daughter,' Miranda said. She glared at Michael, daring him to interrupt. 'She makes me proud every day of her life. She has always put Jack first. *That's* how parenting *should* be. It took me a while to understand as well, but the needs of your young child always come before your own. And that is something *my daughter* knew instinctively as soon as Jack arrived. She deserves much better than the likes of you.'

Michael seemed to have shrunk. Susan was gripping her mother's hand. Again, strength flowed into her when her mum's fingers pressed hers. There was so much fire in Miranda's eyes, she seemed invincible.

'I think you should go now,' Miranda said. Her voice was still strong, but now it was dismissive. 'I don't know if my daughter has the patience to discuss any of this with you. I know I wouldn't, but she's a better person than I am and always has been. Do you want to talk to him, Susan?'

Susan was still reeling. She shook her head.

Michael opened his mouth yet again, but Miranda raised a hand and pointed. 'Go,' she said. 'Go now. You have no right to be here. This is harassment. If you don't leave right now, I'm going to call the police, you understand? Wasn't it your glittering legal career that made you reject *my daughter* and *your son*? You know as well as I do that lawyers who've been in trouble don't get on well.' The fingers holding Susan's were now gripping so tightly it was almost painful, but Susan squeezed back. *Thank you, Mum.*

Michael blinked like a sheep. Miranda was still pointing him towards his car. He stared at her for a moment, then turned and slunk away. He opened the door of his car, climbed in and drove off without looking back.

As the car rounded the corner, Miranda breathed out a long breath. She'd been holding herself so rigid that it almost seemed like she was deflating, but when Susan looked into her face, satisfaction blazed from every feature. Miranda smiled. 'I've been wanting to do that for years,' she said.

'Thanks, Mum.' Susan felt an unexpected feeling of peace. She had no idea how she was going to sort things out with Douglas, but Michael suddenly seemed much less of a threat. She turned suddenly and hugged Miranda tightly to her. 'Thanks for everything.'

They broke apart, and Susan was suddenly aware they were standing on the front doorstep. She felt as if there could be eyes behind every curtain.

Miranda caught her glance and sent Susan a sudden conspiratorial grin. 'Oh don't worry about them,' she said. 'I don't care what they think and neither should you. The main thing is that *he*'s gone.'

'You were wonderful,' Susan told her. They stepped back into the hallway and she closed the door.

Miranda placed her hands together, fingers entwined, then pushed them out in front of her as if stretching. 'It felt good,' she admitted. 'And for the moment he's off your back. I'm not sure what comes next, but right now . . .' she shrugged her shoulders, the movement exaggerated and comical, '. . . I fear our tea may be cold. Will you go and put the kettle back on, or shall I?'

Chapter Twenty-Six

It had been pouring with rain all day and now it was turning stormy. Susan had spent the afternoon entertaining Jack, who had been a little crestfallen to wake up to another wet and windy day. They'd made gingerbread men while listening to a festive playlist and made Christmas cards for Miranda and their extended family and even one for Frostflake and his littermates. It was now properly dark outside. Susan stood up to draw the curtains. Outside the window, beyond the rivulets running down the glass, the white icicle lights on the house next to Mr Gorski's danced back and forth as the gusty wind caught them.

She pulled the curtains on the driving rain and wandered into the kitchen, feeling restless. The euphoria following Miranda's speech had lasted through the night, but now a more sober feeling had replaced the joy.

Nothing with Michael was resolved. Miranda had been very loving afterwards and that was wonderful. But she had made it clear she wasn't going to interfere further. She would leave it to Susan to choose whether she wanted to contact Michael again. 'You know him better than I do,' she'd admitted. 'When he came to the door, I could see you weren't ready and I was angry he was forcing it on you. But it really is up to you to decide what's best for Jack.'

Michael's visit had unnerved her. Though Susan had welcomed Miranda's assertiveness, the fact that Michael had been trying to apologise nagged at her. It was itching at her that she didn't know what he was saying sorry for.

The phone in her pocket buzzed and the usual surge of hope that it might be Douglas rose, only to be quelled when she looked at the screen. It was a message from Mandy.

Hello, it said. *This is a reminder from your friendly neighbourhood man-advisor, that you should call up the lovely Douglas. Go on, cowgirl. Get out your lasso! What's the worst that can happen?*

Susan grinned. Mandy was incorrigible, but she really couldn't call Douglas yet. Not while everything was still up in the air with Michael. Douglas was bound to ask. If she told him the truth, he would just repeat his opinion that it wasn't safe: that he wouldn't risk her happy life with Jack. And she wouldn't lie to him ever again. She had to do this properly or not at all.

I can't, she texted back. *He'll ask about Michael. Mum might have given him a piece of her mind, but I still have to make mine up.*

Frustration rose as she pressed send. This whole situation was stupid. She was hoping against hope that

Douglas would wait for her, like Mandy had said. The spark between them had been real, hadn't it? But no man would wait indefinitely. She had to pull herself together and call Michael. She just had no idea what to say. She wandered back through into the living room. Jack was there, playing with Lamby on the couch, bouncing him in the air and making whooshing noises. They had watched *The Snowman* earlier. Maybe Lamby was flying to Lapland to dance with Father Christmas.

What would be best for you, Jack? she wondered for what felt like the millionth time. Having a dad in his life ought to be a good thing, but only if his dad was trustworthy. She pictured Michael on the doorstep again. Had he really been trying to say he was sorry? But he'd come to the house. It was luck that Jack hadn't been there. Wasn't this just another sign he would continue to force the issue? The thoughts went round and round in her head and she was no further forward. She shoved the worries from her mind. It was almost time to make dinner. Any distraction was welcome.

Her mobile buzzed as she walked through the kitchen door. She pulled it out of her pocket. It was Mandy again. She must be calling to talk about the situation. Maybe she would have some advice. Dinner could wait a few minutes more.

'Hi, Mandy,' she said.

'Susan.' Mandy's voice was breathless. 'Sorry to call, but is there any chance you could do me a favour, please?'

'Of course.' Susan had been about to sit down, but she pushed her chair back under the table. The worry in Mandy's voice was infectious. Was there something wrong at Hope Meadows? With Sky? One of the twins?

Mandy's voice came again, speaking very fast. 'We've been sent a weather warning. There's a massive storm on the way and the Highland cattle are in the high field up by Wildacre. There's a big risk of lightning strike. I'd put them inside myself, but there's a room full of clients waiting. Jimmy's away and Jeremy Loxhill's got a hospital appointment in York – he's all right but it's too far to come back – it's Toby's night off and he's gone to York, Dad's on his way to a calving and I really don't want to ask Mum . . . is there any way you could do it . . . please . . . ?' She trailed off.

Susan wasn't sure what to say. Rounding up the cows with Douglas really was the extent of her experience. What would she do if they ran in the wrong direction?

'It shouldn't be too hard,' Mandy said as if reading her thoughts. 'I've been taking them inside every night for feeding to get them used to the barn. If you open the barn door and the gate, they should just go in. You know where the hay is, don't you?'

Susan took a deep breath and squared her shoulders. Mandy had saved Jack's life last year. If she required Susan's help, then she would have it. If the cows were at risk, they needed moving. 'Yes, I'll go and do it now,' she replied.

'Thank you so much.' Mandy sounded relieved.

'Are the other animals okay?' Susan asked. Wouldn't the cats and dogs be afraid, alone in the house in a thunderstorm?

'They'll manage,' Mandy said. 'They might be frightened, but they're safe inside. I'll need to get on now, but I'll come as soon as Dad gets back.'

Susan shoved the phone back in her pocket and stood for a moment thinking. Was there anything she needed to take? There was no time to drop Jack at Miranda's. She'd have to take him and leave him in the car. She rushed through to the kitchen, opened a drawer and pulled out a torch. If she fell over in the dark, she'd be no use to anyone. Then she called to Jack. 'We need to go and put Mandy's cows inside,' she told him. She helped him on with his boots and a warm jacket, then pulled on her own waterproofs. Together they rushed out to the car.

By the time they arrived at Wildacre, the storm was closing in. The windscreen-wipers flashed back and forth. The rain was near horizontal in the glare of the headlights. Susan pulled up as close to the barn as she could. She felt breathless at the task ahead of her, but she had to stay composed. She turned in her seat and spoke to Jack.

'I shouldn't be long,' she told him, trying to sound confident. 'I'll go and get the cows. Stay in the car and wait for me. Don't get out. I'll be as quick as I can, okay?'

Jack nodded. He seemed to be taking the extreme weather in his stride. Susan glanced at him one last time. He was staring out of the window into the darkness. He seemed perfectly calm.

Thrusting open her car door, Susan leaped out and slammed it behind her. Despite her waterproofs, the rain lashing her face took her breath away. It was freezing. She switched on her torch and made a rush for the barn door. There was a heavy bolt that went into the ground. She reached down and tugged it upwards. A gust of wind lifted her hood and water found its way down her neck as she dragged the door open and ran inside. She shivered. The barn smelled sweetly of hay. Rain was thundering on the roof. She reached up a hand to wipe away a droplet from her cheek and shone her torch round in the darkness. She needed to turn on the lights. In the feeble light, she picked out a switch beside the door. Reaching out a hand, she turned the winged key clockwise and the barn was flooded with soft yellow light. Inside there was a smaller pen with a gate. That must be where the cows should go. She opened it wide.

Stage one complete, she thought. Now she needed to get the gate to the field open and hope the cows would take the hint. She could hear the wind in the trees above the sound of the rain. Somewhere in the darkness, she could hear banging, as if a piece of corrugated iron was loose and flapping. The barn was a haven, but she had to go back out into the storm. Pulling her hood back up, she clasped the neck of her jacket closed. She shone the torch ahead of her as she ran up the short track that led up the side of the house to the field.

She had to let go of her hood to try to open the gate. It blew off and in an instant, her hair was wet through. The gate was tricky. The hinges had sagged and the bolt was holding it up. For a moment, she struggled to pull the latch clear. It was so slippery. Icy cold too: already her fingers were numb. She was going to need both hands, she realised. Gritting her teeth, she shoved the torch into her pocket and tried again, feeling for the cold metal in the darkness. Working the metal pin up and down, she gradually worked it loose and began to open the gate. Close to her ear, she heard the bellow of a cow. The herd must be nearby. If she could get this gate open, hopefully they would run inside, as Mandy had said they would.

A vicious gust of wind whipped through the trees and a flurry of rain hit her neck. Behind her in the lane there was a crash. Still gripping the gate, she twisted round to look. The barn door had blown closed. She blinked the rain from her eyes. She was going to have to go back and open the door again. What about the gate? Should she leave it open? It was too dangerous. If she left the gate and the cows passed the barn and rushed down the lane, they would eventually reach the main road. She couldn't risk it.

Her muscles were beginning to tremble as she struggled to lift the gate back into position. The bolt wouldn't line up. Swearing under her breath, she made another effort and the gate slid from her hands as her foot skidded. The ground underfoot was becoming dangerously slippery. She turned to look down the lane and her blood ran cold. There beside the barn door, struggling to push it open, was a tiny figure all bundled up: blue jacket, red mittens and a stripy bobble hat. Susan could see him clearly in the light from the barn.

'Get back in the car, Jack,' she shouted, but the wind carried her words away.

Her movements were urgent as she turned back to the gate and leaned her shoulder into it. Scrabbling for a foothold, she shoved the wood upwards. *Almost there.* The deluge of water was intensifying. She could feel her hair standing up. There was a flash of light and the night exploded. A vicious fork of lighting struck one of the trees so close that Susan could feel the sound: an immense bang as the electricity discharged. Her heart hammered in her chest. She would have to leave the cows. Get back to the car. Get Jack safely inside.

From the field a bellowing roar reached her. A thunder of hooves. Then the gate smashed into her and the cows were rushing past and she was on the ground as water rushed in rivers down the muddy track.

'Mummy!' A scream rent the air.

Susan felt the shock in every cell of her body. She shoved herself off the ground and sprinted down the lane. 'Jack,' she shrieked. The barn door was half open, but the cows had stopped beside the car and were milling around. Jack was somewhere in the middle of the mob. A flash in her mind. Douglas on horseback, racing to head off the cows. And now she could see Jack standing with his back to the car as the cows plunged around him. Anger surged.

She rushed round the herd to the car. She had to drive them away. 'HeiYA!' she yelled. 'GET ON!' In front of her, the lead cow shook her head. Again that rush of fury. 'GET ON!' she screamed again, and this time, the cows turned. Lifting Jack onto her hip, Susan made a rush for the barn door and dragged it open. 'Come on!' she roared and to her amazement, the herd careered past her, through the open door, made a circuit of the barn and then slowed. She could hear the rasping of their breathing and her own. She was trembling from head to toe.

'Jack?' She bent down to stare into his face.

To her amazement he was grinning. 'I couldn't get the door all the way open, Mummy, but I knew the cows would come if they saw the light.'

For a moment, a flame flared within her, white-hot anger born of fear. 'Why didn't you stay in the car like I told you?' she shouted. 'You could have been killed.'

His face crumpled and for a moment she thought he would cry, but she pulled him into her arms and held his small body against hers, rocking him to and fro. 'I'm sorry, I'm sorry. You shouldn't have got out of the car but thank you. I know you were trying to help.' Tears burst from her eyes and ran down her face and she held him close so he couldn't see her face. She didn't want him to see her cry.

'Will the cows be all right now, Mummy?' His voice sounded small in her ear.

Reaching up a hand, she wiped her eyes. 'They'll be fine now,' she said. She managed a smile and he looked reassured. 'We should give them some hay,' she said. She put him down and took his hand. Together they walked to the corner of the barn where a pile of hay was stacked in bales. One of the bales was open and between them, Susan and Jack carted a few armfuls over and pushed them into the mangers that lined the wall. They would need more when Mandy came, Susan thought, but she had no knife to cut the string of another bale. It would have to do for now.

For all their rushing around, the cows seemed calm now they were out of the storm. One of them was already lying down and chewing cud. Another two stood beside the manger. Reaching up, they pulled a few wisps of the dried grass and stood there chewing. Despite the howling of the wind outside, it was a peaceful scene.

Susan shivered. In spite of her waterproofs, her shirt was soaked through. Jack must be wet as well, she thought. She was starting to feel the bruises she'd sustained when the cows sent the gate flying. Her shoulder felt stiff where she had fallen on it. The wood had hit her face. Reaching up a hand to explore, she winced. They should get home. She could call Mandy from there. Let her know the cows were safely inside.

'I'm just going to turn the car headlights on,' she told Jack. 'Then I'll have to shut the barn door. Do you think you can help me?'

Jack squared his little shoulders. 'Of course I can,' he said.

The rain had not eased. Susan made a rush for the car, just as lightning flashed again. This time it was more distant. She counted in her head, reaching eight before the rumbling thunder reached her. The storm was no longer directly overhead.

She turned the key in the ignition to turn on the headlights, but as she climbed out again, she heard the sound of another car, coming up the track. Square headlights approached up the track and a moment later, Mandy was jumping out of her RAV4. She rushed over to help Jack and Susan close the barn door, then beckoned them towards the house.

'Come in,' she shouted.

Susan quickly turned off the headlights and then they rushed through the rain. Susan gripped Jack's hand tightly. A moment later, they were standing in the flagged hallway of Wildacre. Their clothes were dripping onto the floor. There was a joyous scrabbling of claws on stone. Four hairy bodies burst from the kitchen. Simba, Zoe, Emma and Sky rushed to greet them, bounding round. Emma let out a yelp of delight. The hallway was a heaving mass of fur and paws and licking tongues.

'Hello.' Mandy bent to greet them, as did Susan and Jack. They were irresistible.

They made their way into the kitchen, wading through the tide of dogs. Once there, they stripped off their coats. Mandy lowered the old-fashioned rack from the ceiling and they hung the wet things up to dry. It was lovely and warm. 'Jimmy must have banked up the stove before he went,' Mandy said with a grin. Opening the stove door, she grabbed three logs from the basket, tossed them in and closed the door again. Her damp trousers were beginning to steam.

The fire began to burn up and Mandy turned to look at them properly for the first time. She was smiling, but then she frowned as she looked at Susan 'Are you okay?' she asked. 'What happened to your eye?'

Susan turned to look in the small mirror that hung on the wall beside the window. Her right eye was swollen and turning purple. She would have a black eye by the morning, she thought, but she turned back to Mandy with a smile. 'I'm fine,' she said. 'Just a bit of trouble with the gate.'

'Oh, I'm so sorry!' Mandy inspected Susan with her head on one side. There was still water dripping from Susan's hair. 'I'll get you a towel,' she said, 'and then you can tell me what happened.' She rushed out into the hall and returned a moment later, carrying three towels. 'Here, Jack,' she called. She gave Jack's hair a quick rub down, then wrapped the enormous bath towel around him, clothes and all. Jack seemed warm enough, Susan thought. He was kneeling down, close to the stove and surrounded by dogs.

Mandy pulled out a chair at the table, ushered Susan into it and handed her a towel. 'I'm really sorry,' she said. 'I never expected the weather to close in so fast. Dad came back almost straight away too. I should have just done it myself. I'd never have asked you if I'd thought there was a risk.'

Susan shook her head. The awful scene rushed into her head: Jack with his back against the car surrounded and tiny, but then the memory cleared. She'd sorted it out, hadn't she? It was kind of a rush as she remembered her race to Jack's side. The yells. Standing her ground. Sending the cows on. She had admired Douglas for the way he had rounded the cows up, but when she'd needed it, she had found her own courage. 'It's absolutely fine,' she said. 'Any time you want a cowgirl, count me in.'

Mandy laughed. 'Good to know! Now, would you like a cup of tea?'

'Definitely yes.' Susan nodded.

A few minutes later, Mandy set a steaming mug of tea down in front of Susan and sat down opposite. She glanced over at Jack, and Susan's eyes followed. He had lain down on the floor with the towel covering him. His head was cuddled into Simba's flank and he was sound asleep. Mandy grinned across the table. 'It's lovely when someone makes themselves right at home,' she said in a low voice. She leaned closer across the table. 'There's something I've been meaning to ask you,' she said. She paused and frowned for a moment, then glanced up as if she had made up her mind. 'I never, ever give animals as presents in the normal way of things,' she said. 'But I've been watching Jack and Frostflake over the past few weeks.' She wrapped her hands round her cup, then looked straight at Susan. 'I know Jack has been sad about Marmalade,' she said, 'but if it would be okay, I'd really love for Jack to have Frostflake. They seem to belong together. Only if you're ready of course, and if you're prepared to deal with Frostflake's special needs. What do you think? Would you be prepared to take him on?'

Susan gazed across the table at Mandy's kind, earnest face. The tiniest snore came from the pile of dogs across the room. Zoe's paws were twitching as she started to dream. It would be lovely to have a cat around the house again, and she knew she could trust Jack to take good care of a special one like Frostflake.

She grinned at Mandy across the table. 'I can't think of a better present,' she said. 'Thank you. Thank you very much!'

Chapter Twenty-Seven

Susan took the glass of warm milk out of the micro-wave and stirred in two teaspoons of chocolate powder. Jack was sitting at the kitchen table, drawing. She put the cup down beside him and he looked up and smiled. 'Thank you,' he said.

Susan set her own cup of coffee on the table and sat down opposite him. It was the day after their cow adventure and Susan finally felt confident enough to talk to Michael. But there was another conversation she needed to have first. 'What are you drawing?' she asked. Normally he drew animals, and of late Christmas trees and snowmen. This time there were three people in the picture.

Jack's face was happy as he looked across the table at her. Despite the upheaval, he seemed the same as he always had. She loved him so much that it was almost like a physical pain. He pushed the paper towards her. 'It's you and me and Daddy,' he said.

Susan took the picture. The smallest figure, presumably Jack himself, was hand in hand with the short-haired adult figure which must be Michael. Jack had drawn

Susan herself with long hair. All of them were smiling. She felt a strange pang. This was a picture of what she had wanted, once upon a time. 'Have you enjoyed seeing Daddy?' she asked him, handing the picture back.

She watched his expression. His answer was important; really it was the crux of the issue. If Jack wanted to see Michael, then it was up to her to handle the situation. She needed to talk to Michael. That much she had worked out. But how the conversation would go was partly up to Jack.

'Do *you* like Daddy?' His question took her by surprise, though it shouldn't have, she thought. Jack was a sensitive boy. The last time they'd seen Michael, it had ended in a blazing row and Susan and Jack walking out. It had somehow ended up being all about her and Michael, and not about Jack at all.

'It doesn't really matter what I think,' she said, trying to phrase it so he could understand. 'I want to know whether you like him.'

'Oh.' He frowned for a moment, then his face cleared. 'It was good the day we went to see Mandy,' he said. 'Daddy loved Frostflake. He helped Mandy with the hand-signals. They talked about him lots . . . and he asked about Marmalade too.'

Susan felt a small wave of guilt. She had been busy talking to Douglas. She had missed an important inter-action between Michael and Jack. Catching herself, she looked at Jack and shoved the feeling back down. No use in regret. She must learn from the mistakes she'd made and move on.

'That's good,' she said. 'And what else?'

This time, Jack looked troubled and dropped his eyes. 'I didn't like it when you and Daddy were shouting,' he admitted. He didn't look at her as he spoke. What was he thinking? she wondered. Did he feel it was somehow his fault?

'I'm sorry.' Susan looked at him directly. She had to lift that weight from him. 'Daddy and I disagreed about something, but we should have sorted it out without shouting. If there's anything else, we'll do better next time, okay?'

Jack lifted his head. His eyes brightened. 'So will we see Daddy again soon?' he asked.

That settles it then . . . Susan nodded. 'It does depend on Daddy, but I'll see what I can do,' she said.

Throughout the afternoon, she had surges of doubt about how she was going to handle Michael. Each time, she reminded herself of her reaction with the cows. This was all about Jack. When it really mattered, she could and would protect him. She thought on and off about Miranda too: calm and controlled and making perfect sense. Susan had to stop worrying about what Michael might think and say what she needed to say.

She felt a little breathless as she put Jack to bed. She went down, made herself a cup of decaffeinated coffee, then popped back up to check on Jack. He was sound asleep. Slowing her breathing, she made her way downstairs again, sat down at the kitchen table and picked up her mobile.

She had thought hard about her approach. Michael had come round without telling her. She'd had no time to prepare for the conversation. She wasn't going to do the same to him. She typed in a message. *We need to talk about Jack. Can we discuss when would be a good time please? Susan.*

She half expected a text in return. Part of her wanted the discussion in writing. She could have sent an e-mail so she would have a chance to edit in exactly what she wanted to say, but if she and Michael were going to see one another, she had to know she could speak her mind. She had always worried about his reactions. If she couldn't say what she needed to, if he refused to meet her halfway, it would make the situation impossible. But she had to make a start. Her hand was shaking a little as she lifted her coffee and took a sip, but she ignored the tremor. She set the cup down on the table as her mobile rang. She lifted it from the table. Michael's number. She took a deep breath, pushed her shoulders back and clicked 'Accept'.

'Hello, Susan. So what did you want to talk about?' His tone was matter-of-fact.

Susan had spent half the day considering what she wanted to say. Start as you mean to go on, she reminded herself.

'I want to discuss Jack and the future,' she said. 'Jack wants to see you, but it upset him a lot when we argued. We have to talk about how we make this work for him, assuming . . .' she had been about to say assuming you want to try, but she stopped; it was too dismissive, '. . . assuming you and I can find a good way forward,' she amended. She sat back in the chair, making herself relax. 'So first off, I'd like to know what you wanted to say when you came round the other day.'

It felt daring to be so direct. In the old days, she would have apologised for what Miranda had said, but she wasn't going to do that. He had earned every word.

'Okay,' Michael said slowly. 'Well, I actually came round to apologise.' He cleared his throat, as if he was also finding his way.

'What did you want to apologise for?' Susan asked. It felt almost rude to be so forthright. *When did I get so timid?* she wondered.

'I wanted to say I was sorry for what I said about Douglas on the phone,' he said. 'And about saying I would take you to court. I want you to know I have no intention of doing that.' His voice was a little stiff, as if apologising didn't come easily, but he sounded genuine.

'Thank you for your apology,' Susan said. 'I would hate Jack to have to go through that.'

She was gripping her mobile hard. Consciously, she loosened her grip. *What else? I should have written down everything I wanted to say . . .*

'About Douglas,' she went on. 'I want to be sure that in future, you understand fully. Even if you and Jack have a relationship, nothing is going to happen between you and me. And it is my responsibility to vet the people in Jack's life when he's with me. If I choose to have a relationship with someone, you have no say.'

She couldn't be much clearer than that, she thought. Long silence. Michael seemed taken aback by her directness, but she could feel her confidence growing.

'I'll make sure that's not a problem in future,' he said. Another pause, then he went on. 'I'm sorry about the way I came across. It wasn't just about Douglas himself, though I admit I was a bit jealous. But you said when we were rowing that you weren't seeing him any more. I felt you'd lied to me.'

Susan took a deep breath. She had prepared herself for this. 'I'm sorry if you thought that,' she said. 'When I was at your house, I didn't think I would be seeing him again, but afterwards it worked out differently.'

'Oh.' Michael cleared his throat again. 'So it was a misunderstanding?' He sounded a little unnerved again at her direct tone. She tried to imagine what he was doing. Would he be pacing up and down? He'd always done that during difficult phone conversations. 'For what it's worth,' he went on, 'I do trust your judgement. I know you wouldn't invite anyone into the house if it was bad for Jack. I see that now.'

Susan felt her confidence surge again. So far, so

good. She could hardly believe the way the discussion was going.

'I wanted you to know, I heard what your mother said.' Michael's voice was very even. Had he been thinking about everything he wanted to say as well? 'I put you on the spot with Jack, inviting both of you back to the house,' he said. 'I was jumping the gun and it was wrong. I was thinking about myself . . .' He paused for so long that Susan almost jumped in, but she stopped herself. She wanted to hear what he had to say. 'It was partly about my relationship with my dad and how I wanted it to be with Jack,' he said finally. 'I had the idea I was offering a wonderful home for both of you. I had this perfect picture in my head and assumed you and Jack would feel the same way. I got carried away. I should have asked what you wanted. I'm sorry I didn't. I'll try to make sure I don't do it again.'

Another apology. Susan had expected resistance, but he seemed impressed by her firmness.

'Your mum also thought I'd come round at random,' he said. 'She said Jack could easily have seen me, but I knew he was out. He was at a birthday party. You'd said so on the phone. I really wasn't trying to see him. I knew we needed to talk first.'

Huh. That's much better than I gave him credit for, Susan thought, feeling slightly shocked. She guessed she'd misjudged the situation, much like he had with Douglas.

'There's something else I've been thinking about.' Michael's voice was serious. 'I know there's a chance you won't want me to see Jack again, and I will respect whatever you decide, but I've been neglecting my responsibilities and I want to correct that.'

Susan frowned. What was he talking about now? Was he going to propose sending a backlog of presents for all the birthdays and Christmases he'd missed? That would complicate things.

'I've calculated how much maintenance I should have provided over the years. I have written a cheque and I will post it tomorrow.' He paused, as if searching for the right words, though he had taken Susan's breath away. 'You told me back then that you wanted nothing from me,' he said. 'And if you still don't, that's completely fine. But I really want to do the right thing. I will be sending you a cheque every month from now on. It's up to you whether you choose to bank it or not. I want to be a better father to Jack, and this is something I can do that he doesn't have to know about.'

Susan felt as if all the breath had been knocked out of her body. Maintenance? She had never sought it. She had told him she wanted nothing, but it would have made such a difference if he'd helped. Now here he was, stepping up.

Michael was speaking again. 'The maintenance is yours to take or not,' he said, 'but I've also started to put some additional money aside for Jack, for when he's older. I can pay that into an account of your choosing as well, but again I'll leave it up to you. There are no strings attached and if you want something that says so in writing, we can discuss that as well.'

Shock after shock. Susan held herself in. Every instinct was telling her to gush her gratitude. She should thank him. Of course she should. There was no doubt the money would be more than welcome, if she chose to take it. But she still felt the need to tread carefully, to test his assertion that there were no strings.

If he really means it, he won't mind that, she thought.

'Thank you,' she said. It was heartily said; it felt enough. Her mind was working overtime. Did she want to take him up on his offer of something in writing? It seemed so formal, but maybe it'd be for the best. She shook her head to clear it. She had started this conversation because she wanted to work out how Michael and Jack might come together. Michael had knocked the wind out of her sails with his suggestion, but for once she didn't feel like he'd done it on purpose.

'So what about Jack himself?' she asked. 'How do you want to go forward? Have you enjoyed seeing him?'

A wry laugh came down the phone. 'It sounds corny to say it,' he said, 'but I was really nervous of meeting him. I was worried he wouldn't like me, but he's a wonderful boy. It was amazing to see him playing with Mandy and that little deaf kitten. You must be very proud of him.'

'I am,' Susan admitted. She felt as if so much weight

had been lifted from her that she was floating. 'So would you like to see him again?'

'I really would . . . so long as it's okay with you,' Michael said. Susan couldn't help smiling to herself. The newfound consideration still sounded a little as if it was an afterthought, but he was definitely making an effort.

This was something else Susan had already considered. 'If you'd like,' she said, 'you could come and see Jack in the Nativity play on Saturday evening in the church. Starts at seven.'

'That sounds great.' Michael's voice was firm. 'Thank you very much for getting in touch. Will I see you there as well?'

'I'll be there,' she assured him. 'You and Jack can have a chat afterwards. I'll tell him you're coming.'

'I'll look forward to it.'

Susan sat back in her chair as Michael ended the conversation. It had gone so much better than she had expected.

The offer of maintenance took her breath away, and she felt a little dizzy as the idea sank in. She had always managed on her own wage, and she had been proud of managing all these years, but it hadn't been easy. She would have to give it some thought. If Michael really wanted to be a proper part of Jack's life, it made sense that he was making the offer.

She felt properly buoyed up. In the past, she had been far too worried about what other people might think. But from now on, she was going to be more positive and pro-active. Being firm and forward seemed to suit her. Maybe, just maybe, she should start to go for what she wanted in life, instead of waiting and hoping.

Chapter Twenty-Eight

'This is so exciting!' Mandy beamed at Susan as she met her at the door of Hope Meadows. 'Are you ready?'

'I hope so . . .' Susan had barely been able to sleep with nerves. She felt like a substantial bird was swooping around her stomach.

Mandy led her inside. 'You can wait in the kennels,' she said, pushing open the door only to be met by a volley of deafening barks. Bounce the dog was living up to his name and leaping up and down whilst he bellowed his welcome.

Mandy hushed him, opening the kennel. He launched himself towards her, with whines and licks. 'Oh Bounce,' Mandy sighed, 'what are we going to do with you?' She looked up at Susan. 'I have no idea what we're going to do with him. He barks when he's happy, when he's sad, when he's bored . . . I've never met a louder dog in my life!'

As if on cue, Bounce let out a huge bark.

Susan laughed. 'Fingers crossed that someone hard of hearing wants a dog,' she said.

Mandy pulled a dental chew stick out of her pocket. 'This should keep him quiet for a bit.'

Bounce took the stick and bounded around his kennel before settling down with it at the back.

There was the sound of a car pulling up outside. 'Off I go.' Mandy grinned.

Susan shivered despite the warmth in the kennels. She caught sight of herself in one of the glass doors. Her cute black top was concealed by her coat, but her slim-fit jeans and new cowboy boots looked nice. She avoided looking at her face, with her developing black eye. *I'm ready for this,* she told herself.

She heard the door opening and Mandy's voice, clear and bright. 'Thanks for coming,' she said. 'I know it was short notice. We just need to get a couple of quotes and a photo for the website. Our local business people page, as I said.'

'Just as well I dressed up for the occasion then . . .' It was Douglas's voice. He and Mandy walked in and Susan stepped out to greet them.

'Hi,' she said.

Douglas was indeed dressed up. His smart-but-casual black and blue lumberjack shirt was open at the neck. A pair of black jeans accentuated his slim hips and long legs. His hair was back to its wild spikes. He looked gorgeous. A surge of hope and longing cascaded through Susan, leaving her breathless.

He stopped. His eyes opened wide and he stared at Susan. Shock quickly turned to concern and he frowned. 'What happened to your face?' he asked.

Susan grinned to dispel his worry. 'Sorry if it's frightening,' she said. 'I had a fight with a gate up at Wildacre! If I'm being completely honest, it was Mandy's fault.' She rolled her eyes in mock exasperation.

Mandy laughed. 'She's quite right,' she said. 'My gate, definitely my fault.'

Douglas looked from Susan to Mandy and back again and shook his head. 'What are you two on about?' he said. 'And more to the point, what are you up to? Are you setting us up again, Mandy Hope?'

'Me?' Mandy raised her hands, her eyes wide. 'Nothing to do with me.'

Susan raised a cool eyebrow, though her heart was racing. 'Actually it was my idea this time,' she said. 'I'm taking you on a surprise date. If you have any objections, speak now. Otherwise you'd better hold your peace.'

Douglas's lips twitched as if he wanted to smile, but then he pulled a mock-grave face, took a deep breath, puffed out his cheeks and raised his eyes to the ceiling as if he was considering it. He let out a deliberate-sounding sigh, then stared at Susan, his head on one side and shrugged. 'What happens if I do object?' he asked. 'Will Mandy black my eye too?' He cocked his head, looking from Susan to Mandy.

Mandy looked outraged. 'I haven't blacked anyone's eye,' she declared, 'but if you want to go get my cows in from the field in the face of a raging storm instead of going on a lovely date with my good friend here, you might be lucky enough to get one.'

Douglas looked again at Susan. 'Was that what happened?' he asked. 'Did one of the cows run into you?'

'Something like that,' Susan admitted. He still hadn't answered, she thought. Was he playing hard to get? She put her hands on her hips. 'You haven't answered my question. Will you come out this evening or are we going to stand here all night?'

Douglas shook his head slightly. He looked half pleased, half bemused, but he held out a hand. 'Lead on, Macduff,' he said.

Susan took his hand. 'I think you should know that's a misquote,' she said. 'It should be "Lay on, Macduff." He's inviting Macduff to continue fighting.'

'Really?' Douglas stopped. A look of amusement danced in his eyes. 'Well, in the circumstances, maybe that's quite apt . . .' He grinned his watermelon grin and nodded. 'Go to it, Susan,' he said.

Susan led him out to her car. Her heart was singing as she put in the clutch. As she drove off, she could hear Bounce's barking start up again, as if he was cheering her on.

Douglas's eyes were wide as they pulled up in a sloping field halfway up the valley a few minutes later. There seemed to be hundreds of cars standing in lines on the grass. Susan climbed out of the car and closed the door. The weather seemed finally to have turned. Stars filled the sky. There was a touch of frost in the breeze that lifted Susan's hair and cooled her warm cheeks.

'Where are we?' Douglas was out of the car as well and was looking round in the darkness. The moon was full and its silvery light shone over the sleepy rooftops that huddled in the valley. Christmas lights twinkled from the gables and windows of the tiny houses. 'Wherever it is, it's beautiful,' he said.

'Burnside Farm,' Susan said as she walked round the bonnet of the car to stand beside him. 'Bert Burnley bought it a few years ago from Mr Matthews that used to farm here. He uses the land for grazing and takes his stock down to Riverside for the winter months. Every year he holds a Christmas Barn Dance in what used to be the cubicle shed.'

'Sounds wonderful!' Douglas sounded pleased. As they made their way across the duck boards that covered the wet grass, strains of music began to reach them.

The barn was packed. Looking round, Susan felt as if half of Yorkshire had come to Welford to dance. Streamers and lights had been strung around the walls. Somewhere near one end, there was a band playing. Voices laughed and whooped. Douglas looked round the hall, then leaned in to shout in her ear. 'Wow!' he said. 'I'd no idea it would be such a big occasion.'

'Me neither,' Susan yelled. It had been Mandy's

suggestion, but it had sounded like something Douglas would love. She was feeling slightly overwhelmed now she was here, but she was determined to enjoy herself.

Douglas reached out a hand and she took it. She was glad to hold on as he plunged into the crowd. A moment later, they emerged on the far side of the room beside a bar. Now Susan could see the dancers. They seemed to be doing a line dance, though only half seemed to know what they were doing.

Douglas grinned down at her. 'Brilliant,' he shouted, following her gaze. 'Can I get you a drink?'

'I'll get them,' Susan called back.

A few minutes later, they stood side by side on the edge of the dance floor, each with a glass of non-alcoholic punch in hand. Douglas took a sip and grimaced. 'A bit sweet,' he said in her ear, 'but otherwise lovely.'

Susan sipped her own drink and wanted to laugh. It was so sweet it was almost syrupy. She made a face. 'You're just being polite,' she told him. 'You need to tell the truth.'

He looked at her for a moment, then laughed. 'Okay,' he said. 'It's bloody awful. Honest enough?'

Susan grinned. 'Perfect,' she replied.

Douglas looked around again. The band and line dancers had stopped. 'How about a dance instead?' he asked. She nodded and he took the glass from her hand, pushed his way into the crowd and emerged a moment later, the drinks abandoned. 'Let's go,' he said, holding out his hand. Susan took it and he led her out onto the dance floor.

'We'll be doing some more traditional dancing a bit later,' the bandleader said leaning down and putting his mouth very close to the microphone, 'but for now, another line dance. This one's a Christmas medley. If you don't know it, just follow my instructions.' The accordion struck up a chord, then the fiddle followed into a lively rendition of 'Rudolph the Red-Nosed Reindeer'.

A few minutes later, Susan was in fits of laughter. Douglas was so funny. His attempts at following the caller's instructions were hilariously bad. Within the first few lines of the song he turned the wrong way while standing on one leg and overbalanced, then boomed his apologies as a whole row of dancers wobbled. Three of them fell. Douglas pranced along the line, helping people up, brushing them down and apologising. 'Nobody hurt,' he assured Susan with a huge grin when he returned. He didn't seem remotely embarrassed and Susan could see that everyone was laughing with him, not at him.

'More Domino Dancing than the Slide,' Susan pointed out and they laughed some more. They restarted and within minutes, Douglas was causing chaos again. They finished the dance, breathless, and made their way to the side of the dance floor.

'Want another drink?' Douglas asked.

Susan shook her head. 'Not yet,' she called. 'I want to dance again.'

'Are you quite sure?' Douglas was grinning at her as if he was delighted. 'You wouldn't rather be in a restaurant, or a smart bar somewhere?'

'Definitely not,' Susan declared. 'This is much more fun.' She held out a hand and Douglas willingly followed her back onto the dance floor.

The bandleader looked round. 'Well,' he said, his eye stopping for a moment on Douglas, and then grinning out at the crowd. 'After the last disaster . . . I mean dance, I think we'll go with something a little more traditional. Take your partners please for the Canadian Barn Dance.' He caught Susan's eye and winked and she glanced up at Douglas, who laughed. 'He can't possibly be talking about me,' he said. 'I'm a wonderful dancer. I was just showing them how to do a Highland Fling. Anyway,' he added, 'I know this one.'

A few minutes later, they were polka-dancing round the floor in time to the music. Douglas did indeed live up to his own hype and didn't put a foot wrong the whole time. 'Did that one at school,' Douglas told her as they stood together afterwards. 'And this one,' he added as the caller announced that the next dance would be Strip the Willow. He held out a hand and Susan took it. A moment later, they were whirling so fast that the hall was a blur.

It seemed only a short time until the last dance was announced. Susan was dizzy with happiness. The evening had been a wonderful success. They had danced on and on, only stopping now and then for drinks and to get their breath back. The last dance was a Circassian Circle to the tune of 'Rattlin' Bog', then 'Nelly the Elephant'. They fell apart at the end, gazing into each other's eyes and laughing. Douglas held her hand on the way back to the car. Susan felt as giddy as she had on her first ever date when she was fifteen – and this was a great deal better than limp pizza and a mediocre film with a nervous boy whose name she couldn't now remember.

They climbed back into the car and she drove him back to Hope Meadows where he'd left his car. The moon was riding high over the fells as she drew to a halt.

She turned off the engine and sat looking out at the silvery light. There was a comfortable silence between them: a stillness born of satisfied weariness.

Douglas broke the silence. 'So what now?' he asked, reaching out and taking her hand again. 'I've had a fantastic evening, but you're in charge. Where do we go from here?'

Susan turned to look at him. His hand was warm and dry. Their closeness felt comfortable. 'What I want is more of this,' she said. 'You and me dating.' She stopped. Her heart was beating fast. She was almost sure he wanted the same.

'Can I ask about Michael? What's happening with him?' he asked. He hadn't pulled away his hand, but his face was serious as he searched her face.

Susan counted up to three in her head. She needed

to be completely calm. 'Actually,' she said, 'there's something I want to say about that. I know you were trying to give me space when you decided to go away, but what happens to Jack at the moment is still my decision, and mine alone. There may come a time,' she smiled at him, 'when we make those sorts of decisions together, but for now I'd like you to trust me. It's my job to protect this family, not yours.' Douglas was quiet for a moment. 'I understand,' he said slowly. He smiled. 'Thanks for telling me,' he said.

Susan squeezed his hand. She could feel strength flowing into her. 'What I want now,' she said, 'is for you to take some time . . . a couple of days . . . to think it over. I want you to be absolutely sure, before we go any further. Is that okay?'

She waited to see if he would ask more about Michael, but he twisted his fingers round hers for a moment and smiled gently. His eyes gleamed in the darkness. 'Okay,' he said. 'I'll do that. And thank you again for tonight. It really has been wonderful.' He let go of her hand and turned as if to open the car door, but then he paused and twisted back to look at her. 'Just another tiny query,' he said. He grinned. His eyes gleamed in the moonlight. 'Do you need a formal reply slip for this, or should I message you?'

Susan laughed. 'The Hope Meadows party is in a couple of nights,' she said. 'You can tell me then. In the meantime, I trust I'll see you tomorrow night at the Nativity. Just to warn you, Michael will be there too.'

Douglas laughed, turned again, pushed the door open and climbed out. Then he leaned back in and waggled his eyebrows. 'I think I could get used to this new assertiveness,' he said. He straightened up and closed the door. Susan leaned back in her seat and watched as he loped across the tarmac. This evening really had been a lot of fun. She waited until he had driven off, then turned on the engine and headed the car for home.

Chapter Twenty-Nine

It was steaming hot in the vestry. The children were hyper-excited, as they always were on Nativity night.

Susan had felt an overwhelming sense of delight when she'd walked into the church. The ancient building was beautifully decorated as it had been a year ago, with thick candles on the windowsills and a wonderful tree. But this year, the chancel was set with Douglas's scenery. She had arrived early enough to go and look at all the detail, now everything was in place. The buildings looked almost real, but when you looked up close, there were animals secreted into the paintwork. A grinning spider was lurking in the rafters. A mouse peeped out from the roof of the inn and two white hedgehogs would be joining the group of animals worshipping the new baby in the stable. The colours were amazing: warm and cosy on a cold winter's night.

A shriek from beside her pulled Susan back into the vestry. A pair of excited eyes grinned up at her and she smiled back. 'Right, Christina,' she said. 'Where's your crown?'

'It's here, Miss Collins.' Christina rushed over to the

large oak box where in the old days the vicar had kept his vestments. She picked up the crown and brought it over. Douglas had painted these too. They were gold with glowing jewels. Christina put it on and Susan crouched down and straightened it, tucking a lock of Christina's hair away from her forehead.

'Okay?' she asked, and Christina nodded. 'Got your gift?' Susan checked, and Christina pointed again to the box. It wasn't like her to be so organised, Susan thought, but she was pleased that nothing so far had gone wrong. There was still a lot to do before the parents arrived.

Susan glanced around. The oxen were ready, and for once they weren't chasing the Angel Gabriel around the hall. The lambs were in their fleeces. There were three shepherds to do, she thought, then Mary and Joseph, though Noah's mum was helping so perhaps she would get him into his costume. Jack was already dressed in his shepherd's tunic, tied round the waist with a scarf. The checked tea towel on his head was at a jaunty angle, but that only took a moment to rectify. Kendall was quick to climb into her outfit.

Where was Neil? Susan wondered, looking round. He had disappeared again. She'd caught him earlier, peering rather sadly at the manger. Was he still hankering after being Baby Jesus? she wondered. She took another look around the vestry. He definitely wasn't there, and now the lambs had disappeared. Resisting the temptation to roll her eyes, Susan went through into the main church building. One or two parents had already arrived. Someone flicked the switch that turned on the big lights that shone down onto the stage. There, spotlit, right in the centre of the apse, three fleecy 'lambs' were baaing and gambolling. A small figure was on all fours, crawling around barking and snarling, seemingly rounding them up. He was all in black except for the white scarf wrapped round his neck. It was Neil.

'Neil!' Susan strode towards the stage. 'What on earth are you doing?'

Neil looked up, his eyes stretched so wide with innocence that Susan wanted to laugh, but she stopped herself. 'I'm not a shepherd any more,' he told her. 'Jack said I could be his sheepdog.'

For a moment, Susan wondered whether she should just let it go. But the lambs were giggling now as well as prancing. She had to get the situation back under control or the play would end up in chaos. Keeping her voice low and steady, she held out her hand to Neil. 'Come on now, Neil,' she said. 'We'll get you changed. Jessica, can you and the other lambs stand still please. I need you all to go back into the other room. People are starting to arrive. We want to surprise them, don't we? If they've seen all of you, it won't be so exciting, will it?'

The three little faces had suddenly become serious. Jessica looked out into the pews. 'There's my gran,' she gasped. Hiding her face, she set off at a gallop towards the side room and the others followed. Heaving a sigh of relief, Susan led Neil back and started to help him on with his costume.

Five minutes later, Susan was crouching beside Herbie Dhanjal putting the finishing touches to Mary's outfit. Herbie looked really sweet in her pale-blue tunic with a long white scarf wrapped over her head and round her shoulders. 'That's you done,' Susan said, just as a shadow fell on her. She looked up and her heart missed a beat.

'Hello,' Douglas said. He smiled and held out a hand. 'I just popped in to see how the scenery was holding up.' His grin had widened and Susan felt herself smiling back, amused by his flimsy excuse. All round them, the children were oblivious, caught up in their own excitement.

His hand was warm and dry as he pulled her upright. They were so close. Though only their fingers were touching, butterflies coursed round Susan's abdomen.

'Well, in spite of a bit of sheep rustling, everything's holding up perfectly so far,' she told him.

'Susan?' Armando's mum appeared in the doorway and Susan turned, feeling her face reddening, but Armando's mum seemed oblivious too.

'That's Armando done, but Herbie wants you to come. Something about the manger . . .'

Susan turned back to Douglas. 'I'd better go,' she said, hoping her tone sounded unremarkable.

Douglas sent her another secret smile and a tiny wink. 'I'll go and find a seat,' he said. 'Let me know if the stable needs any running repairs.'

'Thanks, Mr MacLeod,' Susan said. It came out a little too loud and she had to lift her hand and cover her mouth to cover up the grin that had appeared.

She followed Armando's mum to the manger, though she could barely stop her eyes following Douglas. He had taken a seat near the front at the end of a row. He sat there, gazing into space and she found herself wondering what he was thinking about. Was his mind on her? Or was he planning his next drawing? Either way, he looked dreamy.

'Miss Collins?' Susan pulled her attention back to the manger. Herbie blinked up at her with huge eyes. 'Is it okay to put Baby Jesus straight on the hay? It might be too spiky for him.'

'It'll be fine, Herbie,' Susan told her. 'But it's time for us all to get off the set now. Everyone's arriving. We need to start in two minutes.' Herbie gave a nervous smile and trotted back through. Susan followed. As well as Douglas, she had been keeping an eye out for Michael and there he was at the door. 'Excuse me a second,' she said to Armando's mum. 'I just need to go and . . .' She changed direction without finishing the sentence and met Michael, halfway up the side aisle.

'Hello.' He was obviously making an effort. His clothes were smart casual, his expression open, though a little wary, as if he wasn't sure of his welcome.

'Hi.' Susan looked him directly in the eye. She wanted to get this right, here face to face for the first time since all the problems. Firm but fair. That was what she was aiming for. 'Welcome to the Nativity,' she said. 'Jack's been looking forward to seeing you. We'll come and have a chat afterwards.' She paused, then took a deep breath, keeping her eyes steady, holding his gaze. 'Douglas is here,' she told him. 'He painted the scenery and lots of the children know him. As we discussed, my relationship status doesn't concern you. If you speak to him, I expect you to be polite and friendly. Jack will be upset if there's any tension.'

Michael nodded. 'I understand,' he said. 'I'm here for Jack and that's what I'll focus on.' He seemed a little stiff, but there was no antagonism.

'Thank you,' Susan said. She nodded to him once, then turned and marched back to the vestry. He was going to have trouble finding a seat, she thought. The church was just as full as it had been last year. But there was no time to worry about it. It was time to begin.

It was a lovely Nativity. Armando and Herbie were word perfect. Susan felt especially proud of Jack. His fellow shepherd Kendall was nervous, but Jack encouraged her and nudged her when she missed her cue. He said his own lines very clearly too.

Halfway through, Susan glanced out into the audience. Her eyes opened wide when she saw where Michael was sitting. He had ended up beside Douglas. Had he done it on purpose? But there was no antagonism on either of their faces. As she watched, she saw Michael lean in and say something to Douglas. Douglas smiled and nodded. It looked surprisingly congenial. A few more minutes and she could relax. She turned her eyes back to the stage.

'Daddy!' Stripped of his tunic, his hair on end from the tea towel, Jack raced up the aisle towards Michael. Susan followed more slowly. Michael reached out and pulled something from a plastic bag he'd been carrying earlier. It was a present, box-shaped and roughly wrapped, as if by someone who'd struggled. Had Michael wrapped it himself? Susan wondered. It looked very different from the tidy gift-wrap service he usually paid for. 'This is for you, Jack. Happy Christmas.' Michael smiled as he handed it over.

Jack's eyes were shining. 'Thank you, Daddy! Mummy, can I open it now?'

'Yes, you go ahead.' Susan nodded.

Douglas was still sitting in the pew. He swivelled round as Jack began to tear at the paper.

'Look, Mummy!' Jack's voice was thrilled. He held out a nesting box. It had two storeys, one above the other, and was made of rustic wood, shrouded in moss and twigs. It would blend into their garden perfectly.

'How lovely,' Susan said.

'Thank you.' Jack looked up at Michael, who looked pleased.

Douglas stood up and walked over to Jack. 'What have you got there?' he asked, crouching down and smiling as Jack held out the wonderful gift to show him. 'It's brilliant,' he said a moment later. 'Your daddy must have thought a lot about what you'd like. You're a lucky boy.'

Jack smiled, looking a little shy. He still wasn't wholly used to the idea of having a daddy, Susan thought, though he was fast getting used to it. She glanced over at Michael. To her pleasure, he still looked perfectly happy. He and Douglas exchanged nods. Susan found herself smiling. It was all going better than she had dared to hope.

Douglas turned to Susan and smiled. 'Well,' he said, 'I have to be getting off now.' He swivelled round. 'You were brilliant.' He grinned down at Jack, who beamed up at him. 'I'll see you soon,' he said, turning back to Susan. His voice was calm and he didn't reach out. He seemed determined not to give Michael any cause for resentment.

A thrill ran up Susan's spine as she looked into his eyes, but she too kept her voice mild. 'Thanks for coming,' she said. 'Glad you enjoyed it.' And then he was off, striding towards the back of the church with a bounce in his step.

Michael put his hand on Jack's head for a moment. Jack looked up and smiled and Michael smiled back. 'You were the best shepherd ever,' he said. 'I'm afraid I have to go as well, but I want to see you again very soon. I'll arrange something with Mummy, okay?'

There was an expression of pure happiness on Jack's face. To Susan's surprise, Michael crouched down, as Douglas had a few minutes before. He opened his arms and Jack stepped into his embrace. For the first time ever, they hugged properly. When Michael stood up again, there was an unusually gentle look on his face, as if he was truly touched. He too turned to look at Susan before taking his leave.

'We'll see you soon,' she told him. 'I'll call you.'

'Thanks,' Michael said. He gave Jack's hair a ruffle and smiled, then like Douglas before him, he turned and walked out of the church.

Susan held her hand out to Jack. 'Time to go,' she said. It was already after his bedtime, but Susan and Mandy had arranged another surprise for him. She couldn't wait to see his reaction.

Mandy was waiting for them in the porch of the church. She was holding a cat box in her left hand. As Jack walked towards her, she held it up to show him. 'Look, Jack,' she said. 'Frostflake's in here. I've found the perfect home for him. I'm taking him today so he can settle in before Christmas. I wanted your help.'

'He's going away?' Jack's face was so stricken that Susan wondered if they should tell him, but he pulled himself together. 'You mean tonight?' he said. 'Yes, I'll help,' he said seriously, 'if Mummy says it's okay.'

'I'll come too,' Susan told him. 'Then we'll both see where he's going to live.'

Lucy Daniels

Mandy held out her right hand. 'Come on then,' she said.

They walked along the edge of the green. The night air felt wonderfully fresh. Their breath made white clouds in the air as they walked.

'Is it far?' Jack looked up at Mandy, who smiled.

'Not far,' she assured him.

His face brightened. 'Maybe we can visit him,' he said, then hesitated. 'It is someone nice, isn't it?'

Mandy laughed. 'Very nice,' she said. 'I wouldn't give him away unless he had a lovely home to go to.'

Susan watched Jack carefully as they walked. He frowned as they rounded the corner onto the street where Moon Cottage stood. He looked doubly puzzled as they came to a standstill at their own door. He looked up at Mandy. 'This is our house,' he said.

Mandy grinned down at him, just waiting to see if he would work it out. Then Jack's eyes went so wide it looked as if they might pop out. 'Is he going to live with us?' he gasped.

'I hope so,' Mandy said as Susan unlocked the door. 'Will you and Mummy be able to give Frostflake a home? I can't think of anyone better.'

Jack glanced up at Susan. His eyes were filled with hope. She nodded. 'We can look after him together,' she confirmed.

She had half expected Jack to go wild with excitement, but he seemed very serious as they walked into the hall. Susan shut the door. Mandy took Frostflake out of his box and set it on the floor near the door in the living room. 'I'll leave that with you for a few days,' she said. 'It's important he knows there's somewhere safe he can hide.' She looked down at Jack, holding Frostflake against her neck. 'You know it's important he has his own space,' she reminded him. 'If he goes in his box, you should let him have some peace and quiet.'

Jack nodded. He seemed almost overwhelmed as they walked into the living room. He sat down on the sofa and Mandy reached out and set Frostflake in his arms. Though Frostflake seemed a little distracted, he tilted his sweet face up at Jack, then ran up to Jack's shoulder and rubbed his small white head against Jack's face. Jack reached up a hand to stroke Frostflake's cheek. A moment later, his loud purr filled the living room. It was a wonderful sound, Susan thought. Best sound in the world. There was so much happiness in Jack's face that she felt tears forming in her eyes. This was going to be the best Christmas ever.

Chapter Thirty

Susan's heart was beating in double time as she surveyed herself in the mirror once more. Tonight was the night Douglas would give her his answer. She wanted to look perfect. She brushed a tiny speck of white from the skirt of her dress. It was the red skater dress she'd bought in York. She'd thought that she may as well wear it today instead of Christmas, since it was such a pretty party dress. She usually spent most of Christmas Day sprawled on the floor, playing with Jack anyway, so it would have been a bit of a waste. Just as well her black eye had faded quickly. It was barely visible now. As she turned from side to side, the material of the dress shimmered in the light. There were butter-flies flitting round her stomach. Surely Douglas would like it? With a last nervous glance, she turned and made her way downstairs.

Jack was getting Frostflake ready. He had set the kitten's box in the kitchen along with his food and water bowls and several toys. There was a hot-water bottle in the box and a fluffy blanket to lie on. Susan was touched again by Jack's care and attention to detail.

He was determined that Frostflake would have the best home ever. Now he was cuddling the little white body, stroking under Frostflake's chin in the way that seemed to be most pleasurable. The booming purr filled the kitchen.

'Time to go now, Jack,' Susan said. 'Is Frostflake all prepared?'

Jack nodded. He placed Frostflake down on the floor beside his box. 'We'll see you soon,' he promised, then whispered, 'I'll send your love to your mummy.'

Susan smiled and held out her hand. 'You're very good with him,' she said, and Jack beamed.

The reception at Hope Meadows was packed with bodies. Susan and Jack stood together near the door. Mandy had moved the small desk and replaced it with the huge scrubbed pine table that normally stood in the cottage kitchen. Emily was spreading a white table-cloth over the wood.

Susan walked over. 'I brought these,' she said, handing Emily the tin of mince pies.

Emily smiled. 'That's lovely,' she said. 'I'll just put them here. Mandy'll sort them out in a minute.'

Susan moved a little away from the table. She didn't want to get in the way. She and Jack were early. Setting up was still in full swing.

Mandy appeared, carrying a pair of plates piled high with filled rolls. Jimmy rushed in behind her with two huge bowls of crisps and Adam followed, clutching a tureen of soup.

'That looks great!' Mandy surveyed the table, patted Jimmy on the back, then walked towards Susan. She paused for a moment to inspect the decorations that Helen Steer and Rachel, who worked part-time as a receptionist at Animal Ark, were stringing round the room. They had twisted streamers together around the walls and brought in branches of holly, which were bright with berries. Helen was balancing on a chair, fixing a bunch of mistletoe right in the centre of the ceiling. She and Rachel were both laughing. So much so that Susan wondered if Helen would fall, but then something seemed to catch Helen's eye. She stopped laughing, straightened up and pulled her skirt straight. Susan glanced round. Toby had just walked into the room with James and Raj. All three of them were looking around appreciatively.

Mandy finally arrived at Susan's side. She seemed breathless. No wonder, Susan thought. There was so much to do. 'Good to see you,' Mandy said. 'And you, Jack. Did you bring the photo I asked for?'

Jack held out the photo he had been clutching in his hand as they'd driven over. It was the most gorgeous picture of Frostflake. Susan had taken it that morning in the kitchen at Moon Cottage. Frostflake had been hiding inside a wellington boot and Susan had caught him just as he'd emerged.

'Will you come and hang it up?' Mandy asked. She

led Jack and Susan over to the far wall, which was taken up with a collage showing lots of animals.

'Look!' Jack pointed. 'Holly and Robin.'

It was indeed a picture of the two miniature donkeys that Mandy had rescued last year. The photo had been taken in high summer up at the smallholding where they lived now. Mandy helped Jack to pin Frostflake's picture to the wall. 'Thanks for bringing it,' she said.

Jack seemed worried. 'Won't the kittens be frightened?' he asked. 'When all the people arrive?'

Mandy grinned. 'They're very sleepy actually,' she said. 'Pretty sure they'll be all right. Feel free to go in and see them. It's a bit emptier than usual. I moved three of the cats that don't like noise into the residential unit.'

Susan could picture the old residential unit within Animal Ark itself. 'To stop them getting scared?' she asked.

Mandy nodded. 'There are still a few animals here,' she said. 'I'm hoping people will have a look around in between their canapés. All the ones that are here now will be here over Christmas, but maybe some of them will find new homes after.' She held up a finger. 'If you listen,' she said, putting her head on one side, 'you can still hear Bounce, even though I moved him right to the far end of the building. I'd have put him through too, but he'd scare the cats.' She laughed and rolled her eyes. 'One day I might get him to quieten down enough to find him a home,' she said. 'Even though he's a barker, he's not scared of anything and he's a great little dog.'

Dorothy and Tom Hope arrived. Each of them clutched a plastic bag in either hand. 'Must go say hello to Gran and Grandad,' Mandy said.

Susan watched as Mandy went over and helped her grandparents lift the bags onto the table. Between them, they began to draw out tins and boxes of cakes. A beautiful pink and white Battenberg was followed by homemade chocolate truffles and a platter of ready-cut Christmas cake, complete with chunks of white Wensleydale cheese. Emily pointed out Susan's box of mince pies and Mandy waved and grinned at Susan before setting them on yet another plate.

Susan's mouth was watering. She had been so busy this afternoon that she hadn't found time to eat. Six people arrived all at once and Mandy abandoned the table and rushed over to greet them.

'Hello.' There was a voice in her ear. It was Miranda. 'How are you, darling?' she asked, then bent to greet Jack. 'How about you and I go outside?' she said. She winked at Susan and held out a hand to Jack. 'Abi and Max are playing outside and I'd like some fresh air.'

Susan found herself alone in the middle of the floor. It was almost seven o'clock, she thought. That was the official time on the invitation. She turned to see Mr Gorski coming in, arm in arm with his sister.

'Hello.' She walked across to greet them. 'I didn't know you were coming,' she said loudly, looking straight at Mr Gorski as she spoke.

Mr Gorski smiled. 'Wouldn't have missed it,' he said.

'Not after everything young Mandy did for Coffee. Got to support her.'

'That's great,' Susan said. 'If I'd known you were coming, we could have given you a lift.'

Mr Gorski patted her arm. 'It's fine,' he said. 'It wasn't raining. It's good to get out now and then. And Ida here's a great walker.' He nodded at his sister, who smiled. 'Only a few days till Christmas now,' he said. 'Young Jack excited?'

'Very much so.' Susan shifted her feet. She wanted to be able to see the door. 'We've adopted a kitten, did I tell you?'

'From here, you mean? How lovely.' Mr Gorski patted her shoulder. 'Lucky kitten,' he said, his voice a little gruff. 'Couldn't have a better home.' He cleared his throat and glanced round the room. 'Does Mandy have a lot of rescues in at the moment?' he asked.

Susan laughed. 'She's always got a lot of rescues,' she said. 'I think she's moved some of them to Animal Ark for the night, but you'd be welcome to go say hello to the ones that are still here.'

'I might just do that.' Mr Gorski looked pleased at the idea. 'I do miss my little Coffee,' he said.

'She was lovely. Jack and I miss her too,' Susan replied.

Several other guests arrived. It looked as though half the village were there. It was amazing so many people had been able to make it, Susan thought. They must love Hope Meadows. Susan searched the room again. Douglas was not here yet. He was so tall, she wouldn't be able to miss him. Christmas music was playing from the stereo that Mr Hope had carried over from the house. It *almost* covered the sound of Bounce barking joyfully from the kennels.

A movement in the doorway caught her eye and she felt the room come alive. Douglas had stopped and was looking around. To Susan's amazement and delight, he was wearing a kilt. His cream Jacobite shirt was loosely laced at the neck and his broad shoulders made him seem twice the size of most of the men in the room. He looked every inch the Highland warrior with his piercing blue eyes and unruly hair. Susan's breath caught in her throat as he strode across the room towards her. In her peripheral vision, she could see people staring, but she couldn't tear her eyes away from Douglas.

He grinned as he stopped beside her, so close that she could feel the heat from his body. Shivers ran up and down her spine. She breathed in his scent. He smelled of woodsmoke and the wind on the moors in summer. He reached out a hand and took hers and she felt his strength rush into her. *Does this mean it's a yes?*

'Where's Jack?' His first words threw her a little, but he was smiling so broadly she was reassured.

'He's outside,' she replied. She had the strangest sensation that she was floating in the middle of the room, as if she and Douglas were on an island in a sea of eyes.

He glanced upwards. Overhead, the sprig of mistletoe hung from the ceiling. 'That's lucky,' he commented, quirking an eyebrow. He took her in his arms and bent his head.

'Oh so *you* must be Douglas! Introduce me then, darling.' Miranda was suddenly at Susan's side.

Mum! Susan felt herself flushing as red as her dress, as embarrassment and frustration bubbled together inside her. Her mother's timing couldn't have been worse. 'Douglas, this is my mother,' she managed, through gritted teeth.

'Miranda Collins.' She flashed a smile and held out her hand to Douglas.

He took it and shook it gently. 'Lovely to meet you, Miranda. I'm Douglas.'

'Mum, where's Jack?' Susan asked, frowning.

'He's still playing outside with the twins. James is there now, don't worry.' Miranda flapped a hand at Susan.

'We were just talking about something.' Susan tried to give her best *go away* look to Miranda without Douglas noticing.

Miranda finally seemed to get the hint. 'All right, darling. I'll leave you to it, I wanted to have a chat with Emily anyway. Lovely to meet you, Douglas.'

'You too!'

Douglas gazed down at her.

This is the moment . . .

Just then, the door to Hope Meadows crashed open

369

and Jack ran in, with Abi and Max in hot pursuit. Susan thought that this must be the only time in her life that she hadn't been entirely pleased to see her son.

That wonderfully familiar grin split Douglas's face. 'It would seem that this isn't the appropriate place to show you my answer,' he murmured. 'So I can tell you instead. I'm in.'

Susan could feel the hairs on her arms standing up. 'You'd like to date?'

Douglas dipped his head. 'I would.'

Susan felt like she could jump for joy, or explode with happiness. She grinned instead. 'It's a pity there's no band,' she said, glancing down at his kilt.

'Indeed!' Douglas laughed. 'I'd love to have whisked you round the floor in celebration.'

'I'm dancing inside,' she said with a sigh, leaning against him.

'Me too.' He squeezed her hand and they moved apart a very little.

All Susan wanted to do was kiss him, but not in the middle of a room of people who included her mother. Sneaking off wasn't an option either, since she was here with Jack.

'So what now?' he said, looking down at her. 'From past experience, I'd say our dates go better when you're in charge.'

Susan shook her head. 'Not true,' she said. 'Nothing I like better than swinging from trees and rounding up cattle.'

His booming laugh filled the room. It was a wonderful sound.

'But I suppose, as we're at a Christmas party,' Susan told him, 'we'd better do what you normally do at Christmas parties: eat, drink and be merry.'

'Sounds good to me,' he said.

It was a new kind of freedom, she thought an hour and a half later as she chatted to Mandy. Douglas was there. She could feel his reassuring presence. Yet he had not monopolised her every moment. Mandy was laughing as she and Susan stood in the corner of the room and watched him charming Emily. 'I couldn't believe it when he walked in,' Mandy said. 'Isn't he gorgeous in a kilt?'

Susan smiled. 'He really is,' she said.

'And I've watched him when he's been here to draw. Even the shyest animals love him. He's so gentle.'

'I know,' Susan replied. 'And I haven't forgotten what you did. If it wasn't for you, we'd probably be standing on opposite sides of the room, pretending not to notice one another.'

Mandy laughed. 'You'd have found a way without me,' she said, but she looked pleased. 'Wonderful when something turns out just right,' she said. 'Especially at Christmas.' She was clutching a glass of wine and she raised it. 'To you and Douglas at Christmas,' she said.

Susan laughed as she raised her own glass. 'I'll drink to that,' she said.

Mandy grinned, then she glanced across the room and her eyes widened. 'Look at that,' she said. Susan followed her gaze. Mrs Ponsonby was clutching Fancy to her smartly dressed bosom. She was wearing the most uncharacteristically flirtatious look as she simpered up at Toby. Susan had rarely seen such a look of alarm on anyone's face.

'We have to save him,' Susan whispered as Toby took a step backwards. But as she spoke, Helen Steer strode across the room and inserted herself between the unlikely pair.

Susan strained her ears to hear what she would say. 'Toby, I know it's a party,' she said, 'but can you come and check on something for me, please?'

Mrs Ponsonby was left in the centre of the room, opening and closing her mouth as Fancy panted in her arms. 'It's way too hot in here for poor Fancy,' Mandy murmured. 'I'd better go and offer her a bowl of water. Otherwise Mrs Ponsonby is going to be demanding Toby's services again.' She marched off.

The party was nearing its end. Miranda had taken Jack home an hour ago. Susan smiled as she looked up at Douglas. 'Shall we go and have a last look round the kennels,' she said. 'We're here for the animals after all.'

And we might find a minute alone . . .

'That would be lovely,' Douglas agreed.

'You must come round very soon and see Frostflake,'

Susan said. 'Jack is so wonderful with him and he's settling in so well.'

'He's very lucky to have such a wonderful home.'

Susan reached out for his hand and together they walked across the floor. People had started to drift away. Susan frowned as she realised it was oddly quiet. 'Bounce has stopped barking,' she said.

Douglas shook his head. 'Maybe all the barking tired him out and he's asleep,' he suggested. 'Maybe we shouldn't disturb him?'

'Mandy,' Susan called. Mandy looked over. She had been talking to Jimmy, but when she saw Susan's face, she broke off and came across. 'Is Bounce still in there?' Susan asked. 'Only he's gone awfully quiet.'

Mandy frowned. 'He is,' she said. 'And it's not like him to be quiet. We should go and take a look.'

Susan held her breath as they opened the door and walked into the kennel. What if something awful had happened? It would be a terrible end to the evening. But to her surprise, the kennel room was not empty. There was a chair in the corner. On it sat Mr Gorski and on his knee, Bounce lay, gazing up at him, in perfect peace.

Mr Gorski looked up. His eyes stopped on Mandy with an apologetic look. 'I'm sorry,' he said. 'I know I probably wasn't supposed to get him out, but he just looked at me and I couldn't resist.'

Mandy was staring at him. 'Amazing,' she said. 'I've never seen him so calm before.' She shook her head.

Mr Gorski sighed. 'I know it's Christmas,' he said, 'and you probably won't rehome any of your residents just now, but if I came back on Boxing Day, would it be possible to discuss adoption, please? The house is so empty without Coffee and this little fellow and I seem to be well suited.' He looked up at Mandy. 'I can pay for him,' he added when Mandy didn't speak. 'I've made a donation this evening, but I'd happily give more.'

Mandy still looked as if she could barely believe what she was seeing. As they watched, Bounce lifted his head and looked round, studying the faces that were looking down at him. Then he saw Mr Gorski's steady eyes. He lay back down with a contented sigh.

'Mr Gorski,' Mandy began. 'You're right, I don't normally rehome animals at Christmas, but I've made an exception for Susan and Jack.' She paused for a moment as he looked up at her. 'I'm going to make one for you as well. I know how well you looked after Coffee. If you'd like to take Bounce, then I can fast-track the process. I've already been in your house, but if I could come and do a proper inspection tomorrow ...' She trailed off.

Mr Gorski looked as if he could hardly believe what he was hearing. 'Of course,' he said. 'Anything you need to do. Let me know when you're coming, won't you? I don't always hear the door.' He reached out a hand to stroke Bounce's head and the little terrier opened his eyes, looked up, barked twice as if in agreement, then settled back down. His bark was still so loud that Susan felt herself flinch slightly, but Mr Gorski just smiled.

'Well, I will let you know tomorrow,' Mandy said, 'but if you rehome him, I don't think you'll ever have a problem with not hearing your door again. I'll give you a minute or two longer and then I'll come and put him back in his kennel.'

She grinned at Susan and Douglas as they went back through to the reception area. It was almost empty. 'I was starting to despair,' she said. 'I wasn't sure whether I'd find him a home ever, but Mr Gorski'll be perfect.' She reached out and hugged Susan and then Douglas. 'Thanks for coming,' she said. 'People have been very generous. It feels like all my Christmases have come at once. Anyway, I'd better get on. Those plates aren't going to clear themselves away.' She turned on her heel and started to clear up.

Douglas smiled down at Susan. 'I guess it's time for us to go too,' he said. He put an arm around her and led her outside. The moon had passed its zenith, but it was still huge as it hung over the fells.

'It's so beautiful,' Susan whispered. The sky was filled with stars. The chilly air cooled her warm cheeks. There was frost in the air.

Douglas looked down at her. 'You're beautiful,' he said. He leaned down. Susan was sure the kiss she had been longing for was coming. Just then, the door opened again and they sprang apart.

'Susan, dear, I'm so sorry to disturb you, but would you mind dropping us home? Ida and I are quite exhausted. We stayed far longer than we meant to.' Mr Gorski smiled up at her, oblivious to what he had interrupted.

Despite Susan's sinking heart, she knew it was the right thing to do. 'Of course, Mr Gorksi.'

She looked up at Douglas, with a sigh. She saw her own disappointment mirrored in his eyes, but then he smiled and opened his arms.

'All right, lassie, give me a Christmas hug. I'll see you soon.' Susan lay her head against his chest. She could hear the slow steady beat of his heart. She had never felt like this, she thought: so wonderfully safe. She closed her eyes and breathed in deeply for a moment.

Then, Douglas was moving again, bidding a cheery farewell to the Gorskis and the Hopes as he strode to his car.

Next time I see him, I'm kissing him straight away, Susan promised herself.

Half an hour later, Susan let herself into Moon Cottage. Miranda was sitting in the kitchen, drinking a cup of tea.

'I'm afraid Jack is still awake,' she told Susan, wryly. 'But we've compromised. He's playing with his toys, in bed, *quietly.*'

376

Just then, the air was rent by a scream. 'MUMMY!'

Susan was up the stairs in an instant, her heart in her mouth. Miranda was hot on her heels.

'Jack, what is it?' Susan gasped as she burst into the room.

Jack turned to her, his face alight with happiness. 'MUMMY, IT'S SNOWING!'

He'd pulled back the curtains to reveal thick white flakes were falling from the sky.

'Jack, you nearly gave us heart attacks,' Miranda scolded him.

But Susan couldn't bring herself to be angry, despite her racing heart. She knew how long Jack had been wishing and hoping for the snow. It would make Christmas for him. She walked over to the window and opened it a crack, so that Jack could reach out and catch a couple of flakes with his hands. She cuddled him close as he laughed at the cold tingling his hands. Miranda sat next to them on the bed and put her arms round both of them.

The landscape before them slowly turned white. First the rooftops, then the treetops and the gardens. It was like the snow was cleaning away all the problems of the past. In two days' time, Christmas would be here. The future stretched ahead. It was filled with wonderful things.

Chapter Thirty-One

'It's like the North Pole!' Jack shrieked with excitement as Susan drove down onto the Plain of York.

Susan had to agree, it was breathtaking. White, crisp snow, as far as the eye could see.

She had worried that driving might not be possible, but by some miracle, the gritters had been out in force. The roads were blessedly quiet.

'We're driving through the snow, but in a car, it's not a sleigh!' sang Jack, to the tune of 'Jingle Bells'.

'Over the fields we go, laughing all the way, ha ha ha!' Susan joined in.

Jack clapped his hands. 'And we're really like Father Christmas because we're delivering a present on Christmas Day!'

'That's right.' Susan smiled at him in her rear-view mirror. They flashed through a village of red-brick houses. Susan slowed down as she saw a beautiful black horse and rider ahead of her. She pulled out and gave them a wide berth, glancing over her shoulder. The woman beamed and waved as the horse snorted steam and danced a little. It was a glorious day for a ride. The sun had come out and the snow was glittering.

They reached the outskirts of York itself and soon they were at their destination. She indicated right and pulled in to the side of the street. Michael's classy townhouse looked like a Christmas card in the crisp sunlight. Susan turned round in her seat. 'Here we are, Jack. Are you ready?'

He nodded solemnly, then grinned. He looked so happy that Susan's heart swelled. She climbed out of the car and opened his door.

'Daddy!' he cried as she helped him from his seat.

Susan turned to look. The big blue door had opened, and Michael was standing in the doorway. He looked surprised to see them, but then overjoyed as Jack ran up the steps. For once he didn't seem overdressed – he was barefoot and in a dressing gown with a faint trace of egg on the collar. He bent down and swung Jack off his feet into a hug. Then he looked at Susan and smiled. 'I wasn't expecting you,' he said. 'I was looking out at the snow, and there you were. Will you come in?' He opened the door wide, but Susan shook her head.

'Not today. We have to get back,' she said, 'but Jack and I wanted to give you something.'

Jack was wriggling to get down and Michael set him back on his feet. He rushed back to Susan. 'Did you bring my card?' he said.

Susan smiled as she handed him one of the two envelopes she was carrying. 'There you go.'

Jack grabbed it and rushed back to Michael. 'Here, Daddy,' he said.

Michael opened the envelope.

'I drew it for you,' Jack told him. He gazed up at Michael, his face filled with excitement.

Michael inspected the card. It had a drawing of a robin and there was glitter all around the edges. He looked genuinely touched as he looked down at Jack. 'I think it's the nicest card anyone's ever given me,' Michael said. 'Did you really draw it yourself?'

Jack had rarely looked happier. 'Yes,' he said.

Susan climbed the final step, feet sinking into the soft snow, and handed over another envelope. This one was brown and very official looking. Michael frowned as he took it. 'What's this?' he asked.

'Open it,' Susan urged. Her heart was beating hard.

Michael tore open the envelope and drew out the paper. The line between his eyes deepened for a second and then he drew in a sharp breath. He lifted his gaze to meet Susan's.

'I got your cheque and I put it in the bank,' she said. 'It's already made things a bit easier. And while we're righting old wrongs, I thought this was worth doing . . .'

Michael glanced down again at the paper. Susan couldn't help but feel a surge of emotion at the joy that had appeared on his face. It had been short notice, but she had applied for a new birth certificate for Jack. Now the box for 'father' had Michael's name in it. 'Thank you so much,' he said. 'Best card, and now best present too. I'm sorry you can't stay today, but you know you're welcome any time.' There were tears in his eyes. Susan felt her own prickling. Michael crouched and hugged Jack again, then stood up and opened his arms to Susan. After a moment, she stepped into his embrace, they hugged and then let go.

'Thank you too,' she said. 'We'll come back sometime, won't we, Jack? I'll give you a call,' she promised.

A few moments later, they were back in the car and driving back towards Welford. She stopped as they reached the edge of York. Douglas had said he wanted to come round when they arrived back. He had a present for Jack. Susan hadn't had time to buy Douglas anything, but she had rushed round last night putting together a new batch of mince pies. He had eaten three of them at the Christmas party. She sent him a text, *Just leaving York.* Then set off once more, speeding past the white fields.

As she pulled up outside Moon Cottage, she was surprised to see Douglas emerge from around the side of the house. He was brushing snow from a pair of woolly black gloves and grinning all over his face. Susan's heart started pounding as she smiled at him.

'Hello, you,' he said. 'And hello, Jack. Merry Christmas to both of you!'

Jack was jumping up and down. He was as delighted to see Douglas as he had been to see Michael. Douglas held up a hand and Jack rushed over to give him a high five. They were both grinning.

'I got here a bit early,' Douglas said. 'I was just playing in the snow in the back garden. Hope you don't mind.'

What on earth had he been doing round there, Susan wondered, but Jack whooped. 'Can we play in the snow?' He looked up at Susan, begging with his eyes. She was about to say yes, when Douglas spoke.

'Can you wait a few minutes, please, Jack,' he asked. 'I have a present for you, then there's something I want to show Mummy. Is that okay?'

Jack nodded. His face had fallen slightly when he was asked to wait, but it brightened again at the mention of a present. They walked inside and kicked off their boots. The wonderful smell of roasting turkey and onion stuffing greeted them as they stood in the hallway. Susan had put them in the oven before setting off for York. Everything else was prepared. Miranda would be arriving soon.

'Smells wonderful,' Douglas said, sniffing. He smiled at Susan and she felt her heart skip a beat.

They made their way into the living room. It looked very festive. Snow was piled up on the windowsill outside and a beam of sunlight from the window lit up the tinsel on the tree. All round the room there were cards on every surface and there was a pile of Jack's new toys on the coffee table. Douglas sat down on the couch, pulled a parcel out of a bag and handed it to

Jack. 'I made this for you,' he said. He grinned, his eyes sparkling. 'Go on, open it,' he said. He seemed almost as excited as Jack.

Jack ripped open the parcel. Inside was a book. Wide-eyed, he held it out to show Susan. '*The Adventures of Frostflake and Jackdaw*,' she read. 'Wow, it's a special book, just for you, Jack!'

'Thank you, Douglas!' Jack seemed overawed.

Douglas beamed at them both. 'Go on, have a read!'

Susan opened her arms and Jack climbed onto her knee. She opened the book. There on the front page was an inscription. 'To Jack Collins,' it said. 'Merry Christmas.' Douglas had signed his name underneath.

They flipped through the story together. The book was filled with hand-drawn images of Frostflake and his new friend Jackdaw, who somehow managed to look a little like Jack, despite being a bird. Jack himself seemed enthralled as they read the story together. Each time Susan glanced over at Douglas, he was regarding them with a look of utter contentment.

'Look, Mummy,' Jack gasped as they reached the final page. 'Frostflake's out on his own in the forest.'

Susan smiled. 'He's not on his own,' she said. 'Look.' Up in the sky, Jackdaw was flying overhead, keeping his friend safe.

Douglas seemed delighted with their reaction. 'Glad you like it,' he said to them both. 'But I've got something else for you, Susan,' he said. 'Jack, can you spare Mummy for me for a minute?'

Jack nodded. He slipped to the side to let Susan up, then sat down again and reopened his new book. He would be fine with it, Susan knew.

'You'll have to go up to your bedroom for your present,' Douglas said. 'It was all a bit last-minute . . .'

Susan looked at him, confused. *In my bedroom?*

Douglas roared with laughter when he saw her expression. 'Sorry,' he said. 'Misunderstanding. You'll need to look out of the window,' he explained. 'Your present's in the garden. I'll wait here.'

Susan rushed up the stairs. This was the strangest way she'd ever received a Christmas present. But then, when had Douglas ever done anything conventional? She walked across the bedroom and peered out of the window. To begin with, she wasn't sure what she was looking at. The snow in the back garden had been scraped and piled up in odd formations, but then a picture started to resolve before her eyes. She looked down and laughed. It was her, she realised, standing waving her arms as a herd of cows rushed towards her. The cows had shaggy coats and long horns. Susan couldn't begin to imagine how he had managed the detail. How confident she looked. Was that how Douglas saw her? She laughed in delight.

'I love it,' she called down the stairs. 'Give me a couple of minutes. I need to take some photos.' She pulled out the phone from her pocket and took several shots of the snow carving. It even looked fabulous on the small screen of her mobile. She could have stood and looked all day, but Douglas was downstairs. With one long last glance, she turned to go. Douglas was waiting for her in the doorway of the living room.

'It's the best present I've ever had,' she said.

The doorbell rang as she reached the bottom. There was a thud from the living room as Jack dropped down from the couch. Pushing past Douglas, he rushed to pull the door open. 'Nana,' he yelled. Miranda was on the doorstep clutching two enormous bags of presents. She dropped them inside the door and held out her arms. Jack jumped into them for an enormous hug.

'Lovely to see you too,' she said. She put him down and straightened up, then did a rather dramatic double take as she saw Douglas in the hallway.

'Hello again, Douglas,' she said. She batted her eyes, looking ridiculously flirtatious as she held out a limp hand. 'I wasn't expecting to see you here this morning. Did you stay over?' she said. Susan felt herself flushing. Her mum managed to make everything sound as if it was from a soap opera.

But Douglas just laughed and took the proffered hand. 'No, I just popped by to deliver some presents for Susan and Jack. I'm spending Christmas with my dad and my brother's family.'

'Lovely! Well, it's great to see you again. Come on, Jack,' she said. 'I think Mummy might want to talk to Douglas. I've brought you some presents. Shall we go through and open them under the Christmas tree? What do you think?'

Jack cantered over to take her hand and with a wink over her shoulder, Miranda led Jack into the living room and closed the door.

Well at least she got the hint this *time . . .* Susan thought to herself, grinning. She looked up at Douglas who was laughing. 'Sorry about her,' she said. 'I'm afraid she's like that all the time. But before I forget, I've got a little gift for you too.' She led him into the kitchen. The trappings of Christmas dinner were set around the room. There were pans on the stove, waiting to be turned on. A vat of cranberry sauce stood on the side and the newly decorated Christmas cake had pride of place in the centre of a table strewn with candles and Christmas crackers. 'Looks like you're very organised,' Douglas said. 'Somehow, my family always end up having Christmas dinner in the evening no matter how early we start cooking.'

'Well, maybe your present can make a nice dessert.' Susan held out the tin of mince pies. It was an old biscuit tin with a green and gold lid, which she had decorated with a red bow. Douglas lifted the lid and sniffed appreciatively. He looked up at Susan. 'Thank you,' he said. 'My favourite.' He closed the lid and glanced round the kitchen. 'Don't get me wrong, I love this present. But I was kind of hoping for a different one.' He drew her close.

Susan was uncomfortably aware of Jack and Miranda being right next door. She slipped her hand into his and pulled him to the front door.

Outside, the street was quiet, though Susan could hear distant shrieks and yells from the village green. *There must be a snowball fight going on.* Douglas stepped out onto the front doorstep and she pulled the door to behind them.

He was looking down at her. His eyes were so blue. Susan wanted to gaze into them forever. She took a step towards him and he wrapped his arms around her. His lips found hers and then he was kissing her, on and on as everything around her vanished and she melted into him, feeling his heartbeat as if it were her own. It was better than she had dreamed it would be.

As they broke apart and smiled at each other, Susan felt with absolute certainty that everything that had happened to her, every hardship in her life, every twist and turn had been absolutely worth it to end up here, in the arms of the best man she had ever known.

Tiny flakes of snow were falling. One landed on Susan's cheek and Douglas lifted his hand and brushed it away with his thumb. A tiny smile played around his eyes. 'Merry Christmas, Susan Collins,' he murmured, pulling her even closer. She tilted her head and he leaned over. He kissed her so hard that she found herself leaning against the porch railing to steady herself and came up with a handful of snow.

They broke apart once more. 'Merry Christmas, Douglas MacLeod,' Susan whispered back, tenderly, dumping the handful of snow on his head.

He was stunned for a moment, then his eyes crinkled

and he bellowed a laugh. 'Oh, you'll pay for that one.' He raised his voice. 'Jack! Miranda! Come and help me bury Susan in the snow!'

Susan ran away, shrieking, as Jack and Miranda crashed out of the door and they all careered around the garden in their socks, hurling snow at one another.

'This is the best Christmas ever!' Jack yelled.

It really is, Susan thought to herself. As she looked around the garden, at everyone she loved, she felt like her heart might burst with happiness.

Summer at Hope Meadows

Lucy Daniels

Newly qualified vet Mandy Hope is leaving Leeds – and her boyfriend Simon – to return to the Yorkshire village she grew up in, where she'll help out with animals of all shapes and sizes in her parents' surgery.

But it's not all plain sailing: Mandy clashes with gruff local Jimmy Marsh, and some of the villagers won't accept a new vet. Meanwhile, Simon is determined that Mandy will rejoin him back in the city.

When tragedy strikes for her best friend James Hunter, and some neglected animals are discovered on a nearby farm, Mandy must prove herself. When it comes to being there for her friends – and protecting animals in need – she's prepared to do whatever it takes . . .

HODDER

Christmas at Mistletoe Cottage

Lucy Daniels

Christmas has arrived in the little village of Welford. The scent of hot roasted chestnuts is in the air, and a layer of frost sparkles on the ground.

This year, vet Mandy Hope is looking forward to the holidays. Her animal rescue centre, Hope Meadows, is up and running – and she's finally going on a date with Jimmy Marsh, owner of the local outward bound centre.

The advent of winter sees all sorts of animals cross Mandy's path, from goats named Rudolph to baby donkeys – and even a pair of reindeer! But when a mysterious local starts causing trouble, Mandy's plans for the centre come under threat. She must call on Jimmy and her fellow villagers to put a stop to the stranger's antics and ensure that Hope Meadows' first Christmas is one to remember.

HODDER